Children of Tempest

A TALE OF THE OUTER ISLES

NEIL MUNRO

with an Introduction by
Ronald Renton

British Library Cataloguing in Publication Data
A catalogue record of this book is available from the British Library

ISBN 1 899863 99 0

First published 1903
This edition published by House of Lochar 2004

Typeset by XL Publishing Services, Tiverton
Printed in Great Britain by SRP Ltd, Exeter
for House of Lochar
Isle of Colonsay, Argyll PA61 7YR

Introduction

Neil Munro (1863–1930)

Neil Munro, novelist and journalist, was born in Crombie's Land, Inveraray, Argyll on 3 June 1863. His mother, Ann Munro, was a kitchen maid, probably in Inveraray Castle. His father has been rumoured to be of the House of Argyll but there is no evidence for this. Soon after his birth Neil's mother took him to live in his grandmother's house in McVicar's Land and it was in this Gaelic-speaking household that he spent most of his childhood.

He received his formal education at Inveraray Parish School which he supplemented with his voracious appetite for books. About 1877 he became a clerk to William Douglas, a local lawyer, but found the work tedious. Like so many other young Highlanders, however, he found no other satisfactory employment locally and so on 1 June 1881 he emigrated to Glasgow where he soon began work as a reporter. After a number of posts with different newspapers he joined the *Glasgow Evening News* with which he was to remain happily for almost the rest of his life.

He made his first significant mark on the literary scene in 1896 with *The Lost Pibroch and Other Sheiling Stories,* an innovative collection of short stories which seeks to counteract the sentimentality of "Celtic Twilight" writing and to portray the Highlander accurately and in a language which captures Gaelic idiom. In 1897 he reduced his journalistic work considerably to concentrate on literature and in 1898 *John Splendid* was published, a well-judged historical novel of the seventeenth century dealing with the Montrose-Campbell conflict which culminated in the battle of Inverlochy (1645). In 1899 the partly autobiographical *Gilian the Dreamer* appeared, a study of a young boy whose undisciplined sensitivity impedes his ability to act effectively. This was followed by three more novels, *Doom Castle* (1901), *The Shoes of Fortune* (1901) and *Children of Tempest* (1903), all loosely connected with the aftermath of the Jacobite Rising of 1745.

Munro published many humorous sketches in his unsigned column "The Looker-On" which appeared every Monday in the *Glasgow Evening News* and, when they later appeared in book form, he adopted for them the *nom de plume* Hugh Foulis. They included stories about the waiter and beadle Erchie MacPherson and the big hearted commercial traveller Jimmy Swan, but the most celebrated were to be his highly entertaining sketches about the crew of the puffer the *Vital Spark* and their eccentric Captain Para Handy. The first of these appeared in 1905 and Munro continued to produce them for most of his working life.

After the novel *Children of Tempest* (1903) Munro turned to the contemporary scene with *The Daft Days* (1907) and *Fancy Farm* (1910). In the meantime in 1908 he was honoured with an LL.D. from the University of Glasgow and in 1909 he was made a Freeman of Inveraray.

In 1914 he returned to the historical novel written in "the Highland manner" and published what many consider to be his finest work *The New Road.* On one level it is a Highland thriller – the hero Aeneas MacMaster's quest for information about his Jacobite father's mysterious death. At a deeper level, however, like Walter Scott's *Waverley* (1814) it examines the condition of the Highlands and the forces which shape individual destinies. It shows the hero's gradual disillusionment with the romantic glamour of the chiefs as he begins to recognise their vices. Eventually Aeneas comes to understand that only by trade and commerce will the Highlands be "civilised" and the instrument to achieve this will be the New Road Wade is building between Stirling and Inverness. The road becomes a symbol of a more prosperous Gaeldom, but at the same time it will contribute significantly to the permanent destruction of the old Gaelic way of life.

The outbreak of the First World War saw Neil Munro's return to full time journalism. In 1915 his son Hugh was killed in France, near Aveluy. This trauma coupled with enormous pressure of work – he became editor of the *Evening News* in 1918 – seemed to prevent further large scale literary production. He did, however, publish the collection of witty and sophisticated short stories *Jaunty Jock and Other Stories* (1918), and, of course, he continued with his humorous sketches.

In 1927 Munro's health began to fail and he reluctantly retired from the *Evening News* where he was loved and respected. In October 1930 he received a second LL.D., this time from the University of Edinburgh. Two months later he died at his home, "Cromalt" in Helensburgh. In 1935 a monument was erected to his memory in Glen Aray. At the dedication ceremony the writer R. B. Cunninghame Graham praised him as "the apostolic successor of Sir Walter Scott".

Munro's literary reputation declined after 1925 when he was accused by Hugh MacDiarmid of writing escapist literature that did not deal with the great national and Highland issues of the day. Modern scholarship, however, shows Munro's critique of Highland – and national – life to be much more acute than MacDiarmid had perceived. His literary reputation is being restored to its proper place.

The next section of the Introduction reveals some of the storyline. Readers may therefore prefer to read this after they have finished the novel.

Introduction

Children of Tempest

In his journal for August 1901 Neil Munro informs us that 'On 13 August I left Oban with John T. Ewing, School Inspector, on an inspector's tour of schools in the Outer Hebrides. During that tour I got all the essential scenic material for a Hebridean novel *Children of Tempest* and though the concept for such a novel only came to me later, the title occurred to me on the islands.' They worked their way north from the island of Barra to Harris. When they reached Eriskay Munro met for the first time Fr Allan McDonald (1859-1905) or Maighstir Ailein as he is still known in Gaelic throughout the southern Outer Hebrides today. He was parish priest of Dalibrog (1884-1893) and later Eriskay (1893-1905), an assiduous pastor who in working relentlessly for the welfare his people severely damaged his health. He was clearly very charismatic and much loved. He was also a fine Gaelic poet and scholar: he edited a collection of hymns, many of which he had written himself, and compiled many notebooks of folk tales, traditions and vocabulary of the Uists. He also corresponded with and assisted the distinguished folk collector Alexander Carmichael (1832-1912) in his research for his famous *Carmina Gadelica*, (a collection of Gaelic hymns and prayers) the notes to which provided Munro with much of the folklore for *Children of Tempest*, particularly the accounts of St Bride's and St Michael's days. These may, indeed, have been collected originally by Fr Allan himself. Munro was very impressed by him and confirms that he used him as the model for Fr Ludovick, the priest hero of this novel.[1] Much of the novel is set in Boisdale, in the south of South Uist, the area corresponding roughly to Fr Allan's first parish of Dalibrog.

Children of Tempest (1903) is the third of three of novels which Neil Munro set in the aftermath of the Jacobite Rising of 1745. It takes place in the Scotland of 1795-96 and deals with the supposed fate of the famous Loch Arkaig treasure or *ulaidh* of 40,000 louis d'ors (£20,000) which was sent from France to support the Jacobite cause but arrived too late and was buried at Loch Arkaig and then disappeared. Unlike its predecessors *Doom Castle* (1901) and *The Shoes of Fortune*(1902) this novel deals only very loosely with the political fall out of the Rising of 1745 and makes no overt political statement.

Most obviously, *Children of Tempest* is a romantic love story in which two brothers, one honourable and kind and the other unscrupulous and greedy fall in love with the same girl, Anna. The unscrupulous brother, Col, loves her for her money – the Loch Arkaig treasure (*ulaidh*) to which she is heir – and she is later kidnapped by other unsavoury characters who also want her fortune. In the end, however, the malefactors are punished and Anna is restored to her own brother Fr Ludovick and marries the unselfish

Duncan. Although the superficial narration of the plot suggests melodrama with stage villains opposed to saintly characters a closer examination shows that the stark contrast of "good" and "evil" characters invests the novel with the qualities of a parable on the destructive power of human greed. Munro himself referred to his novel as a "fable".[2]

As in many of Munro's stories *Children of Tempest* has as its mainspring a proverb. In Chapter II Bell Vore says, "It is not lucky to save a man from drowning: take its spoil from the sea and the spoil itself will punish you." (p11) This refers to the heroic act of rescue which Col performs at the opening of the novel when he sees Dark John's little boat in trouble on the open sea and rushes out to save him – the sea's spoil – from drowning. It immediately becomes the key idea in the story. Throughout the narrative frequent references are made to this proverb as a piece of folk wisdom and we realise that Col, although intending a kind act, has in fact been guilty of *hubris* in interfering where he had no right. The situation may, in fact, owe something to R.L.Stevenson's story *The Merry Men* with which Munro was obviously familiar where Gordon Darnaway is punished for looting sunken ships – the sea's spoil.[3] That Col, however, should be punished for his kind act seems quite unjust until it becomes clear that the idea of the sea's spoil extends to the *ulaidh* for which he lusts (hidden on a ledge on the remote island of Mingulay and accessible only from the sea) and that Dark John is an evil being. Dark John dedicates himself entirely to Col and is his complete servant but the grotesque imagery which is used to describe him soon makes us realise that there is something very unpleasant about him and he is to be treated with grave suspicion: "He might have been a monster of the deep, some uncanny soulless thing, in the form of man briefly borrowed for villainous devices, slobbering the stuff that feeds itself on ooze and slime."

Like Gilmartin (the devil) in James Hogg's *The Private Memoirs and Confessions of a Justified Sinner* (1824), he constantly dogs Col's footsteps and spurs him on whenever his greed for the *ulaidh* appears to wane:

> A thought came to him with a sense of revelation that this old wretch haunted him, a ghost in moments critical, led him first astray, and always spurred his interest in the fifty years' fortune at any time the same might seem to flag. (p186)

He is a demonic being who drives Col on to his inevitable doom in a magnificent climax in Mingulay. In the yawl which they had commandeered John directs Col to the foot of the cliff below the blood of the Merry Dancers (a patch of red lichen illuminated by the aurora borealis) and, spurred on by his greed, he climbs up. He finds no treasure. Too late he realises the truth of the proverb and death is soon to follow:

> No ease of his mind had been for him since he dragged its prey from the sea, to be the spur to schemes that somehow seemed to end in foolishness and mockery. It was *trom-lighe* [nightmare] – it was Incubus he had lifted from the Barra Sound; there was something after all in the ancient proverb. (p196)

"Incubus" is the term Stevenson used to describe James Durie, the Master of Ballantrae[4]whom he had earlier described as "all I know of the devil".[5] Furthermore the blood of the Merry Dancers which fascinates Col and leads him on to his doom (like the waves in the Stevenson's *The Merry Men*) adds to the effectiveness of the novel as parable for in Gaelic mythology the Merry Dancers were said to be the Fallen Angels rejected from heaven and punished, like Col, for their greed.

As has been noted, Col is selfish and unscrupulous. One interesting aspect about him, however, is that he is a cunning and unscrupulous entrepreneur in a *Hebridean* setting :

> "...but nowadays too many of the curing-barrels belong to Corodale Col, and the bounty and price he pays for the cran are hardly worth a God-fearing man wetting his boots or putting his breath in a net-bow for." (p79)

Along with the Sergeant, his equally grasping but much less subtle business partner, they make a formidable pair. The Sergeant is brutal in his treatment of Anna when he kidnaps her and considerably more so in his treatment of his pathetic and slatternly wife. His ultimate punishment of exile for all his greed, however, is much less severe than Col's, presumably because he did not steal the sea's spoil.

It is certainly possible to see in these two characters approximations to the lowland small town entrepreneurs Gibson and Gourlay in George Douglas Brown's *The House with the Green Shutters* (1901). Munro was familiar with that book and a friend of its author. They in turn may have contributed to the character of the ruthless Gillespie Strang in John MacDougall Hay's *Gillespie* (1914) which was dedicated to Neil Munro.

The character of Dan MacNeil, nicknamed Flying Jib-boom, captain of the sloop "Happy Return" is a "bridge" character between the good and evil groups in the book. Although not without fault, he is, when left to be his own man, a decent person who is in the end responsible for Anna's safe return and for the punishment of the Sergeant. He has a sense of fun and lives to enjoy life. He is clearly a literary predecessor of Munro's most enduring humorous character Para Handy as the following illustrates: "Two or three splendid dances have I lost this week in Arisaig, that I might be the one to take him back. I'm not complaining a bit, though I'm the boy for the dancing." (p204)[6]

In opposition to the dark characters Col, Dark John and the Sergeant we have the characters who represent unalloyed goodness: Father Ludovick, Duncan and Anna – all kind, honest and devoutly religious characters.

Ludovick is a much loved and popular but rather lonely priest whose presence seems to permeate the narrative although his actual participation in the action is comparatively small. He is a mystic who is at one with nature and who very quickly sees into the heart of things and he very astutely sees through Col. At the same time his reputation for justice terrifies Dark John and the Sergeant when they realise their folly in kidnapping Anna. Above all, however, it is the strength of his priestly calling and his attention to his priestly duties which impress us. All along he was in possession of the agonising knowledge that the *ulaidh* had been stolen by Old Corodale but he could not stop the mad speculation and problems connected with it because he could not break the seal of the confessional. But most impressive of all is his belief in the power of prayer: when Anna is discovered missing, perhaps drowned, he goes into his church *Stella Maris* and prays all night. When he emerges from the church he is certain that his prayers have been answered. When he meets her he says: "I knew you were coming ...Since the break of day I never had a doubt of it."(p185)

Duncan, too, is a religious figure. He was a student for the priesthood but left the seminary before ordination. He is a highly honourable young man who, unlike his brother Col, is completely unselfish. Although the older son, he cedes his rights to Corodale to his brother since he feels that enough of the family money has been spent on his uncompleted priestly training. His sense of duty and fairness to Anna forces him to leave her to seek his fortune on the mainland when he realises that people are saying that he is after her merely for her fortune. His return to Uist and to Anna in the end is, of course, right and fitting.

Anna herself, Ludovick's sister and housekeeper, is again a person with strong religious connections. Although she is not portrayed with great depth, she has a sparkling personality and is extremely popular on the island, particularly with the women and the children. Where Ludovick is aloof and remote, she complements this. She suspects Col's integrity but she never fully sees through him. She is courageous and plucky during most of the time of her kidnapping. Above all, however, she is a strong loving personality – as can be seen when she goes back to kiss the Sergeant's feckless and much abused wife when they are leaving Creggans. She is generous to all and a strong force for good.

In addition to Munro's experimental use of Highland English which is, appropriately, sustained throughout this novel and his excellent portraits of the Uist landscape, one of the most interesting aspects of *Children of*

Tempest is the tremendous mass of traditional material of a religious nature which the author introduced to give the story Hebridean authenticity. This adds to the artistic strength of the novel as parable in reinforcing the role of the "good" characters.

The most obvious religious material referred to is Carmichael's collection of *Carmina Gadelica* – hymns, invocations and prayers which cover every aspect of the Hebridean life. The example in Chapter XI he puts into the mouth of Anna as her morning prayer. (This is Munro's own accurate translation except that he omits the fourth line of the original, presumably for rhyming purposes. (p66))

> *Taing dhut Iosda Criosda,*
> *Thug mis a nios o'n oidche 'n raoir*
> *Chon solas soillse an la'n diugh,*
> *Chon sonas siorruidh a chosnadh dha m'anam,*
> *An cion na fal a dhoirt thu dhomh.*[7]

In addition to the traditional Uist hymns he also includes extensive reference to the Latin Mass and, very interestingly, to the Gaelic translation of the *Veni Creator Spiritus* (*O Thig a nuas, a Spioraid Naoimh*) the ancient hymn to the Holy Spirit. Ludovick and the others sing this for comfort as they are crossing the dangerous North Ford (p37):

> Far from us drive your foes
> And award us everlasting peace.

(Munro would have got these lines from the collection of hymns *Comh-Chruinneachadh de Laoidhean Spioradail* (1893) which had been edited by Fr Allan himself.)

The baking of Michaelmas cakes was also traditional in Uist for the feast of St Michael on the 29th September and these were distributed to the island's poor, suggesting a caring and supportive community:

> Some...were running with bee-skep baskets round the poorer huts of the nearer town land, giving, as custom compelled, and their good hearts in any case had prompted, something of their bounty in St Michael's morning food to the less fortunate of their fellows. (p7)

Lastly, there are many references to St Bride, who was particularly revered in Uist. She has taken on the attributes of a previous pagan goddess of Spring and her feast coincides with Candlemas in the Catholic Church. In the novel Anna is rocking Brideag (little Bride) in a cradle when Duncan first comes to see her. Brideag, in reality, was "a sheaf of corn, ornamented with flowers and ribbons". This practice was the vestige of a fertility rite performed to ensure good crops in the coming year and is referred to in

Frazer's *The Golden Bough*.[8] For her virtues and the regenerative spirit she brings to the community Anna virtually becomes identified with the saint. When in the end she is united with Duncan the islanders hear her singing and

> Her voice came over the water from Orosay's lee, a sound enchanting – *Bride's* voice that hushes the children and wrings the hearts of men. (p205)

When we review the novel as a whole, we see that Munro has organised the inclusion of so much reference to Hebridean Christian tradition to suggest the strength of faith in the island way of life which is there to support Ludovick and the other "good" characters and will ensure their ultimate triumph against the brutality of the Sergeant, the scheming of Col and the innate evil of the demonic incubus, Dark John.

Children of Tempest is a love story which graphically evokes the Uist landscape. But above all it is a parable which explores the dangers of human greed and the qualities which can counter it. Why the title *Children of Tempest*? It is not impossible that Munro is alluding to that great Shakespearean parable on human greed of similar name but with a happier ending for all. (Munro knew his Shakespeare as a glance at his next novel *The Daft Days* (1907) will quickly prove.) Is Anna a Hebridean Miranda, Dark John a more depraved Caliban and Fr Ludovick a modern Prospero whose magic is the power of prayer?

Notes

1. "Father Allan." Article by Neil Munro in *Oban Times*, 21st October, 1905
2. Letter for Neil Munro to unnamed male correspondent, 9th July, 1903. See Hermann Völkel, *Das literarische Werk Neil Munros*, Frankfurt; Peter Lang, 1996 p220
3. *Robert Louis Stevenson: The Scottish Short Stories and Essays*, Ed Kenneth Gelder, Edinburgh: Edinburgh University Press, 1989, pp.99-141
4. Letter from Robert Louis Stevenson to Henry James, March,1888, *The Letters of Robert Louis Stevenson*, Ed. Sidney Colvin, London: Methuen and Co.,1901, p.87
5. Letter from Robert Louis Stevenson to Sidney Colvin, 24th December, 1887, *The Letters of Robert Louis Stevenson*, Ed. Sidney Colvin, London: Methuen and Co., 1901, pp.88-89
6. Compare the boast of Para Handy in "The Leap Year Ball": " I can stot through the middle o' a dance like a tuppeny kahoochy ball." Para Handy, Eds Brian Osborne & Ronald Armstrong, Edinburgh: Birlinn, 1992, p.273
7. Carmichael, Alexander *Carmina Gadelica*, Vol. I, No 41, Edinburgh, 1928, p.96
8. Frazer, Sir James, *The Golden Bough*, London: MacMillan and Co. Ltd., 1963, p.177

Children of Tempest

CHAPTER I

Our Lady Star of the Sea

THERE was a woman years ago in Uist who had two sons, one to her first husband, one to his successor. They dwelt in Corodale. That place, remote and little, is like the enormous world and life itself – a mingling of meaningless hills and hollows, suffering the fury of eternal seas incomprehensible; to-night, it may be, wet with tears, to-morrow smiled on by the most jovial sun, and once, though now forlorn, it was exceeding busy with betrothals and bridals and births, and blythe-meats, and burials in Lamasay yard, strife among the folk of it as well as great love. Two mountains stand behind the house where dwelt the widow and her sons – Hecla and Benmore the names of them; close beside in Usinish Glen is a lake so blue that no other water in the Long Isle can compare with it for loveliness. A prince well known in story fled here once from his enemies and hid him in a cave. He came out on a morning, as the story goes, and looked all round him at a wild wan sea and a dripping land, crossed himself, and *"Mon Dieu!"* said he; "how dolorous!" and shivered, poor lad! in his plaid, and looked again at the mist on Hecla, and hearkened, all abashed, to the roll of waves in the creek of the Virgin Mary, the plash of breakers on the rocks of Hellisdale. "What a place for a right tragedy," said he, "if here were people capable of a passion!" Beside him as he spoke was a huge, dark silent man who understood, and smiled to himself, but said nothing to his prince, for whose poor cause a twelve-month later he was doomed to die. He was father to her that lived in Corodale. In this man's mind there slept a score of old fierce tales about the place the prince was looking on; from his own loins was yet to come a story of passion that till now but half-revealed, has made Corodale memorable for many generations. I walked in Uist yesterday, on what were once this dark man's acres; I found Usinish silent, except for the belling of red deer.

Corodale House was gone completely but for the lintels seeking out among the nettles. I cried, with half a hope of something to be manifest – what, I knew not – "Duncan! Duncan!" between the bushes one time coaxed to make a Hebridean garden for Anna the girl of fortune, but there was no answer. Duncan is departed and the girl that loved him; and gone too is Col the brave and wicked: there has been no dance in Corodale for two generations. Still the crash of seas, and Corodale Loch in sunshine blue as an angel's eye: still the mountains but never again the men! Love and avarice, that sought the Treasure of McNeil, blazed high and furious (it seemed), but brief like fires on autumn moors, and all that is left is this tale of the widow's sons, sometimes yet to be heard, half-guessed at, in the shearings, the matter of a song chanted by the fishermen of the Outer Isles.

Not in the neighbourhood of Corodale itself, but on the other side of the island, upon a rock that rose above the sandy macharland, a church-bell rang one morning in September. The scream of sea-fowl and the sound of waters mingled with the summons to Mass in Our Lady Star of the Sea. A high wind blew. The bay was full of idle boats. No shuttle clacked in the looms of the little black town-land houses. From all sides came the people for the Mass of this St Michael's Day, clambering up the narrow paths to the church upon the rock. The men were all fishers, or tillers of the grudging soil, built large, blue-eyed, and slow; the women, almost without exception, wore the gaudiest of plaids and kerchiefs, stepped like hinds, subdued their rover glances from a sense of the decorum due to the occasion, and yet in every roll of the haunches every gesture, gave a hint of fires.

A porringer half full of holy water, brown from some mossy well, stood in a nook at the entrance: they dipped their fingers in it, muttering an invocation, and went into a sanctuary where the odour of peat and new-baked bread was incense, and knelt to their Gaelic *Aves.* All in this chapel of Stella Maris had with them the St Michael's cake – the Michael morning food, seven cornered for the seven mysteries, and later these were blessed by Father Ludovick. Throughout that peaceful service in the chapel on the hill the sound of the quarrelsome sea intruded. Within was calm, one common heart in harmony subdued before the Mystery; outside in the world warred the unregenerate elements, winds unelect by Heaven blustering from Hecla and Benmore, waves thrashing on the little isle of Orosay and striving among the skiffs.

There was one in the congregation who thought of this in the intervals of her priest-brother's exhortations to his people to praise Michael for his guidance and God for His bounty of corn and fruit. She sat in the front of the church, close up on the altar, a figure for daintiness and dress wholly foreign in that assemblage of tartan plaids and kerchiefs, running the beads of her rosary through fingers white as milk and fine as satin, though she was now her brother Ludovick's housekeeper, spinner, darner, baker, and cook. Now and again his glance would fall upon her upturned and abstracted face, and never without a momentary glow of keen affection. He loved his people; but still the very core of his regard was for Little Anna, who was little in their language only because her brother was uncommon tall.

To her alone perhaps of all the congregation came some secular influence with the invading sound of wind and sea; bringing a thought of the wide, noisy, battling, restless world whereof these Outer Isles are but a windblown fringe. A Michaelmas in another land was in her recollection; she heard the morning carol of the birds in the garden of St Teresa; Sister Agnes took her through the streets of Paris again, and the clamour of the pavements, the cries about the booths, were like the throb and shout of seas in the land of her heredity. A wistfulness was in her face: she thought of idle worldly things remote from this high Stella Maris on the rock, filled with humble folk prostrate in their faith, redolent of peats and new-baked morning bread of good St Michael, Neptune of the Gael, patron saint of boats and horses.

It was the chimes of Notre Dame she heard above the tinkling bell that marked the *sanctus, sanctus, sanctus* of the Preface; at the chanting of her brother there came to her the air of a careless song heard on the packet from Calais, when a mariner stood out upon the bows, strong figure of eternal quest and hope, looking for land, and she, the child, the voyager from home, was all agog for new experiences.

And then the Mass was over, the people went forth eagerly with their cakes into the windy world of vacant spaces, of peat-stacks, promontories, dead and crumbling castles, ancient huts of lichened stone that seemed a part of nature, so much in harmony were they with nooks of earth they sheltered in; along the stony footpaths; by the verge of perilous cliffs. On the outer rocks Atlantic burst with thunder or retched through the three Sounds eastward; Hecla and Benmore smoked with mist about their bases. A bleak land it might seem to them that have no inward fires, and yet a land most brave, often most beautiful, acceptable to God, and edifying extremely. On the edge of Kinavreck a piper stood who knew it so, and threw his instrument into his arm, and, full of pride and happiness, charmed the uproarious sea with mountain songs.

Father Ludovick took his sister's hand unconsciously in his as he came out of the church a little behind his people, and they walked together towards the presbytery house that sheltered to the south of Stella Maris. They were, perhaps, the only ones in all the congregation to speak English, though it was not their mother nor their favourite tongue.

"Anna," said he, reflecting, "I think every priest should have a sister. Only one; two would be for any sober cleric's detriment."

"Why?" said she, smiling at his limitation, as she looked up into his face.

He glanced vaguely after his dispersing people hurrying with the Michaelmas cakes to the poor; at the contending sea, at the threat of the horizon. He was a man about thirty-five years old, tall and spare, beloved of his folk, who called him playfully behind his back "Lord of the Isles," half for his mother's name that had been Macdonald, half for his attributes of lovable wise command. A king in some respects, and yet a child in his simplicities.

"Why?" asked his sister Anna again, the wind in her hair, the blue of the sea in her eyes.

"It brings him nearer to the world," said Father Ludovick. "God bless the Long Isle! God bless my dear own people! their very follies make me fonder of them. And yet – *mochree!* – they are somehow, sometimes, so far from me that I need a little sinful sister to make my love for human nature something more than a spiritual passion for the universal."

"Indeed, and thank you, Father Ludovick, for the 'sinful,'" said Anna, and stopped to drop a mocking curtesy. "What a mercy I came back from France to keep my brother from taking wings and flying! Another month of bad baking and a perpetual diet of meagre soup would have made him into an angel!"

"But I wish the sister would not smile to herself when she should be deep in her devotions. It disconcerts her brother the priest."

"I thought of Paris just for some moments," said she contritely.

"I know, I know," said Father Ludovick, "and I, poor dust! – infected through a worldly eye and a Paris cap, thought at the same moment of Valladolid. I heard the wind in its steeples. It was the smell of new-baked cakes, perhaps, as much as my sister Anna's eyes. Valladolid and the guitar – Heaven help me! – and morning in a wayside wine-shop at breakfast. How glad we should be to have escaped the world with all its distractions, and find peace here and the simple way!"

"Yes," said Anna, yet not with heartiness. She loved the Isles for reasons less austere. Her brother did not notice the absence of enthusiasm. With a bent head now and hands clasped behind his back, he picked his way over the rough path that led to his home. "I heard the sound of the sea come in yonder," he went on, "and it seemed the threat of the outer world far away from these little islands, and we so snug and safe here, with not even a lover to steal away my sister."

"Y–yes," said Anna, even less heartily than before. So much less heartily that her brother looked up, awakened from his reverie, caught a fleeting glimpse of some suppressed amusement. He laughed softly, and pinched her slightly on a finger.

"Well, at least, he has not come yet," said he.

"There is no hurry, I declare to you," said Anna. "Why should we talk nonsense?"

"Because we are the children of men," said Father Ludovick. He stopped, and drew her up beside him, and looked at her, dashed upon with smiles and sun, at her wind-blown hair, her ardent open lips, her head upheld in a playful arrogance. "Ah, it will come, it will come!" he said regretfully, and pushed her from him lovably. "The world is not so blind; God the good Artist does not throw away His finest masterpiece upon a desolate rock. And when it comes –"

"It will be for MacNeil's Treasure, and never for my heart." said Anna. "I declare the existence of that wretched gold would make me suspect a fairy prince's wooing."

"It must be for the pure love of the sweetest girl in all broad Albyn!" cried he; "and MacNeil's Treasure will be none of her attractions."

"The good folk of Uist, all the same, make much of my fifty-year fortune," said Anna.

"They will not envy you it, at all events, or I misjudge the folk of Uist."

"Oh no, they do not envy me; they would not do that, I feel sure, if it was blessed instead of cursed as you are always telling them. But I am hearing of it constantly in the huts –"

Father Ludovick gave an impatient cry. "In spite of what I say to them!" said he. "I will not have it! I have told them neither you nor I shall handle this cursed Loch Arkaig treasure. I loathe the very mention of it, because I know its story better perhaps than any man that lives, though maybe there are scores whose purgatory is the more frightful for their new knowledge of how much that devil's dross misled them. What a thought that men – otherwise, maybe, fit for paradise – should tenant hell eternally because some metal, whose glitter they never saw, lay tarnishing under a rock in – in –" He checked himself, and reddened. Anna looked up at him, surprised.

"In where?" she asked him, curiously. "I thought you could not know."

"Nor do I," said the priest hastily. "I have no idea where this wretched *ulaidh* is now, and I wish our uncle had never made it known to folk that he had passed the secret on to you. We are agreed, you and I, Anna, that though to please an old man dying, you may listen, it would be the greatest of errors to try to benefit you by this bequest."

"That is very well, but still I think the Church –"

"The Church!" He raised his arms with an impatient gesture. "Say no more of that; the Church could never touch it, except perhaps to sink it in the deeps of Barra Sound. *Dhe! I* would not risk it even there, for fear our cod and halibut should perish of yellow pest, and our herring come to table with eternal gut-poke for the fever of avarice."

"*Peccavi! peccavi!* I confess, Master Priest, to a small deception just now," said Anna, smiling again. "When I said the Church I meant just a new tower – of the littlest, of the cheapest – for Stella Maris, and perhaps a bottle of Spanish wine more frequently for Father Ludovick –"

"For his visitors it might perhaps be welcome, this extra flagon; myself, I have wine enough in my soul – faith! the juice itself of sun and tempest, carouse on fancies, and walk, when I will, uplifted on the mists of Hecla and Benmore. I own the Isles from Barra Head to the very Butt of Lewis so far as I can ride or sail a skiff; the sea is mine to the dip of it and all the winds come neighbourly to my door; would I change for a display of stone and mortar, and a bottle, the mood that makes me free of all, and one and equal with the universe? The first that mentions your name together with Loch Arkaig's trash – by God! I'll bring him to his bended knees! It was gathered in folly; it was buried in disgrace. Men have lied for it and died for it, and have lain awake at night to think on it when they might in dreams be happier than kings."

"But still," said Anna, – though this was more to herself than to her brother, – "but still I think it would be fine to have a new tower for the dear church, and the extra bottle of Spanish wine!"

They had reached the door of the presbytery house; they went in together.

There was a shiver of autumn coldness in the air; the horizon was broken by a long cloud that looked like a mountain new born in the deep; far off on the flats of Heiskar there was the froth of billows.

And all along the pathways of the island sped the people, hurrying home to break their cakes and divide the ceremonial lamb. Some of them whose dwellings were nearer the church had done so already, and were running with bee-sleep baskets round the poorer huts of the nearer town-land, giving, as custom compelled, and their good hearts in any case had prompted, something of their bounty in St Michael's morning food to the less fortunate of their fellows. Uist the windy complained in tussock and dune, and still gallant above the wind was the sound of young folks' merriment, of children laughing and crying to each other in the fields where they kept the cattle from the unfenced corn, of girls innumerable singing in the spirit of holiday, as, waist-encircled in each other's arms, they walked in groups to outer townships round the bays. A pleasant chatter of voices was carried on the wind, through it, and over all the piper upon Kinavreck giving himself wholly to the wonder of the day, the spirit of the season, breathing his immortal soul into the sheepskin and telling the grumbling sea.

Later in the day there rose a new sound – the thud of galloping hoofs and the whinnying of island ponies bearing the folk to another Michaelmas ceremony. They came from every part of the macharland, men and women and children; Father Ludovick led them to the graveyard first for prayers for all the stout old forefathers, and then to the scene of games. On the great white strand they played. There was running on foot and galloping on horseback; the ambitious contended eagerly for trivial prizes; couples, more wisely gauging the value of all this world can give, sought sandy little dells among the dunes, and there unseen made love with the vigour of the wind, the depth, the passion of the sea. A most merry wholesome world, and frank and simple! Anna flashed, a sunbeam, here and there among them; her brother, the priest, had children tugging at his knees and their mothers crying ironic pleasantries to him. He, too, felt tipsy with the wind-wine of Uist, felt in tune with the everlasting rhythm of all the swinging worlds. So busy were the white sands of the bay that it looked as if the whole isle were here.

All but one man.

The day was growing late when he came – this fellow – along the road from Corodale, and climbed to the back of the church of Stella Maris by a rocky path. He was tall, black, broad-shouldered, curled and bearded like a Spaniard, exceedingly neat in dress. When he reached the top of the rock at the church gable, he threw a glance to sea, sweeping the farthest line of it like a mariner expectant on a raft, then turned his glance with disappointment to the Sound. There was nothing to see there but a tiny lug-sail boat that had rounded Kintra of the Holy Cross, and beat clumsily against dark squalls and a rising tide.

He stood black and tall, and bitterly vexed, it seemed, biting his beard. And then his glance fell on the people at their games.

"St Michael's Day!" he said aloud. "I wondered where the folk had gone, and left their fields so lonely and their doors without a word of welcome. O king! are we not the forgetful folk in Corodale? Had I come here earlier I should have run my head into a Mass that might have cost me sixpence. I came to look for a sloop, and find myself at an *oda.* Well, here's no sloop on the blue, and my skipper is two days late from Arisaig, or met last night's storm and is now at the end of days and all sea-faring, with weeds in his teeth, somewhere under the Minch. I have no luck, devil the bit of it! what else could I look for when I rose on my wrong side this morning, and had mother cry me back in Corodale yesterday?"

He turned on his heel to go down from the rock the way he had mounted, when the open door of the chapel seemed to call him in. He hesitated for a little, bit his beard again, then challenged his resolution, went in with his cap in his hand, and awkwardly dipped a finger in the porringer. The bowl, perched precariously in its nook toppled and fell on the floor, breaking in fragments, and splashing his boots with the holy water.

"God be about us, that's bad!" said he, turning quickly from the unlucky omen. His going had been delayed but a few moments, yet they made nigh twelve months' difference to the life of the man in the lug-sail boat, who was buffeted in the Sound where the black squalls chased each other. For what to him upon the rock was to be the last glance out to sea showed the lugsail shake a moment, then belly suddenly, then the skiff upset and sink.

No one saw it but himself: the lovers busy in the dells the dancers on the sand, the foot-runners striving on the beach, – all the merry, careless populace missed the spectacle. He gave a shout that rang vastly in the wind plunged down the rocky path before the church, and ran towards the cove where the idle skiffs were tossing. "To sea! to sea! *'illean!"* he cried over and over again; and the people looked amazed at him tearing to their skiffs. They were ignorant of the tragedy; they could not guess a reason for his conduct. "'Twas ever the way with Uist at the dancing," he thought angrily; "their eyes in their insteps;" and reached the wall where the skiffs were ranged, and leaped on the nearest, and slashed with a knife till the bow was free, and threw out with one enormous heave of his arms the big brown sail, and steered in chase of a helpless figure clinging to a fishing bladder, driven before the squalls to Kintra of the Holy Cross.

He was an elderly man that grasped the bladder, with a slack foolish mouth in which the rude seas plopped, exceedingly salt and smelling of weeds. To his senses the bladder seemed no bigger than a pebble and no more buoyant as he turned and rolled in the waves. Of windy Uist he could see no speck; but when at intervals upon a crest he opened brine-blurred eyes, he saw the shabby tower of Our Lady Star of the Sea standing miraculous and serene among the waves that swept conquering over the bulging world. His ears were full of roarings, his mind fumbled confusedly over the beginnings of many prayers. Mountains seemed weighed on his feet; his fingers appeared to sweat a grease, and slipped in spite of him from the wood of the bladder; and he sank, and he sank, and he sank, till he hung over the edge of the universe, above the emptiness that is under all things, sea or land.

Down upon him swept the skiff, with the dark man calling, the tiller hard in his arm-pit, the sheets of the mainsail shrieking under his heel; she went round into the wind, her canvas flapping, her bows, annoyed, objecting to the check. The dark man saw a hand, plucked free the halyard, threw up the helm, and dived.

Before the wind, tossed like the bladder or the skiff ahead of them, the two men drifted towards Kintra of the Holy Cross.

And then night fell on windy Uist; the curlews cried night and storm. The wind raved, and the rain slanted over the land. But still were people passing along the road and footpaths; lights shone over all the country. Michaelmas Day was done, and now had come the hour of song and story.

CHAPTER II

In the Black Houses

A CUSTOM of all lonely simple races brings the folk together at night to *ceilidh* (as they call their evening gossips) in these Outer Isles. Storms do not prevent them; storms, indeed, but make these evening entertainments sweeter when the merry groups meet in the larger houses of the townships to sit about the central fires of peat. Tales ancient and heroic, of Fingal the brave and Ossian the plucker of harps, are told; songs of sea and pasture-land, and short love and long war, are sung: guesses are put and repartee abounds. Sometimes, too, a gifted man will fill a sheepskin with a gush of pride and squeeze the most marvellous tunes from reeds and drones, expressing, to all who have the ears to hear, the ecstasy that lies in remembrance and regret, till the folk lean forward on their seats, and with blood-red faces look into the peat-flame and the ember, something with no words for its description, something old and sweetly melancholy and unrecoverable stirring them to tears. Up in the lofts, peeping between the jetty cabars – the peat-stained joists – will lie the children, marvelling, and all eyes and ears, drinking song and tale and pipe-tune thirstily, terrified for the dark spaces of the roof above and behind them when the story is of ghost and sad presentiment, and laughing heartily and uncontrolled when other humours inform the entertainment. The men pleat quicken tethers for the cattle, or twine tough heather into ropes to bind the thatch for the roofs of their houses; the women knit, sew, card, and spin. So have they done for generations beyond number, carrying on by word of mouth the poems, the histories of the Gael.

It was at such a gathering in the township of Dalvoolin, round Kintra of the Holy Cross, the dark man, who looked Spanish because of his curled short beard, found himself that self-same night he had saved an elderly wretch from drowning. He was one that ever loved an entertainment – if it cost him nothing – and felt it good to bask in the praise the Islands of the west will ever accord to a hero.

They called him Young Corodale at the outset, for the name of his family's small estate on the other side of the island: the night passed quickly, but if quick passed the night quicker passed their shyness, and soon they were calling him by his Christian name of Col. For he was one who stood on no ceremony, and liked the brevity of his own name because it came so pat to the lips of all good fellows who had coin to spend. There was no flattery too coarse for him of the Spanish beard. In the spaces between song or tale 'twas "*Oh 'ille!* what courage! In the black squall, too, and for Dark John, an old man without woman or child or a penny of land of his own, who must die soon anyway."

"Amn't I telling the same Dark John that death has surely forgotten him?" said an unkindly spinster woman, dragging rebellious wool through her carding-combs.

"But a trifle, but a trifle, good folk!" said the affable man from Corodale. "I have swam ere now as a lad round Orosay, and to carry this man you call Dark John round the point of Kintra was like bearing a sack of sticks."

"Now that we have dried you, we must wet you hero," said the man of the house, proffering a glass. "Have that, Master Col, and stretch your hand for another; it is not every day, worse luck! a man is on the edge of drowning, and a gallant close bye to save him in windy Uist. Drink, and stretch again your hand."

And Col most cheerfully stretched his hand. It cost nothing.

"It is not lucky to save a man from drowning: take its spoil from the sea and the spoil itself will punish you," said the grumbling woman at the carding-combs. "There would have been a lament and a keening at Boisdale to-morrow, sure, but for this strong gentleman, and I have not had the fortune to hear a dirge for a twelve-month."

"Daughter of him I'll mention not! do you grudge Dark John his life?" cried the man of the house impatiently, and at that the boys in the loft began to laugh, so up with a scourge of broom to them climbed their mother. They ran like mice to their bed, but she was after them, and her switching could be heard below.

"It was not I, mother, not I," cried one of the boys, whimpering carefully.

"Well, never mind; take yon for the sake of company! it will like enough be you on the next occasion. Oh, Mary Mother, what a heart-break are the children of this island!" And down she came, smiling, stout, and panting, no sooner to be seated at her hearth than the faces of the children were at the mouth of the loft again.

Col of the Spanish beard and the trim clothing had an eye that found the very core of whoever he looked at, rendering the shy or the scarce honest uneasy at his glance. He would seem a fellow to be adored by manor woman-kind, so fine in his gestures, so free and bold and ringing in his voice. But the goodwife sitting at his side had his beard between her and the light of a crusie that hung from a rafter, and she must be staring every now and then through it at the mouth below betraying another character She had started by admiring; she grew, like a woman, on the mere aspect of things concealed, to dislike, and her chastisement of her children had been meant in a roundabout way as relief for her feelings.

"Stretch your hand, Master Col," invited the man of the house, who loved a merry party. She gave him a grimace disapproving, and made to end this adulation.

"Perhaps," said she, "our piper will play another tune?"

"The piper has gone over for a while to Geepie's dwelling," said the husband, "but his pipes are here."

"Poor is the bagpipe that is widowed," said she, and could not keep her eyes off the mouth that to all but her was hid below the Spanish beard. Col saw her look: he turned on her his disconcerting eyes; but for once they had no power, because the woman had seen his mouth. "There, or I'm wrong, is the daughter of a bitch!" he thought, for no other reason than that she faced him unabashed.

And then a loud knocking came to the door, setting the hearts of the bairns in the loft thundering in their bosoms. Even the elder company seemed alarmed. It was not on Michaelmas night there should be rapping at any door in hospitable Uist.

"Christ's cross be on us!" whispered the girls. A hollow silence held the house all trembling, outside there was the drip of the thatch eaves, the old search and pity of the wind, but they heard not these, nor the threat of ocean that is ever in the air of the Outer Isles.

"Who knocks?" cried the goodman at last, and manoeuvred to get his wife, a stout one, between him and the door.

"Hail to the house and the household! For the love of Mary will any one give me a place here to lay my head?" cried a voice they all knew, and none better than Col, who had heard the despairing shriek of it as he dived for the man who had lost his hold of the fishing-bladder and was slipping for the last time into the deeps of Barra Sound.

The company laughed, their minds relieved.

"And where would you lay your feet, honest person? Outside to trip the neighbours?" asked the goodwife. She opened the door, and gave entrance to the old man with the slack foolish mouth. "I thought they had dried your skin and wet your stomach, John, and put you long ago to your naked bed?"

"I was there indeed," said the man who entered, blinking with eyes inflamed by the deeper brine, "but wakened and had a strong command in me to seek for the hero that saved me, and in the dark I have lost my way."

"Faith! and in the dark, then, you have had a lover's good fortune and have found your heart," said the goodman, "for here he is."

"Let me put my two eyes on him," cried Dark John. He peered about the assemblage, plainly a whimsical natural character, long and thin and sea-sodden till his skin was all in furrows, scarcely worth saving from the fish he had himself so long preyed on. When he saw the gentleman from Corodale he made a loutish bow. "There he is to you!" cried he aloud and elated. "Master; I could not sleep without coming again to thank you. For more than an hour, *mo chreach!* have I looked for you, and here my fortune brings me to your feet. I dreamt I was in the deep again and the net-bow gone, and the sting of the salt in the nose of me. I wakened with the water glucking at my throat, and felt I must come and make my reverence to the hero that saved me."

"You thanked me enough before, just man," said Corodale, but still was manifestly pleased. "How happens it that a decent man of Uist was fishing alone on Michaelmas Day?"

"It is not a day of Obligation," answered the old man. "I have a wonderful memory for minding things; but of the feast days and the fast days of Isle Uist I am for ever forgetting, being a lonely man without woman or child to keep me to the bit. The truth, O king of the moon and sun and the beautiful sublime stars! is, that I forgot what day this was."

The young folk laughed at his eloquence; the goodwife filled him out a little glass with a foot on it, for the footless glass of the hero with a will is not for men with slack and foolish mouths.

"'Tis no great glass, goodwife," said he, "I could drain it if it was a mile or more to the bottom for I have salt, oh God! such salt, in me. I drink," said he and stood up like a mast, "to the gentleman of Corodale. I am his man from this on. Is it the fire? – there is the hand! The knife for him? – here is the bosom! Oh, the sea, the sea! the tremendous sea, and terrible! I have lived on it, and lived by it, and still I hate it like the very hell when there's but a plank between me and purgatory even though my oars are in the arm-pits of the waves. It serves me right that I should be forgetful of the good St Michael's Day. But I drink to the hero."

"Who has not the best of memories himself," said Col laughing. "We are so far from the ordinances yonder at Corodale, and I am so much from home that even I will now and then overlook spiritual matters. And what luck had you, just old man, at the day's fishing?"

"What but Michaelmas luck?"

"A good catch?"

"No, but very near it; a Protestant from Benbecula who shot a fathom or two to the side of me, had, I am sure, three cran."

"So!" said Col; "the English have a saying that has more sense than most of their sayings – that a miss is as good as a mile; it pertains marvellously to a fisherman who hales empty nets from alongside full ones. And God seems careless enough to be so kind to heretics from Benbecula."

The goodwife looked through the Spanish beard and crossed herself; she had no taste for irreligious levity, and there the *ceilidh* company shared her sentiment, thinking the Corodale hero scarcely considerate of his pleasantries on a Michaelmas night. Dark John coughed to cover the disgrace of his rescuer, and did it so well that it ended in a real convulsion.

"It is there you have the bad cough, old man," said the goodwife.

"He will be wanting another glass," said the woman who was unkind, and teased wool with a gusto as if it were the fibres of bachelor mankind.

"A bad enough cough I'll allow," said Dark John; "but there's many a one in Boisdale burying-ground would like to have it this night."

A demand rose for the dance of Cailleag-an-Dunan – the Mill-dust Man.[1] The piper was called from Geepie's; up he set his drones upon his shoulder and played like a MacCruimen of Skye, while a man and woman made attitudes graceful or grotesque before each other till the woman fell at last upon the floor, play-acting death. Her partner made moan for his dead carlin, dancing still about her body, stopping to breathe upon her palms or touch her with a willow wand. But she did not stir till he had kissed her on the lips, and then she sprang joyfully to life that ever comes from love, and again the dance went on.

Col smiled with an outer aspect of sympathy; but the goodwife looked at his beard, and was annoyed to see his lips.

"You are perhaps tired of our poor play?" said she hastily, jealous for her guests.

1 This should read "Cailleach an dùdain – the Carlin of the Mill Dust". It is difficult to explain how these errors in both the Gaelic and the English translation have crept into the text. The description of the dance is taken from the notes to Alexander Carmichael's famous collection of Gaelic hymns and incantations known as the *Carmina Gadelica* first published in 1900. See note to Hymn 77, *Carmina Gadelica* Vol. 1, Edinburgh: Scottish Academic Press, 1983, p.206.

"On my word," said he, "I have seldom enjoyed myself better. 'Tis ten years, no more nor less, since I saw Cailleag-an-Dunan danced in Corodale. Folk in our part have lost the skill of it." And then he saw that she was annoyed, and she knew he saw it, and was vexed to make a stranger feel uneasy, so she gave him the first word of her flattery that night.

"They have not lost their skill of swimming, at least," she said, "as the old man there has reason well to know. You are a lucky man, that are so friendly with the heartless sea – Mary forgive me that I should speak so of Her Treasury!"

"The sea is no friend of mine, and still I am much on the sea," he explained, "though something of a landlord by estate." He whispered in her ear, "I have an interest in a sort of sloop that sometimes runs a little Barra cordial to the mainland."

"I have heard a breath of that among the men-folk," whispered back the goodwife. "O king! good winds be ever behind you in that. In Barra and Mingulay are honest pious Catholics like ourselves, and well-deserving."

"Doubtless, goodwife, doubtless!" said he of the Spanish beard, "but for once their Michaelmas has gone by without some mainland commodities, for the *Happy Return*, launched by Master Paul, priest of Barra, and with three vials of holy water in her den, is two days overdue. I left Corodale yesterday to look for signs of her, and thought she might have been driven through the Sound by last night's storm, and might be beating in upon this side of Uist to-day, but never a glimpse of the *Happy Return.*"

"Oh righ!" said the goodwife.

> "Blest be the boat
> By our King of the elements,
> Blest be the boat!"

crossing herself the while.

"It is a pious rune," admitted Col of Corodale, "but I wish my skipper may have been depending more on his own seamanship than on prayers."

"But the prayers of the faithful!" said the goodwife eagerly. "Oh! they avail, Corodale. Seven skiffs have I seen brought safe to land through the wildest weather simply through the supplications of Master Ludovick."

Col smiled. "There," said he, "is angelic navigation for you! A good priest, they say, but I fear he could not put all his power into prayer for a smuggler's sloop, for there's some of the cloth are mighty particular nowadays."

"It is true he does not favour the honest free trade," she confessed, "otherwise you might have asked his services. For indeed he is mighty in prayer, more than any other priest in the Long Island, and can wrestle with the worst agents. He might have been among us to-night, for affable exceedingly is Master Ludovick, and loves the old devices; but he has an uncle that is of great years and is near his end, as you may have heard across the way in Corodale, and Master Ludovick and his sister have gone early home to-night."

"His sister?" said Col, with a little livelier interest; "I thought she was in France."

"Indeed, the dear creature! and she was, just man, for five years at her schooling, but came home again three months ago; and long may she be with us, till the right man comes to take her!"

"It was Anna I saw, then, in Saxon clothes among the company at the games?"

"Just Herself, Corodale, just Herself – Little Anna with the fifty-years' fortune," said the goodwife fondly, like one who spoke about a daughter of her own.

"Fortune?" said Col, as if he sang a note of song. She cast a quick glance into his beard and saw greed.

"It is just a saying of the common folk," said she hastily. "They are talking about a treasure; faith! who gets our Anna gets a treasure better far than the red metal of the MacNeil's *ulaidh.*"

When she said that, young Corodale laughed. "MacNeil's Treasure," said he. "You are speaking of the Prince's money from Loch Arkaig? An old tale yon! I am fearing there is little of it to the fore now that Anna's uncle is at his end. I have heard my father" – ("May your father have his share of paradise!" murmured the goodwife, piously crossing herself) – "I have heard my father often speak of this money, and laugh at the notion of any of it being left."

"That may be as it may," said the goodwife, "but here we have another way of it." And stopped suddenly, annoyed at the mouth below the Spanish beard.

"But the treasure would not be Anna's in any case," said Col, with his mind briskly turning over all considerations. "It would more properly be her brother the priest's – no, no, now that I mind of it, the men who made the pact knew better, as my father had the story, and agreed that a priest should never share a second time the secret of the Loch Arkaig *ulaidh.* They were wise in their generation."

"God be about us!" said the goodwife humbly. "Who would touch it till the appointed time?"

A flash came in Corodale's eyes. "The appointed time?" said he, "of course; *Dhe!* have I not forgotten? If there was not another Rising in fifty years, the money was to go to the last survivors or their families. And the last is Master Ludovick's uncle, the old done man of Dermosary. When will the time be up, good woman?"

"I do not know, and I do not care," said she shortly, and cried across to a guest, "Oh, Hector, tell us the tale of Manus!" And the guest started a tale that seemed like to last till the crowing of cocks, but all were happy and all intent upon his story, except the dark man from Corodale.

He made calculations, ticking the years off with his hand inside his waistcoat on his heart, so eager on it, so apt to blunder in his hurry, that he wished he had a score of fingers on each hand.

"Why, by the soul of me!" said he to the goodwife at last, a light in his eyes, and his mouth to her more unpleasant than ever – "there's no more than a year to run. Come next Feill Michael the treasure will be Anna's. Lucky indeed was Anna – if the tale were true." The goodwife paid no heed. "Twenty thousand pounds!" he said to himself softly in English no one there could understand. "I have heard my father mention it a score of times. He believed the stuff was still wherever it was hidden when they brought it to the Isles, and many a day he searched for it when fishing had been more profitable. Twenty thousand pounds in louis of France, crusadoes of Spain, and English guineas! Lord! what a hole it would cobble in Corodale's brogues, that's like to suffer again by the loss of the *Happy Return*, stove in maybe on Barra Head or Mingulay." He lost himself in thoughts the most indulgent, the most luxurious. What could he not do with twenty thousand pounds? No longer-this ridge of rock, this narrow life among unable simpletons. With half twenty thousand pounds he could take the world for his pillow, and see to the very end of things – travel, adventure, purchase, love and win. Twenty thousand pounds; God! twenty thousand pounds! In the hands – as it were – of a schoolgirl! What days and nights were in a tenth part of that sum! And still – and still – not so very much in itself after all; some people ill-deserving had far more – but in what a bold spirit could make out of it. He turned over in his pocket some coins that had been his first care when he was dragged ashore with Dark John drenched; he turned them over, and they felt singularly lonely and insignificant. What might be made of twenty thousand pounds – the stuff itself being but dead dust? A bigger sloop was in a fraction of it, perhaps two or three; no need to run risks in the free trade; himself his old ideal – master of a bigger fleet of fishers, or briskly trading between Uskavagh and the mainland, with curing-stations round every creek in Uist beating the encroaching east coast merchant at his own devices. Twenty thousand pounds – and every pound a bait for twenty more!

And all this was in the keeping of a girl! He felt a grievance against her, though he had never seen her close at hand since six or seven years ago, when she was but a child with no interest for him.

The night passed quickly in the house of entertainment dance followed story, and song came after dance. "More peat: more peat!" the hearth glowed, the bairns still looked down from the loft, lying on their bellies, some asleep for weariness, and one of them fell among the company and suffered his mother's lovable harmless chastisement. The cattle in the byre turned noisily in their stalls, a pony fastened at the gable beat wildly on the ground. Smells of mordants, of the herb-dyed clothes, of peats and pungent byres and the sea perfume – the clean, good, zesty perfume of net and line and oar – prevailed. And outside in the night there was the storm rising with the rising tide. The lights of the islands grew less; townlands were gone to bed; the ocean tore round Kintra of the Holy Cross, and growled like a beast furious on Rhu-na-faing. Far off on Heiskar, like a star afloat upon the sea, there gleamed a beacon-fire – Heiskar was guiding in the herring shoals or warning off the foreign mariner.

And Corodale the hero, on the hero's seat beside the goodwife, turned his silver *tasdan* in his pouch, feeling the indecent lust for gold, the goodwife glancing through his Spanish beard the while, liking him less at every look though there were half-a-dozen girls in her company who would have gone barefoot with such a noble fellow to the other end of Albyn through the storm.

"What would you do with twenty thousand pounds if you had it?" he asked her suddenly, coming out of his noble dreams.

"Fine I know that!" said the goodwife quickly. "I would make mirth in every patch of tenant land in brindled little Uist of the sheldrakes. Tochers for the brides, and silver crown pieces of luck for the little fists of the darling new-born babies; hale nets for the fishers, and braver boats. Where the land is blanched, I would spread, sow, and build. O king! what an opportunity! I am all hot to be thinking of it, sure! Good would it be indeed to be the free giver out of such a store. And first there would be a guinea for Nanny Veg, that needs a new loom. and there would be five to bring the blind man's son back from the bloody wars – oh, it would take the night to tell the marvels of merriment there would be in twenty thousand pounds; but very early and above all there would be a new tower for the chapel."

Corodale laughed.

"*Oh Dhe!* I daresay the Church has had its claw in the stuff ere now," said he, "though a priest by the pact was never again to know its whereabouts."

"Heaven forgive the thought!" said the goodwife humbly. "There would be a curse on any that handled it before the time appointed; and indeed Master Ludovick calls it cursed in any case, and has a red fury on him if he hears us call it Anna's gold."

And now the night of song and story was done; the folk, humming the airs of the songs they had heard, went forth in groups for their homes. Loud indeed was the storm on the islands; no distant star was to be seen except the flame of Heiskar or the twinkle of some crusie light in Dalvoolin. Corodale went forth to his lodging in the tacksman's dwelling over the burn, pondering on hidden gold, never heeding the wind or rain, unhaunted by any tender strain of song. One by one the lights went out in windy Uist, and the night was conqueror. But in the waste and middle of it, when the storm was wildest and the hour most dark, fathers and children came out and got upon the roofs to keep the thatch from flying. They sat on the slopes of heather and straw, beat on by rains and choking to the gusts, and sang together: –

"God shield the house, the fire, the kine,
And all who take their peace within,
Hold care aloof from me and mine,
And Mary keep us all from sin,

This night, this night, this stormy night
O Lightner of the stars that shine,
Pity the women, pity the bairns
Bring peace to man, and horse, and kine!"

They sat all night on the frail roofs along the shore singing these and suchlike runes and hymns (if ships were passing and could hear, the seamen must have thought the waves enchanted); and there the morning found them when he came, gladly and with peace, over the hills of Hecla and Benmore.

CHAPTER III

The Widow and Her Sons

COL went back that day to Corodale, walking, to begin with, on the pleasant sandy plains facing the Atlantic, that turned and basked in the bosom of the world, murmuring a little in the creeks, and showing a curl of grey on the distant Monach isles. The road soon left the shore and brought him into the country of the lochs, past dark and thoughtful barps knee-deep in the rushy tarns, past ruined duns where ravens pecked in the eyeless gables – old strongholds of the tribes, remembering. Beyond Askernish and Mingary, Ollay Loch and Ormaclett Castle, and then he departed from the country of habitations and went through grave Glen Dorochay, seeking the Pass of Hellisdale that comes out upon the east of Uist.

A pleasant land to travel in upon such happy weather; on every hand the folk so rude and strong, coming along the way with cheerful salutations, engaged with natural easiness upon their season's occupations – the reaping of oat and barley, the herding of sturdy little cattle red and brown, the driving in of peats. Long strings of little horses, led by girls and boys, came out of the east where cried the lapwing, where sometimes blackguardly old Loch Boisdale sea-gulls screamed to the little rustic birds the taunt of far-travelled mariners, and every horse had its panniers laden with the turf to light and warm innumerable *ceilidhs*, to make pictures on the hearth-stones for the tales in the winter nights to come. The huts gulped smoke, the doors stood open; he had many invitations to go in and drink milk and rest.

It was pleasant exceedingly to see the young folk smiling; it was good to travel in such a land of hospitality, but Col stayed to enjoy neither one nor the other, walking quickly, and full of thought about his fortunes.

He came down the pass on Corodale when the sun was at his height and grandeur, saw the lake in Glen Usinish shining like an angel's eye; and far away, dim and faery, a vision like Ibrysail, land of eternal youth, a bard's thought breathed in vapour on the horizon, he saw, unmoved, the cliffs, the peaks of Skye.

At a place beside the cave where Charles Edward Stuart skulked when all his fights were done and his hopes destroyed, Col met his mother, with a bright *tonnag* of tartan wrapped over her head, as if she were for travelling.

She was altogether unlike her son, this widow woman of Corodale, notable in the isles till to-day as the best who ever danced there, so little in stature that he might have lifted her like a child. She ran to him with her arms outstretched, and, never at ease in the English tongue a new gentility was bringing to the best families of the Outer Isles, though she knew it very well, she cried "O Michael Saint! my son that was lost is found again bless the sacred Name! And come away within this moment, and have something to eat."

She turned to walk with him towards the house, that stood in tall walls sheltering such lowly shrubs as alone will thrive upon the wind-vexed Hebrides.

"For two days I have not touched bread," said she hanging on his arm and all trembling. "For two days! And as for sleep in such storms, with a door shut upon my son, it was impossible. Col, Col, where were you?"

He smiled, kindly at the eyes (whatever might happen below the Spanish beard). "There's news to tell in that," said he. "I was on Monday at Loch Eynort, spending the night with our friends at Kirkidale. Yesterday I took my feet out of there with me and went west to Boisdale, and –"

"On Michaelmas Day, O king! to be travelling on affairs. Col, it is not right. Were you at Mass?"

He felt annoyed to be so questioned, but did not show it. "I went to Our Lady Star of the Sea," he said.

"My good Col!" cried out the happy mother. "And saw Master Ludovick?"

"Yes," said Col, never mentioning how brief and secular had been his seeing. "There is no word of the sloop," he hurried on. "She has been heard of neither in Loch Eynort nor on the other side. I thought she might have been driven through Sound Eriskay on Monday, and it was that sent me over to the machar side of the island; but there the sea is blank. Three days ago she should have been here in Skiport, but now I'm thinking there may be empty kegs about the Minch and dog-fish in the hold of the *Happy Return*. There was my last chance!" He became exceeding bitter in his tone.

"*Oh Dhe!*" she cried in horror; "to have such a thought, and make so much of the vessel and so little of her men! I will excuse you, because you must always be putting the worst face on affairs; and it is not at all likely that so skilly a man as the skipper was anywhere else than safe in Arisaig yesterday waiting the end of the storm. He will be here to-morrow; and now I must go and comfort his wife."

"And still," said Col, "I wish I had the comfort of but the one look of the sloop, and her with her mast standing. This north wind takes three days before its heart is broken –"

"– And this is the fourth," said she, determined to make him more cheerful, "and look what a day it is, with the sea, as the men are telling me, all shivering with fish. We went to Mass yesterday, in St Mary's, Duncan and I; but my Michaelmas morning cake is still on the board: I had not the heart to go among the poor people. But now I'll be hurrying among them, seeing you are back again. It was wrong of me to stay at home."

"There is nothing in that that heaven will not look over, for we are poor enough ourselves."

"Not so poor," said she blythly, "but there are others will be thinking us as wealthy as the kings, Col."

"That is Duncan's way of it; my own is greatly different. By all the old great stones, I have had such plans!"

"Plans, *mo chreach!*" said she. "It is richer you would be, my son, with plain contentment."

"You are learning Duncan's lesson very well," said Col, and stared ahead of him as they neared the house in the glen.

"We could have no more than we have," said the mother. "Here's a comfortable dwelling – praise Mary! and the good building of your great-great-grandfather! Here's our own land with Mary's Treasury lapping at our door, and every fisherman will bring his basket for us to pick from before he takes a fin to his own fireside, even if he must live himself on the dog-fish afterwards."

"It is good, mother, that you are so easily pleased. I have other notions myself of what is comfort. But indeed what am I to be complaining, that am only your second son?"

"You are the only son of your father, my goodman – peace with him and his share of Paradise!" said the little woman, her face exalted. "Duncan – dear heart! – would be the last to think of things in that way."

They had come to the garden wall. Corodale House, that was as high as a tree in this treeless glen, and as grey as the rocks, and speckled with windows, blind or lozenged, had one gable of greater antiquity than the rest, with broken gun-ports for a hint of other days. Col stopped and looked at it, struck for the first time in his life with some sense of its humility.

"Where's Duncan?" he asked suddenly.

"He has but new come home," said the mother. "Like yourself he has been gone all night."

"All night!" said Col, astonished. 'And where was he all night?"

"I was anxious about you; I had dreams, I saw you swimming for your life –"

"By the name of God!" cried Col, and faced her, "you were not far amiss. I had to do some swimming last night down at Boisdale for an old man who but for me would never sup crowdy nor set eyes on Uist again."

"A drowning man," said his mother, with a start; "a drowning man, and you saved him. I am glad, and I am sorry, for whoever takes its spoil from the sea, the spoil, they say, will punish."

"The saying's a silly one," said Col, uneasy to hear it so soon again. "Where's Duncan?"

"All night the poor lad searched on either side of the fords and is just come home, and is now at a melancholy meal."

They entered the gate. In the shelter of the old house that had seen wars there was every sign of calm affairs, – a barn with cockerels pecking grain; a byre where a cow was being milked by a servant-maid, who sat on a stool with her cheek against the flank and sprayed the milk in the frothing cogue, looking from the dusk out into the dazzling sun. Pigeons, too, pure white, paraded with trailing wings about their loves before the door, and a hundred starlings chattered on the ridges of the roofs. A pleasant, flourishing place enough, and yet Col of Corodale felt it more than ever mean.

"Duncan, Duncan! here is Col!" cried out his mother at the door. A man inside laughed gladly with all his heart, laughed as a boy might laugh in his sleep at some keen joy tickling his dreams. So the well laughs in the mountains when it tumbles into linns among the heather and the fern. He ran out, sweeping his brown hair from his temples, and caught his brother by the shoulders and shook him playfully, crying the while, "Son of the one I'll mention not! here is a fine joke upon the mother and on me; come home, vagabond, come home!" He was slighter than Col but every inch as tall, brown where the other was black, scarce so handsome, and yet more pleasant in the countenance, clean-shaven, womanly at the mouth, and glanced from a tranquil eye.

"Come in and eat, lad!" he cried, with the universal welcome of these isles, seizing his brother's arm. He spoke in English. "I have been spoiling my own dinner these twenty minutes with the foolishest speculations about you; now I'll make up for it."

But when they were before the food it was Col who ate the heartiest after all, while Duncan, eating little, listened to the other's story.

"Bah! Col," he cried, "it's ever the worst look-out with you. Your skipper is too good a seaman to lose the *Happy Return* or to be caught in yesterday's weather anywhere west of Arisaig. I wish he had other cargoes – but no; no, no; I'll say nothing of that now, Col; take your meat like a man! A stuck priest should be sparing of his homilies, in case the world laugh at him."

Col frowned, plucking his Spanish beard.

"I have heard you often on that tack, Duncan," said he. "My small ventures in the free trade seem to be spoiling your sleep. You are more particular on that score than the clergy themselves. Faith! many a keg I've had Flying Jib-boom slip in at the presbytery houses in Moidart. But that's all done with, perhaps, if the *Happy Return* belies her name for once. If you want to know, I'm seeing a gloomy time for us in Corodale."

"The last year I was in Passy," said the other, sharing none of his apprehension, "there was a French student there who saw ruin in every washing-bill. His face turned whiter than the linen each time the *blanchisseuse* unpinned her account from her basket. On the last day of his term he fell heir to twenty thousand louis, and without a moment's swithering he gave it all to the Jesuits."

"Twenty thousand!" cried Col with a start. "The luck of the world seems to run in twenty thousand. I like the ring of twenty thousand; it sings itself like a good song: more than twenty thousand would be awkward, less would be scrimp –"

Duncan laughed.

"Keep a close grip on your envy, lad," cried he; "doesn't our Gaelic proverb say it is the second cousin of avarice, and wears the same tartan?"

"I think nobody can call me miserly," said Col.

"I thought nothing of the kind; I meant that there's the root of it in every man that has imagination and a love of power."

"You talk about Passy!" said Col. "Now let me tell you, I wish to heaven you had gone through with it; faith! it seems to me silly enough to boggle at one or two doctrines of the Church and swallow all the rest without bocking."

He saw his brother's face show vexation, and hurriedly begged his pardon; then plunged into the bitter recitation of evils that had of late befallen all his ventures. Two seasons' fishing had been failures; cattle had died, sheep had been lost by the trembling, two cargoes of Barra cordial had been confiscate by the excise.

"And yet what the poorer are we, Col?" asked his brother. "We sleep as soft, we eat as well, we are sheltered as securely, and clothed as warmly as when Corodale was at its best."

"It took five hundred pounds from Corodale to teach you what your notion was about the Church," retorted Col, again angry. His brother gently smiled, his eyes half-shut upon the other's rudeness.

"I could make an easy answer to that, dear brother."

"Yes, I know, I know," said Col, hurried and more bitter still. "Out with it, Duncan, man! out with it! Corodale is none of mine, and I am but the beggar for your bounty. It is yours I have ventured with and lost – do I not know it?"

"I have not said a word of that, brother," said Duncan; "I had forgot; I gave up all for the Church."

"It was not on paper," said Col, pulling his beard, and mentioning the fact as if it were a grudge.

"Our parents meant me for the priesthood and you for the world; there was no contract needed between us; what money there was at hand seven years ago went to keep me in Paris and make it plain that Duncan, son of Ranald, was not the stuff priests are made of. All I got from the money spent on me was that I found myself and lost a calling. Col, *'ille!* 'tis I that am the beggar, ashamed to be here but half-employed. All I expect from Corodale is shelter, till I have decided what to make elsewhere of the trivial learning it cost Corodale so much to get for me."

"If things go on as they are doing, I must go elsewhere without even the learning. If I had had it instead of you, I might have made more of it than you did, but the one thing is certain, there is little room for two of us in Corodale: perhaps if the sloop is really lost, there is little enough for one."

Duncan looked on him with some surprise: this was not altogether the brother who had gone away two days ago. And so, someway, thought the mother; and so too, thought the workpeople of Corodale when that day Col went out among them.

Many a glance he cast to sea but never found a sloop upon the rollers. The women loading and leading peats upon the moss found him changed: he that had hitherto gone among them anxious to have the best of their labours, but always with some jocundity, now drove without a smile.

"God be about us! what ails the poor man?" they said, lading up the creels or binding corn, and speaking before their master freely, as they always do in Uist. "His Michaelmas cake must have disagreed with the stomach of him, for black's his aspect, as black as his father's before him."

"What ails the brother?" they asked Duncan, when he in his turn came smiling and hearty among them. "He has got a turn through Boisdale reek, and come back with his face like thunder."

"Worry, good folks, just worry! the worst dog in the pack. There is no sign of the sloop?"

"*Oh Dhe!*" cried the labourers, "St Michael keep off all dangers! What would become of the widows of her crew?"

"They would starve – like the rest of us," said Col, overhearing, and left the field.

He spent a sullen day; at night he went early to bed, in an upper room below the roof of Corodale House. It had been lit by his mother with two candles; he pinched them out, and looked from the little window into the garden and over the fields and out as far as he might upon the sea, that he had robbed of its spoil, and now – it might be in the first of its revenge – had robbed him of his sloop. The moon, enormous, stared upon the Isles.

CHAPTER IV

The Fifty-Years' Fortune

FOR little Anna there were many by-names in the Isles. So rare indeed they thought her that, following the Gaelic custom, which makes us seldom speak directly of the thing we love, lest heaven or the jealous elves have their remembrance called to it and something happen, her just cognomen was scarcely breathed among her brother's people. She was in the language "Herself," or "Yon Little One," or "The Lady of the White House." But oftenest was she "MacNeil's Treasure" – a play upon the island story of the fifty-years' fortune.

When she went through the townships scattered among the hollows round the rock of Stella Maris, bringing the wind in her wonderful flowing garments, a dash of the sun in her hair for the blackest hut, the folk would for ever be wondering how Uist had got on without her while she was away in France. The households she could gladden in a little short winter afternoon – oh, 'twas a miracle entirely! and yet 'twould be by trivial acts as natural to her as smile or song – by no more than a word of merriment or a turned pillow for one bedridden, or a housewifely question for that other busy at her loom with the crucifix over it; by a sort of timid make-believe at manly pleasantry for burners of kelp, that made them laugh as she passed their kilns near the rocks of Torrisdale, or by a distant call to fishermen barking their nets along the shore.

"There's Herself!" the young fellows would cry, seeing her gown flap in morning breezes as her airy figure ran down the hill from the White House, and she sped for a hut where possibly some poor creature could not believe it morning till Herself appeared, the true dawn, the best of sunshine, at the door. And they would stand – these bold admiring lads – among their nets or jump upon a thwart to look after her, but always with some other thing to do suddenly if she should happen to look round and see them. Her presence among the little clustered dwellings seemed to change the air, as was said; the busiest housewife at her fire knew the girl was there without, and would hasten to her door to see Little Anna, and to say "God be between her and harm!" When she entered a house the gravest smiled without knowing why; when she had gone, dulness seized on the blythest company, and there was an understanding that at any *ceilidh* she should be the last to leave for home. There was one, indeed, a tacksman, a gallant sentimental man, who, when gatherings were in his house, was used to seek the loft and go to bed before she had departed, having a happiness in hearing her voice below, yet trying to fall asleep before this blessing had gone from under his roof-tree, leaving behind the commonplace. Girls loved her garments, unlike any they had ever seen before, magnificent beyond words, made for her, as the bard of Hellisdale said in verse, "from the melody of the birds." The boldest would venture to finger her cloak unnoticed, delicately, tenderly, as if it were a portion of her body. As for the bairns, dear hearts! Herself was another Mary: how often the wildest boys on their knees in Stella Maris were looking at her and making of that their true devotion? Outside they would stand in bands open-eyed, admiring, ready to join her laughter.

The best gifts we get are from those who have nothing but themselves to give us. The Lady of the White House gave herself in affection, in understanding, in the help of her wit-and her hands. She had left the Isles when she was scarcely more than a child, and shy beyond expression; she came back a woman, at ease with herself and the world, to be the mistress of their hearts. In three months she had grown as needful to the happiness of Uist as the very chapel on the windy hill.

But from Michaelmas Day till All Saints' Day the townships had to be doing without her presence, so that bleak season seemed more bleak than usual. The old man her uncle was dying, and they sat up with him – as they say – waiting on his end. For himself there were three things only to make him sorry to go travelling – he had a craving to see England again, that he had marched through when scarcely out of his teens on an escapade with Charles Edward; he had a common vanity of his race, to make up the tale of his years to a round four score and ten, and yet a twelvemonth was awanting; and he wished to see Little Anna the veritable mistress of the Loch Arkaig gold.

She valued the prospect of such a fortune no more than a handful of shells, except for the opportunity it might give of bringing happiness to others. To get a new tower for Stella Maris – an old project of the poor people, who had built the church with their own hands (the children carrying up the sand) – was one of the earliest notions that entered her head; the mention of it always found her brother Ludovick cold. For him the hidden fortune was trash unspeakable; that a priest should have gone to hell for the sake of it made him count it, from the days of his own frocking, a thing cursed. The folk of the island soon discovered how bitter the Lord of the Isles could be upon this topic – the only one that ever seemed to rouse his anger. Between his uncle and himself the mention of it was never breathed.

And now Dermosary was dying. There was no doubt about it. He had been anointed for the grave. He had been wild in youth, and fierce beyond mid age, a man of rock, and the sea waves salt and beating in his veins so deceiving him that he insisted every day he should sit up and keep death out of him by clenching his teeth; but each day he was a little more humped in his chair, his teeth more frequently fell apart.

That the end had come was, in the long-run, first discovered to the people by a boy. He had been playing with his fellows round the White House byre on an early evening and hid behind a door. Standing in the dark there, breathless with his running, and chuckling silently to himself, the boy put his hand upon a plank that shared his concealment. It was broader than a boat's thwart, polished to the touch, higher than a man. For a little he held it in front of him and cried upon the others, and then his finger went inquiring along its edge. He felt the plank swell out above his head and then fall in again, – to any boy in Uist that shape of wood was eloquent – he had come upon a stretching-board! His horror would not have been greater had it been the body itself for which the stretcher was intended; he went out screaming and ran home, as we say, on the four oars.

Twenty minutes later old MacNeil of Dermosary was dead. The black house people, called to the lee of their dwellings by the boy's alarm, knew it from the yellower glow of candles in the room where he had so long been prisoner.

"God sain him!" said the women. The men took off their bonnets. "May the Possessor keep him in His keeping!" said they, and thought just a moment upon some stuff concealed beyond their discovery between the Mingulay rocks and Ronay. Some went up to the White House and sat the night through with the candles round the body, silent and discreet for the sake of Herself and Father Ludovick, though in any other home in Uist they would have passed the evening differently. At morning, too, others came with funeral gifts – cakes, halibut, and fowls; and the day was silent, with no noise of looms or oars, as if it had been a day of Obligation; not that such was customary, for death is too frequent in the Isles, but that, loving their priest and Little Anna, the good folk felt that thus they must honour the clay below their roofs. Even the children were kept indoors, and the wind had it all its own way, without a challenge from laugh or song.

Born and bred among tempests, he went properly in tempest to his rest; for very high and shrill blew the north wind that day on Uist of the sheldrakes. When the people were at Mass the sea-pyet came on glancing wings and cried around Our Lady Star of the Sea, its call breaking the solemn silences.

CHAPTER V

Three Islands

OVER three islands Dermosary went to his burial, the lairs of his name being at Trinity Temple in the other Uist, now cut off from the grace of Mother Church, astray and heretic. The cart he rode in – as comfortable for a corpse as any hearse with feathers – had to cross the two fords, dreadful in November weather, for all their sandy miles are mournful with the whimpering ghosts of ancient tragedy. He went on a Wednesday that he might be under turf on Thursday, for Friday is the cursed day (and yet for us how blest!) on which Christ died.

Father Ludovick and his sister and a dozen of his people rode north in the face of the wind, first traversing the plains, and in the afternoon threading among the little lochs that lie unnamed and without number in Uist and Benbecula, forgotten when the Lord relented and blew back the waves from all the bens and Ararats.

Three halts they made for refreshment, and built three cairns for a memorial, and at the mouth of the evening they came to Creggans – a hamlet of the ancient monks, that sees St Kilda itself far out on the deep, with its mountains exceeding dim.

Creggans had an inn, an ugly place, two-storeyed, square, and black with rain, thatched with withered ranach. It stood by itself drearily in the middle of a desolate patch of sandy soil near the margin of the sea, that always looked like leaping on it and sweeping all within it through the lattice windows, leaving the tangle of the outermost deeps upon its sills and astragals. Here the mourners meant to spend the night. When they came towards it at first there was no sign of occupation, far less of hospitality: no smoke came from the chimney, no person was visible in its neighbourhood, but when the cart was stopped Father Ludovick hailed the house and the household. A pock-marked red-haired man of an aspect unpleasant and unwelcoming came hurriedly to the door and touched his cap.

"Who in the world is this that travels?" said he with a glance at the mortcloth on the cart.

"One that was a man last Monday, innkeeper," said the priest, "and travels no more in this world; my uncle of Dermosary."

"Dermosary! Just so! just so! a good man; peace with him and his share of Paradise," said the innkeeper, with a buttered mouth. "I am out of the world here, and never heard a word of it. You are making for Teampuill Trianaid, Master Ludovick? Then you cannot cross till break of day, if you will not cross in the dark."

"That was in our calculations. With your will we will stay here till the morning ford is open. I daresay you can provide a room for my sister, and the rest of us who cannot make a shift with a chair at the kitchen fire can get accommodation in the outhouse."

"I will do my best," said the innkeeper, with a hesitation. "It is not every day we have a true gentleman of name as well as fortune to bury." He made to help Anna from her saddle, but she was on her feet before he could offer her a hand. At that he gave a cunning smile.

"Her ladyship is very light," said he, "for twenty thousand pounds."

Father Ludovick gripped him by the arm. "My good man," said he, "it is not the hour for wit."

"Take my excuses, Father," said the innkeeper, his pitted face as red as his hair. "It's an old tale in the isles of Uist, her ladyship's fifty-year fortune, and I meant no offence." And then he went to the outhouse where his wife, a drab, was curing dog-fish, and gave her his mind in English oaths she luckily could not understand. She looked on him with terror, trembling, as dumb as a stalled beast. "Here's a funeral," he said to her, "from Boisdale – old Dermosary – and not a bed made. *Mollachd Dhe!* but have I not the useless slut, barren of wits and work and weans?"

Dermosary for the night slept under his mortcloth, in the barn; two men kept him company with a crusie, and played a game of cards; a few sheltered in houses near Gramisdale, Father Ludovick and the others sat up in the kitchen of the inn, and Anna tried to sleep in a room above. But the inn of Creggans was not meant, that night, for sleep. It was for ever shaking to the wind, its carpentry creaking, its doors and chimneys abominable with continual moans. She lay staring in the darkness and the first touch of the dawn at her window was very welcome. Up she got and said her island prayer, and looked upon a landscape she had not seen since she was a child, a landscape that many a time in France she had thronged in dreams with folk of terror or romance. Miles of sandy strait lay between her and the hills and plains of Northern Uist Deep sea-pools were there, and rivulets of escaping tide; rocks – very black – very cruel – very cold – were scattered upon the sands on which the sea-gull and the curlew went staggering before the wind. The light of Carinish was still shining on the other side, a wan eye for guidance to the traveller, and the tall Mount of Eaval was unseen, but already the ford was thronged. Some women with their gowns high-kilted waded knee-deep in the pools, spearing flat-fish; others bent to seek for bait. Little ponies, saddled with rugs of pleated bent-grass and bitted with rope, with streaming tails, plashed in the morning wind at a cheerful trot across the rivulets; others stepped leisurely, long streams of them laden with panniers of peat. The day indeed was come, and it came hardly any sooner than her brother, who was not astonished that she should answer dressed and ready for departure, to his summons at her door.

"I knew it," said he. "No sleep, Anna? I could not sleep myself for the certainty of it, and there's an innkeeper here has talked about what he calls 'life' – his blackguard life of the barracks and the sea, of wars, and smuggling ships, and blacker crafts I'm thinking, though he dare not mention them to the priest, – till I could have gone into a trance had I not the knowledge – a constant pain over my eyebrows – that you were lying, *m'eudail!* staring in the dark and hungry for daylight."

"I am so glad the day has come," said Anna, looking about the room that had for so many hours seemed dreadful to her wakefulness, and they went to the poor slattern's notion of breakfast. They were in the midst of it when Father Ludovick took a thought and cried upon the innkeeper.

"You have not seen any sign," said he, "of a friend of mine from Corodale?"

"Corodale," said the innkeeper, and showing a slight confusion, – "Col, or Master Duncan?"

"Either," answered Father Ludovick. "I sent a message asking them to the funeral, and hoped to meet one or other of them at the south ford or here. But the bidding was something of a piper's, as we say, and it is unlikely that any of them would come all the way from the other side of Benmore in such weather."

"Weather, Master Ludovick, is a thing that never troubled one of them in Corodale: there is something in the race of them that they would sooner have the brash of rain in their necks than a sunburning."

Anna could not but smile to her brother, for here was his commonest sentiment – a preference for the storm, that made him often wander out upon the shore at midnight and revel in the onset and the fury of the sea.

"If he comes, then, – but I do not look for him now, – he will have counted on the open ford, and will be here presently," said Father Ludovick, and the innkeeper went out to make inquiries.

"I was not aware you had specially invited Corodale," said Anna when they were alone.

"I did so at the last moment," said her brother, "and on a curious impulse, for it was our droll friend, Dark John, hinted at the compliment, and offered himself to travel with my message. I thought if one brother could not come, we might be honoured by the other."

"Dark John – poor fellow! it will be long before he forgets his thankfulness. Since Michaelmas Day he has been constantly praising Young Corodale to me. Many a time I have blamed myself that I did not that day see the man who risked his life to save a few more years for John. What is he like, this Col?"

"Like? Oh, just like the world, my dear, that we luckily never see the inside of till we die: pleasant enough to look at, and reputed of many accomplishments. It may be no more than the scandal of Uist, but he has the name of trafficking in contraband between Barra and the mainland, a wretched enterprise surely for one that has no excuse of poverty to justify it. I have been vexed myself that I found no opportunity to talk with him when he swam ashore at Dalvoolin on St Michael's Day; it might have been lucky. I had that high impulse on me at the time I could have wrenched the soul from him."

Anna wanly smiled. "It would have been taking an unfair advantage," said she, "of a soul soaking with the brine of the Atlantic. Your human intuitions, dear Ludovick, are fortunately much better than your spiritual ones sometimes."

He sighed at that.

"Well, I no more than saw him landed, and assured myself that he and the other man were safe. As you know, I went to the tacksman's house again in the morning and found that Col was gone. He had come over from Corodale to look for a sloop that was thought to be foundered, but has since turned up and plies her trade as wickedly as ever – so I hear – between Mingulay and Moidart. I would like to meet the man for the sake of his soul and his brother Duncan."

"The heretic!" cried Anna.

"Hush! my dear; a most unholy epithet. That a man has abandoned his intention of taking orders is no impeachment, surely, of his faith. Duncan has his own sufficient reasons, as no one will admit more readily than I, that know them best – 'faith, better than himself, maybe. You have never seen him, and can never know how good a heart he is – so frank, so bright, so honest."

"My dear brother! And are they the qualities that spoil him for a priest?" said Anna, smiling again. "If it is so, I wonder that some folk I know are doing not so very badly in Highland chapels."

"I have not met him but once since he came back from France," said Father Ludovick, unheeding of her humour, "and I hoped that he, if not his brother, should be with us at the Trinity Temple."

But neither of the sons of the widow in Corodale had come to Creggans before the ford was fully open, when the funeral party set out again upon its convoy of old Dermosary to the place where his folk were sepulchred. The innkeeper stood at his door and watched them trailing behind the mortcloth to the side of the ford, and "Fair wind to you! brethren," said he; "if there's one I cannot stand much company with, it's his reverence from Boisdale."

The cart laboured in the sand, and splashed axle-deep in the rivulets that in the north ford are never dry; behind came the mounted mourners, Anna the only woman among them. Once and again on the ford, she let her pony fall behind a little, to gaze curiously at the spectacle. This way and thus, she thought, had come many burials; this way had come fierce bands of cruel soldiers from the north, scourging the poor islands; this way had come lovers, fiery after waiting weary hours upon the cold shore of Benbecula or Uist, to meet the lady.

Her company, crossing the sand without a sound of hoof or wheel or whinny, was like a vision: as her little pony walked doucely under its fairy burden, she half closed her eyes and sank (for she had something of her brother's habit) into the trance that sometimes came to her from rare landscapes, from unusual aspects of sea or cloud, – a trance where, in a sweet half-dream, she saw the mourners as ancient old eternal folk, travelling through time for a goal unattainable, the sport of the pagan gods, with one that was her brother, a dreamer and a priest, leading them on a tall horse, his head, half sunk on his bosom, thinking. She saw, too, Eachkamish in the west, barring the way to the open sea, and busy with birds above it like a dust, though so far away she could not hear their screaming: Isle Grimisay rose in the sands, half-way over the ford, low and rank and dark, a sandblown rock whence came the women spearing flat-fish in the pools. The men they passed stopped their labours, arrested their ponies, and doffed their bonnets to the pall; the women – if they were of the ancient faith – let down their garments, waded from the pools, knelt upon the sand and crossed themselves, murmuring –

> "O Mary! Mother of Christ
> A soft path for the far traveller!"

"Dear people! dear people!" said Anna, passing them: they wakened her from her reverie, and she urged her pony to a sprightly pace that brought her up beside her brother.

They rode wearily through the unending sands of the Great Bay, and passed among bareheaded heretics at the Ditch of Blood, and reached the grave beside the Trinity Temple about the hour of noon. Anna looked round the company at the grave, half hoping to see the man from Corodale, but he was not there.

CHAPTER VI

The Lost Lady

THE last turf was hardly upon old Dermosary, and the spades were still at the smoothing of his bed, when the storm, that had all day threatened a renewal, made its bold and unmistakable appearance in the west. The afternoon smelt suddenly salt; there came a boom of the surf from Eachkamish; wild-geese flapped, tuneless and harsh, in wedges hurriedly over Benbecula; the skua slanted like a lance across the wind. Then it was that Father Ludovick's face clouded, though his thoughts were not upon the weather. He was one that had curious gifts, and felt the influence of the elements quickly, – felt them not in warmth or chill, but in premonitions and inward impulses that answered to the tiniest rainfall of the spring, even when he slept, and made him glad in his dreams for all the flowers, and rejoice with the thirsty mountain grasses. He had communion with the sea and wind; could tell when they must rise and shout, or when their hour of rest was come for them – not a trivial gift of fisher-lore, but the knowledge of the smaller gods. "I am Boreas to-day, my dear!" he was used to tell his sister when she came seeking for him, with a hat and plaid, knowing him of old, and finding him all uplifted, breathing deep in hours of storm upon their island, tramping the sands of the beach, or bareheaded, with flying curls upon his temples, and an abandoned neck, standing on the farthest promontory crying Gaelic verses to the day.

"Boreas will excuse me for interrupting his business, but he must not be catching cold, and it's wise he would be to come to dinner," she would cry through the gale laughing, and stand on tiptoe to clap his hat upon his foolish head, his plaid upon his shoulder, then gently tug at a wet sleeve to bring him home. "Come in, Boreas, come into thy cave and use thy breath to cool thy broth! It is good broth, for I myself made it. O king! am not I the unhappy woman to have a brawling wind for brother? Father Boreas, consider the poor seamen that are tacking for home, and that I am a useless doctor for quinsies, and that my humble human broth is waiting your reverence's leisure."

"It will clear in half an hour," he would tell her then, perhaps, though the sky seemed angrier than before, and he would go with her calmly, laughing, a little ashamed of his raptures, and by-and-by, as he had said, the ocean shared his impulse and was stilled.

No less was he the instrument of the dulcet hours. "To-morrow I will shine, I know it!" he would say, on a night no matter how black and menacing, and to-morrow for a certainty it would be a world of light, and he would spend the day from house to house among his people jocular and hearty, the very sun itself, and yet – and yet at times between the dwellings, with just a little touch of sadness as he looked upon the ground and thought of all the earth's futilities. "You are the master of them all – Boreas or Sol," would Anna say on such occasions, sharing in his gaiety, for was not that, too, her nature? but more deeply feeling in her breast a pang of the Gaelic melancholy. "Yet on my word I am liking you best as Boreas for storming is a brisk business that needs no meditation, and when it's shining we must be, it is so easy that it gives too much time for thoughts."It was true; he had in marshalling the stormy elements a rapture that he never found in the days of calm. And she knew why. "It is just this, Ludovick," she would tell him; "you and I are bairns of tempest, and feel that it is better to fight and die than rest and rot. For me, give me the pots and pans and something sensible to be doing."

As he stood at the grave, hearing the pat of the spades, his thoughts were with the conquering worm that crawls in the chamber of dreams and glory; and with the angels that are no nearer earth anywhere than in the Outer Isles, so that he saw nothing of the mustering clouds, and had no calculation of the weather, and yet Boreas frowned upon his face, and at a gentle touch from Anna he wakened with the full knowledge that it was time for them to make for shelter.

"A bad night, people," he said, hurrying them from the graveyard. "It will last, this stormy weather, till the quarter moon, and to-night we must keep well together in crossing the ford. We will go by Gramisdale."

But Gramisdale or otherways, the ford was gulping full, and they must wait its emptying. Between the isles the channel ran boisterously with waves, every fang of rock upon the strait – Grimisay Isle, and the Grey Isle, Thin Isle, and Trialabreck, and the Islet of the Dead Women – white with the spray and spindrift. Benbecula, flat like a bannock, that they had walked from in the forenoon, was but dimly to be seen on the other side of this new-born sea. It seemed a change incredible to Anna. That the hoof-prints of her pony Gaisgeach should be for miles below that noisy sea, and that there, where the fish now sported, she had tranced and dreamed behind the mortcloth of her uncle Dermosary! Was it possible that the tide, filling this channel to the brim, would flow back to the west again before night-fall, and leave the bare dim sands as they had been before?

They were in the country of heretics, but still an isle of hospitality. Folk came out to them, and proffered shelter till the ford was open, and of this kindness they availed themselves until the evening, when the ford was almost dry. The storm was worse than ever; but the priest was confident of a lull, and delayed their departure until it came, as he had said, at the utmost slack of the tide.

"Gramisdale, and in a hurry now," cried he, leading the way on his pony; and Anna, warmly wrapped in a plaid, comfortable on a Spanish saddle, kept close by his side, never afraid the least, but almost glad and eager for this new experience. They went before the wind down the Big Bay, as it might be the gullet of the sea, and at the end of it turned to the west. The driver of the cart sheltered his head and shoulders with the mortcloth, and a man who rode beside him carried a torch that flamed noisily in the slackened wind and hissed in the raindrops. It called about them shadows and shapes of fear, and drew to their neighbourhood, too, screaming sea-birds that might very well be ghosts; but worse than all, the flambeau brought the night about them like a wall, so that no matter how quick they rode, they had with them always the one same little bit of sandy desert.

"We would be better without the light," at last said Father Ludovick, for the second time confused by the shadows, and unable to see the rocks that are the beacons of the ford; and so the torch was stamped out in the moist sand.

The priest went on his way, with his grey eyes searching into the very deeps of the darkness, humming the native Veni Creator –

> "Ur naimhdean fuadaich fade bhuainn,
> 'Us builich òirnn do shish gu buan."

The air, the sentiment, commanded him at last; his voice increased, as challenging the wind, and Anna's joined it. There were runners to cross, rocks, and pools like tiny lakes to pass round, quicksands familiar and ill-reputed – some of them with horrible stories – to evade; but these things they accomplished as in a dream. Conquered by the music was their company too, and, carried away upon the hymn, they began to separate a little.

"Keep together! keep together!" cried the priest. "I have no notion for any of us to pass the night on Trialabreck, and it is the poor best that could happen to whoever missed his way here."

He caught his sister's reins.

"I must not lose you, at any rate," said he.

"And am I to be the only child of the company?" she asked with a touch of spirit, gently releasing them from his grasp. "No, no, Ludovick; I can do as well as my neighbours. There is no fear that I shall lose myself."

"If you did," said he passionately, "I should wade or swim between Eachkamish and Grimisay all night long looking for you; but there must be no talk of losing you or any other. Poor girl! I'm sorry to have you out in such a night."

"I am happier here than I could be at home in your absence," said she, and fell again into the humming of the Gaelic hymn, her head bent down against a wind gaining its strength anew, some loops of her hair beating lightly on her cheek.

No lights shone that night in all Benbecula, or, if they did, the clouds concealed them. Some there were behind them if they turned to look – pale crusies, weeping through the rain in the little windows of the Protestants, and one or two in Grimisay; but they grew dimmer and dimmer and died at last suddenly, as if puffed out at a breath.

"Keep together! keep together!" cried the priest, sure that some of his company straggled, though they were not all to be compassed even vaguely by the eye, and he wheeled his pony about to circle round them and gather in the wanderers of his flock. Anna followed, so that she might obey his behest and keep by his side. She had no sooner turned her pony's head than he was seized by longings for the shore of Northern Uist, for the hard salt turf he had come from last, for a stall where he had ease and oats and none of the sleet and rain that now began to fall. He dashed sprightly over the sands with one little snort of pleasure.

"Gaisgeach! Gaisgeach!" said Anna with reproach, struggling to stay this shameful retreat, but the pony could not be stopped till something so suddenly checked him that he almost threw her from the saddle. He flung back his head with a whimper, plunging with his forefeet as if they had been hobbled: he had come on quicksand, and was sinking!

The girl was as calm as if the hour had been noon and this the highway. She dismounted hurriedly, coaxed the animal for a little in vain, then urged him free at last. He stood with his nose on her shoulder, all trembling.

"Poor Gaisgeach!" said she, soothing him, while the wind

boomed over the flats and the sleet whipped her forehead. "Poor Gaisgeach! home was happier than this; but never mind, we'll be there to-morrow." He raised his head to whinny, still trembling at the neighbourhood of his terror, and she caught him by the nostrils to prevent him, lest it should alarm her brother and call attention to her accident. The night was deathly dark; her friends were wrapped in it and no sound came from them, but yet she had no fear that she could not speedily regain her brother's side. Mounting again, she forced her pony to a canter. She rode for five minutes – nothing rose before her but the black wall of night, she rode for ten – the world seemed governed all by darkness, and tenanted wholly by sleet and the sounds of the sea, and the sands had swallowed up her company. Then she knew herself lost indeed, for she came on a group of little rocks, and beyond them a great pool that the good guidance of her brother would never have brought them near.

"Ludovick! Ludovick!" she cried, stopping her pony, and bent against the wind to listen. She got no answer. New fears came down on her – dogs of darkness and danger – she set the beast to a gallop on the sands, finding more runnels, rocks, pools, and quicks. The sleet stung on her eyelids and the wind struggled with her gown. With her growing terror there came a thought half-envious, half-despairing – of warmth in St Teresa, and Sister Agnes snug with a book beside a fire: she could have sworn she heard the chime of bells.

"Ludovick! Ludovick!" she cried again. Only a sea-gull answered from another pool greater than the first she had encountered. Ludovick could not hear; he was far off to her right, ignorant of her absence, driving his flock before him, his face uplifted to the sleet, Boreas again, exalted in this night of hazards.

"I must trust in God and Gaisgeach," said Anna, and at guess trotting through pools, with a loose rein, on ways that appeared to lead nowhere. She seemed to herself to travel thus for hours, but always with hope – till at last, with a splash of her pony's feet, a thought struck cold at her vitals.

She was crossing many streams for this to be a falling tide!

The tide was coming in again; the ford was filling!

She had heard too many tales of disaster in this place not to know the horror of the situation. It was she that was all trembling now; her pony was indifferent. "We must hurry, Gaisgeach!" she said. "We must hurry. Dear Gaisgeach! fellow of my heart! Gaisgeach, my hero! Gaisgeach, we must hurry! Ludovick! Ludovick!" She cried again, shrill against the wind that tore her voice in fragments; the horse began to share her fears, and raised his head and whinnied as he did before upon the verge of the perilous quicks; she felt the sense of swooning, and gasped a prayer for heaven's assistance.

Her answer came at once in the stumble of her pony on some stones and in the odour of grass. Here was safety of some kind – if it were no better than Trialabreck that her brother had spoken of. She dismounted, led her pony over the loose stones, and reached with difficulty a summit tufted with herbage, where, all worn by her fears, she threw herself upon the ground, under a heavy overhanging reef of rock, and burst into tears.

The rain had ceased; the wind bellowed more fiercely than before, and seemed to challenge her intrusion on the haunt of gull and gannet. Many a time she cried like a soul lost in the chaos of the latter days – a poor little tender, gentle soul, and white and fragile, perched on a rock uplifted from the waters. They ran round the base of the islet now, and sent her to speculate whether she should be safe in such a night even here. The pony lay beside her, and gave her shelter. She heard the wind grow larger and larger until it seemed a world of sound; she grew more tired; she was not cold; she was not uncomfortable; she could sleep. She would have slept but that a curious sound startled her into full wakefulness and something of her native Gaelic terrors. It was the plash of footsteps as if some one waded to the rock. The sea has a thousand wonders in the Outer Isles; there still haunt the sexless and nameless things that are in olden legends, storms enticing them from profound green beds that they may sport on sea-beach and on shallow. She stood up trembling, little left in her of all her foreign scholarship, a cry kept back upon her lips.

The plashing footsteps came near, – unmistakably some one walked in the rising tide. They reached the rock; she heard breathing, some one stood – she knew though she could not see him – on the level below her, and a man's voice cried "Anna! Anna!" over the darkness. And it was not her brother's, nor that of any one else she knew.

CHAPTER VII

Followers of the Sea

A SLOOP had come in on the day before to Uskavagh on the east side of Benbecula, and her seamen walked across the island to the inn of Creggans on this afternoon. The five of them were rogues: a Maclean of Corbolst; two brothers – Macleods, incomers from Loch Vaternish in Skye; a Lowlander with a name and language beyond the knowledge of his comrades, who, when they wanted his attention, had to jog his elbow or thump him on the back; and the skipper, a man of Barra answering to the by-name of Flying Jib-boom, who had, by all accounts the mark of the lash on his back, and wore earrings like a woman, could sing a song in a way to make folk weep for pleasure, and between the stanzas – if the need arose for it – was capable of cutting a throat. They came over the island in the spirit of boys, capering upon the way, chasing each other in childish gambols, laughing, swearing, singing choruses to the lead of Flying Jib-boom, playing tricks upon bairns in the bye-going, or jocular with women working in the mosses which they passed. They were in the very height of merriment until they reached the inn.

Was ever an inn that was not welcome to a mariner? And yet this inn of Creggans might have been a church, so sudden their aspect changed.

They went forward to the grey gable-end of it with steps that grew slower and slower, till at last they stood together a little bit from the corner they must round to reach the entrance; and there they clustered to debate who should be the first to venture in.

"I'll take a little of the air, lads," said the skipper, beating upon his breast, "and will be after you in a moment." But the others closed about him, and refused to let him go.

"What's this of it?" said one of the Macleods. "Who should go first but the skipper himself, that has the command, and the two languages, and can take – if need be for a quirk – to the fine and convenient English?"

Flying Jib-boom was pleased at the compliment, but still reluctant. "It's not that I'm feared for the brute nor for any of his name," said he; "but here's the whole of you shivering in your shoes because a man has a rough tongue in him, and such cowardice puts me in the nerves."

"Well, just go on, skipper; let us go round the house three times sun-wise for luck, and pop in and clap down," said the man Maclean from Corbolst, drawing his hand across his mouth. "I'm dry. He can but talk; and at that same, skipper, lad, there's few your equal on a deck."

"On a deck maybe, but this is different. Give me the soles of my feet on timber and I am the boy that can roar; but there's something weakening about the land, and I was aye too jolly when it came to inns. I cannot talk here unless I lose my temper; and how can I do that just now, I'm asking you, and me in such a jovial key?"

"O king! I'll warrant he'll give you the excuse for temper," said Maclean.

They all crowded, and pushed, and nudged, and shuffled; but still no one would lead the way, till a man in rags came running across a small field to them and cried, "Brave lads! are you looking for some one to have your morning bitters with?"

The question was so bold and strange they had to laugh.

The very man we're seeking for," said the skipper, putting two fingers through one of the holes in the fellow's coat, as if it were the gill of a fish. "It is not till this time of the day we would be putting off our morning bitters in the month of November and in bleak Benbecula of the agues, but here's a gallant youth will lead the way into the Sergeant's inn. Put your bare feet to it, lad, and I will pay your morning tankard."

But the native drew back. "Not a bit of me!" said he. "It's too much honour to be marching before my betters. I thought perhaps I might slip in at the hinder-end. Besides, the Sergeant –"

What more he might have said remained unspoken, for the innkeeper himself at that instant came round the gable of the house and threw them all in a confusion. He stared at them with a contempt he took no trouble to conceal – surely the most unusual attitude for a man who kept a tavern!

"God's splendour!" said he, putting his hands upon his hips, "have I not here Jib-boom the brave and his lice? Here's a corps of stout fellows fit for the gallows; there's not one I could not send there if it was in my mind to do it, and yet they'll stand shuffling at my honest door debating about who'll come in first. Gentlemen, gentlemen, don't be feared; it is not the jail of Inverness nor the confessional."

"I am in the hope that you are very well," was all that Flying Jib-boom could say, for he was not yet in a temper, and, following the innkeeper, he went within, followed in his turn by his crew, who clung together like schoolchildren again, nudging and winking to each other, – the Lowlander, who knew no word of Gaelic and could only guess the situation, making a gesture of contempt with his palm upon his breeches.

"My trouble! there's the gallant lads now!" said the ragged man to himself, thinking on the thunder of the Sergeant's visage, and then went lothfully and took a drink of water at a neighbouring well.

Once in the house it was plain how seriously the seamen had to fear an entrance. For the Sergeant was their master and their bully. He threw some liquor on the table before them at the skipper's order as if they had been dogs, and, "What's this I'm to credit for the honour of your call to-day?" said he. "I thought I ordered you to take the sloop direct to Barra, and here you have her, I suppose, at Uskavagh."

"Well, Sergeant, I would not say but she might happen to be in Uskavagh indeed," confessed the skipper, hurriedly gulping his drink, as if it were the last he was to have on earth. "My God!" he thought, "I must make haste and get wild. I must get the red fury on me at once, or he will have the whole advantage. That's the worst of singing and of songs, that they put a man out of the right key for business with a person like this."

"You're not denying it?" said the innkeeper, folding his arms. "There was little need for you, because I knew it. Just let me look at you." He bent with a hand on the table and looked from one to the other of the five men sitting round it. "Between here and the other end of the kingdom," said he in English, "I would be beat to find a blacker lot of ruffians. I would say nothing about that if they could be trusted the length of a cable-tow with any business that demanded common-sense. I'm not paying high wages for handsome looks or for even-down honesty, but, God! that I cannot get my plain orders carried out the way I put them!"

"I will have no parley in English, – there you have the whole advantage," said the skipper; and to himself, "The devil's in it that I cannot get an anger! It's the worst of a good humour that there's no getting over it."

"What's all this gang wanting here?" asked the innkeeper, back to his Gaelic.

"The skipper said we were to come," said a Macleod, "or on my soul you may be sure I would never have put a foot in Creggans Inn this day. There's plenty of good company about the world elsewhere."

The innkeeper paid no heed to the Skyeman; but, to the skipper,

"I suppose," said he, "you could not trust them alone on the vessel? They might sell her keel for sinkers to the fishermen."

"Well, it's just this of it," said the skipper, "you would not be expecting any man to come from Uskavagh and go back in the dark again without some company."

"It's at Uskavagh you had no right to be. I said Barra, did I not? I said Barra. You know the place? You've been in it often, drunk and sober. You have ears in your head by all appearance, and I said Barra. Take the cargo into Barra, I said, and –"

"Yes, yes, the cargo!" said the skipper, and slapped his drinking-horn upon the table. "Was I not sure there was something of small importance I forgot? We did not go to Barra, Sergeant, because – well, because there is no cargo. Is my face red, Macleod?" he asked, turning to one of the men of Skye, who said it was. "Then," went on the skipper, "there's an end to peace! I am telling you there is no cargo, Sergeant, and make the worst of it! We lost the stuff at Arisaig; but there's plenty of cheap drink among the Macdonnels of Morar, I'll warrant, since last Thursday, for the gaugers never got it any more than we did. There's news for you! You are very fine with your tongue, Sergeant, very fine, if one will listen to you in the English; but give me the Gaelic and fair play, and timber to my feet, and I could burst your ears with conversation. The cargo's lost, man. There's news for you!"

"Do you think it is, sea-pig?" said the innkeeper. "I knew very well what brought you here to-day, for I had the news from Corodale in the morning. It's the third cargo; another loss of the kind and I am a ruined man."

"And when you're ruined, Col of Corodale will not be very wealthy too, whatever," said the skipper, sitting back in his chair with a great indifference. "So you'll have good company."

"Col has nothing to do with her."

"It's a lie, Sergeant, a red lie," said the skipper; "and who would it be but Col that sent you the word from Corodale?"

The Sergeant grew grey with rage. "The first man that credits Corodale with it I will give him my knife in his neck," said he, and drew a *sgean* from his armpit with a flourish.

"Knives!" cried the Skyemen, starting up with much enjoyment, and kicking the stools away from their feet, but the skipper stopped them. "Put back that!" said he. "If I had my full fury on me I would slash his lordship here in ribbons for a pipe drone, but I am not more than just a small bit vexed."

The knives were all returned; no one more readily put back his weapon than the innkeeper, who was a good judge always of the lengths it was safe to go in quarrelling with islanders. "I have told you before, skipper," he said in English, "that Col has no more to do with our business now than his brother, and the brother's not to be vexed by hearing any such rumours as that. You hear? This loss is mine – and that's the worst of it; I would not mind having any one to share it with, but we all know the close fist of Col. Your last misfortune put an end to his patience and shut his pocket. He has had his last day at the free trade."

"I am very glad to hear it," said a new voice, breaking in upon the company, sitting in a room dark under any circumstances, but now more dark than ever, for the evening was falling fast and the sky was blackening with storm. Duncan was standing at the door and looking in on the skipper and his company. "Hail to the house and the household!" said he, shaking the raindrops off his hat. "I came over for Dermosary's burial, and am late by a night and day through no fault of my own, but because a witless messenger would have his own way."

The smugglers stood to their feet and went out for the sake of good manners, leaving their betters together.

"You're welcome at my door," said the Sergeant, looking anything but truthful. "It is the first time; I hope it will not be the last, and that the next occasion will be different. Master Ludovick and his sister and their folk took the morning ford, and I half looked for them back by this one, but they have likely gone south by Gramisdale, – at any rate, they have not come this way. A dozen of them at least – a most genteel and notable funeral. The priest and his sister spent the night here."

"My brother Col was not, by any chance, was he, of the number?" asked Duncan.

The innkeeper jumped to his answer. "No," said he, "Col was not here, but Master Ludovick said he had looked for one or other of you."

"Ah!" said Duncan, "that's vexatious too, for though I was late, I thought he would be here before me and make up for my absence. He left Corodale last night before the messenger came, and I fancied he might have happened to hear of the funeral otherwise. Where he can be is beyond me, for some folk on the way tell me they saw him come in this direction."

"Well, he has not reached this length, I'll assure you," said the Sergeant, taking to his English, which was the sign, as most folks knew but the man he spoke to, that he saw some need for lying. "I hope he is very well, your brother?" he went on, and moved to the door with Duncan.

"Was it ever otherwise than very well with Col?" said Duncan, answering him in English. "A stag's frame and a hind's heart; there is not, for many things, the equal of him in all the Isles. You have heard of him swimming at West Boisdale on Michaelmas and saving an old fellow's life?"

"Faith! and I did that, from the very man himself that he saved. He was here at the last market, and Col of Corodale was his first word and his last. The thing was not without its hazards, for you know the saying, 'Take its prey from the sea, and the prey will punish you.'"

"I have missed my purpose in coming here," said Duncan, paying no heed to the proverb. "But I will not be counting the journey unrewarded, seeing it has given me the assurance that my brother is – is –" He hesitated, from a consideration of the innkeeper's feelings, but he might have saved himself the trouble.

"Out of the *Happy Return*," said the Sergeant, finishing his words for him. "Oh, it does not matter for me. I have a living to make some way, and folk are too particular. Your brother, Mr Duncan, was an ill man of late to get on with, and I am glad that he has taken his money elsewhere. I'm all the better pleased at it because my skipper and his men there have come to tell me they have had another misfortune and lost a cargo."

"So we heard at Corodale last night," said Duncan. "If there's any consolation in the fact, I may tell you that Col was as much put about as if the vessel was his own. It is another proof of his good heart –"

"There's one thing about it," said the innkeeper, "your brother Col has a very good-natured brother. In some respects he's on the narrow side is Col."

"Narrow side?" said Duncan, drawing down his brows.

"Has he not faults?"

"We have all faults, Sergeant, so we should have little to say of the faults of others. 'Narrowness,' you say; what would be the wonder, seeing so much has gone wrong with him in business these few years back?"

"Oh, a gentlemanly vice I admit, sir," soothingly acknowledged the innkeeper, "but apt to grow on one. I have always stood up for Col when people said he would sell yourself for a shilling."

"There is too much Col in our conversation, Sergeant and I'm the last to hear his credit cried down. I'm for off to Gramisdale; perhaps

I may meet Father Ludovick and his people coming back there. Good night!"

He left hurriedly, angry at the insult to his absent brother, angry with himself that this reading of Col's character should coincide somewhat with his own. But as he sped towards Gramisdale on the verge of the ford he grew glad that his brother was at last clear of the Sergeant and the *Happy Return* and her nefarious traffic.

"Fair wind to you also," said the innkeeper, when Duncan had gone in the darkness; "I hate priests, half-baked or wholly cooked," and listened for a moment to the sound of surf booming in on Eachkamish. "By the seven stars! there's a night of it coming on," he said to himself. He looked about for sign of his ship's company, but they were gone; with their unpleasant message delivered, they had taken the opportunity given by Duncan to disappear, and they were now as gaily as before crossing the island, schoolboys, and brave, and careless, whooping in the townships, tapping at windows, playacting wraiths and ghosts, to the terror of mid Benbecula.

CHAPTER VIII

Crafty Col

HE heard the last haloo of the seamen on the verge of Ollavat Loch; it came through the gloaming, a sound so plainly telling of merriment, of hearts free from all anxieties, of a spirit so different from what the men had shown when in his presence, that he felt a touch of envy and of anger. He had followed the sea himself. He had splashed in ports; he had in his time known the satisfaction of a day on shore with no man to pay wages to, with the price of a glass – perhaps no more – to jingle in his pocket, and now he was a landsman of substance, in the slack-water of mid-age, possessed by his inn, chained to Uist by what fools considered his good fortune, and the paymaster of fools. The inn, square among the windy sands, with the salt of brine on its very lintel, that night, like many a night before, stirred up by its gloomy aspect all his old dissatisfactions. He forgot the gentleman of Corodale and the noisy careless seamen when he turned and looked at his own bleak walls. "It might as well be a tolbooth," said he aloud, staring gloomily. "A fine spot for a man who has been round the world to clap himself in at the hinder-end. It was my grumble in the barracks or at the sea that I never had a place to lay my boots; now, by God! I cannot put them down in this damned barn, but what I have a task to find them."

He went within, and his wife made to fly before the menace of his visage, but came at his command and stood on the other side of the fire facing him.

"*An do ghluas e fhathast?* – has he stirred yet?" he asked her, looking over her head at the steep wooden steps that led to the upper floor.

"I have not heard him moving," said the woman.

"What a brock to sleep! Time he was on foot if it's Corodale for him this night," said he, and lit a candle, and went noisily up the stair into a narrow cam-ceiled room where Col lay fast asleep in his clothes, a hand in his pocket and his mouth open. He had been there since morning, after travelling all night from the other side of the island to tell his partner of news so unwelcome it might very well have kept for twelve hours longer. The light of the candle that the Sergeant held revealed the meanness of the features, that, awake and watchful looked so handsome. "He has the mouth of a skate," thought the Sergeant; "it is a blessing for us that there's the beard." He pushed Col till he started up and stared about him.

"It gets late," said the innkeeper, "and there's a gale brewing; if you must be making to-night for Corodale, the sooner you start the better."

They went down the stair together without a word more till they stood at the kitchen fire. The peat-smoke checked by the wind at the outlet, swirled about in the rafters; the sea on Eachkamish was thundering. "Faith 'tis time I was taking my feet for it and stepping," said Col, but made no move.

"Skate-mouth – skate thirst!" thought the innkeeper, and drew a horn of ale for stirrup-cup. Col pulled in with a chair to the table, glad that twopence was saved. "I slept, on my soul! like the kings that are under flags in Icolmkill," said he, stretching himself, "and I wish I was at it again, to forget this cursed quirk of fortune on Arisaig. The third cargo in a twelvemonth! Luck like that again and I may take to the Lowlands roads for it with a blue gown and a beggar's pewter badge."

"I wish I had as little cause as yourself to grumble," said the innkeeper. "With you it's a penny lost and whining for a pound. The men have been over from Uskavagh while you were asleep up yonder, Jib-boom ready to defy us."

"The cod-head!" cried Col, slamming his palm on the table. "It's as well I was not down to meet him, for I would send him about his business. You should have wakened me?"

"You have the memory of a crab when anger's on you; what have you to do now with the sloop and her losses?"

"That's true," said Corodale, "did I not forget? And there's this in it, that Flying Jib-boom is the cheapest man we could have for the business. He's gone, I suppose?"

"Half-way to Uskavagh by now, him and his men howling like wild cats round the edge of Ollavat. And who else do you think was here a quarter of an hour ago? Your brother Duncan."

Col gave a start. "What!" said he. "You did not mention to him that I was here?"

"You need hardly ask! His coming could not have happened better for us, for he was standing in the door there before I noticed him, just when I was telling the skipper it was all by between you and me and the *Happy Return*. I can assure you he was glad to hear the news. The trade might be kidnapping to see the satisfaction it gave him to hear you were clear of it."

"The fellow's a lump: I'll say it, though he's my mother's son. What in God's name was he doing here?"

"He came a tide late for old Dermosary's funeral."

"A funeral fits him. He must be hard up for diversion when he would come over Uist and Benbecula without any bidding."

"The bidding, so far as I can see, was for yourself," said the innkeeper; "but the man who went last night to Corodale with it could not deliver it, seeing you were from home."

"Faith! my luck sometimes stays with me after all," said Col with satisfaction.

"I'm not so sure of the luck of it this time."

"What way that?"

The innkeeper made no answer, but bade his wife throw more peat on the fire. She hurried to his bidding, and from a wicker creel piled up the turf. Col put down the empty horn and watched her with a grudging eye. "A spendthrift slut," he thought, "to build a peat-fire in that style at this time of night. If we had her at Corodale she would know different." Her task done, she took to her stool again, as far in the shade as possible, and continued her spinning.

"What was that about luck?" said Col after a little, showing he had not forgotten.

"Just a notion I had," said the innkeeper, and seemed to change the subject. "I have Macodrum to pay next Wednesday," said he; "I suppose I can be counting on yon fifty pounds?" They spoke in English because of the wife who span.

"Forty-nine eighteen, to be strict," said Col sharply; "and I'm not sure but with justice it should be a shilling or two less, even."

"Forty-nine eighteen or forty-nine nineteen: the point is, can I depend on getting it from you, Corodale? I'm risking plenty to be taking the whole credit for the sloop without having to pay all the losses and give you half the profits."

"When there's any, – when there's any, *loachain,*" said Col. "If my memory's not failing, I have not had my hand on any profits since Whitsunday."

"Just so, just so! no more have I; but to come to the bit again, can I count on the money from you by Wednesday?"

Col rose to his feet and walked the floor with his hands in his pockets. "By God!" said he, "if this had not happened at Arisaig! I'm like this, that I'm at the last steever nearly, and where am I to turn to?"

"There's another story besides that," said the innkeeper. "By all accounts you have what will do your turn, though you aye put such a poor mouth on."

Col's eyes snapped, and he stood dumfoundered. "They're saying that, are they?" said he in a little. "Well, well; let them! just let them! That comes from the displays of my mother and our stuck priest, that must always be going about with as much bravado as if he had found MacNeil's *ulaidh.*"

"MacNeil's *ulaidh!*" thought the innkeeper; "the thing's in his mind that I was thinking of." "You can't deny but you're pretty close," said he.

It was not a charge for Col of Corodale to take offence at, but he felt that it was one he must not pass. "That's where you misjudge me," said he. "I have to keep a watch on myself or I would spend what I have at the one bang. For the stuff itself I have not that regard that I would walk a mile out of my way to the seashore for it. But I am my father's son; you know the way he had of making money go when once he got his hand on it, and he had his own glisk of good fortune? I have – I have dreams. Tell me this, Sergeant. Are you content to rot among the rain in this bannock of sand they call Benbecula? You have travelled; you have seen things; there was a time when you did not sleep every night of the year in the same bed under the same roof. I would think it would be happening often that in winter nights like this the dark and narrowness of Isle Benbecula would be worse than hell." He stopped, his face red. The woman was so struck by the vigour of his utterance she let her thread break in the heck of the spinning-wheel. The sea was noisier than ever on Eachkamish, and the rafters creaked with the wind.

"You will have another horn," said the innkeeper, and waiting no answer, ordered his wife to put it down. He tapped with his fingers on the rough table they sat at, and seemed to fall in deeps of thought.

"You're gey good at a guess," said he at last, speaking very slow and soft, without looking at Corodale. "You have not been far –"

"Once in Rotterdam, when my father was alive, with a cargo of cured herring, and it cost us a guinea to tie up to the Boompjies."

"You have not been far," repeated the innkeeper; "the thing with me is that I have been wherever the winds blow from. *Dhia na grace!* I have not missed much, and here I'm in Benbecula with a business, and no way out of it, so far as I can see, but feet-first on a couple of spokes. For twenty years I never kent where I would lie tomorrow, and cared as little, so long as I had my stomach and enough to put to it. I have followed the sea; I know the smell of so many harbours I could not mind the names of them in a day; and that's not the whole of it, for I sogered in the Royals. Am I content? says you. Man! there's whiles I lie sweating all night cursing the day I stranded here, where the sand is in my very palate."

"I can well believe it," said Col, "and I'm a native."

"It used to be, when I was at sea in dirty weather, at dirty work, and little for it, or when the corps was in America, my whole notion was for a tavern or an inn. What way it got into my mind God knows, but I thought if I had a business I would not call the king my cousin, as the other one said. But there's men that's meant to go roving, and men that's meant to keep inns for them, and I'm in the wrong place. I never see a ship going past there but I'm just sick. 'There's the Long Island,' I think I hear the captain saying, with his thumb over his shoulder, 'fifty miles off Scotland; there's not a tree on it,' and feels the way I have felt about some rock with gulls on it in the Indies, and no name on the chart. That's a place for a healthy man to have a business in, is it not?"

"Oh, the place has not done so badly by you," said Col, a little jealous for his native country-side.

"That's all your consideration, Corodale, the money that's in it, and I'm ruing the life wasted. You're a man, yourself, that if you had the spirit of a louse and less greed of the siller, you would be dashing. It would not be Uist for you. What's here for the like of you and me?

Rock and rain, and peat and lochs, and rags and black cattle."

"I'm telling you I have had my dreams," said Col. "You know that fine yourself. I never got a chance. You're always on that key of your travels, and smit me long since with notions of going somewhere myself. Well, it's your own choice that you gave them over, and planked yourself in Benbecula. I have as much spirit as them that think themselves my betters; and if I did not throw my money in the sea when I had it –"

"When you had it!" said the innkeeper, and whistled meaningly.

"When I had it, just! I'm telling you again I care no more for money than for a handful of sea-dulse. Let me get out of this bog we're in, and I would not be content to be breeding black cattle in Corodale and running cargoes underhand in a half sloop –"

"But let us come to the bit again," said the innkeeper. "I want to know if you will let me have my money by Wednesday. I must have it."

Col groaned, with his head in his hands and his elbows on the table. The woman finished her spinning, put past her wheel, and slipped out of the kitchen.

"You said something about my luck a little ago," said Col again. "What did you mean by yon?"

"Just a notion I had," said the innkeeper, inwardly satisfied to have the interest come round exactly where he wanted it, and without any tugging on his part. "You thought it was lucky you were from home when Father Ludovick's messenger went to Corodale, and I was thinking to myself it might be luckier, perhaps, if you had been there instead of your brother Duncan, and caught the north ford in the morning."

"It took me all my time to catch the south one," said Col. "I don't understand. I was never particularly keen for funerals; and I don't see for what reason the priest should want either me or Duncan at Dermosary's, for there was never much coming and going between the two families."

The innkeeper went on like a man with a task by rote. "You mentioned MacNeil's treasure," said he. "It would be luck to come on it without putting the islands through a riddle and raking the sea-bottom as some folk – and one of them your own father – have had the name of doing."

"It would be lucky to be born a duke," said Col; "but most of us never discover that till we're too old to arrange it. There's plenty of talk about the treasure, but who kens where it may be by this time? Twenty thousand pounds – so they count it. Lord! it's sheer romantics to think it could be fifty years without some one dipping in it."

"I'll swear old Dermosary never touched a coin of it, at any rate. The man lived to the last like a cotter."

"But the priest, Sergeant – the priest!" said Col, like a man convinced, and yet keen to have his conclusions set at naught. "Another priest had pickings from it when it lay in Loch Arkaig, and I would not put it past this one."

"Ludovick!" cried the innkeeper, and cracked a thumb. "Pooh! The man is in a mist continually. I am as dubious of the tribe of them as yourself; but I'll uphold that this one could not find the time to go and lift the stuff even if he was less honest. The *ulaidh*, whatever it be, wherever it be, is yonder yet."

A map of all the isles of the Cat – the bony ridge of the Uists, and Barra and Benbecula; the multitude of rocks drawn about the fretful borders of them, the lakes innumerable, flashed in the mind of the man of Corodale.

"Yonder!" said he, "and where in the name of God is yonder? I'm not the fool my father was, to think I could put the islands through a sieve and come upon the treasure that way. It might as well be somewhere in the stars."

The Sergeant splashed another horn of ale, – "And you have no notion of a way to save yourself the trouble of riddling it?" said he. "What about the woman?"

"The woman? what woman?" said Col, and put up his hand, pretending to hide a yawn.

"Anna."

"What about her? I have not seen that bairn for years."

"She's on the unhappy side of twenty, and little of the bairn, I'll assure you. The fortune's hers –"

"In a twelvemonth!"

"In a twelvemonth, as you say. You appear to have considered the thing yourself. The fortune's hers, and there she's at an age for marrying. Your father made a fool of himself and gained – if I may say it – no very good repute, by hunting for the *ulaidh*. It would be like the common luck of life if his own son got it with no more trouble than just to throw his bonnet at a lady. By God! the girl, to look at, and by all accounts, is worth consideration if she had not a groat. Do you hear me, Col! Here are you with an old name, with a property – though you'll be telling me fifty pounds are ill to squeeze from it – and just about an age for marrying – it's stretch your hand and help yourself. The *Happy Return* is the only thing against you."

Col smiled and took another look at his adviser.

"Upon the soul of me!" cried the innkeeper, "here am I talking, and you are wiser than myself. I see now your anxiety to have your name clear of the sloop, and this new craze of yours for an honest reputation."

"If one could be sure the stuff was there," said Col.

"It's there, I'll warrant you; and you're the man to get it. Twenty thousand pounds more or less."

"One could do a power of good with half of it."

"No doubt; and who could do it better than yourself, if you had the inclination?" said the innkeeper. "You should have been here at Dermosary's funeral; that's the point I'm on. The messenger went for you, and it was not the best of luck, though you say so, that he should have only got your brother. They're a softening influence, funerals; I count it an opportunity lost."

"Oh, there are other days," said Col. "We'll think of it."

He rose to go, hastily. When he opened the door the fury of the night astounded him; he swithered on the threshold. "*Mo chreach!* I had no idea it was so serious."

"You can stay for the night, if you like," said the innkeeper.

"Two days running out of Corodale!" said Col; "not I! I can be doing with two nights of it, but not two days with such a clan of drones. I must be yonder by the cry of day. Good-night with you!"

The innkeeper listened to the footsteps plashing east. "Skatemouth!" said he to himself. "The idea was boiling in him till the bubble of it was at his eyes, and 'We'll think of it,' quo' he. And 'One could do a power of good with half of it,' quo' he. There's a bright one! And he's off skelping for fear I would mention the fifty pounds again. Not I, crafty Col, not I; there's more than fifty in it."

Far away towards Griminish were the sounds of people calling; at least it seemed like that at first, and the innkeeper cocked an ear. He heard no more. "The birds are wild to-night," he thought; "the funeral folk are well to stay on the other side, and I'm glad myself I'm not on the road, like the two Corodales."

CHAPTER IX

Night Sounds

THERE are two ways a person on foot or horseback may cross the ford from the upper Uist to Benbecula. Having come to the trough of Gramisdale, that is three-fourths over the passage, he may either make Gramisdale itself of it or turn to the right for the sake of a mile more of sand that is smooth and pleasant to walk on, and thus he will come at last to grass and the road that goes down by the backbone of the three isles, busy at most seasons with people and herds. Whether Father Ludovick and his folk should come out of the ford at Gramisdale or Creggans, Duncan could only make a guess at, but he fancied, on a night like this, the shorter way was the more likely, so for Gramisdale he made when he turned his back on the man who so scurvily kept an inn, reckoning that what time he had to wait for the opening of the ford he could shelter in one of the houses that gathered in sand-blown hollows by the shore, to catch in times propitious the magnificence of the sun that goes down in such a glory there in the west, the folk can never doubt there is a Paradise.

He drew up his horse in the midst of the township, that was half Catholic, half Protestant, according as things had happened, and Catholic or Protestant all was one to him (in a sense) that greatly liked his fellows.

"I will tie my horse at a gable," he thought, "and pass an hour or two in *ceilidh*;" but what door he should make a first venture at in this place where for years he had been something of a stranger, he could not at once make up his mind on. The night was as black as the bottom of a bog; his pony and not himself had found the path from Creggans: as he stood by its head now in a clachan that seemed barred for ever against night and tempest, with nothing to show it was tenanted except a line of light here and there in the chink of doors and the pale glow of inward peat-fires coming through the holes in the roofs, he heard break out from a backhouse the sound of a reel-tune softly whistled.

"Well, here's gaiety whatever of it!" thought Duncan, who loved a pleasant omen, and took a liberty that one may take with the gay heart he may never attempt with the doleful, for he led his horse to the back-house and drew aside a sack that did for both glass and curtain in the hole that served for window. There were four girls with bare feet dancing discreetly on the clay floor, and a fifth that puckered her lips to the reel-tune, all of them so busy that they did not see that some one pried on them.

"Well done, daughters!" said he; "faith, and it's in there yourselves are hearty on't."

"God's grace!" cried the whistler, and all of them stopped and stared at the window, where Duncan smiled.

"Not so hearty on it, stranger," said the whistler, finding nothing more than human in the interruption, – "not so hearty but what if things permitted, and men were not so noisy by nature, we could be doing with a lad or two at this reel that suffers from too many petticoats and a direful want of trews. Come and be good, and you can pick a partner. You have a dancing face on you or I'm mistaken."

"I have a dancing heart, I'll give you my word of that at any rate," said Duncan, "but I cannot indulge it to-night, for I'm here on a solemn occasion."

"My grief! You cannot have come to be married?" said the whistler, who was a rogue, by all the merriment and freedom of her countenance, "or we would have had some news of it."

"No," said he. "I'm waiting on the ford and some friends over in Uist at a funeral."

"Is that it, good man?" said she that whistled; "you're in luck that it's not your own, and are spared to see such beautiful dancing. We're here five maidens in the fear of life and the fear of death that the minister may come on us at a step or two of reeling, – for the dance, like the song and the pipes and the fairy story, and all that is not dismal, is left nowadays for the Papanaich."

"Fortunate, faith, are the Papanaich then!" said Duncan, "and I'm glad for that, if it was for nothing else I'm a Catholic myself. What I'm wanting is a ring to tie a horse to and the right side of a fire for a while till the ford is open."

They opened the door, and in the light of it for the first time saw his figure.

"Och, now, is it not a gentleman we have here?" said the whistler, the only one unabashed. "On the other side of the wall I took you, by your freedom, for a plain person."

"There you are again!" cried Duncan. "There is not a plainer person in the three isles though I am not wearing home-made clothes. A gentleman would not have come without a bidding to look at your dancing, and if I was here on another errand, I would try to make amends with four good reels, and one-and-a-half for the musician who can whistle in a way to vex the lark."

They laughed at his compliment, and showed him to the best house in the clachan. He went in with "Hail to the household!" and found there was bedrid in it a woman of age, propped on pillows, with a staff at her hand, who mastered a widow daughter and three tall pretty grandsons straight as fir-trees. The grandsons looked to his horse, and put his seat for him; the mother set his plaid to dry, but the old one in her bed it was that gave him the words of welcome.

"Just that! just that!" she said to his explanations, "just that! honest man; and it is from South Uist you have come now? Indeed! indeed! A kind country, and well I know it. If manners would let me, I might have been asking whether you came from the east or west of it! But I am not inquiring. I have known good folk in both."

"The best in the world's there yet," said Duncan – "except such of them as may be in Benbecula – and for the particular bit of it I come from Corodale."

"Corodale!" cried the dame. "Corodale of the corri and the pass! Was I not, O king! once young there? On my soul, but that's tidings! You speak a scholarly Gaelic, not like us riffraff of the Benbecula black houses. There would not be much wonder on me if you were of the one notable family in Glen Usinish; and if that were so, I carried your mother to her christening, being myself a girl in her mother's kitchen."

"Then," said Duncan, "you carried one that is a good mother herself – faith, the best! – and worthier of a better son."

The woman was almost blind with age; she made an eave to her forehead with a trembling withered hand and peered at him out of two pits, seeing him all the more dimly because he was between her and the light. Putting out her stick she caught him with the crook of it by the arm and drew him, laughing, over to her bed. "Let me look at you!" said she, and put her face up close to his. Then she smiled herself, and pushed him lightly on the shoulder. "I have had thee in my lap, son, and the hide of thee was mottled like the back of a Druidibeg trout. You're not the Col one, but the priest one, Duncan, the son of a tall and manly parentage. Have you walked? If you have, my girl must bathe the feet of you. No, you have ridden! – then these large good-for-nothing lads of mine must look well to the horse and seek beds elsewhere, for here you will stay this evening."

"Grandmother," said Duncan, "I am much in your reverence; but I am going back to-night to Creagory, and am waiting here but an hour or two for the opening of the ford that I may meet the priest of Boisdale, Master Ludovick, and his people, who have been burying old Dermosary at the Trinity Temple. I missed the occasion by a tide through the foolishness of a fellow they call Dark John."

"Dark John!" said the woman. "Is that old vagabond to the fore yet, and better folk in Purgatory? And Dermosary is dead? Peace with him and his share of Paradise! he was a wild man, and I'm wondering if he kept his fingers out of the fifty years' fortune. If not, then the Worst Place is his portion."

Duncan stood back abashed a bit, and spoke of going out to see what night it made.

"You will not put a foot over the door," said she, "until my daughter boils some eggs. Your mother was a lady; there was more than pickings of bones in her house. Your father, her first man, – I'll say nothing of her second, – had charms for rich and poor. Not a foot till eggs are made for you, master. You cannot live like the herrings, that thrive and fatten on the foam they make with there own tails."

Duncan promised surely to come back in a little, and went out to look at his horse, to see how stood the tide, and, if possible, find a *ceilidh* party, for he loved the ancient tales.

It was nine o'clock; the storm was at a lull, though out on Eachkamish the surf was booming. In the dark above him there were the most wonderful sounds: the beat of wings that seemed never to have a conclusion; strange contending cries of birds – pictarnie, and skart, and swan – travelling in hosts on their own purposes, which man can never hinder nor divine, winging their way over the islands, a humming in their feathers, no share of the thoughts of the human world in the heads they craned cleaving the darkness. The ford, by the sound of it, was almost empty: he put hands behind his ears to listen for any rumour of the funeral party. But there was none. Away to his right a mouth yawned, and breathed a cloud of light; there was a kiln there where folk in other seasons made kelp, and he walked across to join them.

Four men were having a little *ceilidh* round their furnace, men of the true island kind, counting themselves the equal of the best, speaking frankly yet always with consideration for the stranger, who had to say to them but the name of Corodale to make sure of his welcome. Duncan sat long with them in the shelter of some drift-timber, and talked with them of the seasons and the activities and interests of the Long Island; of kelp prices and breeds of black cattle, of fishing and peat-cutting, and all the things that are of moment in life. There was one that was a wit, and told stories – true *sgeulachdan* generations old, of happenings with giant and dwarf and treasure.

Let tales or songs be going and Duncan was ever the man to listen; he forgot that eggs were at the boiling for his delectation, hearing of Conol Croibhidh and Manus, and told a tale for himself that night as good as these, a tale that is in the Greek books, with never a passage to come in it that his hearers could not have guessed before they heard it, – for there is in all lands, with simple folk, but the one true way to carry on a story and make the same things happen freshly every time.

While they sat round the kiln with the driftwood over them, the wind got up again and sleet began to fall. Duncan, with a sudden recollection of the girl who was with the funeral company, brought his story to an end and put his back to the furnace to look into the darkness. He could almost fancy that Benbecula rocked in the sea torn from her old foundations: women came to the end of the town and cried for their husbands, the men who sat before the kiln, and they ran up to save their roofs, so that Duncan was left alone. He went to the margin of the ford and put an ear to the ground to listen. At first he brought from the tangle of the storm only the tern's "wheel-ah!" the "keevy-keevy" of the red-shank or the scream of a skart, and then he made out the oddest sound, of human voices drifting about the darkness outside, like souls in black perdition. It came in cries and murmurings, the desolation of the sands tenanted with the ghosts of the people of its terrible tales.

"They come at last," said he to himself, wondering how the girl had fared, thinking of her as a child with hair hanging down her back, and shy eyes as he had seen her last, seven years ago.

But the voices came no nearer; they hovered strangely on the sands, blown about like feathers.

"They must be making for Creggans," thought Duncan now, and determined to go out and see. He hurried up to the little town, and threw the saddle on his pony; ran into the house that had meant to entertain him, and got his plaid.

"You will not leave the house this night till you have the eggs," cried the old one with the *cromag* in her bed, "though they are as hard as stones by your own waiting."

He laughed, and declared he had no appetite, kissed a child that stood sleepily on the floor looking up at him, said he might be back, and went out. The pony baulked at the verge, but answered to the heel, and cantered out upon the sands with a splash in tiny rivulets. "A neaptide," thought the rider, "and filling early." He heard no more the sound of voices; the wind mastered all till he reached the trough of Gramisdale, and here he came upon a man that bellowed, running his horse about in foolish circles, plainly not knowing what he was doing.

"My God!" he cried to Duncan's question, and took to whimpering. "My God! is not Herself lost – the darling, and Master Ludovick in the half-horrors?" And he started to cry the name of Anna like a man demented. He did not utter another word of explanation, but gave his horse her head, and galloped up the ford. Then Duncan, standing still a moment, heard again the sand noisy with murmurs and distant cries, and the name of Anna fighting here and there through the wind. He knew the ford as he knew the inside of his own pocket, for a hundred times, as a boy, he had followed his father's wandering droves of cattle over it to the market. The thoughts of what was possible to the girl – of quicks and pools, and aimless straying till high tide – came horrible and confounding to his brain; and he, too, rode across the sands crying her name.

CHAPTER X

High Tide

SOMETIMES he stopped and put his hands behind his ears to gather the wandering sounds, but no answer came to his calls. The others who cried were for a while far to the west, and then went drifting – by their declining cries – eastward towards Grimisay, and the night held him alone when he sent his voice among the huddling rocks and over the little islands. He tried the region of the quicks, and felt the silvery shriek of the sand under his pony's hoofs. He circled the deeper pools, crying the name of Anna till his throat burned, and still found every isle and rock and all the plains of sand unoccupied except for the birds of the sea that heard him with astonishment, and rose to sweep complaining overhead. So much was he mastered by hopes and fears that he made no count of time nor of the tide, till he came to himself with a shock when a dash of spray struck him on the cheek. For a moment he stopped considering. If he turned now he could make the land with safety, but there was still the island of Trialabreck to visit, and the girl might very well be there. Indeed, now that, with all the best of him stiffened to a crisis, he thought calmly, there was nowhere more likely; but if he searched Trialabreck he must stay there till the ford was dry again. The last consideration scarcely found its image in his mind when off he set among the splashing waves, making the wind his compass, and came in a while to the island. For a moment he stood on the verge of it, silent, afraid to put it to the test and lose the last of his hopes.

"Anna!" he cried, at the end, with some odd sense that he would not cry this time in vain, and a great happiness filled him when he heard an answer.

"A lucky man who knows what he wants has but to shut his eyes for a little or go out in the dark and find good fortune at his feet," he thought, leading his pony over the stones. He could see nothing, but he could hear another pony's whinny, and "Who are you?" he was asked, in a voice that surprised him, for all the time he had pictured such a child as he had slightly known in Boisdale before he went to France, and this was something like a woman's utterance. He put his answer and his explanation in a sentence, coming up beside her where she stood in the hollow below the rock.

"I am so glad you have come," was all she said, almost like to break in tears, and smiling in the darkness as if he could see her, and so discover there were no womanly terrors here. "I am so sorry to trouble you."

"There is no trouble about it," said Duncan, "except that I have not come upon you sooner. With a little more judgment I might easily have done so, and now I am sorry to say we must remain where we are till the tide ebbs, for even if your whereabouts were known there is not a boat on this side of Benbecula to face such weather."

"My poor Ludovick!" said Anna, with a pang to think of her brother desolate till daylight. For herself now she had no fears: there was something in the voice of this new companion of her misfortune to set her wholly at her ease. She explained briefly the cause of her misadventure.

"If you are safe and well yourself, so far, that is the first consideration," said he, busily. "The tide will not reach us here, and we will not be the first who have passed a night on Trialabreck. Are you cold?"

"No, not so very cold," said she, clenching her teeth to keep them from chattering, and wondering a little at the want of a deference she was lately grown accustomed to.

"Cold enough to be the better for a plaid more," said Duncan, "and you must have mine when I have seen to the ponies; "but she would not consent to this deprivation. He took the saddles from the ponies, and for a little was thus engaged, while she stood by, weary in every limb, and thinking it odd to have the company and service of one whose appearance she could not even guess at. He made her saddle into a seat for her, put his own beside it – very close, indeed, she could not but think, for a new acquaintance – and seating himself, threw his plaid about their knees.

"Are you comfortable now?" said he, maintaining a composure lest the child should be too easily induced to tears.

"Oh, I am very well, thank you," said Anna, and could not resist an irony. "I – I hope you will make yourself comfortable too," she added, and no sooner saying it than she felt ashamed. But he had no suspicion of her humour: in spite of her voice he went back to his old conceptions of a Boisdale hoyden with her hair flowing. "I am so pleased to have found you that I'm almost forgetting how unhappy the folk on shore will be till morning."

"My dear Ludovick!" said Anna again, and then Duncan felt a touch upon his sleeve.

"Could we not – could we not shake hands?" said she timidly. "It was so brave of you to come, and I would just like to shake hands."

"Shake hands!" said he. "Of course! of course! How stupid that I should forget!" He felt for her hand in the darkness, found damp chilly fingers and a warm palm, which he pressed hurriedly.

"On my word," said he, "I ought indeed to be shaking hands with you, for I might have been *each uisge* coming out of the tide on you in this fashion."

"I'll admit I thought of *each uisge* – of the water-horse – myself when I heard your pony's splashing first," said Anna.

"And so much of a stranger, too! We have both been long away from the islands, have we not? But we'll have time to make better acquaintance before the ebb."

"My poor Ludovick!" said Anna yet again. "I wish it were ebb now."

"Of course, of course!" said Duncan, with a smile in his voice, "though the wish is hardly a compliment to your present company. Let us think how glad your brother will be to find you safe; it will make more than amends for his anxieties," and he drew his saddle an inch or so nearer, till their shoulders almost touched, giving her further shelter from the wind that whistled round the rock they leaned against. Smuggling, thought Anna, was a trade that gave considerable elbow-room to the manners. She would have preferred the deference to start with, but must confess to herself that after all it was not the hour nor place for ceremony; for together in the night they might be the sole survivors of a ruined universe, or the first creatures set in a new and dubious Paradise of storm.

A bud of light suddenly showed itself on their right over Gramisdale; it blossomed into a flower of flame.

"They have started a beacon," said Duncan. "I wish we could reply, but I have the material for neither light nor fire." She stared at the distant flame, sighing, half for her overwhelming weariness, half for longing, but found some comfort in the signal.

"The time will pass quickly," he assured her, and put a light, encouraging, kindly hand on her shoulder, where a damp strand of her hair lay astray from its fellows. She started at his touch. "I beg your pardon!" said he, wondering how old she was, and whether she was good-looking. For a child with her hair hanging he thought her manifestly over-sensitive. It was likely, he thought, that she was on the point of a hysteria, and he hurried into a conversation about the funeral (always with their eyes on the distant beacon), and he explained the reason for his absence.

"My brother looked for you at Creggans," said Anna, but did not tell that she had, herself, a notion to meet a notorious hero.

"That I was not there," said Duncan, " was no fault of my own, but must be the blame of your brother's messenger. He came to Corodale, by all appearance, with a bidding only for my brother, who was from home; and for his own reasons, that have puzzled me ever since, he misled me by a tide, and brought me to the ford six hours late."

"That is curious, certainly; for it was yourself the man was most anxious to have here with us, and there is none whose name is more often on his lips."

"Then that is odder still, I'll assure you, for I never, to my knowledge, saw the man between the eyes till he came last night to Corodale."

Anna started. "Oh!" said she, with a gasp, " I took you all the time for Mr Col, and – and –"

"And by worse luck for you I am merely his brother Duncan. Plain Duncan, Anna, no more nor less. And that's the mischief of the thing! Col, I feel sure, would have had his wits about him, and tried Trialabreck first of all, and got you off before the tide was too high. Well, I'm lucky enough myself to be just in time to keep you company."

There was a good deal of "Anna" in this for a first acquaintance, thought the girl, and sat in the darkness speechless.

"Are you cold?" he asked again, at a loss for anything else to say in such a coil of curious circumstances.

"No, not now, only weary, and a little sleepy," she replied, her eyelids like lead. "It is so stupid of me, but I could not sleep last night in that inn on the other side."

"The sooner you sleep the sooner the morning will come, then," said her companion, and then there was no more between them. She leant against the rock, all her body so relaxed of life she feared to swoon, and fighting her fear she fell asleep.

He watched the flame, that was the only evidence of another world than this. It never failed, though for some hours more the ancient furies possessed the isle of Trialabreck, and he had some comfort in the certainty that it was her brother's beacon of hope. He could not hear her breathing, but felt the pulse of it, and by-and-by her head slipped from along the cold hard pillowing of the rock until it found a place at last upon his shoulder. "Poor child!" said he, feeling very pitiful. He had a thought to put his arm about her, but feared she might awaken, and so he sat with her head on his shoulder. Her bosom rose and fell on his arm – surely somewhat generous for a girl so young – and set him wondering again upon her aspect – whether she was like her brother; upon her mind – whether she had brought back from the convent-school the bleak innocence he had found in girls of that experience. And full of these reflections he drowsed, himself, so that the Long Ford of Uist had a marvel, in a rock tenanted by a man and a maiden who had never seen each other and still were sitting dreaming in the dark together, upon the cheerless sanctuary of the gannet and the tern. The sea clanged, the wind declined to dry gusts, the tide began to turn.

The creatures of the ocean, the sea-folk of the *ceilidh* tales, that romp in billows and ramble in the weedy deeps came to Trialabreck to see what God saw once, and only for a little, in His Garden.

CHAPTER XI

The Awakening

IT was not for long they slept, out of the world and life and yet on the edge of them, happy because heedless, victorious over perils and temptations, and indifferent because unaware. Her hair billowed on his shoulder, and her body was warm against his arm: if he had listened closely he might have heard her placid breathing – surely to some moods of ours the most pitiful thing in the world. But he was in the other dream that contains and commands us as much and as truly as that we inhabit in daytime, unconscious that here was Eve – Eve with the flowing hair and lips untried, sometimes sighing in her sleep.

He was the first to waken and find his shoulder was still her pillow. He did not move, but sat watching the light at Gramisdale. The wind had dropped from its thundering to a melancholy coronach of sound in the distance and a whisper among the rushes of the islet. There was no booming out on Eachkamish; the smell of fresh ooze and new-bared wrack was in the darkness – the tokens of a falling tide. But welcome more than all the rest to Duncan was a patch of stars over Grimisay and a faint portent of the moon; in an hour at most they could quit Trialabreck.

He was not sorry. He had given her all his plaid an hour ago, and Adam was cold and Adam was hungry, with Eve not much in his mind, and he was thinking how much wiser he had been to have pocketed the eggs that had been made ready for him in the hospitable house in Gramisdale. But he thought of Father Ludovick too, grief-stricken on Benbecula – on the priest's plight more than on his sister's, for he knew that strenuous ardent heart, and could imagine it beat to bursting over where the beacon flared and folk were waiting for the fallen tide. There, he thought, was a man forlorn in the world, though surrounded by people who loved him and that had his inmost heart, for he soared over the mists of Hecla and Benmore like the golden eagle on his thoughts, while they, except when they felt stirred to accord with the simplest of his raptures, trudged the macharland and peat-moss, tethered to the rocks. His morning walks were bounded by the same sea-strand and the same cliffs that marked their own, but they did not walk with him that loved them, they did not understand. A lonely man – though often exalted and happy – and over yonder in Gramisdale he was in despair for his sister.

As thus he was thinking, now with eyes on the tiny garden of stars, now on the withering bloom of the beacon upon Gramisdale, Anna wakened too. She lifted her head quickly, seemed stunned for a moment by the mystery she had come to, then saw the beacon-light of her brother, had everything flash to her understanding, and shrank abashed at her own indelicacy. Duncan understood, not by thinking, as it might seem, but by some magic message through every pore of his body. Eve was awake, and wise, and frightened, and ashamed! Well, Adam was a gentleman; he pretended that he still was fast asleep.

She listened for a moment to his breathing, laid the plaid about his knees softly, and rose gently to her feet. She stole to the islet's edge and found the sea receded and almost calm. How glad she was that very soon she might escape from this imprisonment and join Ludovick over at the beacon. Upon a little patch of grass she knelt and said her morning prayer – the matin of all these Isles –

> "*Iosda Criosda*, thanks to Thee
> That brought me from the deeps of night
> Into the solace of the light,
> Through blood atoning shed for me;"

and bathed her face and hands with another tiny prayer of the Islands, as for a lustration. If the uncanny tenants of the deeps were haunting round the edge of Trialabreck then, be sure they must have taken fins for it and swam far out and deep into their offensive caves; and if the others were there – the maidens that sing riding free on billows with half souls and wistfulness when they look on the wholly blest – be sure they were kneeling about her on the strand, loving this sweet half-sister Anne.

When she returned to their shelter she found her companion of the night awake. "So you have not run away and left me?" said he craftily, when she stood before him, a figure taller than he expected, though still to be seen but dimly. "I think I must have been sleeping for hours, – the thing's a gift in the family."

"Oh, I was almost dead for sleep myself," said she, relieved to think he did not know. "And now I am quite refreshed. The ford is drying; we may go soon, and have Macfarlane's lantern with us, for the moon is rising."

"We may set out in less than half an hour," said Duncan, looking from her dim figure to the patch of stars, and mildly wishful to see her face. The coronach on the isle was only a whisper now, the water was lapping round the edge of Trialabreck with a friendly sound in the way of hidden pools round ancient keeps in the deep old glens with the kindly sounds of old friends, old cronies that have had many gallant times together. And the birds flew seaward again, high over them, sometimes blurring the garden of stars, chuckling together as they flew. The wan eye of Garinish, the lamp that guides the wanderer on the ford, shone through the dark behind them, and the beacon of Gramisdale, fed with fresh timber bloomed again. The morning air was fresh and clean giving a gladness to the man and woman as if they had drunk wine.

"Oh, I must rise and go away!" hummed Duncan, in the words of MacMhaister Alastair's ditty, and took to the saddling of the ponies, while Anna stood apart and looking on, curious as to what fashion of man was this that had so strangely borne her company. The last faint breath of the wind – that was like a sigh to leave her – blew a stray lock of her hair across her cheek; she hastened to trim herself before the moon revealed her. In the upper space the clouds flew hurriedly across the heavens; it grew clearer every moment; at last the moon jumped in among the stars that faded and died of envy, and Duncan fastened the last buckle, and turned about to find a woman with a wan face regarding him.

"*Mo chreach!*" he thought, dumfoundered; "have not I been a fool!" He had nothing to say for a moment as he looked at her there in the moonlight, composed and pale, her face upheld, and her eyes eager.

She guessed the cause of his silence and had to smile.

"Shake hands," said he at that, with his hat off. "Shake hands again, and forgive me all my liberties. I am like the man in the story; I went to sleep when you were a child, and I wakened to find you grown into a woman. I was so long away in France that I did not know. I am afraid my manners –"

"Were not French," said Anna, as he stopped for want of words. "If they had been, I daresay I would have been less at my ease. You have been very good, and I, and I – oh, I have been so rude. I think – I think, I – I slept."

"Faith! I know I did," said he, and dwelt in her eyes, that were lit so wonderfully by this tardy moon. "I did not know my own good fortune – there I am like the man in the other story – I did not know my own good fortune. If it were not for Father Ludovick over there, I could very gaily be taking the saddles off and sitting down again at a more respectful distance, and talking till daybreak, just to show I am not wholly so stupid as you must think me."

"What!" cried Anna; "and spare me no chance of proving I am fairly clever myself! But I'm afraid all that must stand for another occasion," she added more gravely. "I can only be thinking of Ludovick."

"What a happy man is Ludovick!" thought Duncan; and to make her happy too, the sooner, he proposed that they should try the ford immediately.

They set out in a world of light – the shallow waters like a floor of gold under the riding moon. They saw Hecla and Benmore before them sombre and high above the beacon. The tide ran fast; by-and-by they trotted upon grey sand strewn with birds, and heard before them the inquiring cries of human voices. Duncan turned in his saddle and took a last look at Trialabreck, feeling friendly to that cold islet where he had spent a night so curious. A little later Anna was in her brother's arms.

CHAPTER XII

The Dead Months

NOW were the dead months, as they call them in the Uists, – November of the fogs, December of the hurricanes. Seamen going past from warm lands then, must pity the poor isles, as high on spars, astounded, they saw them of a sudden through the rain, or leaned on the bulwarks and had compassion, maybe, on the people sentenced here to a perpetual banishment, suffering for ever the harassment of winds, the anger of the Sounds. But Uist, none the less, was happy even then as any land of lighted cities. They saw black thatch rain-rotted – these tropic mariners; they saw the reek of townships to all appearance knee-deep in morasses, but they did not see the warm peat-fires within. They heard perhaps the *langanaiche* – the sad inquiry of the cattle wandering over the salt plains; but they never had a guess of evening melodies in the huts. The dead months – but it is then there is most leisure in Uist of the winds and sheldrakes. There was a saying once that a new song was put together every day somewhere between the two Bernerays, and seldom was the poem doleful, so quick, and clever, and content the folk of the Outer Isles. There must have been a handful of such ballads fashioned in Uist each day that tempest blew, for always the Island spirit feels its best when the world is thundering. Then Ludovick, when he saw the great round moon rise rolling through wrack of clouds, Hecla and Benmore dragging through them, brave companions of carouse, belated, the sea of a sudden revealed, and its vexatious slumbers, thought on the words of Genesis, "And the earth was void and empty." He would say to Anna, as they watched together, "I have it here!" and beat on his breast, "I have it here; I share God's gladness at the Creation." He had eighty pounds a-year – little enough for a partner with God in His operations, and yet for that same reason all-sufficient; eighty pounds – and Valladolid to remember, and good wines, music, pictures, cheerful folk with sparkling conversations, but he put that all behind him with no pang, relieved and gay to have done the day's duty, loving his people truly. There are no gardens in Boisdale, for there, too cruel, blows the wind, but Father Ludovick had a garden that bloomed in these dead months: his fancies flowered; he came with perfumes from the soul to the huts, sedate or smiling. Then the people had leisure to talk with him, and many were their conversations. They speak in Uist sensibly, with that simplicity that was common with the old great kings, mingling gravity and mirth, saying nothing merely for its cunning or display. He moved upon the surface of things in these fine talks on food and fire, cattle, ships, men, women, work, all the matters that most affect us; but sometimes he must long to indulge himself in depths his people could not reach to – sometimes books palled, the hours hung heavy, and Anna often tried to make him have a holiday.

"You are looking ill, Ludovick – as grey as a ghost," she would tell him. "You must take a jaunt and a rest on the mainland, or I'll soon be a widow woman."

He would glance in a glass and laugh to see the healthy tan of his countenance, that told him she was but manœuvring.

"Well, if you are not, you ought to be," would Anna say then. "I am vexed to have a common barnacle for a brother, that sticks on this rock from year's end to year's end and never goes anywhere to bring back a new story for his sister, or give her a rest from her continual toil and moil for his lazy comfort."

He would put a hand through his hair and laugh again at that.

"Let us take a month's travelling," she would propose.

"What!" he would say, "and leave poor Uist shepherdless? Besides, there is the question of money, girl Anna."

To that she had an answer in her mind, but it never got expression from her lips, for one matter was between them that was never mentioned.

"Travel!" he would say. "I can be travelling every day from Portnan-long to Pollacher and see the world there."

"Yes! yes! but not the pictures in Italy."

"The pictures in Italy were made by men who stayed at home attending to their own affairs. Have we not the morning and the evening on Benmore? And there is nothing to be found in travelling but what you take with you in your trunk. But – you will go yourself, dear," he said once on a sudden thought, and off he packed her to the Lowlands that winter after the death of their uncle. She was scarcely out of sight of windy Uist when she knew that she was rooted, too, among the dunes, and this travelling was something of a folly.

The dead months for once seemed worthy of their name to Father Ludovick. He missed her singing in the kitchen; he would lie awake at night trying to see her over the dark and over the sea, three hundred miles away.

In November came a great change to Corodale, also; for the mother died, and Duncan was the master. He was that at least in name; but in truth our stuck priest relinquished all, and was no better than a servant without wages. He would have gone away, but there was much to do in the interests of the ancient patrimony. Now was Col more busily on foot than ever, an owner of many skiffs, hirer of many crews, though he could protest at last he was at an end with smuggling. It was then he got the name of the New Man. By-names are found in these islands at a flash, to tell a story in a word or paint a portrait, and to him the name New Man attached because of the sudden change that sent him regularly into Boisdale for the Mass, though his confessions must be elsewhere. The *Happy Return* still plied between the isles and Moidart or Argyll, and went now and then to the Lowlands, and sometimes seeing her careen off Corodale, Col would lament to Duncan the old days unregenerate when he shared her fortunes. They were not unhappy then, the two of them in Corodale, where Duncan was the stay-at-home, more greatly admiring his brother than ever, for his handsomeness, his skill at many things, his bravery in all. He thought he had his brother's inmost confidence. But there was a Col that would have puzzled him had he known, sitting up at nights in his upper room whereinto the moon had looked enormous on St Michael's night, – a Col who had gathered books from every airt where they could be borrowed – narratives of the wealthy, of domestic splendour, of travel and extravagance; and there in the upper room with a candle he would sit reading and thinking long after the rest of Corodale was asleep and the lights were blown out in Uist. Let Duncan have his *ceilidh* as he will; for Col the tales of far lands to travel in, of gallantries to buy, of people vastly prodigal. And when he tired of reading and of thought he filled pages with itineraries, of lands he would go through like the others, or with estimates of moneys he would spend on buildings, and boats, and horses, and cattle.

It was remarked how often nowadays Young Corodale's business brought him into Boisdale. "There will be tales to tell of this," said the spinster woman who carded wool that night he saved Dark John; and the good wife of Dalvoolin, who had seen his mouth, kept out of his way when she saw him coming along the road, for fear he should discover what were her thoughts about him. He went to chapel always when he happened to be in the neighbourhood of Stella Maris, and always dipped his fingers awkwardly in the porringer that replaced the one he broke – the only awkward thing he did in life. Father Ludovick gave him the welcome of the priest and of the Gael commingled, the open hand and no inquiries. He would rather it had been the other brother, but Duncan never came to that part of the island, and indeed this Col had qualities to make him likeable by a priest that loved wit, and was too much the dreamer to comprehend how sometimes it might but poorly compensate for the lack of other virtues.

It was the day before *Nollaig* – it was on Christmas Eve – that Anna came home. The little boat that took her ashore from Scalisdale's lugger was hardly on the land when she was eagerly over the bow of it, with a thrill to feel the sand below her shoe-soles, the smiles and the tears of joy on her face, all her being moved tremendously to be back with them that loved her.

"Who is that?" she asked Father Ludovick, when the greeting was over and they moved up to the house, and she indicated a tall figure, black-bearded and straight that stood a little way off, watching them.

Her brother looked into the setting sun, and he saw Young Corodale there, jetty black against the coppery west, a figure enormous and unnatural, so aloof in some way from this happy world of home-returnings and content. He wished it had been ordered otherwise just for this day, though the arrangement had been his own, and that Col the New Man was at home in his own country.

"Oh, faith!" said he, "'tis Corodale, I forgot that he had expressed a wish to be here at your home-coming, and that I asked him over for this Christmas Eve."

"Not – not Duncan?" said she, searching with all her eyes.

"His brother Col. He has been very kind; he gave me much of his company in your absence," said Ludovick, and at that her staring ceased. "Duncan is doubtless better engaged in Corodale. I'm like yourself, perhaps, in preferring that it had been Duncan; but seeing it was the other I had e'en to make the best of it, and indeed one might have worse society. The fellow has some curious charm."

"Oh, as to preference –" said Anna hurriedly, and stopped. "Well, to tell the truth, I wish it had been the other, too, for all that's come and gone, as we say. I'm afraid he's of the notion that Father Ludovick's sister must be anything but a credit to him, for I was out of my wits on Trialabreck, and he has never given me the opportunity either of thanking him or of showing that I was not so stupid as I looked. And this is Mr Col, is it? Upon my word now, Ludovick, one may be a smuggler and pass, so far as the looks go, for a gentleman."

"Smuggler no more, my dear," said Father Ludovick in an undertone, for Col approached them. "And, I assure you, quite the gentleman, like all of his name. Here, nowadays, we know him as the New Man, for very creditable reasons."

Col came forward, with a breeze of the heartiest welcome in his manner.

"Miss Anna," said he lightly, and still with the warmth of sincerity, "there's an old word of the Barra fishermen that bids the sea-bird welcome, after it has been south, 'Come home to the isles, for fortune is in your feathers.'" And then he felt dumfoundered for a second, for the word "fortune," that had come in all innocency to his mouth, was the last that, on reflection, he would have chosen. But, luckily, no one noticed it but himself.

"You are very good," said Anna, laughing. "It's true enough of Edinburgh bonnets this winter," and she made a motion of her head that set the dark plumes waving there. "Only I wish you had not mentioned it, for I had not intended to tell my brother what they cost until he had eaten his favourite pudding, that he must be weary for, to-morrow. But he's the sort of creature who would never have noticed them if they were tickling his very nose."

"Now! now!" said the priest, with admiration, "I assure you I thought there was something unusual rare and fine about you."

"Oh *mochree!*" cried Anna, "here's gallantry after all the Lowland lads! And my fineness is in my feathers! Mr Col, I have an eye for the practical cavalier if you please, and I should like to make you my brother's tutor in some polite arts that are not studied much in the isle of Uist. Tell him, will you, there can never be anything unusual rare and fine about any lady under forty; she's for ever at the pinnacle of her splendour, or else she's not worth looking at."

"Now that you're back," said Col, taking the step by her side, "we'll be at our practice immediately; what excuse could we have in honesty for our compliments and Miss Anna away?" He pulled his beard to a peak, threw back his shoulders, and felt a man come into a world he was born to ornament. There was astonishment in his mind if it was not in his face, for this lady, so self-composed and beautiful in the way of the wild-flower, was as different from her he had expected that for a minute or two at least he forgot she was first and foremost the girl of fortune.

"You are come for our Christmas Eve," she said as they rose on the brae to the presbytery. "I am so glad, for I have Edinburgh cakes."

"Not a bit better, I'll wager, than the ones you could have baked yourself," protested her brother.

"Thank you, Ludovick!" said she. "We're getting on at our gallantries. Your influence, Mr Col, is for the very best, I can see that; but my Edinburgh cakes are so good, as you'll find, that I'm only sorry you did not bring your brother to share in them."

"Oh, Duncan!" cried Col, and no more than that, but a great deal in the accent of it.

"Exactly," said Anna, reddening at the tone. "And why not? Who, please, has a better claim on the gratitude of myself – and Ludovick? Let me tell you – no, I will not tell you; I must not be rude. But I must hurry to my kitchen if this bannock eve of ours is rightly to be celebrated, and you two can follow at your leisure." And off she ran for the White House, all the way annoyed, for some reason that she did not tell herself, leaving admiring eyes behind.

Col saw he must be cautious. He found he had a different spirit to contend with from what he had expected. Plainly it was to take all his knowledge of the mind of man and woman to keep Miss Anna outside of him upon the plausible surface. She had, perhaps, the piercing eye, but was too modest yet for that to be seen; she had certainly the understanding ear that comprehends the spirit of all spoken words, and is cursedly dangerous to any but the man of single mind. He looked after her as she turned the corner of the presbytery, and marvelled to see how much of an air of the domestic and refined she gave even to the white-harled walls of that austere old dwelling. It was but a priest's cell before; now it was a home.

"Yes," said Father Ludovick, following his eyes, and with more certainty than surmise, – "yes; she does! she does! she makes the place as jolly as if every day was a day of weddings. I am glad you came, Col, to share our bannock *Nollaig*, what were these isles, so unkindly dealt with, as I sometimes think, by God, but for the genialities of man and woman? I'm telling you" (he turned to his Gaelic, that was for him the language of the deep emotions), – "I'm telling you on my own soul, and on the life of me, that I brought her home simply by the wishing for it. She was not to be here for another fortnight, as we had planned it when she went away, but I lay at night in my selfishness and said over the sea and over the night, 'Come back, come back to Uist,' and I'll warrant she heard me in her dreams."

"I'm not denying it," said Col, "but what are sea and darkness when there's but the one wish between them?"

"Do you think so? Do you think so?" cried this foolishly fond priest, all glowing with pleasure. "Well, well, I would not say."

'Twas a merry night that night in Uist of the winds. All the lamps were lit, the townships blythe and hearty. Lovers stumbled against each other in the paths that cross the isle, poorly lighted by a grey moon in her black boundaries; the songmen – the guisards – went in masquerade from house to house at their diversions. A calm night, with the kindness of May, so that when supper was done, Anna and Col and Ludovick went out on the hillock to hear the long roll of the sea in the creeks, to see the sparkle of the dwellings, to listen to the choruses. The night was full of sea-scents and the odours of turfen fires. A hundred skiffs lay in the bay, to every one a lamp in token of festivity, and as they softly rocked in the waves from side to side, they seemed like tall flowers of the night. The priest looked from them to the chapel lights – for Our Lady Star of the Sea was being made ready for the Mass; and he thought indeed the world was good and beautiful, and Col counted the skiffs and summed up their profits, and Anna sighed with content that she was home again and the tang of the ocean in her nostrils.

"Oh," she said, "it is good to be back! The folk were pitying me when I was leaving to come home, for what they called this hermitage on an island. Ludovick – Mr Col – can you guess what I said to them? 'It is I that will be pitying you, poor dears, in your houses and your grey streets of stone, the same every day and every hour of it, when I'm looking from my window at the miracles of the sea, and feeling the heart in me like a bird.'"

"Ah! 'tis blest to be happy and young!" said her brother, with the air of the pastor.

"True, true, Father," said Anna; "I am glad to have the confirmation of antiquity. Is he not failing with age, this brother of mine, Corodale? – six-and-thirty if a day – but so tremendously wise!"

"I'm not Corodale, strictly speaking," explained Col, as her brother moved away to speak to some of his people grouped close at hand waiting the hour of chapel. "The honour of the name's my brother Duncan's."

"And I am sure he will do credit to it," said Anna, a little more heartily, as she felt in a moment, than she had intended.

"More than poor Col could do, I confess to you," said he. "What am I but a rough home-bred one, half porpoise, half mole, that has never been long enough away from his birthplace to get the peat-reek of home blown out of his clothing?"

"Nor the warmth of it out of his nature, I'm hoping, Mr Col."

"That Duncan should be master is in the way of nature; and, as you say, it best befits him –"

"You are scarcely complimentary to my manners, Mr Col," said Anna. "It has been the misfortune of my brother's house that you have been too busy to let us see either of you there to give us the chance of judging any of your qualities or of letting you know our own. I hope your brother has some of your bravery – you see what a plain blunt speaker I am, Mr Col? – and that you have some of his gentleness. I am not like to forget in a hurry his goodness that night I sat in Trialabreck trying my best to be courageous like a true MacNeil, and swallowing my heart like a woman every time a gannet cried in the dark. You will do this for me, Mr Col, will you not? – you will send your brother to Boisdale when it may earliest suit his convenience, so that I may have a chance to thank him – what am I saying? He – you – must think me very bold to say that. And still I should like –'

"Naturally, Miss Anna, naturally," said Col. "The scamp has been ill-considered in his manners that he has not been here before now to inquire for the lady he had the good fortune to be of a small service to. He is a man of many charms, Duncan – there's not a nobler fellow in some ways in the Long Island – no, nor for many a hundred miles about them; but he has that ridiculous interest in his duty, as he thinks it, to Corodale, that as you know is not in the best condition at present, for all the pair of us can be doing to amend it – that – that –"

"That he cannot spare the time," said Anna coldly. "Oh, I understand! I hope I will never come between any honest man and his duty. I must say to you, though, that it's pleasant the sinful world is not always so set upon its duty, and that though Mr Duncan has been too much engaged to visit us, his brother got the time to come for a crack occasionally with Ludovick, who valued such a thing all the more in the absence of his sister, that perhaps has too much to say. To tell you the truth, I daresay I was less anxious to show my gratitude to your brother than to have an opportunity of showing him what a very clever young lady I was in spite of all the evidence to the opposite that night he kept me company on the ford. Are you astonished, Mr Col, to find Father Ludovick's sister so vain and foolish? It is because I'm in the dark I can tell you this: if it was light, you would be seeing a very demure and modest person, I assure you."

There was something so sprightly in her manner, so unexpected in her moods – now proud, now soft – that it fairly captured Col's fancy, and his character for the moment took – as was often the case with him – its colour from that of his companion. The darkness favoured him, as it had ill favoured his brother on Trialabreck, and, escaping the scrutiny of her eyes, he could freely discover in himself emotions he had not felt for many a year, and experience a sincere satisfaction in her company. It came out in his conversation, in his very accent. For once he fairly shone, a better man than ever he had been before. He felt no sense of the intruder that night at Mass in Our Lady Star of the Sea.

CHAPTER XIII

Over to Boisdale

"FATHER LUDOVICK has been asking for you over in Boisdale," Col said some weeks after, to keep himself right with all the possible circumstances, but never a word of Father Ludovick's sister, still supposed to be on her mainland travels.

"I hope the good man is well?" said Duncan. "I had the thought once or twice to go over, but the intention may stand till slacker times. You will give him my remembrances when you see him next, and my excuses. If there's anything in the tale of the ninety-and-nine, he'll think more of the lost sheep Col as a casual visitor than if I called, myself, on him once a-week."

"You will please yourself on that score," said Col. "It is of no account to the lost sheep."

Duncan, who always felt the whip himself in any innuendo about his past, begged his brother's pardon quickly.

"No offence, I assure you," said his brother, "none in the world! If it was lost sheep we had to discourse on over at Boisdale, the most notorious would be yourself. I, for one, was never within the four walls of their clerical fank in France."

"Neither you were, Col, neither you were!"

"And that puts me in mind of a thing," Col went on. "Do you know who brought you back from Paris?"

Duncan reddened. "I could say with truth that I did not," he said, "but I'll admit I have had my own suspicions that Father Ludovick himself was at the back of that. Mother said as much. She once told me that when father was near his end he sent for the Boisdale priest. They talked long and they talked late, and the outcome was that I was taken home. That I came willingly, because I felt all along I was unsuited for a priest, has nothing to do with it. I came home."

"And here you are!"

"And here I am, as you say, Col. From that day till this I have never been able to learn the reason, indeed, to tell the truth, I have always been a little afraid it was one that I would be happier not to know."

"A priest's reason like enough," said Col, thinking deeply, "and of little account among ordinary men."

"Anyhow, here's a sheep that has escaped the shearing, and not very sorry for it. If Father Ludovick it was that advised my recall, I feel he had his own sufficient reasons. Once I would have given a good deal, from natural curiosity, to know them; now I keep out of his way, from a feeling that there might be some displeasure in their discovery. Do you follow me, Col? The chapter's closed. It's a wise man that takes things as they come without too much inquiry, if they turn out in the end to his advantage. But how did you come to think of the priest in that connection?"

"We were talking of father – the priest and I, last Wednesday – and the legacy left to him and the crazy schemes he spent it on, and the priest sat without a word and damned uncomfortable, I assure you, by the look of him, till I mentioned your name, and said it was a pity for all your years in the college wasted. He let the thing drop to me unawares there. 'On my advising,' said he, he came back on my advising; it was the least that could be done,' and no more than that, but shut up like an oyster, with his face pretty red and a look at his sister."

"Miss Anna!" cried Duncan. "You did not tell me she was back."

Col's face became indifferent. "Did I not?" said he.

"I could swear I did, but it does not matter; she came back at Christmas."

"Faith, then, I wish you had said so sooner, and I would have had a jaunt to Boisdale. What do you think of her?"

"Oh! – I'm no judge," said Col. "If it was a quey, now, or a filly –"

"You're a clever man, Col," said Duncan, laughing, "but now and then, in some things, I'm thinking I could give you lessons."

Duncan went over to Boisdale for St Brigid's Day in February, when the men of the Outer Isles start the longline fishing on the banks, when the raven begins to build, and the larks get their new voices. The early morning had been frosty, but now it was wonderfully bland; the sea was calm – the air so clear he could see the Monach Isles twenty miles away in banks of purple on the blue, and the rocks of them grey in the sun.

The fisher of the Uists begins no enterprise but in the spirit of prayer, nor rises at morn nor sleeps at night, nor kindles crusie light nor smothers an evening fire, without some invocation of the saints. Beholding the sun at morning break, gorgeous, through the sea, he takes the bonnet from his head and feels again the early awe before Columba.

On St Brigid's Day the fishermen went to chapel and heard their priest exhort them to ways of justice and peace in all their traffic on the deep. When Duncan came first in sight of Stella Maris, he could see the men, with Mass over, clustered near the quays casting lots for their places on the fishing-banks – themselves boisterous like the sea itself. On the southern wall of the chapel was a seat where old men gathered, guessing at the possibilities of the opening season. For them the wave no more, nor the pull on hard-rimed oar, nor the swelter at the line. They looked out on the old friend – the old enemy – lying there so crafty hiding her thoughts, and tried their ancient skill to find the darting gannet against the dazzle of the east They would have been contending at the quays too, and not here at the chapel's gable, were it not that it is unlucky for the young to meet the old when the young are going a-fishing. Seven of them sat with their humps to the wall, and gallantly feigned a satisfaction with their fate.

"We are lucky to be out of it, brave lads, and our fortune made before the trade was done," said one, whose fortune was six sons that wrought for him. "There has not been a notable fishing, my grief! since the year of the yellow snow. At the best of it I was always thinking the long lines no gentleman's occupation. The cod and conger – they are the churls of the sea, daundering around in singles like the raven of the land: give me the herring of the summer-time, that moves from place to place in jolly bands, and is a king's fish, and was never caught by the greed of its guts with worm or cockle, but went to his death, like the great Macleans, in noble armies. Long lines! long lines! to the Worst with them! – give me the nets at her, bow to back, and the brine of the curing-barrels."

"It was very well in its time, but nowadays too many of the curing-barrels belong to Corodale Col, and the bounty and the price he pays for the cran are hardly worth a God-fearing man wetting his boots or putting his breath in a net-bow for," said another little red man like a gurnet at the gills and the nose of him. "They're calling him the New Man, my heroes; but the New Man's as close in the claws as the old smuggler."

"I'm not so sure about the old smuggler," said another; "Col's brand is still on the ankers of the *Happy Return*, and I hear he's often across at the Sergeant's inn at Creggans. It was never the morning bitters brought Corodale there."

"Well, he's here at Mass often enough, and makes plenty of profession," said the gurnet.

"Here at Mass and friendly with Master Ludovick; but *'illean*, have you seen him bungle at the holy water? I take it for a sign. The New Man! faith! who gave him the name but Dark John that thinks so much of his life saved on St Michael's, he would throw it away for Col – in any manner but drowning. By the Book! and there's his brother Duncan himself."

Duncan passed with a smile and the word of day for the oldsters at the gable-end; stood for a little apart from the fishermen loudly bickering over the luck of their drawing, and went to the jetty where women were passing the vials of holy water into the dens of the skiffs. Father Ludovick stood on the slip and beamed in the lovable banter of his flock.

"You rogue!" said he to Duncan, "where have you been for a hundred thousand years? Am I a leper, Corodale Og? Or has the tale gone about the islands that Father Ludovick's Spanish wine is sour? At least a twelvemonth back from – at least a twelvemonth home, and all I have seen of you was a phantom on a wild morning on the Long Ford, when I was too demented to make much of the opportunity."

"I have been so busy," said Duncan.

"It is the worst of fevers; I hope it is not catching. Your brother Col was not so busy but what he could find time to be civil and give us a call occasionally. Let me warn you that you'll have a cold reception from Anna on the head of your neglect. There was a good deal of Mr Duncan in her conversation before she went to Edinburgh, but now that she's come back to find that very throng gentleman has never looked the road her poor brother was on, all the time of her absence, but left his neighbourly courtesies to Col – h'm! well let me tell you, sir, it is a different tale with her. You will go up to the house at once and make your own explanations and apologies; and what is more, I cannot just now go with you for a backing, for I'm here at a duty that cannot be left. Go up and have something to eat and drink – if her ladyship will forgive you enough to be hospitable – and I'll follow by-and-by. But let me tell you again, sir, you compare but poorly with Col."

"Was it ever otherwise," said Duncan, laughing. "For that you must blame nature and not myself, and I do but the best I can."

He went up to the house with but a dim conception of her presence or of her mind. He had seen her white and cold and disarranged, her thoughts all flying, and that sufficiency that is the finest gift of woman altogether wanting. It was indeed to meet one that was still a stranger to him he left Father Ludovick her brother.

No sign of life was round the priest's house except the smoke of its chimneys; but when he came close he heard a woman singing in a voice so full of thinking and of soothing that he could have listened for ever. For a while he stood on the sole-sod of the porch with his hands on the jambs, indulging himself, and made out the air of a Gaelic lullaby. It had the fondness of maternity, conveyed that wonderful confidence that sets asleep bairns startled at the terror of the world; it made him young, it made him happy. Reluctant he rapped at the open door. The singer was too fully possessed by her song and did not hear, nor hear indeed when he rapped again, so he stepped within the porch, intending to try the inner door.

But the inner door, too, was open, and showed him a curious spectacle. Anna sat with the side of her face to him, knitting, and while she made the needles flash she rocked a wicker cradle with her foot and sang. "O Bride!" she sang –

> "O Bride, Brideag, come with the wand
> To this wintry land;
> And breathe with the breath of the Spring so bland,
> Bride, Bride, the little Bride!"

She was dressed like one that had been at an assembly, in a deep-tucked gown of white, short-waisted in a recent fashion, a green sash round it, a fillet of green staying the tumult of her hair, where nestled a spray of the primrose that blooms on the isles when the rest of the world is barren. He stood astounded at her occupation, at her beauty, and felt some sudden flush of soul that never before had been in his experience. She seemed the very spirit of all he thought of when he thought upon young and beautiful maternity – something lush and happy like the summer fields. A madness touched him for a second that she was his own, and he, the tired householder, come home.

"Duncan!" she cried with the freedom that the Hebrid Isles are happy in, when she turned and saw him. "Duncan!" said she, her face on fire with pleasure or surprise, and came with outstretched hands – an action so spontaneous and so much in harmony with his thoughts that he was almost swept away on his delusion.

"You have come at last," said she, "and of course with your old luck you must be finding me at a disadvantage."

"I declare, Miss Anna," said Duncan, "that I could not find you better engaged. The baby and you must pardon me for spoiling the song."

"The baby!" cried Anna, and seeing he was in earnest, laughed outright. "Bonny on the baby! come and see our Brideag!" She tilted over the wicker cradle and let him see it held only a sheaf of corn, ornamented with flowers, and shells, and ribbons. "Have you been so long in France," she asked, still laughing at his confusion on this discovery, "that you have forgotten the little Bride? Ludovick must be always laughing at my playacting, but even himself he is fond of the old diversions and ceremonies, and lets me lead the girls in procession on Brigid's eve. We made her yesterday – look, Corodale! is she not the darling now? and so good-humoured to be of my quarrelsome sex. Twelve of us in white took her round the townships, and the others took her here this morning and bedded her, with all the luck that is with her, in the house of Father Ludovick. Aren't we droll? Now, if you laugh at us –"

She searched him for a sign of contempt, but this was the last humour he could have found amusement in.

"Miss Anna," said he, "I am not laughing."

"Well, you can be if you like, then," she said. "I give you liberty – though, if you had laughed without my permission, I would have been much offended. Of course a man must think me daft to be rocking the little Brideag; it was so childish. Just like – just like the little girl you came to on Trialabreck island? I quite forgot, and at my knitting, my feet went to the rocker without thinking, and the song of 'Crodh Chailin' came to my lips without any idea of what I sang."

"Indeed, and where better could the song be than there?" asked Duncan, twinkling with his eyes on her lips till she bit the under one as if it had been stung.

"O my young man, my good young man, you must be kept in your place like the rest of your family!" thought Anna.

"Gallantry seems to run in the blood of the Corodale folk," she told him. "I can only say 'Thank you.' And now that you have found me at my doll – that some of us are fond of in our hearts till we are well matured, let me tell you – and have again an advantage over me, I must ask for your excuse for paying no attention to our invitations that we sent to you by Mr Col."

"Father Ludovick warned me of a cold reception," said Duncan cheerfully. "What excuse can I make but that far is the cry to Corodale, as the saying goes in Lorn and that Col is so busy with a hundred notable ventures abroad, it takes me all my time to look after the trivial ones at home."

"Your brother was most considerate, in spite of all his engagements. He did much to cheer Ludovick in my absence. And let me tell you, Mr Duncan, I'm fair in love with him – though, to be sure, it's a thing I would not care to have mentioned to himself, lest it should add to the conceit of him, that is not very small already."

Duncan felt for a second a new and curious pang. The thing was said in sport, he knew; but yet, could anything have been more natural?

"It's the first good luck he has had, then, in the twelvemonth he and I have worked together," said he, not too seriously. "And who better deserves it? As brave as a lion –"

"Oh! you are very complacent and agreeable. There are as brave –" said Anna, contrairy, looking at him, and remembering the night on Trialabreck.

"As handsome as a prince –"

"And who knows it better than himself? But that is a matter of taste."

"As honest as the day!"

"H'm! who is denying it? Mr Duncan, it looks to me as if you had plenty of practice at pleading for a brother who is very well able to look after himself, I assure you. And now that I think of it, I declare I could never love a man quite so perfect as this you are describing to me. I take back my word – as a woman is quite at liberty, surely, to do when the mood comes to her – and I make it 'like' instead of love."

"*L'amitié c'est l'amour sans ailes*," said Duncan, and Anna laughed.

"Without wings, indeed; and that minds me, Mr Duncan, that I am a goose to be so frivolous. It comes of this little Brideag," and, reddening again at the sight of the cradle and its occupant, that she had been discovered so ludicrously playing with, she caught it up and thrust it into an inner room.

"There!" said she – "the last of my dolls! And because you must laugh at me, I'll be the very sedate woman all the rest of the day."

CHAPTER XIV

Tir-Nan-Oig

DUNCAN felt that he talked as a man dances when it is a happy night with him, every fibre of the flesh of him in a compact, and soul as well as body part of the dancing tune. When Ludovick joined them – the tall man, with eyes half-shut and twitching at the under-lids as the eyes of mariners do that constantly look on sun-struck seas – he found the sinner forgiven and the pair on a footing of drollery. It had been so between her and Col, but even Ludovick could feel that here was something of a difference, – that in Anna, this time, was no reserve. For a little, a cloud came over him – some dim breath of doubting, of regret, for what, he knew not, as he looked at them. For the first time in all his knowledge Anna was gone from his world, and farther off, he felt, than when the waves of the Minch and the dreary mainland miles and the darkness sundered them. And Duncan – so elate, so sure – what had come to this recluse from Corodale who in his brother's report was for usual so engrossed in the material affairs of the world, on herds, and crops, and correspondence? If love was an ailment that seized on one at sight as the solan on the saithe-fish, and not a thing that grew about the heart in years as the lichen creeps on rock, as his affections had grown about Anna, he would have thought that this stranger had in an hour, by some magic, got into such a surety of comprehension and possession as he himself enjoyed.

At noon the boats set out for the fishing-banks upon a sea blue beyond comparison. It would gladden the most indifferent eye, as sunsets do, that in their grandeur have a message and a hope that man at the end of all may not be for the maggot, that he may be cheerful, that he should be brave. Duncan felt it – saw it – heard it – in the rolling deeps; he knew to-day in the very bones of him that the world was magnificent and all well, he felt every dreary hour in Corodale, every doubt that came from his strained position there, uplifted on the cold clean washing waves that rose in the bay and struck the steadfast rock. And Anna walked beside him – he hoped she shared in these delightful influences.

Father Ludovick busied himself amongst his children, coming from his abstractions to haul laughingly on tack and halyard, with "There you are, Master Ludovick! is it not the splendid fisherman was spoiled in you when they made you into a clerk?" from bantering fishermen, stout junks so thickly clad in home-spun wool that when they laughed it was like trees in hurricanes. They asked him what of the weather, though there might be none of them that had not skill elsewhere than in the presence of this magician Lord of the Isles to know without an error what the sky told, the shoulder of Benmore, and the birds; he glanced neither to the right nor to the left, up nor down, but promised at once a night of calm and three tides more of it.

Children gathered round Anna, brown like the winter brackens or the young leaves of the early oak, laughing in a chorus for no reason that was visible, the luckiest that were nearest burying their heads in her gown, convulsed with happiness; and she laughed too, in a ripple of hilly brooks on mossy green stones, with the spirit of Spring in tiny woods, – not the great and brooding where dwell reflection and remorse – not loudly at all, as if the joy were something out of herself, but as if the secret of content was in her bosom. The women, come to see their men off, laughed too, bewitched, infected by herself – the darling! Oh, surely to-day there was no care in little Uist of the sheldrakes; surely this was Tir-nan-oig – the land of the eternal young. No more nights of storm for Uist; no more rain nor cold, mist nor hunger, sorrow nor farewell. "Come back, come back, little scamps, little heroes, and do not vex the lady!" cried the mothers, but did not mean it in the least, loving to see their children there, knowing there was but one joy between them all – the joy of the Spring – that Brigid's white wand had touched them all, the innocents! and opened their inward eyes to the gardens of Tir-nan-oig.

The sun made the sands pure gold, dazzling beside the blue of the sea; the far-off islands hung angelic in the heavens. From the houses along the bay, once mean and dark, now by the magic of Bride made sweet and simple and clean as garden hives, the smoke of peats came blowing to the shore, not only the scents of buried grass and shrub and of all the ancient flowery summers, but the incense of domestic gods – *glastaig* and brownie and dwarf – that had sat for generations round the hearths.

"Come away, come away, little rogues, and let the lady be," said the mothers – hypocrites! "No, no," she cried, and put her arms about as many as she could, bent over them – Bride herself, pure white, with the primrose in her bosom – and in a sweet fury shared her lips among them as they fought for her favours. Some strands of her hair were drawn from her temples, and beat about their mouths as they ravished her caresses: they knew a perfume that they had never perceived before, that pleased them wonderfully – the breath of birchen leaves from mainland woods, that brides in the Outer Isles make use of for the bathing of their hair in Spring.

"Come with us for luck," cried a lad on the last skiff, leaning, all aslope, his weight on the oar he thrust with from the beach, his face like that of the olden Lochlanners who handsomely scourged the isles when heroes moved about the world in galleys, his figure tense and strong.

"Oh well would I like it, Magnus," cried Anna, her face bright at the notion; "but I have the pots and pans."

"Well, lady," cried the fellow, so handsome and bold, "say three times 'Luck to you,' and we'll come back in the morning up to the gunnel."

"Good luck! good luck! good luck!" cried Anna, and kissed her hand.

"O Christ!" said the fellow under his breath to the others of his company, and in a true devotion, "look at yon, and I so poor!"

Duncan felt an aimless yearning: the world of itself was perfect, but something within himself was incomplete.

"We might take a little boat and follow them out of the bay," said he.

"And I never thought of it!" said Anna. "Ludovick, will you come out to the point on the little *Ron?*" she cried. But Ludovick had affairs in chapel, and asked to be excused, so the little boat went out with Duncan and Anna alone at its stern, blown under a fanning breeze that was like a sigh, in the wake of the skiffs departing with their brown sails softly flapping and their sweeps splashing the blue. He held the sheet, she sat beside him, close against his arm, for the *Ron* was heavenly narrow. The odour of the birch-leaves was between them: he swooned in some wood of France, or in some mainland garden as the boat nodded on the sea, scarce moving through it. If this was not Tir-nan-oig, if this was not the land of eternal youth and honeymoon, Tir-nan-oig was there before them – Barra with the beads of pearly islets round it, Orosay and Fiaray and Fuday. A bird's song suddenly rose from the bay behind them – the confession of the linnet, bird of Bride, sounding passionate after the shrill of the sandpiper, the sea-swallow's cry. Over their shoulders the isle they left was flooded with the sun, and every hill and hollow was majestic. The skiffs stretched out before them, and suddenly the fishermen sang. They put their bodies to the oars and their spirits into an *iorram* of the ancient unperplexed old days, singing in unison as men do that ride on horses upon serious affairs, or as did the Lochlan kings. It rose, the boat-song, as if the sea itself thought it and must tell its great desire; and hearing it, Anna murmured a counter so sweet and mellow that it made the *Ron* as it were the sole possessor of the song.

Duncan looked at the swell of her throat and the surge of her breasts where the primrose lay, and felt again that yearning aimless and serene. A thousand times had come to him in happy hours a brief conviction that between him and bliss's very climax something less tangible than a web of gossamer lay; but how to break through these bounds, that were on trial more durable than ramparts of stone! Now the sense of it was in every artery; his heart, he felt, was tangled in her hair, though he never had the thought in words but in a shiver of the being. He saw that she was what he once had thought the world was – in its morning, before the curst sophistications. The boat-song floated over the sea, the linnet piped on land, the waters were blue to very ecstasy – the very heaven itself – and in the heavens they floated free from the influence of the clod.

She had been looking before her into the west, out to the far horizon, as if her thoughts were there, content in all her being, her eyes half closed on the dazzle of the waves, her lips scarcely parted as she sang her counter to the seamen's air.

"What are you thinking of?" he asked her.

"I did not think at all, I was so happy," said she, with her eyes still on the sea-edge. "But now that you have made me think, I think – I hope – oh, I hope I shall never be forlorn," and suddenly she glanced about her – at the pearly isles of Barra Sound, at the land behind them basking in the sun. A tear came to her eyes, the wellings of that strange chagrin that comes on all the sensitive who know that beauty is so brief.

"Forlorn!" said Duncan, passionate. "Whoever can be moved by days and scenes like these can never be for long forlorn;" and then of a sudden there came to him, as he saw the curve of her neck, the throb of her bosom, the conviction that the world without her would indeed be desolate. Now he knew the gossamer web that lay between him and the complete surrender of the soaring lark, the unalterable contentment of stars for ever inseparable, – it was that they were apart. And yet – in that perfume of the birch-woods, hearing the distant song of those men labouring at the oars, there was another thought and baffling, that she was sweeter not in his possession. He loved her – and yet he knew that she was better wild and free.

Anna turned to him and saw his eyes, so strange, and guessed why she was happy. Her own she cast down for a moment in confusion, wondering and mute; then, "I think we must go back," said she.

"We can never go back," said Duncan, putting about the boat and heading for land; "we have gone too far from the old dull land for that. Tir-nan-oig! Tir-nan-oig! who comes back from Tir-nan-oig?"

She did not ask him what he meant, but sat now silent, the faintest flush on her countenance. Over Uist the people were dispersed; Stella Maris stood grey-white on its pinnacle above the land, constant in this world of changing fancies, exceedingly earnest, certain, and austere. To its south they saw Ludovick rising on the brae, his tall figure bent against the furrows of a little field beyond his dwelling. When he reached the summit he stood dark against the sky. He stopped a moment there, and turned and looked across the islands and over the sea, the genius of the place, a lonely figure.

CHAPTER XV

A Messenger

THE old men who sat at the gable-end, lazy-content to the marrow, nudged each other when a man passed at a distance who had not a fortune of sons at work for him, and though elderly was not so very old, yet was not with his neighbours that went a-fishing. Michaelmas Day had brought Dark John to the boundary-walls of valour, as they said in Uist, though he was the last himself who would have owned to it. From that on, he had, more than ever he had before, a horror of the deep, so that the thickest plank in his boat seemed under his feet like paper, and a heel of a half-inch in a puff of wind made him gasp like one that slid into perdition. Ailments and omens he made much of after that – no pretext too scurvy to keep him from the hazards of the open Sounds; and he caught the fish he lived on mainly in fresh waters or in the sheltered bays of the east in calm weather, where he went spearing flounders in the pools after the women already had had their pick of them and had gone home. He fancied he kept his secret cunningly, but there was neither man nor wife in Uist who did not understand.

To-day he waited till the long-line men were gone, and now came down with a lobster-creel to his skiff, that had, like himself, been salved from a grave in the sands of Kintra. Father Ludovick, a little way off, standing on the hill-top, sweeping the world with his glances, feeling benign with all his happy flock, gave him a wave of the hand as one of God's own creatures, and pitied him in spite of a repugnance. John touched his cap to the priest, uneasy, for this was a person who knew all things, even before they came to the confessional. He shuffled on his way more slowly, for some women stood on the quay-head exchanging scandal in the shelter of their new spring shawls, and seemingly in the key for some diversion now that the men were gone. He would have fled from an encounter but for the knowledge that the old folk at the chapel-wall were watching, and that the women themselves were fit for any escapade that might discomfit him.

"Here comes the *gioltair* – here comes the poltroon," said one of them, half in pity, half in contempt, and all of them turned about with interest, and unfriendly, for might their own husbands not some day come to this – their husbands and their sons, that dared the wildest weather, and were out at night in the welter of the Minch when this wretch snored sluggardly and snug at home?

"There you go, John!" cried the boldest of them – the virgin who carded wool on Michaelmas night. "You are late, just man; put a pace on you, and if you do not catch the head of the fish, you will maybe get the tail."

"Good day to you, dames," said John, most blandly. "*Oh righ!* and isn't this the weather?" and cast a flattering glance at the sunny hollows of the island, at the gold sand and the cordial sea.

"You could not have it calmer if you were the witch of Mull herself, and had, just man, the making of it," said the spinster, her bosom swelling with satisfaction that she should be blessed with such an opportunity. She had had a lover once: he had been drowned.

"I am going out to the Stallion rock just for a little pot of lobsters," said he, throwing his creel into the boat with much pretence at manly bustling.

"A fierce, fierce fish the lobster, John," said the spinster; "you must watch, courageous man, that you are not bitten," and the other women laughed.

"Daughters of she-dogs!" said John to himself and scratched his neck, then thrust some shreds of dulse seaweed in his mouth from a store he always kept in his waistcoat pocket. He was ever one who feared and hated the creatures that eagerly hunt for man and live in petticoats: this gathering of the pack gave him a sort of terror, but he put the best face he could on it. "Ladies," said he, "I will not be detaining you," and made to pass, but not this way was Bell Vore the virgin to lose her opportunity.

"There would be more money at the fish than at the lobsters," said she, hugging her blubbery self in her plaid with the greatest satisfaction. "You should be with the men, Dark John."

"My end! my hope! my loss and my losing! there good dame, would I be for certain but for the fact that I drew but a notable barren bit of bank for my portion, and it was not worth the going to," said Dark John, who never swithered at a lie.

"Och! the devil, now wasn't that unlucky?" said the spinster. "It would be a bit too far out now, I'll wager?"

"And I would never have put an oar to it this day of days in any case, for the first I clapped eyes on in the morning when I set my foot over the sole-sod of the door was a red-haired woman. Red-haired women are good for love (as they say) but poor for fortune, pleasant dame, and are the worst of omens for men that are starting on the day's exploits. I did not venture forth till I thought the road was clear, and here, on my word! was a Dalvoolin red-haired woman sitting with a bundle of her husband's sails on the road before me. I would as soon have met the Worst One himself and he in his red wroth."

"Oh John, John!" cried the woman, "but you are sore on us poor creatures. Is there not, now, between yourself and me and the creel you are carrying, one woman among all the kindly girls of Uist you could be thinking of in an evening or counting lucky to meet at the start of a day's fishing?"

"I would be gaily telling you that, Bell Vore, my darling," said he, with a crafty smirk that was laughable, "if there was but yourself, and these other ladies were not listening." The other women laughed at this and made off, leaving the pair of them, and at that Dark John, though he sometimes feared this woman loved him, got a little of his courage. He chewed his dulse with relish, and felt that now he was on equal terms with her.

"There's but the one woman in all Isle Uist," said he, "I would consider lucky for me to meet of a morning and I on my way to the banks."

"Who might she be, honest man?" asked the spinster, who had never abandoned hope.

"Who but Herself? Many a time I'll be sending a boy out of the house before me in the morning to see if Miss Anna is on the road, and if she is, I run out and past her, and I'm the stout fellow then for the fishing."

"Then you have not been seeing her much since Michaelmas?" said the spinster sourly, "for you and the banks since then have been strangers. And Herself is in demand to-day, for look! – she is out at the fishing on her own account, and I'll swear she has made her shot, and found a spot and haled him," and she pointed to the *Ron* drifting in the lee of little Orosay.

"*Mo chreach!* now, do you tell me?" cried Dark John sharply. "Who is with her?"

"The stuck priest from Corodale," said Bell Vore.

He stared at the boat, dumfoundered, forgetting at once the virgin and her mockery, swearing mutteringly to himself in the words that Gaelic borrows from the English, then, fired as it seemed by some sudden decision, threw his creel into the boat, turned his back on the woman with a sentence of excuse, and hurried over the quay cobbles to the shore. He rose on the brae, determined; skirted the vacant gable of Our Lady Star, following the road north with long sliding steps that never took his shoe-soles from the gravel, his mind turbulent and his eyes with no engagement, so that he walked without seeing anything for an hour, and turned Dalveen and its broken walls to come face to face with Col.

"Here's a man in a hurry," cried Col. "The like of this I have not seen in leisurely Uist since the Norway bark was wrecked on Fioray, and every one wanted timber for building of byres."

"I'm in better luck this time to find you; and, my grief! that it was not so before, when I went seeking you for a funeral," said Dark John, wincing, a hand to his side, for he had come like the very wind.

"Your news first and then your grumbling," said Col.

"It's just this, that there's a fellow yonder in Boisdale I need not mention by name, and he in a place where I would much prefer his half-brother."

Col's face grew furious. "You damned fool!" said he. "What is this to me that you should break your legs to tell me? I hope you let every gull in Boisdale know you were coming here to carry me such piper's news."

Dark John shrank before the vexation of his master, as this man was, who never paid him wages, yet, because of one gallant impulse, could command him to the pit's mouth. "Allow me for that, Corodale!" said he. "Dumb's the limpet, but more dumb the rock it hangs on, and the rock a gossip compared with me, myself – Dark

John, and your humble servant. I thought, on my word! the thing might interest you; but it seems I have worked my legs for nothing. Well! well! I will know better another time. If the thing was of importance, I would have remarked that the one I mean – and no names mentioned – sits in the *Ron* with his arm about a fortune and speculation is already among the clattering jades that watch them from the shore."

This time he struck the mark, for Corodale was plainly staggered. The messenger saw his trip was not in vain.

"Just so!" said Col, and plunged in a meditation. The tidings did not sink into him all at once, but found his ears as words unpleasant. Then grew within him a sense of wrong and deprivation that poisoned every channel of his body. He was a man with vision, so that he could image a spectacle more actual than he could see with eyes: he saw, in that space of time he stood on the road facing this wretch of his own saving, Duncan and the girl together on the little boat; heard the voice of Anna with its revelation of a nature great and kind, felt the warmth of contact, and realised the fascination she must have for his brother after twelve months' hermitage in Corodale. Every quality that before had seemed admirable in Duncan now appeared a blight.

"Just that!" he said again, his mind far off, as Dark John saw. And Dark John knew. He was satisfied that he had accomplished what he had hurried from Boisdale to do, however much Corodale might attempt to conceal it.

"It's a matter of no importance," at last said Col; "but it's scarcely to his credit; and though I was bound for Boisdale myself, I'll put off my business till I can go there with a better countenance. What were the women you talk of saying to it?"

"It was not what they said but what they showed in the shrug of their shoulders, and that's the way of women for you always," said Dark John. "But one of them made so bold as to say what I myself took the liberty of thinking, and wished it had been yourself instead of Duncan."

"By the Book! and I'll have none of my affairs cackled over by Boisdale hens!" cried Col, furious to have his worst fears so confirmed. "And who put this pair together but yourself, with your fool's notion of sending my brother to her uncle's funeral! Not that it matters much to me."

John chewed dulse and rubbed his hands together till they seemed to creak. "It was the last thing I would be thinking of, Master Col – the very last," said he. "For yourself I went, as you know, and for no other, and for a reason you were clever enough to guess, but you were not there when I reached Corodale, and your brother got the start of you, though I did my best, and put him wrong by a tide."

"He's a tide ahead of me still," said Col, but that was to himself. To the messenger he presented, with an inward struggle, a countenance untroubled, and protested again that it mattered little.

"It matters twenty thousand pounds – the whole of the stuff from Arkaig," said the other, with a face uplifted. "On my soul, and on the life of me, oh king! there's twenty thousand tarnishing somewhere within halloo of us. By the Book! I have but to stamp my heel, and you will hear the money jingling. Put your ear to it, Corodale, Corodale!" He stamped violently on the road where he stood. Isle Uist, in the calm and clarity of the air, appeared to shudder, and Col, so mastered was he by five months' dreaming of the stuff talked about, plainly heard the tinkle of gold, enormous stores of it, blind and caverned in the moss of Uist, crying to come out and be merry again among men. He looked down at Dark John's hand, and saw that the old rogue had done the trick with twopence in his palm.

"The Arkaig treasure," he said with an effort – "an old wife's tale! It was known to Ossian and the Finne. I could never credit that it had existence except in lies told on winter nights round *ceilidh* fires."

"I have told you before that I have seen it," said John. "I was at the freight of it from Arisaig in my grandfather's generation."

"Were you, faith! I clean forgot," said Col. "How did the history go, just man?"

"We carried fulmar-oil from Mingulay to Arisaig in the lugger of old Colin-Calum-Angus, and there was with us Dermosary, on a purpose we could make no guess at till he had the yellow on board. Oh, the devil! 'twas the sight that was there when a box burst! I have not seen a woman's gathering of cockles more plenteous on the beach than yon was. A man might count himself rich all the rest of his life if he lived to a hundred, if he got but the one look of it."

"The look was all you got of it, anyway," said Col, who had heard the tale over and over again, and ever with a growing fascination.

"As much as I could make any use of," said Dark John, quite cheerfully. "But for a fellow of enterprise, now – for a true gentleman of parts with the art of spending – *oh righ!* hark! –"

He stamped his foot on the ground and jingled his pence again, with the most amazing look of cunning and regard for Col of Corodale.

Col knew it was but twopence in a dirty palm, but heard the clang of fortune in that coppery pretence – heard the creak of halyards throwing out the sails in his own great fleet of sloops, the clatter of his own horses and cattle trotting to Lowland markets, heard bells in towns, and felt the glory of command. He put out his hand and caught the old man by the shoulder, grasping cruelly.

"You rotten – you rotten wizard!" he cried, half in anger at this deception, half in the agony of desire; "what's this, and what's the use of talking? We cannot be digging up the whole of the Isle of Uist."

Dark John looked at him and turned dulse in his cheek, satisfied.

"Your brother Duncan," said he, "is like to find what he wants without much digging," and turned his gaze away from a shrewd rude delicacy.

"Then let him," said Col; "it's the luck of the elder born," and felt exceeding bitter with his fate.

John chinked his paltry twopence again, and drew closer to speak low, as if some other listened. "I know a stuff," he said, "foxglove, butter-burr, nine stems of fern, three bones from a man's grave and him ancient, all cindered, and thrown against the north wind at her –"

Corodale snapped his fingers with contempt.

"Charms! If charms availed, then my father himself would have found the naked gold, for many a time he tried them. I have something surer than charms."

He put his arm through John's, and in a red heat of invention filled his ear. The old man listened, now and then nodding his head and trembling with excitement.

"I'm the man who can do it," said he, when he had heard all; "no one better. I know! I know! love will close a thousand eyes and waken ten thousand jealousies."

Col went back to Corodale, and Dark John went home.

CHAPTER XVI

A Confession

INDEED Bride's wand had given the magic touch to Anna. In days succeeding that one – golden, and for ever to be remembered – when she floated in a fairy galley to the verge of Tir-nan-oig, she went about fevered with her happiness, so that her presence brought the sourest an infection, and Ludovick, ever the child of fancies, extravagant to madness in a brother, surely, sometimes thought he saw her in an aura, such as one may see in pictures of the saints. From morning till evening she sang, if not aloud, in throaty murmurings as the pigeon coos in spring. Even Ludovick, who had never known her otherwise than sweet – the very essence of that womanhood 'twas his willing but cruel fate to lose in a great renunciation – sometimes waked to wonder what was this so novel in her. Birds, that she had liked always, now became her passion; much she loved to press her lips in the heart of the flowers that scantily grew in the shelter of Stella Maris; for her brother she showed an affection almost devouring. He pondered on it long, this change in her, and came to the conclusion that she suffered from some fervour of the religious spirit, and at that he was alarmed to find himself regretful, thinking of the nunnery. Once he tried to discover her mind upon the matter. It was a day on which she had been more than ordinarily radiant. She had said something of his sermon, expressing her agreement with its great convictions.

"Anna," he said hastily, "I hope I have not of late been too eloquent. I would carry conviction to these dear souls, and give them, if I could, the supremest joy that is in fellowship with Christ and the saints, for theirs is a destiny poor when that is wanting. But you, my dear Anna – you – you –" He hesitated, afraid, as it were, of his own words. "You are as good as I would care to have you. I am not going to have you any different, do you hear? No different. You always reminded me of our mother – peace with her! Where she was, there was Paradise, if her acts were to be judged from the sentiments that inspired them. It is enough of religion for you to be like her. I wish – I wish sometimes – perhaps I am a poor priest and unworthy, – I wish you were less often of an evening on your knees in the chapel there alone."

She reddened, distressed to think how far had been her thoughts from spiritual things often when she went to these orisons.

"A reasonable practice of it," he added, "is enough for such as have a shrine in their hearts, and make an altar of the table they spread daily with love and kindness for others."

Anna felt she must either laugh or cry. The guilty sense of deception knocked in her breast. She had for weeks been loading her brother with attentions, lest he might suspect this sweet unrest in her; and to show she had too well succeeded, here he was crediting her with the fervour only of the devotee!

She looked across the table at him, and her sense of humour got its way. She laughed, much to his disconcerting. "O Ludovick!" she cried, "upon my word I am ashamed of you! That I should hear such heretical doctrine from the priest of Boisdale! Myself too good, indeed! – *oh righ!* and I your sister, and I have never learned a tune on the harp. Father" – she went on, chanting in an intonation – "I will confess. Let me think – yesterday I lost my temper with poor Gaisgeach and called him *son of the devil*, only it was in the Gaelic of course, because he slipped his bridle in the field and would not let me catch him. Then I had cream in the milk you had to this morning's porridge, though I denied it when you asked me, for why should all the cream go every day to that lazy widow that had a cow of her own and lost it through her own carelessness? And I put three eggs of our own to old Mary's score when she came with them yesterday, so that you might think her more generous than she is by nature, poor body! And that is not all – oh, I could take a week to tell what sins I commit in an afternoon – I was nearly crying with envy when I read to you from Lily's letter yesterday her account of her new gown. And – let me see – here is a dreadful sin before your very nose, – I have eaten the last of the scones, and I meant it for you."

"*Ego absolvo te!*" said Father Ludovick, stretching across their little breakfast-table to put a hand on her head. "Sin no more, child, in the matter of the cream; I am not old enough yet for fattening. And when did this new vanity for gowns take hold of you? I never knew a woman who had less of it before."

A shrewder eye would have seen something suspicious in the start she gave at this; but Ludovick, deeply learned in many things less important, did not know the world and was utterly deceived when she ran round the table with a flutter and put her hands on his shoulders, with "Oh! I could shake a brother so stupid to say such things. No vanity for gowns indeed! – that would be a pretty failing in one that desires above all to be in most things like the rest of her sex. I will never be ashamed of my fancy for fine clothes, and I cannot be so very like our mother after all, Ludovick, if you did not long ago discover that, for, as I remember the dear, she never looked so much like an angel as when she was trying on a new gown, and I'm ready to hate you, just, for not knowing that I have had two since Christmas, just to please the eye of a man who might as well have been blind for all he seems to have seen of them."

"I did not know, upon my word I did not know!" cried Ludovick, laughing, leaning back to seize her by the hands, and looking up into her face. "Now, how was I to know that you considered the priest in your toilet?"

"Whom else should I consider, poor man? Whom else is there in Uist with eyes for these things?"

"I don't know. There's Corodale, now: I'm sure he has a taste in such matters," said he in all innocence, whereupon she screamed that he hurt her hands, released them suddenly, and proceeded noisily to clear the table.

He sat watching her through eyes half-shut, seeing her head dark against the window. Beyond was the Atlantic, its waves white-crested, and a curve of it lapping a horn of the bay, where women and men were gathering wrack, up to their waists in the brine, forking the weed in heaps and bearing it off in creels. His thought went out of the room and wandered there; his mind busied itself upon these industries of the isles, and he was startled when he heard Anna sigh.

"Why, Anna, what is wrong?" he asked her, rising hurriedly to his feet, seeing now for the first time perturbation in her manner.

"Nothing at all," she answered, then gave way and melted in tears. "O Ludovick! I wish – I wish we had our mother!" she cried with a sob that could not be suppressed.

He went to her and put his hand upon her head, caressing her hair. "Yes, yes," he said; "I know, I know. I have often wished she had been spared, for you must be lonely. This place is solitary for you. There is no one but myself – so much from home in mind if so little in body – so ill-equipped to understand. Are you unhappy, Anna?"

She threw her arms about his shoulders, her head in his breast, broken for the first time since she was a child and came to her mother's lap with childish griefs. "O Ludovick! I am unhappy – no, no, I am very happy; and – and my heart will break," she sobbed, and then, to his astonishment, he saw her smiling through her tears. He set her down in a chair.

"On my soul!" said he in Gaelic, quite perplexed, "you act like a girl in love by all I ever read of it."

She dashed the tears from her eyes, rose, red with shame, and storm in her bosom, proceeding again to her duties, while he stood by bewildered at such hysterics in their calm dwelling. "Yes; just like a girl in love," he repeated, walking bewildered up and down the room.

"You must always be at your nonsense, Ludovick," she said. "As if – as if it were a thing you knew anything about."

"I was no MacNeil if I did not know the effects of it."

"And what are they?" she asked, not for information really, but that she might gain time to recover herself.

He turned and looked out at the window to see the ocean – the masterful, the unalterable, the bitter, the terrible – roll from heaven's edge into Boisdale Bay, where men and women toiled and children plashed in the spray his dear parishioners.

"Love," said he; "it is a thing so honey-sweet it must be sometimes salted with our tears; it is the age of true gold returning. God! it is His very name; there is not a pleasure under heaven that is finer than the pain of it. It is seeing the world at its best – hearing for the first time the music of the stars, and comprehending the blackbird's song. The stars and the birds are my brothers then, and the littlest flower beside the way has sudden life. A day given up to it is recompense for a lifetime of griefs; it makes the beggar equal with the king. Uist of the sheldrakes, Uist of the storms – she may be bare, she may be bleak, but she becomes a garden when love lifts up the curtain of the eyes."

Anna was silent for a little. He still looked out at the window, his face elated.

"How do you know?" she asked.

"Because I have it here," he answered quickly, with his hand on his heart. "I am so full of the very potion of it I must walk through Uist and the world with caution, for fear I jolt some over the brimming edge. How do I know? By God! it is my happy torment, for it makes me dread that it may be heaven itself, and that I, Father Ludovick, the Boisdale priest, am passing the open gate."

She came to stand by his side at the window and put her arm through his, and with him look out into the bay.

"What do *you* think it is?" he asked her.

"It is a distraction," she said quickly, lest she should lose the courage to express what welled in her. "It is lying awake at night for fear that one should sleep and find that the waking had been dream and the sleep was the reality. It is more scent on the heather, more blue in the sea, longer days of fine weather. Before it, you think the happy times were the times of childhood, when all the folk you know were young and careless like yourself; when love comes then you know that the young days had something wanting because they had no fear. Fear – that is what gives love its piercing."

He wondered, but he did not look down, for he felt her trembling. He had spoken from his brain, she from her bosom: his was the abstract passion of the priest, whose love compassed the living universe, and had no central object; hers was the voice of a closer experience. How blind he had been not to know it sooner!

"You rogue!" he said softly in a little, "and I was blaming you for piety. Is – is it the welcomest wind that blows from the north-east?"

"It is," said Anna.

"From Corodale?"

"From Corodale."

"Col?"

She shook herself free in vexation. "O Ludovick!" she cried, on earth again, "how in all the world could you think so?"

"Well, he has known you longest."

"But Dun – but his brother has known me all my life; he showed me that in an afternoon."

Father Ludovick looked at her perplexed. "It is strange," said he. "With Col you were all gaiety, with Duncan you have been so silent and cold, I sometimes feared he might consider himself unwelcome."

Anna laughed. "That would have made any other than yourself suspicious, Ludovick," she said. "And I think – I think – though I am sorry – we shall after this see less of Col. He has been here but twice since his brother came; but he was not so blind as my loving brother, and he saw, I feel sure, what wind blew welcomest to Boisdale presbytery."

Her brother took her hands in his and smiled on her. "I am pleased with your preference," he said. "I am as happy as yourself, for I have long been grieving that I was the means of taking him from the Church, and now I rejoice that I can make amends and give him to love and my little sister."

Anna put her arms about her brother's neck, drew down his head and kissed him, all rosy with her shyness and her joy, then ran from his presence.

CHAPTER XVII

Lovers' Moons

HE might have been blind, this brother going about for ever in his raptures; but Uist, that always liked a lover, was watching with open eyes. Duncan never came trudging over the miles of gall and grass and sand that lay between Corodale and the rock of Our Lady, but every township on the way knew of it. Anna never went shyly walking along the dunes of the machar but some sea-bird rose crying before her, so that men and women busy with the wrack turned to look and smile and speculate. Brave for many things, but bad for courting, Uist, so flat and frank, hiding nothing on its surface any more than the sea does. You might walk for a day on that peering open isle and never come upon a nook where you might kiss the willingest so long as it was daylight. That, perhaps, was the reason for Ludovick's blindness. When he saw his sister and Duncan together it was always at a distance most discreet, – an arm's length from each other. He was not close enough to see their eyes or hear their words, and that made all the difference.

Of course there were the little dells close on the wider bay, where it was possible to sit upon the sand, and love as the bird loves, unnoticed. But only Anna knew that, and Anna did not tell, for to be seen on any day but a festival coming from these sandy hollows was to Uist women the unfailing sign that weddings were at hand. But there was the little *Ron*, the fairy boat. No hesitation need be about the pair of them sailing out to Tir-nan-oig, for no one knew but themselves that Tir-nan-oig was there, and often Duncan, in that cheerful spring, would take the tiller, and she snug up beside him, glad in his arm, desirable exceedingly, her voice in his bosom. The *Ron*, – the Seal, unfitting name for this good boat, this galley of joy! it should have been the *Eala Bhan* – the wild white swan, proud strong bird of the islands, and beautiful and free, – the *Ron* swam in these days round the coast and into lonely creeks, where only, from the cliffs, the fulmar's cry was to be heard, its wedding-song. Long and far would they glide silent through the waters into shallows where brown burns from the bog-lands stained the froth of tides incoming, and birds twittered among the shelisters and sedges, and little fish plowted in the pools, and the spout-fish thrust from the sand, parched with the sun, but seemingly finding the heat delightful. Silent, the two of them, like as it were a swound they sailed in, and she could hear his heart beating at her ear.

Uist, garnering wrack, up to the arms in the cold salt weeds of the sea, used to stand shading its eyes with a dripping hand and look at them holidaying in this busy world: the old would sigh for something gone, the young would envy.

Or it would be in the nights of moon, the Islands floating in golden fire, Hecla and Benmore abrupt and clear against the east, every rock that jutted from the Sound jet-black. Drifting then at the will of the gentle wind, they saw dim Barra lit with kelp-fires; the scent of bracken and peat came from the shores they skirted; in townships close upon the beach they could hear the bleat of lambs and sometimes the sound of a pipe lamenting, but sweet, oh! sweet beyond words, in its very sorrow. They were out of the world as if they tenanted the remotest star. How often in these evenings must a man have come out before his prayers and stood to yawn, his hands in his pockets, a very clod in the moonlight, in the sound of the small shy waves of the ebbed tide, wondering to see that tiny boat drift across the gold, and guess in a little 'twas Herself and him of Corodale, and feel an influence that if he had been bard would have found itself in song. He would go back, be certain, to his low door, and call his women out to share the spectacle. "*Oh m'eudail!*" would the women say, wooing her with their words, out yonder on the gold, glad to see this. How great a joy in the Hebrides is night and a moonlit sea and a boat coming home across it! Who that remembers, and sees the black sail blown across the highway of the moon but does not, even into age, feel vague ardours, pleasant profound unrests?

Yes; Uist saw. But Uist said nothing, only "God between her and harm," as says the Gael in all lands though sea-divided, and went roundabout roads on its business, so that it might not meet her and her lover and put her to the pain of blushing in his presence. But when the women had her to themselves alone in their cabins then they teased her, – oh, they teased her!

"We are busy at present, oh yes! but busy or not we must be turning to the spinning speedily, for there is many a cupboard and kist and napery-press in Corodale." So would they say slyly, bending over their husband's nets, plying the wooden needle. Or "Hens will have to be at the fattening soon here, good lady, was ever a Boisdale wedding without its hundred hens?" Or warn her – as if in ignorance – of marriage as a pact too easy made and ill to unmake, like the flounder's wry-mouth, that came to him in one tide for his mockery of the cod, and has stayed with him a thousand years.

A month ago Anna would have been their equal with retort, but now her art was gone: she so poorly replied to them, and smiled so helplessly, they tired of their new diversion, and started in earnest to the fattening of their hens.

And then all of a sudden the air of Boisdale was poisoned by a doubt set round in whispers, in half-sentences, and shaking of heads at *ceilidh* fires, before kelp-furnaces, and in waulking-sheds, where women gossip between the choruses as they full the home-spun cloth. How the doubt arose no one could say: it came up like a north-west storm out of the most placid weather, and the overcome of it (as they say) was "MacNeil's Treasure". It was recalled that the Corodales were always keen for money. Old Corodale, the father of Col, had in his time been the only man in Uist unprincipled enough to search for Dermosary's secret, and to spend a whole winter trailing among the rocks, dragging lochans, and digging holes in search of the *ulaidh* which he had died without lighting on, though what he would have done with it had he got it was plain from the folly with which he scattered in harebrained schemes another fortune that had come to him from a relative in the Lowlands. Like father like son, said the doubters, even with a stepson, and Duncan's interest in Herself began to look less pleasant in the eyes of Boisdale. Anna, with a mind less wrapped in her own affairs, might have noticed a sudden change in the manners of the women who at first had bantered her about wedding napery and wedding fowls. They dared not hurt her feelings by expressing what was in their minds, but they were silent in her company when her mood was the most joyous; and instead of feeling pleasure when Corodale was in the neighbourhood, they stayed indoors and scowled.

She went one evening to a house where a woman was bathing her child in sea-water warmed; went down on her knees beside the tub and doted on the rosy body, her throat full of gloating little murmurs, touched the velvet skin, and could have smothered it in kisses. Every sign of ecstasy added to the mother's annoyance with an innocent man in Corodale. They have a bathing hymn in Uist that the woman crooned as she put her palms full of water on the child: –

"A palmful for the age of thee,
  And the neck of thee like milk;
Spoils for thee and love for thee,
  And the green gowns of silk,"

There are many verses in the bathing hymn, the last an allusion to treasure and gifts, and as she was singing it, the mother let a fast glance fall on Anna at her knees laughing back to the laughter of the child. "No, no treasure," she added, stopping her hymn; "better wert thou, my darling, wanting it and going about the world with the face of thee for all thy fortune."

"Faith! a little money would do no harm at all," said Anna, without thinking the remark had any application to herself. "We must be letting the little Morag have a tocher," and dipped her hand in the water, and poured a palmful on the baby's bosom, laughing. "That's for treasure, sweet," said she, "and that for the contented mind," as she added another palmful.

"Your own treasure is your worst fortune," said the woman, and Anna's countenance fell. She had forgotten all about her reputation as an heiress to old Dermosary's secret.

"My fortune, *oh righ!* is just my face and a chest with two large drawers at the bottom of it."

"A pity, indeed, it was no more," said the woman hurriedly drying her child, and Anna went away wondering what lay behind the words. She had not long to wait for an explanation, for she met next day the one man in all that part of Uist who had been at the start of the change of feeling in her neighbourhood. It was Dark John. He met her coming radiant from her prayers upon the rock, for prayer had taken a new meaning for Anna now that she had sampled the delights of Paradise. So much she brimmed over with content, she was in the mood to take even Dark John to her finest graces. When she hailed him with her usual cheerful affectation of the manly one, the equal, he was touched for but a little with remorse, but then remembered Col his master. "The knife – here is the bosom; the fire, here is the hand," he said to himself, recalling his words on St Michael's night.

"Oh, love of the domain and of the universe!" said he, in that lofty manner not uncommon with the simplest people of the Isles; "why, by the king of the moon and of the sun, are you not for marrying, and you so beautiful?"

Anna laughed. "Oh, thou love among men!" said she, in his own manner, "how can I marry, and bachelors so numerous and alluring? I am in the state of Peter-of-the-Foxes, so many partners are to my mind that I am beat to choose one."

"It is unkind, good lady, on all of them," said John, chewing a shred of the dulse that he always carried with him. It brought the briny taste of the deadly deep to his palate.

"Perhaps," said Anna. "Still they seem wonderfully thriving for fellows with broken hearts. 'Tis one result, maybe, of a bad example; you are the last, yourself, just man! to blame anyone for leisure in coming to the altar."

"I had no attractions, on my soul!" said John, a thing so manifest on the face of it that one less considerate would have laughed. "I was notable in my time for the one thing, and that was just the dancing; oh yes, I had the name, in many parts, of a powerful, strong dancer. But otherwise, at his best, there was nothing curious about Dark John to please the ladies. Just a plain man, with a knowledge of boats and fishing, and the rearing of small cattle, and no time for trifling. And consider, *oh righ!* the risks that are in taking to house another man's daughter. She may be beauteous as the bird, as timid as the mullet of the sea, till the spinsters strip her for her bedding (if I dare to mention it), and turn out in the morning a manager. No, faith! I know who's in my house when it's myself alone is there, but I might never be sure of it if I had a wife. A plain man – that's all of it, lady; a plain man, and plenty to do with himself. I had never the art for the ladies."

"O John! let me tell you it is simple enough for any man who has baited hooks for the long lines."

"That is the worst of the baited hook; you never can tell what it will catch – biorach or turbot, or the devilfish himself. I knew a fellow once who married a most plausible person, and he was hardly over the chapel door when he learned that she was plain-soled, so that water would not run under her feet – the most unlucky person a man could take for partner."

"He should have given her high heels for her plain soles, and it might have happened that she had a soft hand for a sick-bed."

"By the luck of things she went and died on him before he had a chance to learn whether her hands were hard or soft."

"Then he might have counted her flat foot not so unlucky after all, if it ridded him of a woman that was unsuitable."

"The poor man got the wrong wife anyway," said Dark John, turning the dulse in his cheek.

"Perhaps it was the other way about, as I've sometimes seen it happen, and it was the poor woman got the wrong man. We are but simple creatures at the best, Dark John."

"So they tell me; so they tell me! I am but a plain man, and have had no experience; a busy man all my days, and without a scrap of learning. Foolish the women, indeed, as they tell me."

"It must have been a married man let you into the secret," said

Anna, still in the key for the old rogue's humour. "A man unmarried would never suspect it, for we are too cunning to let it be found out too soon."

John grew weary of this banter, that brought him no nearer his object. He saw her brother in the distance, and feared he might come up before anything was accomplished, drew in his breath again upon the dulse, and got the flavour of the floor of Barra Sound, remembering all he owed to Col of Corodale. He edged a little nearer Anna, with his eyes like beads in the furrows of his face, every furrow full of cunning.

"They're talking about the hens for a wedding," said he.

"Just so!" said Anna, cold and proud on the moment. "The geese must aye be cackling about their neighbours."

"I'm a plain man, and it is myself, perhaps, who should not be so bold as to mention it," said the man, drawing in his lantern cheeks.

"Indeed I do not differ," said Anna, moving to quit a conversation that pity for a wretch lonely more than any other creature in the Isles had made her carry on longer than was wise. "I would leave the cackling to the geese: 'tis unbecoming in a man to hawk the clash of women in waulking-sheds about the country-side." He was not to be beaten, and kept for a little by her side as she moved towards the presbytery, – her chin in the air, her eyes cold, and her shawl drawn tight to bursting about her shoulders, a sign in that cordial weather that storms were in below it, but no sign at all to Dark John.

"On my back be Conan's curse, lady," said he, "if I did not tell them it was but women's chattering. I would be on my knees to beg your pardon for mentioning it otherwise. 'Neither the one nor the other in Corodale,' said I, 'would soil a hand with her fortune.'"

The blow struck to her inner heart. The pleasant land, the glowing sea, grew dim, and her limbs shook under her. She stopped a moment, commanded her countenance by a miracle of effort, and looked at the wretch who was her torment. He chewed his dulse, felt the flavour of the deeps, and wondered what she thought; but that he could not have discovered from her face if he had had a million eyes.

"Good man, John!" said she; "you may mean well, but you have a fool's tongue." Then left him hurriedly, where he stood chewing dulse and scratching his neck.

Her brother had gone into the house; she passed the gable, without entering, making for the township. They say that nature does not heed poor man's anxieties, and will not cloud nor weep with him when he is hurt nor smile when he is glad. Never a heart broke in the Highlands or the Islands but a mountain frowned; Uist sorrowed for her daughter stricken. A mist gathered over Hecla, a rain began to fall weepingly on her shoulders. She heard the bleat of lambs in Salachry – Christ! the little lambs! – His very emblems, and born to delight so brief and the inevitable knife. She saw her dear native place mean and dark, the people in the field, whom she now avoided for the first time in her life, bent with toil.

CHAPTER XVIII

The Blow

HER first thought had been to fly to Ludovick, but what could she tell him beyond that an old rogue babbled? Then she reflected that the first of her apprehensions did not rise to-day, but sprang from some words of the woman who refused to bathe her child for fortune. She was hurt there first; she would go there for healing, if healing could be had: and once a little apart from Dark John, she quickened her step until she came to the cluster of dwellings they called Ballavon, in such a hurry and in such an inward turmoil she saw none of the queer sights that always gave her interest when she came to it in ordinary good spirits. It was built in a ring – this Ballavon – every door of it affably open to the doors across the way; the grass in the middle of it given over to stirks and hens and ducks and children. The rain was already gathering in little pools, where the ducks waddled in content and the bairns plashed; the hens stood under the broad eaves of rannoch or bent grass, chuck-chucking, laughably like old women in drab gowns and red caps sheltering from a sudden shower on the way to Mass. And in every doorway there was a wheel humming, or a barrel of nets repairing, or a creel of hose at the darning, with the spinners and the darners briskly carrying on a conversation across the open space, where their youngsters paddled with the ducks, and the yearling cattle lowed and nibbled the scanty grass. Could the princesses of the world have a more useful or more cheerful convocation? A month ago or less the children would have run laughing to Anna, and the women would have checked their wheels or put down the needles at once, and made some excuse for attracting her attention, but now Herself, who used to bring the ease of mind, the mood of idleness, brought unrest. The women kept their eyes on their wheel-hecks and pinched hard at the woollen rollags, making their feet go faster on the treadles till the hum arose of bees in heather; the hose demanded closer attention. As for the children, they stood open-mouthed or smiling awkwardly, ankle-deep in the puddles, so enraptured with the welcome rain after weeks of sunshine, they let her pass without interruption. When she had dashed into the house of healing, as she hoped it was to be, all the wheels and needles stopped as if at a command. The women looked across the common at each other and nodded their heads; nothing was said, but all Ballavon, saving only the bairns and the hens and the stirks and the quacking ducks, had one idea – Miss Anna was in some distress! Who can bear to see a neighbour in trouble that cannot be relieved! – not the soft-hearted folk of Uist! Ballavon abandoned the doorways and went into the dim hearth-side with its work, and wished it were last summer and Herself the cause of no vexation.

"I have come to put but the one question to you!" was the first words Anna said when she entered the house, to meet a very startled woman singing the song of "Crodh Chailin" over her baby.

"Wait till I put this one to bed," said the mother, bending over the cradle to gain time to think what her answer should be to a question that she could guess the nature of before it was uttered.

"When I was here on Wednesday," said Anna, when her chance came, standing on the floor, refusing the seat offered, her limbs trembling, her mouth parched, "you said my fortune was my worst possession."

The woman had made up her mind to lie. "Did I? faith!" said she. "If I did, I must have been wandering. I cannot guess what would put that into my head, for unlucky indeed would the fortune be that yourself would not adorn."

The house was dim in the sudden falling of the afternoon; but she could see that some tumult was in the girl's bosom, her face unusually solemn, and her eyes distressed.

"I did not ask you at the time what you meant when you said it, for I thought it might have more than one meaning, and be no more than a fancy of your own."

"Indeed, darling, and what more could it be?" said the woman, glad to borrow the notion. "Just a foolish fancy of my own! You could not ask any one in Ballavon but they will tell you I have the name for talking nonsense."

Anna was not for a second deceived, and it was the agony of the woman that she saw this. The girl stood on the floor in silence, not as if she wished any more to listen to the other, but as if she strained to hear sounds far off; her eyes absent, a most pitiful stillness come to her body. She saw in the woman's evasion a confirmation of her dread; she was the object of pity to all Uist, because the fools thought her reputed fortune was her attraction! She could stand their pity, – but that Duncan should be thought so foul! 'Twas that overwhelmed her. Duncan! The man who had brought her all the riches of the world, who laughed at the vulgar ambitions of common men! It was unlikely that he had ever heard her inheritance mentioned. It had been a vexation to her before; now she grew red with shame to be associated with it in any way, and with the old man of Dermosary who had made her the victim of his unhallowed bequest she felt a grievance. It extended for a little to her brother, who, in his odd caprice, would neither make use of the treasure nor get rid of it. How gladly to-night she could throw it into the deeps of Barra Sound, if all Uist could be present to see her doing so. But as things were, how helpless was the situation! Tears came to her eyes and trembled on her cheek, she surrendered to one sob that brought the woman lamenting motherly, seizing her by the arms, herself in tears. "I could take my tongue from the roots," said she, "for saying a word about it."

"Oh! you need not vex yourself for that," cried Anna; "what you said, of itself, would have troubled me little, but I have heard the same thing elsewhere, and now I know it is the common talk of Uist."

"I would not be heeding it, if I were you, my dear; sure Uist was ever fond of gabbling!"

"The pity is that Uist should have the excuse! but that is no fault of mine. I am hurt, I am hurt, good woman, and none to blame but the wind that brought a prince to Scotland to sow trouble. Some of it grew at once and fell before the hook, and there was an end of it; but what was sown in the sods in Arkaig is now coming up in Uist for the pain of those who never had anything to do with it. I am going home now. There is no more to be said. I am going home. Good woman, how it rains! How is the baby's chicken-pox?"

She went out of Ballavon, for the first time in her life without seeing a soul at its doors, for all the women, so averse from grief, were busying themselves inside, and now she knew the reason. She was glad herself they were invisible, for she would never have been able to present a front of unconcern to them. Besides, she wanted no distractions just at present, for she was nursing a hope that had been born when she stood on the floor of the house she had just left. There was one way out of this horrible affair: calumny could be still diverted from the man of her adoration. Very simply, too; Ludovick had the remedy in his hands. She had but to get his consent to the dispersion of this wretched money, and his assistance: once he knew the grief it caused her, he would no longer take up his old position. One thing was plain (she could admit it herself now) – the curse he had spoken of was certainly in it, and she would not finger a single coin. Of course Ludovick would easily settle her difficulty. She knew how much he, too, loved Duncan; how horrified he would be to learn that Uist thought Duncan capable of alloying his affection for her with a thought of that vile trash tarnished by intrigue, and known in history as a relic of defeat and degradation and ideals long abandoned. She grew almost glad as she hurried home to the presbytery and it was without a single doubt in her mind that all would be well in a moment or two. She came in upon her brother, where he read from the Venerable Bede.

"I had almost gone to look for you, Anna", he said laying down his book and looking up at her with a smile of relief. "Surely you were not out in the rain all this time: I cannot think Dark John's conversation so fascinating as all that."

"I – I took shelter in Ballavon," she said, and dropped in a chair.

He saw something disturbed her. "What's the matter, Anna?" he asked anxiously.

"O Ludovick!" she cried, "I want you to do something for my peace of mind. I promised I would never mention Uncle's bequest any more, if I lived to the age of a hundred; but then I did not – I did not know Duncan."

The priest's face clouded. Surely he could not have misread the character of young Corodale.

"You must not be angry with me, Ludovick; but if you will, you must just be so. I cannot help it, for I must speak. This money must be given away."

"It can't," said Father Ludovick.

"Listen, Ludovick, dear," said his sister, warm and eager, sure she had only to show him how unhappy she was to have him consent to anything. "Listen, I refuse to have the name any longer of owning this wretched Loch Arkaig *ulaidh.* Let us give it to the Church –"

"I have said before I would not if I could; the Church has lost already, and direfully, in souls by it. It is cursed."

"To the poor, then!" said Anna eagerly.

"What! and convey the curse to them, Anna? No, my dear. If you were our mother from heaven that asked it, I would still say no; it cannot be. I could tell you in four words why, but for two or three reasons that do not affect us, and particularly because it was once a secret of the Confessional. Why do you bring this up again, Anna when it was understood between us we should mention it no more? Let the stuff lie wherever it may be; all the evil it may do accomplished –"

"It is like to do more evil under a rock in Mingulay than ever it did above ground," said Anna. "It has already brought the name of Duncan into disrepute."

The priest started. "What!" said he.

"They are saying – the very folk that I have always thought my friends; he – Oh! I cannot tell you, Ludovick," she cried, and her tears began to fall.

He paced the room nervously, waiting her composure, hard at meditation, his guess far distant from the actual nature of her grief.

"What could they blame *him* for?" at last he asked, stopping and facing her. "*His* innocence, *his* honour, are beyond question. For why should he be blamed because – because he comes from Corodale? He has paid, poor lad! enough for that already. And how came out the story? I thought the Mingulay rock could have kept a secret just as well as any priest."

Anna sat stony, bravely restraining her tears, now certain hope was gone, and little heeding her brother's surprise.

"Come!" he said again, "tell me what you have heard, Anna."

"You know very well," she said.

"I have a notion," he confessed; "but in what form did it come to you?"

"The form it came in matters very little," said she "for the lie is on the winds. I see it in every face, that Duncan is thought to have as much interest in the Arkaig *ulaidh* as in myself."

"What!" cried Ludovick, much amazed. "Is that what he gets blamed for, that he courts you for your fortune?"

"Could he be blamed for worse? My dear Ludovick I told you long ago that something like this would be the consequence of my reputation. There's not a soul in Boisdale to-day but thinks my Duncan mercenary."

Father Ludovick did a strange thing – he sat him in a chair and laughed. The presbytery rang with his laughter – his that usually never got beyond the grave, gruff undertone of merriment. He held his sides, his eyes streamed with tears of frantic entertainment. Anna was amazed and indignant.

"I am sorry to look stupid," she said; "but if you took me into your confidence I might laugh too. Till you tell me where the humour lies I cannot see it for myself."

"Faith! Anna, I'm certain of that," said her brother more restrained. "You must excuse my want of feeling, but this revelation of yours is not exactly the one I had reason to expect from the distress you showed."

"It seems as serious to me as it well could be," said Anna incapable of understanding why Ludovick, usually so sympathetic, should be for once so inconsiderate. Then she fancied she saw the reason – he thought such a charge against her lover merely laughable. "I know it is ridiculous," she said; "but remember that our neighbours do not know Duncan so well as we do."

"Then let them learn," said Father Ludovick, growing grave. He came over beside her. "Come, Anna," he said; "do not distress yourself over a piece of folly."

"It seemed to me it would be so easy for you to make everything clear and pleasant if you wished it, and I never thought you would refuse," she said, now dry-eyed.

"It would, if it could be, but it cannot, more's the pity; and there's an end to it. I thought you were in love. What sort of love is it that lets the opinion of the world, regarding its object, dull for a moment its own delight?"

"I will love him all the better for the injustice done to him by the thought: it is not because I know of it that I am vexed, it is because I fear he himself may some day know. His spirit would never brook it."

"What! is his love so delicate, too, it could not suffer the suspicion of fools?"

"Ah! you do not understand," said Anna. "He would suffer for me – that Uist should think I took second place to my fortune would hurt him more than that he should himself be thought a traitor."

"I did not think of that," said Ludovick.

"No, for you were never in love, my dear," said Anna. "And you cannot help me?"

He showed a visage distressed exceedingly. "My dear, my dear, I cannot," he said; "that is more assured than ever, but time may do what the Boisdale priest cannot."

CHAPTER XIX

The Great Carouse

A FEW days after this there happened what was long remembered in Uist as the Great Carouse. Once upon a time carouse had been common enough on the island, – a fever that swept among them after lucky seasons flushing them at the face and making them merry and noisy, and generous to that degree they scattered pence among the very seagulls that quarrelled round the gutpots. But 'twas a brief fever at the worst, and harmed no one very much, and left behind it a whole winter's telling of foolish spectacles and laughable mad exploits. Father Ludovick put an end to the little carouses. Himself, he had always wine for a friend and a gardevine of spirits for the very sick, and would countenance the passage of a judicious glass on a proper occasion; but on recklessness he came down with a king's hand. Not commandingly – he knew the men of Uist better – but with the influence that came from their regard for his respect. Let the boats come home from the east, every man's pocket bulging with silver, his heart light and free, – no matter the day nor hour, Master Ludovick had some excuse to be in the neighbourhood of the ale-house door. They might be thirsty as old brine-barrels that had gaped for a summer in the sun, but he had no mercy on them. He marched up and down between the drink-house and the quay, hard (as it seemed) at cogitation on his next sermon, but never without the tail of his eye on the door. Four hundred men back from Loch Hourn and the money burning in their pockets could thus be thrown past temptation, as it were, at a shrug of the shoulder from the Lord of the Isles. They must be into their own houses before he left his post, and then he would go home chuckling, and tell Anna, "Praise God, they are with their wives and mothers, and now will be picking of pockets."

But the Great Carouse happened at a time when Uist had no money in its pockets and Father Ludovick was away at a funeral Mass in Eriskay. His being there, indeed, had something to do with the planning of the carouse. Planned it was beyond a question. Col of Corodale, sitting very close to his own affairs and rarely venturing abroad, heard his brother one day let drop that he meant to go over to Boisdale on the day after the morrow. The news left him envious and angry, but he could do nothing, for he was still on a footing of open brotherliness – though that same somewhat cold and selfish – with Duncan. But a remark of the person that Duncan spoke to, that Father Ludovick was to celebrate a Mass on the day that Duncan meant for his trip to Boisdale, suddenly sent a plan into his head. He sat late that night and laboured with the Gaelic muse until he had fashioned some verses of a ribald song to the air of "The Little Black Pot"; made an excuse the next day to visit Benbecula, and rode to the inn at Creggans, where he had a long sederunt with the Sergeant, who found an escapade to the fancy of Jib-boom.

The day of Duncan's visit to Boisdale was moist and warm, with a fog so thick on the sea there could be no fishing, so at the foot of Our Lady Star the boats lay hull to hull in a long row, lazily rocking in the swell of the bay, where the guillemot and the diver boldly ventured in beside them. The men sat on the thwarts or lay on the half-decks, passing the time till evening, with no more thought in their heads of carousal than of Christmas, when suddenly there came down upon them from the open the form of a ship. For a moment she was vague and great – a phantom – then she was the *Happy Return*, the smuggler, her name white on her bows. She swept past them with a froth at her counter; the fishermen started to their feet astonished, expecting to see her thrown on the shore; but this was the hour of display for Jib-boom: he scraped the very edge of safety, turned on his heel, and came to his pick of an anchorage at the end of the row of skiffs. His sails came down as if the halyards had been cut; the anchor roared.

"By the Book! and I'm the finest sailor in the Islands," said Jib-boom, and looked to his men for the admiration he counted no more than his due.

"I'm not bad myself," said one of the Macleods of Skye, and drew his cuff across his nose.

"You!" cried the skipper. "By the grace of God I was sailing ships when you were supping brose out of a horn spoon with a whistle on the other end of it."

"Like enough, like enough; we were aye the lads for music in Isle of Skye," said the Skianach; "and perhaps yourself was content to take it with your fingers."

The skipper aimed a blow at him in good-humour, then caught a stay, and stood upon the bulwark to glance over the long parade of skiffs. "It could not have happened better," he said to himself with satisfaction. "If I give them a glass I'm sure of a hearty chorus."

The fishermen looked with admiration: they make much in the Hebrides of a man who can handle a ship with skill. "Good for yourself, skipper!" cried the nearest, and clapped their hands. "'Tis you are the boy can do it! Did we not think you were making yonder for Master Ludovick's garden and planting of kale; but you put her about when your keel was crumbling the cockle-shells!"

Jib-boom kept a calm face, but felt warm and satisfied within him.

"Too thick for the banks, lads?" said he.

"Too thick altogether, just man!"

"That's fisherman's luck for you, O lads! Glad am I that I was bred to the big boats and not to the blowing of wind in net-bows, and shelling of mussels, and that I trade with fish that follow the scent of their noses."

The fishermen laughed. "True for you, skipper! true for you! But we're here, and we're not complaining so long as we have our health." And indeed they looked contented enough – the rogues! – to lie on their backs on the thwarts and take advantage of the idleness that Providence sent them.

Aft in the *Happy Return* the man without the Gaelic started to make ready a meal. "To the devil with your skellit!" cried Jib-boom. "Have up a jar of Barra, and let us keep the fog from our inwards."

The jar came up like magic. Jib-boom took a wooden *cuach* from his breast and drew the full of it of spirits, which he threw in the sea for luck; then helped himself less generously again. "Here's to the little black pot that reeks so sly in the burns of Barra!" he cried – a smuggler's toast; and his men were not long in following his example. The jar gurgled at the neck most pleasantly; briskly about went the cup! In the solemn bay of Boisdale there was at once a jovial spot. For a while the sloop had all the cheer to herself, the skiffs but dumb spectators; but Jib-boom at last bellowed across the bay, "Gather round, lads! gather round, here's a letter from home!" The fishermen laughed, thinking the invitation was not serious, but soon he made them see he meant it. Round came the skiffs, till they hung on the side of the *Happy Return* like a bee-swarm on a branch. An old Nantes keg came rolling from the chains where it stood marvellously ready. The bung came out with a "tloop!" and the stuff they make in the black pots of Mingulay and Barra was splashing in a hundred vessels. It swept like a spindrift over the skiffs, gaiety with it. Jib-boom was the king of a jovial corps.

"*Sguab as e!* – drink it out, friends!" he roared; "I'll warrant there's plenty more where that came from; sure the barley's in braird in Barra already. Pass her round fast, boys – Lord, I'm in the key! Pass her round, I'm telling you; she's the genuine."

"I declare I do not feel the least taste of Parliament off the good stuff," said an old fellow, with his nose in the can and his eyes twinkling.

"I'll warrant you not; Geordie nor his gaugers had a finger-nail on that keg. Pass her round, lads! Hearty, hearty! so long as I'm in the key. Pass her round; to-day for fun, to-morrow for repentance. Make her go with a splash, and to the Worst with all your shirkers."

He stood on the deck of the sloop, high above the other vessels, his shaven face filled with devilment, his eyes dancing, his long black curls blowing across his mouth, and his earrings making him look like a foreigner – there was no refusing to keep abreast with the humour of such a gallant fellow.

Once or twice the haze rose on a gust of easterly wind, and showed the island sombre and cold in a drizzle of rain; the chapel gaunt and hard over all, the houses of the townships very small and dull; then fell again more close than ever about the boats, shutting them off completely from the world of sober duties. The spindrift of folly, of the Barra barley-fields, went over and over them; the youngest felt that now he had found himself, that now he might be brave, that he had only to open his mouth and speak the finest wisdom, and that he could command the circling of the stars; the oldest felt just on the verge of some magnificent discovery. Just on the verge, just on the verge – another glass would do it. All grew noisy, breaking into gusts of laughter or loudly arguing. They began to spang from boat to boat, and brag and challenge.

"I am thinking it is time for my little bit song," said the skipper to himself, and started "The Little Black Pot": –

"Fisherman, fisherman, what is your fortune?
  Empty nets and a mail to pay;
To the Worst with sorrow, and God bless Barra
  For her small black pot will make you gay.

Sheoladair, sheoladair, what is your ruing?
  A rotten ship and a foul land-fall.
That was to-day, to-night be drinking
  From the small black pot, and forget it all."

He stood with his back to the mast, and sang with a rollicking voice that would tempt the soberest on the highways of folly.

"Man! am I not the singer whatever?" he would say, taking breath while the others chorused, and glance at his crew for admiration.

"No doubt, no doubt; but here's a poor fellow from Isle of Skye that's doing his best, and would like a little of the credit," said one of the Macleods. "God! I wish I knew the words, and I would be showing you!"

"Stop you, timber-tune, till I'm done with this song and I'll give you my hand on the half-head," said the skipper, and proceeded with his ditty. He looked as drunk as his company, but spilt more from his *cuach* than he drank, and always kept an anxious eye around to see that the stuff was flowing freely. "It's time for the Sergeant's verses now," said he to himself, and started a verse they had never heard before: –

> "Duncan, Duncan, what is your wishing?
> A crock of gold and an easy life.
> Come over from Corodale, then, and welcome,
> To make the crock of gold your wife."

"*A risd! a risd!* – again! again!" – cried the fishermen, laughing, and Jib-boom sang it again and again, and two or three more verses of its kind that he had learned himself no later than that morning from the lips of the Creggans innkeeper. In ten minutes the words were common property, and the new verses were counted better than the old.

> "Duncan, Duncan, what is your wishing?
> A crock of gold and an easy life."

They bawled it over and over again, till a diversion came in the outbreak of a fight between the Macleods and the crew of a skiff beside them.

"Give me but the one stroke at him and I will make a popish burial," cried the elder Macleod, and jumped into the skiff, with his brother after him, who cried, "Dunvegan! Dunvegan! Dunvegan never was beat!"

"Children of Satan," said Jib-boom, unaccountably vexed for a man that dearly loved a ploy. "Are they going to spoil me altogether? Come back this instant!" he cried to them, looking down into the skiff; "come back, or I'll take to the fists myself, and Isle of Skye will be the sufferer, I assure you." But a Skyeman never came back till his blow was struck.

"The one stroke and I will be content," said the MacNeil who had started the quarrel, and found next moment his enemy stumble over a bundle of lines and into his very arms. They grappled and fell, and the others in the boat got into grips for the sake of company.

"I was never in all my life in a better key for joviality, and here you're vexing me with your arguments," said Jib-boom, shaking his fist. "Come back, Macleods, and I'll give you the best of satisfaction myself."

The Macleods paid no heed, – they were too busy; so Jib-boom caught a stay and swung himself in among them.

"I'm fair affronted," said he. "They'll be putting the blame of this on the decent stuff we carry from Barra." He caught the elder Macleod by the collar and breech. "Come out a minute till I whisper to you," he cried, and with a heave had him over the side of the skiff and bobbing in the water. "There you are, Callum," said he, "and good you were when you were in your senses: I have seen the day it was not two cups of Barra would put you out of them." The fighting stopped; everybody laughed at Callum climbing on board the sloop.

The tide was ebbing, the skiffs that were farthest in were already aground, and Jib-boom was the first to see it. "Five o'clock," said he; "time you were on shore, lads, to see if your wives and Isle Uist are still to the fore."

"Is the keg empty?" asked one.

"To the dregs," said the skipper, and tilted it over with his foot.

"Well, it is time to be steeping the withies, then," said the fishermen, and stepped from skiff to skiff till they were all ashore, splashed through the fringe of the tide, and got to the grass. They went in noisy bands. For the first time their women learned there had been folly, and came out to the doors amazed.

"*Oh Dhe!* here is the work of Jib-boom and his blackguards," said they. "And Master Ludovick away in Eriskay! There will be cracking of heads before the mouth of evening. Just listen to them singing – *och*, indeed there will be cracking of heads!"

> "Duncan, Duncan, what is your wishing?
> A crock of gold and an easy life."

There was not a man of them who had not the words of Col's song; it was to be heard on every road.

"There they go!" said Jib-boom, listening from his deck. "Have I not had the diligent scholars?"

CHAPTER XX

Half-Brothers

THE lovers, who had been at Loch-an-Ealan, a favourite haunt of their privileged hours, where they could have wellnigh a world of their own, had come back to the presbytery, and were parting in the porch. Anna had been happy almost to an aching of the sense of it; at the very sight of Duncan every apprehension had departed. There was, in this last hour, something of Arcadian simplicity in their dalliance – the flying and stolen salute of the fields, the warmth and pressure of dusky barns and shy sheepfolds, little repulses, tempting mockeries and defiances, mild contentions and easy triumphs, for it was not often they found themselves alone, and Uist, as we know, is not in one particular at least a lover's land except in darkness or the hour of the sagging moon. If Duncan never heeded to grasp the material benefits of the world leaving even his own due of these to his brother, he was greedy of the rarer blisses, the fragrant ones, that have no pang of disillusion following after them, that Heaven puts in the way of her poorest sons, and he was never so much the man complete and confident as when he had Anna in his arms. She had a waist so pliant with young strong life, it gave him the old savage joys of the possessor and protector. When her laughing tame resistances broke down shamefully, he valued her lips the more for the contest, and to get them was to know he was a captive himself, for they drew out his very soul. Breath of the mountain thyme, cheek that lay to his, ravishing soft and silken, sweeping him into a delirium only to be dispelled by the laughter of her eyes! She was no languishing lover, – the breed of them is not in stormy isles, – she did not, like most women, show her nativity in her character, otherwise had she been more mist than sun, mysterious like the brooding lochs of Uist, solemn like the moors and the wave-thrashed macharland. It was said there was a drop of Spain, three hundred years old, in her family; perhaps it was that and the school in France that gave her less of the long thought that bodes in the Gaelic bosom. She was no languishing lover; that she was altogether his was a thing she would have him know without her showing it; that and a spirit of playfulness made her loving the more sweet.

The hour had come when Duncan must go; she stood silent in his arms.

A sound of rude minstrelsy from the direction of the bay brought them back to the human world: Anna raised her head, leaned back from his breast to look out at the porch window, and saw the bacchanalians scattering about the bay and the township.

"What a pity!" she said, distressed. "These men are making fools of themselves, and Ludovick from home! How vexed he will be! I'm afraid the Benbecula smugglers are to blame for this: their boat is in the bay, and the fishermen have not been out at the banks today."

Mercifully they could not make out the words of the song the fishermen ranted, though the air was familiar to Duncan as a favourite of his brother's, and the women of the township were out in a panic lest Herself should hear, coaxing or commanding their men-folk home.

"I am so glad Col has no more to do with that pack," said Duncan.

"So am I – for the sake of his brother. But if it were nor for you I do not know that I should very much care. I always thought the traffic half respectable because Col Corodale was in it: the trade just gave him that – that air of romance that sits well on a handsome man who cannot control very lofty thoughts."

"You sinner!" cried Duncan. "I think him all the better, if not even the more romantic, because he is honest and busier now about reputable affairs."

"Too busy to see much of Boisdale presbytery nowadays, at any rate," said Anna. "Ludovick has been missing him at Mass."

"Perhaps I'm not wholly blameless for his sinful state. Corodale can ill afford to have the two of us making weekly trips to Boisdale. I have a notion that there's but the one thing he envies me, and for that I cannot blame him, the wonder would be if it were otherwise."

"And what may that be?" asked Anna, smiling, and knowing very well, as her lover plainly saw.

His answer was to kiss her.

"On Sunday – I shall be over on Sunday," were his last words as he left for his long walk home. She did not come part of the way as she was used to do, for the noisiness of the fishermen made it inadvisable; but she stood at the door to look after him, feeling the day for the first time chill and dreary. He turned round once; she would have preferred that he had not done it, for Uist always deems the backward glance bad-omened, and then she went indoors, a little pensive.

Duncan went on his way with the glow of the lover still in him, and hardly hearing the sounds of revelry that were constantly in front, though every group of singing men he came up to stopped the chorus before he got close enough to hear the words. Some of them did so guiltily, shamefaced, but Duncan did not see that; others because their women rushed out as he approached and silenced them. It was so till he drew near the huts of Milton, and here seated on the last of a stack of peats, was a group more melodious than any that had gone before. He took up the air, hummingly, himself, so pleasant was his humour, thinking of the Sunday.

> "Sheoladair, sheoladair, what is your ruing?
> A rotten ship and a foul land-fall.
> That was to-day, to-night be drinking
> From the small black pot, and forget it all."

The men stopped as he came up to them.

"Faith! and it's yourselves are merry on it, lads," said he cheerfully.

"Middling, middling, Master Duncan," said an old fellow soberer than his neighbours. "Jib-boom was for once in his good vapours, and gave us the freedom of a keg yonder, and we're not accustomed." Some young men laughed. There was something odd, Duncan thought, in the way they looked at him, but it might be no more than Uist's interest in a sweetheart, till he had gone a dozen paces past them, when they broke into their song again –

> "Duncan, Duncan, what is your wishing?
> A crock of gold and an easy life.
> Come over from Corodale, then, and welcome,
> To make the crock of gold your wife."

The rhyme burned into his consciousness as something never to be forgotten, he seemed to have known the words all his life, and yet they puzzled him for a moment. What gold did they speak of? Did they think life in Corodale so profitable or easy? Let them try it for a while and find how much happier was their own. Then the meaning built itself among his rambling thoughts – this had something to do with Anna and the Loch Arkaig legend he had never once had a thought of since he was a lad, when it was a tale that gave heroic interest to the person of old Dermosary. He had an impulse to run back at his insulters, but a thought of Anna and the scandal this might raise prevented him. By Askernish and Mingary, Ollay Loch and Ormaclett he went, and in the dark through Dorochay Glen, and the Pass of Hellisdale – three hours of amazement, of speculation, of anger, of self-examination, of distress. There was no rain when he reached Corodale; a quarter moon struggled among clouds; the sound of the sea beating on Rhu Hellisdale oppressed the night with a melancholy he shared, and seabirds whistled dolorous above the waves that are their home. Corodale House looked black, abandoned, a fort empty, eyeless, full of old considerations, moaning in the wind like Kismul Castle, only a shred of light in the upper storey, where sat, he knew, his brother Col. Once it had been gay enough in Corodale House, when his father was alive, his mother young and beautiful, and himself a child; when the pipes went and the trump as at a fair, and neighbourliness prevailed. By-and-by it would be so again, and Anna's bower would rise in the garden and her evening lamp gladden the darkness, all happy and all well; but he could not guess that, and God! to-night how dolour held the place! So sad, so strange, so unwelcoming, so cold!

Col, in the upper room, sat at a congenial occupation. He was no common miser to gloat on the metal stamp of his possessions. The sound of his gold, indeed, was apt to startle him, because it proved that it was something talkative and foolish, calling attention to itself. What he preferred was the discreet dumb record of it on the written page. Though there was more money in that upper room than Duncan could have credited, knowing the constant complaints of his brother, its owner never cared to look at it except to assure himself that it was safe: the very candle might have been a spy, to see him open the box and glance so quickly in and shut the lid so suddenly again. If his hair was getting thin on the top, it was not with holding up the lid of his chest to count his money, as Corodale cotters said. No; he much preferred his book – to see the column grow by guineas, ay! even if it were only by shillings. It was with joy he came to the foot of a page and summed it. He would search his pockets on Saturday for a coin, no matter how small, to make up the column; for his fancy was a column complete in the week, and great was his ingenuity to make it out in sums small or large. And then when the page was turned, O Lord! it was a sweet indulgence carefully to ornament the virgin page with the sum brought forward; to that went his finest penmanship, yet when the figures stood by themselves he was unhappy till some others went below them, and the week's accumulation had manifestly again begun. More than once had he stayed from Mass on a Sunday to put his contribution to the hoard, so that the week might open auspiciously. He had had always in his mind an ideal sum that, once attained, should mark the bounds of his ambition, and set him free to spend gloriously upon the schemes he had made out for his years of leisure. It had grown and grown – that ideal figure – as his secret store, as his actual possessions, had grown; the day of his liberty receded every week, till now it was further off than ever.

But to-night Col was not even at his book; he was intent upon a chart of the Outer Isles. It had been his father's; he had remembered seeing it as a boy, and of late had searched about the house and found it. To-night he narrowly conned it, the isles of the Cat to the southmost – Barra, Uist, Benbecula, Eriskay, Hellisay, Lingay, Flodday, Pabbay – all the rocks that fret the Minch and feel the churn of the Atlantic. The map was freckled with red crosses, and every cross accompanied by a date in his father's hand of writing. Col knew now what that meant, though the puzzle as a boy was beyond him – each cross marked a search for the Arkaig treasure, and these were the dates of his father's expeditions. He could not but marvel at the patience and the industry manifest on this tattered sheet of paper; his father seemed to have drawn a comb through all the Outer Islands in his hope of raking a treasure to the top. Many had been his systems of search, based on the foolishest things – not on legend and rumour alone, but even on dreams and omens. And yet how hopeless a search too – among the broken fangs of the girning tides, among Atlantic spume, or in lonely plains of sand, or on the shores of lochs, and through these ancient temples, cairns, castles and barps, hags and mosses. Col, with his gift of imagination, felt in himself each time he pored on it his father's travails, chagrins, and despairs. For fifteen years his father quested; the last had been at Mingulay, twelve years ago by the date on the chart. It was the time something of fortune came to him from a lowland speculation, and how poorly he proved himself capable of husbanding the same!

Col heard his brother come into the house, and rolled up the chart hurriedly. "By heavens!" he thought, "but for him I might have had it now. I wonder how my bit song went."

He came downstairs. Duncan sat at the table, white-faced, his brow disturbed, eating his food and finding no savour in it. Col gave but the one glance at him, and saw the hour had come for craft.

"Holloa, lad!" said he, cheerfully, coming into the room with a seaman's red shirt tucked in at the band of his breeches, and taking a seaman's pace back and forward on the floor, his hands in his pockets, his figure straight as a young willow. "Holloa, lad! Home? You have had a sharp walk of it. And how's his lordship of the Isles and all the folks at Boisdale? I'm in the hope that they are well."

"Well, well, very well," said Duncan, in a voice empty of all interest, fiddling with his fork and spoon, looking at the wall before him and seeing nothing, but with the overcome of a song sung fifteen miles away dirling in his ears.

"Struck! struck badly, by God!" said Col to himself, and waited for what was coming. For a while there was a silence in the room – for one at least, to Duncan the air of the "Little Black Pot" was louder far than the boom of the wave on Rhu Hellisdale. He could not eat with that drunken chorus so oppressing him; back he pushed his plate, and plucked from his aching heart the mystery that troubled him. "Did you ever hear of the Loch Arkaig *ulaidh?*" said he.

Col laughed. "To the devil!" said he; "did I ever hear of my own great-grandfather?"

"But I mean of late."

"Late? No later, if you want to know, than yesterday when – well, no matter, no matter! with a man of more importance I would have given him more than he got for it."

"Is – is it thought to be still to the fore?"

Col stopped his walk, looked pointedly at his brother, and laughed. "Come, come!" said he; "who knows that better than yourself? By all accounts there's nobody has a better right."

Duncan's face grew whiter than ever. "By the living God! Col," he said, with a fist on the table, "I never gave the treasure a thought for ten years, except perhaps to think it a curious fairy story."

Col laughed again, more slyly than ever. "Well, who's denying it, lad? I have thrieped all along the thing was never in your mind."

"*Mo chreach!* Was it necessary to assure any one of that in Corodale?"

"Well, not in Corodale – let them venture to say anything about it in Corodale and there's me to reckon with! – but elsewhere in the Islands here and there – here and there – oh! I would not make too much of it, but here and there things have been mentioned."

Duncan groaned. "And you never hinted it to me?"

"Not I," said Col readily. "I'm the last to put a spoke in the wheel of any man."

"But such a blackguard thing, Col – that they should think that of me!"

"Just so!" said Col, shrugging his shoulders. "That's it, but I would not mind the thinking so much if they kept their mouths shut."

"But Col, Col, surely you did not think it was some dubious coin in a crock that sent me over to Boisdale."

"Here's my bit song! bravo for my song!" thought Col. He put up his shoulders again. "Bah! Donacha, there's no need for play-acting between the pair of us. You'll admit I let you go your own gait, and never asked you anything about it. Damn it! man, I agree with you that youth and good looks and a handsome tocher are no drawbacks to a woman; they're all things that time will cure, – Corodale would be none the worse for any of them."

Duncan felt the infernal pang, he was struck to the core. He leaned with his arms on the table and his face in his hands. The house was dead; the room, indifferently lit by peat flame and a lamp, had Col's blood-red shirt for the brightest thing in it. Col could count, if he liked, the pulse of the waves on the shore of the promontory, but Duncan heard nothing save the echo of a song.

"Then this is it, Col," he said, looking up in a little. "I'm to take it that all Uist, including my own mother's son, believes I'm the rogue that this implies?"

"Oh, well –"

"Come, Col, come; no shuffling, man! the hour's gone by for that between us." He stood to his feet and went up to his brother standing with his back to the fire, and presented a determined and compelling front, with his face like flint and his eyes flashing.

"Well, you know the world; it's cursed seldom it gives the lover of a moneyed lass the credit for having a single mind on her person only."

"By heavens! let me meet one other man to say to my face what you hint at, and I'll stretch him dead at my feet."

Col cracked his thumb. "*Dhe!* Bonny bloodshed for a half-priest, Duncan," said he. "If it's to stop the tongue of Uist on that business you're bent, you should go about with a gun and bring the clan with you and make a month's holiday of it. Faith! there's damned little sport in the island anyway."

"But Col, Col, man," he said bitterly, taking his brother by the shirt-sleeves, "did it not seem horrible to you that I should be so mercenary?"

"Well, I admit the business annoyed me," said Col. "There was no doubt a roguish element in it. For here were you – if I may take the liberty – a little – a little marred by your reputation as – as –"

"As a stuck priest; yes, yes, don't bock at it, man! – as a stuck priest, yes, Col, yes! Well?"

"And wasting your time, too, in a certain way of speaking, at Corodale, a poor place at the best of it, without a penny behind your back –"

Duncan winced. "That is true, that is true," said he. "I never gave so important a consideration a single thought. I was bold enough, by Heaven!"

"Now here's the way I look at it: the girl of herself is worth the best in all Albyn."

"It is so."

"And with Dermosary's fortune –"

"Her only blemish, Col; as sure as death I think it so And I never knew of it."

"You'll admit it looks bad for you, in all these circumstances, to be hanging at her heels."

"For me!" said Duncan, smiling bitterly. "Man! Col, that never occurred to me; what I am thinking of is how it looks for her. A stuck priest – as you say – a fellow that has neither present position nor prospect of it, so poorly thought of even by the folks that know him best that they must believe him capable of the most filthy meanness – I was contemplating a pretty partner for the woman who, as you say, deserves the best man in Albyn Thank God, the blunder is not beyond remedy!"

Col found this mood beyond him; he had nothing to say, but wondered what his brother would propose.

"To-day I was so happy," said Duncan, as if he spoke to himself and no one else was in the room. "I would not have changed my place with any man in Europe. Tonight I envy the poorest hind in the Hebrides. Well, one thing's certain, Col; 'tis all bye with Boisdale."

Col's face lit, but his brother had no eyes to see that. "I would not mind their gossip a docken leaf," said he. "You may be poor, but you have come of the very best; many a man has cobbled his brogues with a bride's fortune before to-day, and –"

"Stop, stop, Col!" cried Duncan; "you mean well, but you hurt me. I am going out a turn to do some thinking."

He pushed past his brother and went out of the house. Col stood a while in the room, guessing at the outcome of a crisis he had so cunningly brought about. He waited a while. He heard his brother's footsteps pass the house front. "Well, let him take it!" he said, with a shrug of his shoulders as if he threw off all responsibility, but honestly wished his ends had been attainable by other measures, for they had in other days been happy enough together. By-and-by he went upstairs and into his room and prepared for bed. When he blew out the light he looked a moment from the window, and could see, by the light of the moon, his brother walking up and down between the barn and the boundary-wall. He cursed anew the need for what he did. "We'll see in the morning," he thought, and went to bed, but could not sleep. The sea was sounding over all the island, beating at high tide on the spit, but he fancied he could hear, in spite of it, Duncan's footsteps crunching on the sand. Old days came into his recollection – days when they were boys – when they guddled for trout in Usinish burn, and drank whey from the one bowl in the summer shearings and slept in the same bed every night. "Ach! the best thing that could have happened him," he told himself with a shake, "a touch up to his manhood!" But could not sleep. What would his brother say in the morning? He did not need to wait so long to learn. By-and-by the outer door opened and shut softly; Duncan's footsteps were on the stair, the bedroom door was opened. "Are you asleep, Col?" Duncan whispered.

"Not yet," said Col, and wished to Heaven he was.

"I'm for off the Islands," said Duncan; "there's but the one thing for it."

"Indeed," said Col. "You might do worse, but we'll talk it over in the morning," and turned on his pillow. Duncan went down the stair again.

CHAPTER XXI

Duncan's Departure

HE sat below for hours, sometimes falling into a doze close-packed with horrors, that he waked from aching like one who had been stunned. The night was cold; he broke the carefully builded peats that were meant to keep the fire alive till the morning, and by-and-by it went out altogether: what did it matter to him who was all fires within? It was not that on leaving the island he had any hesitations, – pride and the unreasoning impulse that sweep away his kind on the most frantic enterprises had soon determined that for once and all; but what he spent the cold hours pondering was whether or not he should see Anna again before leaving. If he did what every pulse in his body craved for, he would go to her to-day. But then there would be the need for an explanation, and the most delicate he could offer would be a coward's blow. Besides, he could not tell how far his resolution would stand the test of a meeting; he might be tempted too much. There was but one way of honour, though its seeming cruelty made him shiver to think of it. He must be on the sea before she had his farewell. But that determined on, he had still to frame a message. With paper and ink he made a score of attempts to put the situation in words that would torture her least, and would leave her free, and still would make it plain he was the same to her, and was not hopeless of a happier time.

"... I have found myself, and lost all else that was worth having, since I left you," he wrote at last. "It would have been better for both of us if it had happened sooner. I have discovered that I have till now had but small consideration for your interests, and let my vanity and my selfishness put common justice to you out of my mind. What I have thought of you, *Anna bhig*, – what I think at this dark hour, more deeply than ever before, – what I will always think of you so long as I live, is not to be expressed on a sheet of paper. But it is a poor bargain that is all one-sided, and I have just been thinking that while I was ready to take the best gift in the world, I came for it without deserving it, and with nothing of my own. I have been happy, *Anna bhig*, and so rich in thought of you, I clean forgot that I was only the prodigal come home, and without a penny and without a calling. I think too much of you to tie you at your age to so poor a prospect as mine is like to be unless I take some step to mend it. I am leaving Uist, and I must not see you before I go – that's the one thing dauntons me. Where I go and what I am to do must lie with chance; I take but two things with me – love and hope. But I am asking, *Anna bhig*, no promises; for that my future is too dark. If fortune favours me you will hear speedily; if not, then I would, if I could, be asking you to forget...."

When the letter was finished for the last time, he was astonished at the scrupulous and studied penmanship, ashamed of the shabby words, so worn-out in the use of common everyday affairs. There was not a throb of his heart in them; not a single drop of the tears that were in him deep as wells. So much for scholarship! – it could not make him in a hundred years express what he could make plain with one glance of the eye to her that owned him. It was not this way went abroad the fellows who ride in *ceilidh* tales from maidens desolate, and in the shearing songs; no splash of sour ink with them, nor chewing the head of the grey goose quill.

He wrote a line to Father Ludovick too. "You have been good;

you have been kind. And I have been a fool, and showed poor gratitude. Think what you will of me but that I can ever forget."

Sour ink! sour ink! black marks on some of Col's accompt paper; not a drop of blood in them – well, it could not be helped! they must stand for the best he could venture. When it was done it was the dawning and swallows fed their young in the deep barn eaves. Wild weather promised; the sun came up from black seabounds and sea-birds lined the beach, and Rhu Hellisdale was white with them bickering on the shelves. He put out the light, and gave the room to the pallor of the day. In came a servant yawning, startled to find him there before her, and busied herself to set the fire.

"My grief!" she cried, with hands uplifted to find the embers of her gathering peat grey and cold. "Och! och! Master Donacha, here's misfortune; you must have spoiled the *griosach* of the fire. Something will come of it worse than sneezing," then set to the task of rekindling it, humming softly to herself the lines of the grace for fire –

> "Within my heart oh kindle Thou
> The lowe of love for every neighbour;
> For foe, for friend, for kith and kin;
> The brave, the knave, the thrall of labour."

"Have you not been in your bed this night, Master Donacha?" she asked in a while, stopping her puffing at the fire. "Och! now is not that a poor business? If it was Col, little would be the wonder that would be on me, for night or day was ever the same with yon one: the world, the world for him, and the father that went before him."

"I have been writing, Morag," answered Duncan, with a weary smile. "I am making ready to take a turn to the Lowlands."

"And if I might take the liberty – when may you be back, Master Donacha?

"That will depend on many things, like the start of the lazy man's sheep-shearing."

"Ochanoch! is that the way of it now, Master Duncan? It's ill to keep the black-cock always in the heather, and I knew it would come to the wings for it sooner or later. Faith! I daresay I'll not be staying long myself in Corodale. I was thinking to myself it was better I was where I came from, in Benbecula. *Tigh gun chu, gun chat, gun leanabh beag, tigh gun ghean gun ghaire*." (A house without dog, without cat, without child, a house without liveliness or laughter.)

Col came down that morning from a night of the pleasantest

dreams, with no more doubt of what his brother would do than that he himself should make a hearty breakfast, for all his craft had been built upon what he knew so well of Duncan's character. But while he was assured that his brother would go, and felt content in the prospect, he was not going to show too hearty an agreement with his step.

"What's this about going, lad?" he asked. "Did you come upstairs last night to tell me that, or by any chance was I dreaming?"

"I wish you were, Col, and I too," said Duncan. "I have had pleasanter nightmares than this that troubles me. I'm going with the first vessel for the mainland I can get a chance of. I have been wasting far too much time in Corodale; there's neither two men's work nor two men's reward in the place, and any one less considerate than yourself would have told me that sooner."

Col, just for a second, thought the words were mockery, but no! he saw a frank and affectionate face before him; his brother was still insensible of his own rights, and had no suspicion how much they were encroached on.

"It's the God's truth, Duncan!" said he, "there's scanty kail for two of us in Corodale. Kelp at less than forty, and half the scamps on our shore cheating us out of even our honest share of that; black cattle and ponies at that ebb where I could be giving them as Fair-day gifts to my friends; the white-fishing the one week as boss as a barrel, and the next with good hauls made into manure for the want of salt. You'll admit I never troubled you much with accounts, Duncan, for I was swears to vex you; but you have had your eyes, and see the struggle that there is to keep things going."

Duncan could have told as much by the experience of his palate and the emptiness of his pocket, for every day saw his brother's management more frugal. Of late the latter had had a new dream of a mainland house – perhaps in Edinburgh, where lairds of smaller lands than Corodale nowadays kept their winter quarters in something of state, even with kelp at forty.

"I know," said Duncan. "And there's one thing troubling me."

Col winced, for he knew very well what that was. His brother could not be thrust off the edge of Uist without some money, and curse the need for it that started at the top of a new page!

"But what for should it be you to go?" said he putting off a while the unpleasant moment. "You're the elder-born, and I'm in the second stall. Corodale's yours. If it's furth fortune, as they say, I'm the one to be packing the haversack and you to look after your own here, though I could not be wishing you joy of it. East west, north, or south, I hope I'm man enough to face what any airt of the world offers me. By the Book! I could gaily start to-morrow."

Duncan felt thankful for so generous a heart; this was the Col of his imagining!

"No, *ille!* indeed I start to-morrow, or as soon as may be, and you know the reason. I could not set a foot on the wester side of the river Roag after this without being affronted. Man! they're making songs on me, – but I'll vex you none with that. Corodale's yours by every wish of our mother and our father. I wish you may make a fatter living out of it in the future than you made in the past."

When it came to a consideration of what money was needed, even then the younger brother must be true to his nature. He hummed and he hawed. The times were so terribly bad; if it had been Whitsunday! at present he had not the wherewithal exactly at his hand. But he would get an accommodation. Was it not as little as he could do for Duncan? The Sergeant over at Creggans was due him money still for his share of the sloop, he said, and he would ride up to-morrow and get enough from him to set Duncan forth with something in his pocket.

"I wish it could be to-night," said Duncan, "for the sooner I'm off the better, and a chance might offer at any moment."

Col was glad of the excuse for hurrying, and he went that afternoon to Benbecula, catching the second tide upon the lesser ford.

"Well," said the Sergeant, as they sat over a horn, "you're there, and you're not ill-pleased by the look of you. I can guess, whatever you meant by your song, it served its purpose."

"It did that," said Col. "He's going off to the Lowlands – yon one – for good."

"Now, by the Seven Stars!" said the innkeeper with a scoundrel admiration, "it is you have the ingenuity! I was fair beat to understand the demand for song. Struck! He must be a greater fool than I gave him the credit for, and that's saying a good deal, by your leave, or without it as it may suit. But you did not come over to lament with me about such dire intelligence."

"Not a bit of me," said Col. "I came for a small accommodation. He wants twenty pounds from me."

"Just so," said the innkeeper, very dry; "just so. And I make no doubt he'll have it: your heart was aye a credit to you, and the season has been good."

"Not so very good; and there's no cream on a cat's milk. I declare I cannot tell where to lay my hands on so much unless I get it from yourself."

"Twenty pounds, h'm! That's back where we were before, and I would have thought you might have tried the little poke in Corodale before coming again to Creggans," said the Sergeant, who had always his own reason for lending on such prospects as Duncan's departure left. "But you'll have it, *loachain*; the sloop did fairly well on her last trip. Twenty pounds! – a cheap riddance, eh, Col? And out of a bit song! –

'Duncan, Duncan, what is your wishing?
A crock of gold and an easy life.'"

He sang the verse jocularly. "That was well contrived," said he. "Jib-boom will be giving me the credit of it; he learned it with a gusto, but I could neither have had the notion nor made the song if my life depended on't."

"He would never have gone otherwise," said Col; and stopped suddenly, for he saw the Sergeant's wife at the stair-foot – listening, it was like enough; and she could understand them.

"There is no harm done," said the Sergeant, turning to the English, when he had given her a scowl that sent her flying; "she has not the brains of a hen. When does he start, yon one?"

"With the first vessel he gets a chance of."

"Well, there's the sloop herself; she is leaving Uskavagh with a cargo of fish and a trifle of Barra for Clyde to-morrow; what would hinder him to take a passage with her?"

So Col rode back to Corodale through a stormy evening with his twenty pounds and his brother's departure all arranged for. He gave him the money with a grudge, but still got some satisfaction out of it, for he kept a quarter of the Sergeant's loan.

The sloop came off Corodale next day in the evening and Duncan went aboard. He had given his letters to his brother to send across to Boisdale. If Col had been of late on closer terms with Father Ludovick, and of a nature different from what he was, he might have looked for him to be the messenger himself and make the blow less cruel. But Col, he knew, was not the man for any office of the kind where delicacy was demanded; the letters must speak for themselves. Till the very last he was eager for departure, yet when the sloop was under sail and he saw the islands sink behind him, Hecla and Benmore in clouds, and the coast noisy with the breakers of a north-east wind, he felt the greatest sorrow of his life.

CHAPTER XXII

A Stricken Heart

COL himself it was, nevertheless, set out for Boisdale in the morning, riding a short-legged Barra pony clean-clipped and shod, with a great deal of hurry in the blood of it, the rider amazing long and large on the back of a beast so small, and busy with his heels, being cheery over one thing done and eager to be over with another. The Minch was grey as a gull's back, contemplating offence; skiffs with well-reefed mains scudded for sheltering creeks or harbours, knowing what was coming soon or late, but the day was dry, and the wind, blowing behind Col, set him out of Corodale and past the foot of Hecla with the spirit of a bird. He could have sung – so jubilant he felt – if the only tune that could find room in his memory at the moment had not been "The Little Black Pot," and some dregs of decent sentiment kept him from giving that one utterance, though the words he had made himself to the tune of it went humming in his head. People in his fields looked up and wondered to see him pass so brisk and blythe on it, so hearty in his greetings, that was of late morose as Macailin's boar. Yesterday he had been quarrelling with his tenants over the rents of kelp, and threatening all the paper laws they had no understanding but a great deal of dread for: now he passed them with a smile on his good-looking face. He kept his mind, as well as he could, from brooding on his task. Up rose the rain-goose – the black-necked diver – from his nest beside the tarn, crying "*Deoch! deoch! deoch!*" rose, too, the mallard—Mary's duck – in swelling circles the higher it got, then darted like an arrow to the Sound. The island was alive and throng with brave and zestful things, and interesting for a man on a horse with leisure to look on them, and Col, who ever liked the creatures of the wild that live on no man's crop or manger but on the broadcast bounty of God, found his travelling to his mind so long as he kept his thoughts from its object. In the bounds of Corodale his own folk knew him, gave small return for the smile and brief courtesy to his salutation for they felt that now were come the days of bitterness since Duncan was gone. But out of his own lands, on the western side of the island, where the ways were thronged with people, he rode like a noble gentleman, high-renowned for courage. So friendly, so affable his mood, he took a child once to ride *biolag* on the saddle before him, and the passersby were charmed to see such kindliness in one true-born, the real *duine-uasail*, saying, "Och! there's the good heart now for you! May he never have care on the saddle behind him!"

But when he came to the top of the brae that gave him a sight of the white house of Boisdale, the chapel on the rock, and the townlands scattered far and near of Father Ludovick's parish, the coward rose in him. He drew up his horse in a fright at his first idea. He could not be the one to break the news. Let them have the letters today, and he would come again himself to-morrow when the lamenting was over. So he found a messenger in one of the wayside houses and set him on with Duncan's letters to the presbytery, then turned and rode home again. He came back next day to Boisdale at dinner-time; the paltriest considerations were beginning to count a good deal in his economies.

"I am glad to see you, Col," was Ludovick's welcome; "you are just in time to join us," and Anna felt her heart expand, for now there would be explanations, and all would again be well. Col, who had not held that hand in his nor looked in her eyes since Duncan took possession, felt his treachery would be justified even if the girl had not a farthing. He was as nearly in love with her as any man might be that had his heart in a ledger.

"Not a word about the letters till we have eaten a morsel," said the priest, less elated by the visit than his sister, for he had read the letters over and over with a deepening sense of the severance they created, and small hope that Col brought consolation. "Not a word till we have eaten; there was never a complication that was not the easier understood after vivands." Anna, he saw would have had it otherwise, but for once he must have his own way, so down they sat, no very cheerful party, to a meal that only Col could relish. He helped himself with a liberal hand to Ludovick's Spanish wine, and felt his task was to be less disagreeable than he had feared, for here was the girl, showing some signs of a natural distress, it is true, but joining bravely in the snatches of conversation that her brother started on subjects far from their settled thoughts, and so trivial that their interest was exhausted in a sentence or two. What the priest designed was plain when the meal was over: he looked at his watch, and said he must go at once to the blessing of a new skiff to be launched at high tide.

"I'll be back in half an hour," he said, and gave Col a glance that commanded the gentlest consideration for the girl.

This was better still, thought Col, who found it ill to get over a fear that the priest at any moment might come down from the clouds where his thoughts dwelt generally, and might shrewdly understand him and discover. It could not have been planned better than that Anna and he alone should discuss the situation. When her brother was gone she turned on Col a face that, in spite of her brave restraint, was showing her hope and fear.

"Well?" she said. "It was kind of you to come; it was what I should have expected from you. We heard you rode across with the letters yourself yesterday and sent them on by another hand: I think I understand – and I am grateful. It has given us time to think. It was kindly considered; but for some time after I got the letter I was in a mood to saddle Gaisgeach and hurry after you."

"On my word, Miss Anna," said Col, calling all his craft together, "I came with the intention of giving you the letters with my own hand; but – but I was aye the coward when the duty was unpleasant, and I baulked at the first sight of Boisdale presbytery."

"I understand. Perfectly. If Duncan – if your brother – had been half so considerate, he might have vexed his friends in Boisdale presbytery less. To go like this! without a word of warning, without good-bye; it is not our custom, Mr Col, is it?"

"What! without good-bye!" cried Col. "Come, now! that is news I find ill to believe of Duncan."

"It must have been a sudden decision?"

"Sudden enough, at last, I'll allow," said Col; "but that should surprise nobody who knew Duncan, in many things as variable as the sand."

"Indeed, I was not aware of that peculiarity in his character," said Anna coldly, feeling that consolation came more slowly than she looked for.

"I'm the last, perhaps, who should mention it, and to tell the truth, most of his vagaries had the very best motives at the back of them. He came home on Tuesday night with his mind made up on leaving the Islands

"And he's gone?" said Anna with a sunken heart.

"On the other side of the Minch by now."

Then was he gone indeed! She knew from her own experience how widely the Minch could sunder. "Friends even less intimate than myself – than Ludovick and myself – might naturally expect he would have mentioned his intention when he was here on Tuesday," she said.

"What!" cried Col again; "and he did not say anything of it? I thought at first you did not mean exactly that. Too bad! too bad! I declare I'm fair affronted; I thought he came over here for no other purpose, and that his letter was a mere formality."

Anna's face, if she did not turn away to hide it, would have made it plain that this was anguish. "Then – then you were not taken by surprise?" she asked.

"Not a bit of it, Miss Anna, I was long expecting it Who could wonder at it either? Corodale's no very hearty place after some years of Paris. Do not be telling me he never let a word drop of his intention."

Anna could not answer. She had been sitting before him searching his face for hope or consolation, but as the prospect of either melted with every word he gave her, she rose at last and walked to the window, for fear she should demean herself. Could it be possible? Was any man – and Duncan before all capable of so cruel a deceit as was in every word and look and act of his when she saw him last in this very room? Could he laugh as he had laughed, and coax, and banter, and kiss as he had done if he knew that in a day or two he was to wound her worse than with the dagger? Heedless of her visitor, she drew the letter from her bosom and searched it again for a key to the mystery, though every word of it was visible to her inward eye, a separate sting in her memory. She was young (she had reflected), she had not the acquaintance of any women like herself; she did not know for certain what her due was from him who held her heart in the hollow of his hand; but surely, surely the trivial fact that they had made no promises did not make their claims on each other the less! Promise – he said he "asked no promise" – was the man mad? She had almost found excuses before; now in the knowledge of what his brother told her, the letter was an insult: a wild proud anger whelmed her; she walked to the hearth tearing the paper in pieces and thrust them in the fire.

Col slyly watched, guessing her thoughts, indulging an admiration. She had never seemed more desirable for her own sake: a girl so fine would be thrown away on his brother, even if she had not a farthing. The burning of the letter greatly pleased him, – he could have cheered when he saw it flare, no more warmly than her face that now she turned on him in a very different spirit from that she had before.

"Your brother has been rude," she said. "The poorest cotter in Uist would not have treated us so, and I think we deserved some more consideration, Ludovick and I. He was here on Tuesday, he said not a word that gave a hint of his intention; indeed his last words were a promise to be here on Sunday, and that he should steal away like this is disgraceful. His letter makes his rudeness all the worse: I would sooner he had sent his good-byes with yourself or some casual messenger or omitted them altogether."

"You will not do poor Duncan an injustice," said Col, in a great display of mortification. "I felt sure he told you he was going; but as he did not, it may well enough be that he made up his mind only after he met you."

Anna laughed with no gaiety.

"That would be a poor compliment to my attractions, Mr Col," said she.

"I mean he may have decided between here and Corodale."

"Surely a step more momentous was never determined on upon so short a journey. That was the variable sands indeed, as you say. You are anxious to excuse your brother, and I cannot but think all the better of you for it, but – Where is he gone to? I hope I am not prying too closely into his private affairs; if so, you must excuse me."

"Not at all, Miss Anna, not at all," said Col, who could not have had her in a mood to please him better. "Who has a better right to ask?"

"I make no claim to the honour," Anna hastened to explain. "I have no right at all so far as your brother is concerned."

"Faith, luck is with me there again," reflected Col who did not think she could have been free for such a declaration. "Beyond that he makes for the low country," he said, "and will write first from Edinburgh, I know no more than yourself, Miss Anna. What he will be after depends on chance, and we'll learn in good time, I daresay."

"Oh, there's no hurry, I assure you," said Anna. "Just a woman's curiosity on my part, you know. And Ludovick might be asking. Perhaps your brother will write us by-and-by if he can find the time. I am sorry to seem so curious, but an old friend of your brother's may perhaps presume to take the liberty: the reasons for so sudden a departure must have been grave?"

"What brought him to the bit he never told me, but Corodale is not Paris as I have said, Miss Anna, and it has long been in Duncan's mind since he came back from the college that Corodale was scarcely the place to keep two idle gentlemen."

"Idle gentlemen? So far as I have heard, neither of you was idle; your brother gave yourself the credit of working early and late. I hope we did not trespass too much on his time in Boisdale."

"Well, I have always done my best, and he was active enough, himself, there's no denying it."

"And you are said to have done very well with the Corodale skiffs this season," said Anna, who had the ears of a housewife.

"Middling, middling," said Col hurriedly. "I'm far from complaining. It's not an earldom, Corodale, and it's not plain *fuarag* for breakfast!"

"So far from that, it's very good indeed by all accounts," said the housekeeper.

Col eyed her quickly. "Did Duncan say that?" he asked.

"Your brother never brought his business affairs to Boisdale, Mr Col," said Anna, reddening a little; "and I'm not very sure that he knew himself."

Col laughed. "Well, the place can still keep a man and his wife at all events," said he, with a purpose in telling the truth for once.

"And if one of you had to go, the younger son –" She stopped suddenly, fearing she went too far.

Col was quite ready for that suggestion; had he not prepared for it?" That, Miss Anna, is the very thing I told him. It is true my father's and mother's notion was for Duncan to follow the priesthood and for me to look after the property that would have been out of our hands long ago if my father had not had his stroke of luck in his later years: but I have always treated Duncan since he came back as the head of Corodale, and offered to go away myself. Home or abroad, it is all one to Col, I assure you. Thank God, I can sail a ship or hold a plough if need be. But my brother had his mind set, and so I'm here to smooth his awkward leave-takings, it seems, and with no great capability, I'm thinking."

"You do very well," said Anna, sick of a conversation that fell on her ear like blows. She drummed on the arm of her chair with her fingers; her lips were parched, an outraged pride possessed her, so that for the time her love and grief were gone. She sometimes smiled when she spoke; she sometimes even laughed; a high colour had come frequently to her face, and Col was quite deceived. After all, he thought, madame was no way badly hit but in her self-esteem, and that was its own cure: there was nothing settled between Duncan and her. This return to a siege he had abandoned for Duncan was opening full of promise. She was a rich woman, she was a fine woman, he had never seen her looking better than now, with her girlishness taken flight miraculously. But for the misfortune that had found him from home when Dark John came with a bidding to Dermosary's funeral, things might have been on the best of footings ever since, and no need for plots. In three months Anna would be more beautiful by twenty thousand pounds: he must ply a fast suit now that there was the opportunity.

Ludovick came back to find his visitor laying bare a score of enterprises by which Corodale was to be as wealthy as in the days of his grandfather, when kelp was at two hundred shillings, and Anna courageously listening, and joining, to all appearance, in his interest, but with a face her brother saw revealed there was no consolation. What an idiot was this, to be so talkative about his miserable ambitions that he could not see the tragedy before him!

"O Ludovick!" cried Anna, when he entered, turning on him eyes that prayed for release; "Mr Col has been telling me that we have done his brother injustice. It seems he has always been keeping his ambitions in check, and that the poor Isles are at last insufferable."

"Is that it?" said the priest blankly, bewildered at an aspect of Duncan's character he had never seen a sign of, downcast for his sister's sake who so gallantly hid her torture. A trying stillness fell upon the three of them till Col's good sense came tardily to him, and he rose to go.

"I hope," said he airily, "it will make no difference in your friendship to myself. At the worst the thing was a stupidity I did my best to put a check on."

"Of course not, Col – of course not!" said the priest; "come over as often as you can to see us. We have few callers at Boisdale. Your brother was always welcome. Ambition!" he laughed sadly. "Well, that's beyond me; a world I cannot set a foot in, but no matter. To jostle in the market for the upper hand, isn't it? to plan for the best of every packman's bargain, to sweat for place and fortune – alas! poor Duncan gone so far adrift from Corodale and contentment."

"Not contentment, Ludovick," said Anna. "I am afraid you and I have been very dull. Not contentment, his brother assures me."

Afraid for his sister, the priest almost hurried his guest away. They had not rightly left the door when Anna fled to her room. She stood for a little there calling back her indignation, that somehow now scurvily deserted her; but the storm in her bosom found escape in tears, even as she struggled for control. Then she came down and rued most bitterly the burning of her letter, that was now grey ash on the hearth-stone.

CHAPTER XXIII

In Shealing Days

JIB-BOOM and his sloop came three times over the Minch from Lowland voyages (for Corodale's trade was thriving): thrice, Anna, hearing the *Happy Return* was back at Uskavagh, went to bed early to hasten her happiness, all in a tremor that kept her awake thinking, "To-morrow! to-morrow! there is sure to be word for me to-morrow"; but the morrow left her desolate. Col would come on these occasions with a face drawn as long as a fiddle, and empty-handed, with not a scrap of news, blaming his brother in a heat of manly annoyance, but cunningly mixing brotherly excuses and the sentiments of a noble loyalty with his blaming. Anna prized his awkwardest advocacy, but somehow was always dubious of her visitor. She was glad to see him go, and still he would be no sooner gone than she must long for his returning: he was her hope, he was her single bond with the mainland, where Duncan had so strangely vanished. The weeks, for all but her, went past on birds' wings, as Uist says. Summer came with the mouth of melody and exceeding bland, songs on the mountain, pipings and twitterings along the machar and in the sounding sea-arcades. Atlantic in that weather dozed in the yellow bays – the seamen's friend; west winds fanned the reeds; the tranquil islanders turned the taste of soft sea-breezes on the palate, smacking the tang of it as if it were a liquor, and with their tilling done, passed their days awhile in an idleness that was blessed to soul and body. Of every household in the Isles only Boisdale presbytery did not share the season's influences. Not that Anna, though grieving, was without a smile, or went abroad with a face inviting compassion. She was Herself as much as ever (to all but Ludovick sometimes and her evening pillow), and even Col, eagerly watching for his own encouragement, could see no sign that she had more than a temperate interest in Duncan. Col was the New Man again, diligent at Mass, constant in attendance at Boisdale presbytery: seeing Anna as brisk and cheerful as before, the delight of the townships, jocular with plain folk, diligent in her housewifery, as perjink as ever in her attire, it was little wonder he deluded himself with the belief that his prospects brightened. There was nothing in her manner to tell him that the wound to her pride was clean forgotten, and that she was back to her old devotion and hopeful of being made happy by-and-by.

It came to the time of the summer shearings, when the cattle grazed on the uplands till the corn of the levels should ripen for the hook. On a day in early June the people of the island rose and gathered together sheep and cattle and horses, and drove them to the hill recesses and the table-lands of Hecla and Benmore. All the world went – women and men and children, and sang on the way; God's flame, the butter-fly, the *dealan-de*, no airier among the flowers than the Boisdale bairns that romped in the wayside hollows or clambered up *eas* and corri, the lark shaking his soul out in the blue. Father Ludovick having prayed, and blessed their going, looked after them, with Anna, from the chapel rock with something of envy.

"There goes mankind at its simplest, and best, and cleanest!" said he.

"I'm in the humour to admit the simplest, and will even stretch a point, and say the best, but not, sage man! the cleanest," answered Anna playfully. "Did you not see Dark John? He looks as if his terror of water extended now to the very wells."

Ludovick did not hear her; he was lost in his abstraction, stirred within by vague associations roused at the sight of that wandering band. "I declare," said he, "the shearing season always makes me wish fortune had made me something else than a priest. My pasture on the machar here is bare enough, God knows! with a constant nibbling at the same old doctrines. I wish I could take my flock into some place of juicy grasses in among the hills, lush fresh grasses of the mind, and breezy hills of speculation. I'm tired, I'm tired!"

He looked uneasy at the huddled little hamlets that gathered round Stella Maris, children of the church, God love them! how he felt for them!

"Just the vapours, Ludovick, nothing else," said Anna putting her arm in his and very tender, "come home and I'll make you a dish of tea. You'll be much more comfortable at night in Boisdale presbytery, I assure you, than in a hole m the wall of a shearing bothy."

He laughed at himself and her, but still was mildly sorrowful, half for parting with his people, half for his inability to go with them.

Indeed, it was no wonder a poor priest should crave for Airi-nam-bo. What better could Eden offer than that green garden of mountain grass and flower on the slope of high Benmore! When at noon the people reached it they could not but think it blessed, looking on Loch Eynort, looking out upon the Minch and far to Skye with its peaks snow-silvered yet, and the purple deep of glens looking to Tiree and Coll, the flat fat granaries of the Isles – green rafts floating on the sea, looking to Arisaig and Ardnamurchan vexed so much by storm, and Mull of the mountains. While the men repaired the bothies and the women cooked the shearing feast, how the children of Boisdale played! Dark John, who had come with the cattle of a better man at sea, could not but stop his mending the pleats of a wicker door to look at them noisy in the haunts of last year's holidays, startling the sea-fowl from the cliffs and chasing the trout up mossy burns. Households clustered on the grass when the meal was ready, the wilderness was festival.

"Draw in, good man, draw in," said the Dalvoolin woman to John, who, being no wife's man, was the guest of any that would take him. "Draw in, just man, and try my good-daughter's cheese. It is not every day we kill a wedder. Long's the way you have to go back to-night, unless you will be sharing some *crupa* and biding till the morn."

He spat seaware, and took a seaman's knife to the kebboch. "Not a bit of me," said he. "I must be at my trade this very night, and my trade is on the leaping sea."

"With your trews rolled up over the knees and you wading with a fish-spear," said the virgin woman Bell Vore. "Could you not be content in the burns of Airi-nam-bo with the baggy-minnows?"

The men and women, sitting in a circle of stones, laughed at John's vexation that made him dumb. He put his hand in his pocket and took a little dulse, the stuff that makes men brave who have plumbed sea-depths, and had the vision yellowed, and filled their stomachs with the bitter beginnings of creation.

"Come, John! Bell Vore must aye be sharp as the shelister: never mind her, but stretch your hand and try again my own good-daughter's cheese," said the kindly dame of Dalvoolin. "'Tis sweeter by far, I'll warrant, and fuller of nourishment, than that seaweed. God! that a man should waste his stomach on such trash!"

Dark John took cheese again and a thick oatcake, with butter spread inch-thick by the goodwife's thumb. He wished that he were gone, for he feared the women, and the virgin most of all, certain of late she had some plot to marry him. The families were scattered on either side of the burn where the children waded; great talk and laughter sounded everywhere but at his group; the smoke of fifty peat-fires rose lazy in the air of the afternoon, and a diligent man was tuning a pipe to a dance-tune in a cave of the cliff below them.

"Fine I know the reason for your hurrying, just man," said Bell Vore, at him again. "You are not going back to Boisdale at all this evening, but are bound for Corodale."

"It was in my mind, I'm not denying," he confessed, alarmed at her divination of a thing he had never mentioned. "But who could have told you that, Bell Vore?"

"Oh, I guessed," said she; "you were not within a handful of miles of Col without communication. You are very chief of late with that fine gentleman; 'tis not, I'll warrant, what you get from him of jingling wages."

"Daughter of the one I'll mention not, sing dumb, sing dumb, I'm bidding you?" cried John. "There's not his better in the three islands! *Oh righ!* did he not save my life!"

"More shame to him, the meddler! and let him take what he'll get for it if there's any truth in proverbs."

"I wish Herself had not so much to do with that same Col," said the goodwife. "Have you seen the mouth of him, neighbours? Take a look at it if you get the chance on a sunny day or on the right side of a crusie-light, and you will see the miser. I do not like to see that *biorach* mouth so much in Boisdale chapel, nor his foot so often at the white-house door."

"Och! there is nothing wrong with the fellow at all, at all," cried some of the men who were hacking the cheese. "The prettiest man in the islands, and a back on him like the gable of a house."

"Oh, very well, very well!" said the goodwife. "You can have it what way you like, my loves. Ill would it become me to call myself a judge where my goodman was before me. Indeed it is well enough known that wisdom abides in breeks. But I'll be keeping my own opinion."

"Hush! hush! I'm putting command on you," said her husband; "you must not be judging the gentry –"

"Gentry indeed! he's that but on the half-side; what was his father but Para Dubh? so mean a fellow he would not let his kitchenmaids pare the rinds off their cheese."

"Oh men! men!" cried the spinster, and looked at Dark John as if he had been dirt.

The sweat broke out on him. "On my soul!" he thought; "there's the devil himself in that woman: she'll have me yet if my luck leaves me."

"Have you seen him at Mass, men and women? I need not be asking the girls – faith! they see nothing else. He has his eye more often on Herself than on Master Ludovick. And little I like his affability, neighbours, with his sweet word of day for rich and poor, his Master This and Goodwife Yon: be sure I'm telling you he has his reason for it."

"Och, men! men!" said the virgin again, and put her tongue a little way out at Dark John.

"Oh yes, I'm away with it! she has got her eye on me, and I might be her father; five-years-and-ten-and-three-twenties of age come Martinmas," thought he, and his sea-weed had as little taste as shavings.

"Corodale is of the very best," the men maintained, – "not the beat of him in the Isles for sport and for ability. He was on the top of the brae when courage was given away and good looks were going."

"It's the truth you have there, lads," said Dark John, and started to tell again for the hundredth time since Michaelmas last how he felt when the waves swept over him and he tasted the deepmost brine. It was a story he told in a wonderful way to make women gasp and men uneasy The horrors of it ever grew with each narration: from other fires men and women ran across to listen; the children, seeing his movements and hearing his voice so high, ran up too; he put the blood of his heart in his thinking, and held them in a spell.

Only Bell Vore, the virgin woman, kept her own humour, and when the tale was done she was back to her jibes again.

"Yes, yes, he fished you out, and I'll warrant he'll make you pay for it. You might be Corodale's *gillie cas fleuch*, to see you coming and going upon his errands."

"I would go to the Worst Place for him," said Dark John, and banged his fist on the rock he sat on.

"Och! you will go there anyway, and Corodale will have to be putting up with your company," said the woman, who found that folk enjoyed her humour. "My grief! my loss! my hope and my losing!" thought Dark John, "here's a woman sure with her love on me, wasn't I foolish this day to come to Airi-nam-bo?"

"It's busy your master is nowadays at the courting; but if his brother, a better man, was here, Herself was better pleased, I'll warrant. Och! it is a scandal – a scandal! Col Corodale never came over the moss so often unless he had a greedy man's purpose. Pity on me that I was not her mother, to bid her beware of the gled."

"I'm thinking now we need not be bothered about that," said the goodwife. "Master Ludovick, who knows everything, will be sure to have the sight of him, and indeed she makes it plain enough herself that she has no taste for him and his Spanish beard. Do you not see it, neighbours? When it was Duncan was after her we dared not go round a corner without a cough for the fear of meeting them, and her with her face like the fire for shame. If she has to take a step from the door with this fellow she will go out of her way to meet the like of you and me, and stop and gossip till the man is yawning."

"It is right enough you are there, good woman," said the neighbours. "Have we not seen it ourselves?"

"And the *Ron*, now – the little boat – did ever yourselves see her set foot on it since this fellow took to the wooing?"

"Not once!" said the men, who in Duncan's time had so often called their women to the door to see a boat in the splash of the moon in the Sound.

Dark John in his trouble at a new discovery forgot that the spinster hunted him. If Col was courting in vain, farewell to the fifty years' fortune! He had thought things went well, his notion being that women by nature took to the man who came handiest.

The men stretched themselves lazily, the sun hot on the backs of them, and rose to their occupations. Some were fishers, and must return to their boats in Boisdale, for the white fish ran till the end of June. They left their wives and daughters in the shearing, and set off on their way across the heather. Cows came in for milking; women put their cheeks against the flanks, and the milk purred in wooden cogues. Still Dark John stayed in Airi-nam-bo, fearing Bell Vore, and yet in a fascination. She paid no heed to him, but that did not deceive him: well enough he knew that she was wishing him, and if she had no pity, he was gone, that had so often boasted never a petticoat should master him and spoil the peace of his home. He chewed his sea-weed, roamed from door to door of the summer-huts, green with winter mosses, but always found himself, sooner or later, drawn to the side of the spinster woman, where she eyed him with contempt and to his great confusion.

"It is time you were off to your master," she told him at last, but in a way, he thought, that dared him.

"There was never a man that mastered Dark John," said he.

"Nor a woman that called him master either," said the spinster. "Och! poor creature!"

"Saints help me now!" he thought; "she'll drag me, right or wrong, to the Boisdale altar. To the devil with them and their courting!"

"I'm asking you this," she said on another tack; "what took the other one away?"

"Who?" asked John.

She put out her tongue at him: he saw there was no use beating about the bush with this Bell Vore. "It's more than I can tell you, I declare," said he, "unless it was his feet."

"Sharp! sharp!" said Bell Vore. "There's a tongue wants clipping. The man would be a fool that would tell you. If it was not that they quarrelled, and the like has happened before with sweethearts, your man has put between them, with his eye on the *ulaidh*."

"The other fellow had his eye on it too, if there's anything in the song; and if fortunes are going, who but the cunningest deserves them?"

The spinster stopped her milking, and rose with her cogue to make for the bothy. "It's time you were off," she told him again; "and you may be telling your master there'll be day about with him for this. Some of us know very well how came the song and what sent Master Duncan to take the world for his pillow. Are you hearing, *gioltair?* – are you hearing? Tell him we'll have his brother back in Boisdale before the heather."

He stood dumfoundered where she left him. Faith, this was news more dire than ever! If Col's plot was known to women like Bell Vore, it was as good as published to the world in another week, and Col's chance was gone. Who could have told her? It was something more than a guess. He chewed dulse and hung about the shearing for another hour, hoping he might learn more; but nothing came of it.

Then he made for Corodale through the Pass, and skirted the shore, where wild geese – barnacle, lag, and brent – answered the gander's loud "Honk! honk!" The night was before him at Corodale; stars as thick as herrings in a trammel-net gladdened the sky, but Corodale House was black; and his old ill-luck in that house was with him, for Col was not at home. He was in Benbecula, the women said.

CHAPTER XXIV

Sand Drift

THE inn of Creggans, rimed with the salt of nor'-west storms, its rannoch thatch rotting to dust in the summer weather, was a place that of late the world avoided. The tenant was a brute – so went the estimate of the two Uists, – he kept poor ale, and thrashed his woman. Folk crossing the Long Ford now made their way by Gramisdale, and Creggans was left for weeks forlorn, with not so much as a drover, drunken and wandered, or a man with a pack, to bring it news of the out-world. When door or window opened it gulped the sifted sand. Round the sea-side of the walls of it the sand swept in drifts as if it had been snow, and so thick was on the window-sills that the cockle might have bred there. Sand was ankle-deep on the path that led to it; sand smothered the poor garden, where stunted kale never took heart; sand was in the tankards, sand in the meal. In windy days the place was in a constant stour; and in calm bright weather any one who saw it from the ford, sand-grey like the skull of a ruined keep, was bound to think it desolate and forbidding.

"Christ! that I should come to this, that have had other chances and have seen elsewhere!" was the Sergeant's constant lamentation.

He would stand by the hour at his door, not hoping any more for custom, for that was plainly gone for good elsewhere, but speculating in a gloom upon the prospect. The sand, he thought, would creep up, and up, on Creggans Inn till it choked the windows, till it reached the roof, till it closed the chimney, and he and his wife were buried – the slut! that crept about the house in terror of his eye, long since beat to keep the place in order. For weeks on end of fine weather the ground about him was smooth as a board with the sand. One morning when he rose and looked out, he saw it trampled – people had ventured to the place, and in the dawning gazed at it and gone away again without knock or halloo, plainly thinking the inn abandoned! He felt at first when he looked at the footsteps then like a man shipwrecked on an isle, and a ship gone past him when he was sleeping; and then he was in a fury of rage at what he thought an insult, all the worse because it was not so intended.

It was the more vexatious because from his door he could see the traffic of the Isles pass over the trough of Gramisdale. In his neighbourhood there was only the cursed life of the wastes. The bittern would be rising there, booming in the dusk – its voice an exhalation of the stagnant pools, the very breath of dreariness and decay; the whaup night and day went mourning there. That, perhaps, was not unusual: what he felt the most was when grey-lag geese, tenants more properly of the outer rocks, came in before Atlantic storms and cleaned the sand from their feathers almost at his door, manifestly thinking Creggans no better than a lifeless boulder of the tide.

And no farther off than a mile or two the world was in so fine a bustle! For hours at a time he would stand in blasphemy to see the open ford in a constant throng, crossed by cattle, horse, and sheep, by men and women for kirk or market, avoiding him and his inn as if he had a pest there.

He was standing at the door in that mood, the sand searching over the mouth of his shoes, when Dark John from Boisdale came in view of the inn. The Sergeant, with a seaman's eye, caught sight of him as soon as his head showed over the brae on the track that so rarely knew a footstep, and he turned to bellow to his wife that some one came.

Dark John drew forward, wearied to the bone by his travelling, dragging his feet through the sand, casting an astonished look at this forbidding tavern.

"Hail to the house!" said he, hawking dust from his throat and rubbing his smarting eyes. "O king! but this is the spot for an alehouse! Let a man of any parts and the right accommodation be here but for a day or two with the wind from a proper airt, and he would have a happy drouth that would drain every cask on the gantries."

"What is't you're wanting here?" said the Sergeant with a black brow, keeping his breadth in the door, for Dark John was not like to be the most desirable of customers.

"The sand from my throat first, and then a word with Corodale," said the visitor, chinking some coppers to show he had the wherewithal. The innkeeper let him in and beat the dust from the bottom of a can. "I have not clapped an eye on Corodale for a fortnight," said he.

"My own soul! You're not saying that?" cried John, astonished. "Och, may the devil take all bad counsel! Have I not been wearing the soles off my feet since yesterday in search of him, and his own servants said he was for certain in Benbecula? My grief! such walking! Not an open door on the way with the folk being at the shearings, and I with hunger and thirst and sleepiness. Fill her again, master, fill her again; that was no more than a damp spot on my thrapple, a dew on a kelp-kiln! Once upon a time I drank the sea. Faith! your tankards are meat and drink I If I'm not mistaken I gulped a spout-fish yonder. One would not need to go to the strand for bait in Creggans. Corodale not here!"

"Not since Saturday was a fortnight, I'm telling you, unless he sank over the head in the sand-drift at the door," said the innkeeper, who was in the bitter state where he could scoff at his own misfortunes. "It's no great odds to me except that it's a saving of money, for when Corodale's travelling this way his purse keeps house at home. I make no doubt if he's in Benbecula he's over at Uskavagh keeping his eye on the sloop, for fear the letters she brings across the Minch get into the wrong hands. He's an anxious man, is Corodale, about his letters."

"Is he indeed? Now, are you telling me?" said John, blinking into his can and pretending he knew nothing.

The innkeeper gave him but the one look, and coughed.

"I need not tell you," said he, "for you know very well already. You and Col are pretty chief, and it's there you're like myself."

"So far as that goes", said Dark John, and stopped with a troubled face, his hand in his waistcoat pocket. "You do not happen to have the least bit dulse about you?" said he.

"No, man, I'm clean out of the thing just at present," said the innkeeper, who knew the old man's oddity; "but I would not wonder if you got it growing against the gable of the house."

"I must just be doing without it, then. I happened to take the droll notion for a taste. As for Corodale, I'll admit I'm in his reverence. You'll have heard about his diving for me over at Kintra last Michaelmas, and I'm like yourself, I would do him a good turn. I would have liked to see him; for nothing else have I been walking all the night, except for an hour or two in a loft at Carnan."

"You'll have news, likely, good man? take another horn of the ale with me for company."

"Your health! I heard a matter yonder from a woman they call Bell Vore in Airi-nam-bo, Loch Eynort."

"My wife's second cousin: if gossip were going, there was no surer place to get it."

"It was that the other fellow, Duncan, was likely to be back soon, and I had the notion that the news might interest Master Col," said Dark John, who knew how came the song to Boisdale.

The innkeeper put down his drink when it was halfway to his mouth. "What!" he cried, and swore most foully. "His brother coming back!" His pock-marked face was grey with astonishment and vexation. "Tut! tut! that was the thing I was always thinking of. Now what the devil should bring him back at this time? A more unfortunate thing could not have happened."

"That's what I'm thinking myself," said the old man, with his eye on the innkeeper's wife, who passed through the kitchen. "Go out of this at once and feed the hens!" her husband bawled at her, and she fled at once, a most obedient woman.

The innkeeper spilled out more ale, turned the grit on his tongue, and fell in thought. To the door went John, dragged there in spite of himself to sniff the weed that festered in the sun. It set him craving. Over the sand he went, and the bent-grass, to the sea-edge. Some rocks stood out a little, the sea lapping the wreck that grew on them: out he went, wading over the knees, and plucked the dulse in a ravenous handful, cramming the sappy salt weed in his mouth and chewing it like a glutton. He might have been a monster of the deep, some uncanny soulless thing, in the form of man briefly borrowed for villainous devices, slobbering the stuff that feeds itself on ooze and slime. The sea-birds did not fear him, – they wheeled and squealed about his head. He came back to the inn refreshed, his pockets stuffed with the dripping dulse, and found the table roughly set for a meal.

"You'll have a bite with we," said the innkeeper, very genial They ate in silence, Dark John's hunger gone, sparing even of the ale, and preferring the taste of the seaweed on his palate.

"Ah!" said the Sergeant, when they were done and his wife had cleared the table, "and the other one's coming back, you're telling me? That's news! it's not to Col's advantage."

"Just so! just so! 'tis the truth you have there, and I'm here for nothing else but to tell him that: mo *thruagh!* that I must be hunting for him other wheres."

"No hurry for that, – he'll learn it fast enough if Bell Vore is in the secret." He leaned across to whisper, with a side-glance at the door for fear his wife was listening. "How are affairs at Boisdale?" he asked. "There's a white-house yonder and a woman in it – eh? Does he come any speed?"

"If you have seen a buckie-whelk crawling, that's him for the speed of him. So the women tell me. Praise Mary! I'm a plain man myself, and no judge of sweethearting, though many a one's been after me; and one no later gone than yesterday – bad death to her! Unless he stuns Herself with an oar, and drags her to the altar before she gets her senses back, she'll never be made to marry him. And that's a thing beyond me; for look at the fine, big, gallant fellow!"

The innkeeper rubbed his chin and scanned the face before him, wondering to what lengths the old rogue could be trusted. If Col could put his trust in him, surely he could do so too?

"There's a lump of money in it," he ventured. "It's likely you'll have heard?"

"Before you were born, good man. Was I not at the shifting of it fifty years ago from Arisaig, and myself a halflin lad?"

"So they tell me; I have heard Col mention it. It's a pity he comes such poor speed – particularly if his brother Duncan's likely to come back so soon before there's anything settled. Twenty thousand! a fine round hearty figure."

"I saw it myself with my own two eyes, and no one else's, running out on the deck of Colin-Calum-Angus's skiff like cockles from a basket. The sound of it, I'll warrant you, was noble, noble."

"O Lord! 'tis a pity Col comes such poor speed, and you and myself so willing to help him," said the innkeeper. "Do you think there is no chance for him to marry the girl?"

"No more than there is for myself, and I am not thinking to ask her."

The innkeeper rose to shut the door; looked from his window over the sand, from a custom that might very well be done without, to see if any traveller came, and drew his stool closer to Dark John's. He spoke fast, like one that burst with a project commanding every passion.

"We're a bonny pair of fools!" said he; "egging on this Col to a fortune he has so little chance of getting, and would neither share with us nor thank us for if he got. Duncan's coming back, you're telling me; very well! that settles it for Col, and it's an ill wind that sits in nobody's sail. Are you hearing? The money's yonder somewhere, and she's the only one knows where it is, for the priest himself said so. What's to hinder two well-deserving fellows like ourselves – eh?"

Dark John saw the speaker's thought, – ground his teeth through the sea-weed, felt the horror afresh of Barra deep, and made up his mind. It was plain Col Corodale's interest was here to be protected.

"And how would we be getting it, Master Sergeant?" he asked. "Tell me that!"

"Fifteen years I followed the sea and five was in the Royals. I know women, on my soul, better than any man that walks Long Isle sand."

"Then you know the one thing beats me, myself, Dark John! She and the sea – my loss! they're terrible! terrible! terrible!"

"Put yon one before me here and me with my hand on her –" the innkeeper clenched his hands together with a shake of them as if he had a thing to crush, his pockmarked face purple, his eyeballs bloodied at the white. "What's this Corodale but a miser? I could knife him often for the way he scrapes about his feet for ha'pence and no need for it, for there is no man wealthier between the Barra Head and Berneray. MacNeil's Treasure jingles every bit as well wherever it is just now as it would do if Col got hold of it Little we would see of it if he married the girl and handled the stuff to-morrow."

The old man chewed his dulse and said never a word, but looked like one who sympathised.

"Mine is the seaman's motto and he on the last spar Every man for himself. Are you hearing, old fellow? What's to hinder the pair of us taking a turn at fortune, seeing Corodale has had a fair chance and made nothing at all of it?"

"I'm not of the marrying kind myself," said John, "and next door there's your mistress."

"Twenty thousand," said the innkeeper, paying no heed to this humour, "and in a place where the priest of Boisdale says it will lie till Doomsday. The wonder's on me that you could see it once and can sleep at night without an envy to be handling it."

The old man blinked and nodded his head, like one that had a new idea given to him.

"Bring her here," said the Sergeant, "bring her here! Give me half an hour of her in Creggans."

"My God, not murder!" cried the old man, staggered.

"Marriage, nor murder; are you taking me for a fool? I'm telling you I know women: half an hour of her in Creggans – not a second more. I'm sick of this Benbecula; there's nothing to lose in leaving it in a hurry but a cheap burial in sand."

"Just that!" said the old man; "but getting her here?"

"I had her once before when she came to Dermosary's burial; the room's up there she lay in. Thinks I at the time, 'twenty thousand pounds on my wife's bolster!' I could have her here by the week's end and the money ours by Monday if I had yourself to help me."

"I would not be the man to see you beat," said John.

CHAPTER XXV

The Kidnapping of Anna

SO Col saw the sloop on Monday beating to the south, and wondered where she went to, for his partner the Sergeant had mentioned nothing of a trip so soon. But Jib-boom was a skipper given to vagaries: he would shift his port on any jovial fancy that might come to him; the rumour of a wedding in any seaward part of Barra or of Uist was enough to set him hoisting at his anchor or throwing from the pawls and spreading sail in prospect of diversion. "A dancing somewhere, or a drunken wager," thought her half-owner as the ship lay over toward Boisdale Loch with every stitch of her straining. He looked at her with discontent from Corodale hill, grudging the chafe of cord and canvas that cost good money. If he could have guessed her object he would have cursed to himself on the hill more heartily than he did; but he was still the persevering lover (as the pipe-tune goes), and this new venture at the Treasure of MacNeil was out of his cognisance.

All the Hebrid Islands lay that day in a feverish heat that lessened the bounds of the thousand lakes, and made the rivers and burns whisper where ordinarily they cried: the sea itself had a look of shrinking, only the mountains swelled, and when at the fall of night the sloop ran through the Sound of Eriskay, its rocks and skerries seemed more numerous than they had ever done before. She cast her anchor in Boisdale Bay. Dark John, hovering like a bird of bad luck behind the townships, watching for her coming where himself would attract no attention from the few folk left at home there while the general world was at the shearings, saw her with a satisfaction.

Anna was in chapel, almost the only woman there. A couple of lug-sail boats from Castlebay were in the harbour that would otherwise have been vacant; some of their crew came up the hill, dipped calloused fingers in the holy water, and entered awkwardly on tiptoe, squeezed into seats here and there in the dim chapel, indulged but a single glance at the lady on her knees, and then began muttering their Gaelic prayers. Perhaps they had not so much to pray for as Anna, – at least their prayers were sooner done, and they had another glance at her as they left the chapel to set out on their evening toil.

She was, herself, the last to go. A troubled world waited her at the threshold, for up from the west, sudden and enormous, had come a cloud that raced the natural nightfall; and she had scarcely reached the shelter of the presbytery when thunder, horrible and abrupt, burst high above Benmore. There was but one wild peal of it, that seemed to shake the island. "Poor Ludovick!" she thought; "he is to have a wild night coming from Kilbride."

The night was warm, but she built a fire in readiness for his coming though he might not be for hours yet, put out dry clothing for him, and set a table for his supper, taking delight in these domestic offices, as if she were to entertain a company. There had been but the single thunder-peal, yet the living things that haunt the shore and the moor were terrified. Sea-gulls that had been quarrelling before the curing-sheds had disappeared, plover and whaup were dumb. The fowls that Anna kept behind the house ran frightened under the thatch-eaves of the byre, where a calf lowed pitifully, as if it felt some dread of the wide mysterious universe it had never seen.

She drew the curtains of the little window, and the last glance from it showed the anchor-light of the sloop that had taken Duncan from her, and as yet had brought back no word of comfort. It set her sadly thinking. Her hopes since he had gone were centred there, in the *Happy Return*, – the very name had a cheerful omen. If she could find no excuse for him when her pride was wounded first, she could readily now have found a score. He might be ill; he might be too far off to let her know so soon, he might, indeed, have written already, and her letter might be on the way, for in these days the written communication came to the Islands in ways precarious.

She sewed, she knitted, she read; no occupation could very long command her mind that night, so full she was of a distressing apprehension. Some trouble menaced: it was as one feels that wakes at morning having gone to bed with grief, and, seeing the cheerful common day, cannot for a little remember what the sorrow was, but feels its pain. They say in the Isles when such a spirit seizes one the danger is for others; Anna was bound to think that something threatened one or other of those she loved. There was a keepsake she wore at her neck – a Virgin Mary nut, the bean of the Moluccas – that Duncan had picked up on the Long Ford that morning he had spent with her there, and had mounted in silver; her fingers often went to it for comfort. Boisdale presbytery had never seemed so solitary before, horribly silent in the stupor of the night; the air heavy, the night oppressed with some tremendous purpose.

What came oftenest to her mind was that a person walked outside.

It was not that she heard anything, but the conviction grew that some one walked and some one waited. She went to the window and drew back the curtain, but nothing was to be seen when she looked out except the empty night, the light of Jib-boom's sloop its only star. She had just made sure of its vacancy when a loud knock came to the door. She stood speechless, doubting her senses, till the rapping was repeated. This was human life; she boldly opened the door. At first she was dismayed to see the man who stood there – Dark John, in the porch, his hands in his pockets, a shred of dulse in his cheek, and his jaws busy. He met her questioning look with an evasive eye.

"Take my excuses, mistress," he said quickly; "I saw the light."

"Master Ludovick is from home, John," said Anna, thinking he had been sent by some one for her brother. "I hope no one is ill."

"Not a bit, not a bit; we have all our very good health in Boisdale, and little else except that same to brag of. There was just a notion came to me yonder, when I saw the light in the window, that I heard Jib-boom make mention of some letters that were for you on the sloop, in Master Duncan of Corodale's writing."

A great joy gushed in every vein of her – ice gone, the barriers broken, the happy river running free again.

"For me, John? Are you sure? Come in, come in!" She took his arm, and almost pulled him into the room, that she might see his face more clearly, and assure herself that there was no deceit. His face was like a rock, his eye with no sincerity, and he chewed like an animal, but he was beautiful there and then for Anna.

"Jib-boom was on the quay a while ago: you know our ways in Boisdale, mistress; he got to his gossiping and mentioned it."

"He would have been better employed, the wretch, to fetch me in my letters," cried Anna. "And now, I suppose, I must keep my patience till the morning."

"Faith! it's myself would have taken a small boat and gone out for them, if that was all that was in it, mistress; but Jib-boom had a message for yourself or Master Ludovick. Did I not clean forget his reverence was over in Kilbride, or I would not have troubled you? When I saw the light, I thought to myself in the Gaelic he might be taking a turn out in the *Ron*, and that I could be taking the oars for him."

His voice was drowned in a thunder-peal that burst frightfully close at hand and clanged across the island. Rain fell in a sudden torrent, drumming on the dry hard ground; the house was full of noisy patterings. But Anna heard thunder nor rain, so loud her heart beat at the man's intelligence.

"I will go out myself, John," she said, determined, rolling up her hair that had been hanging in a pleat to her waist, her face rosy, her lips shaken with gladness. "I will be ready in a minute if you will row me out to the vessel."

"*Dhia!* it is impossible!" cried the man, himself abashed at the thunder. "The rain! just listen to the rain."

"Oh dear! poor Ludovick! how wet he will be! It is so good of you to come and tell me, John. We have been expecting some letters: they are important. The skipper's message may demand immediate attention, and a drop or two of rain will not keep me from learning what it is to-night. If you will sit here I will be ready in three minutes."

She picked up a candlestick, and ran upstairs with her great delight. "Och! isn't she agile, now – the creature?" said Dark John, and he sat with an absent eye, too deep engrossed in his project to look about him in the unfamiliar gentility of Father Ludovick's dwelling-place. So loud, so often, the thunder roared, so heavy the rain fell, that at first he was afraid the girl might baulk at the adventure. This storm was a misfortune: if she lost courage and forewent her resolution, a very fine scheme, for the time at least, was a failure. He was assured when he heard her come down the stair again, humming the air of a song.

"The element's there!" said he to himself. "MacNeils! MacNeils! weather is in the blood of them: this one, or I'm mistaken, would swim to the sloop if a small boat was not handy. Are they not all alike, the women? for the prospect of a man they take the fancy for, they would walk to the Worst Place."

He had some fear for himself now, so wild the night was sounding. Anna saw it in his face when she came downstairs wrapped for her adventure.

"On my own soul, mistress," said he with his knees to the fire and grudging to leave the comfort of it, "I'm not fond of the task for you. Master Ludovick will be blaming me for taking you out in such a night."

"It's the other way, and I am taking you," said Anna. "If we lose no time about it, we may easily be back before my brother."

A thunderbolt burst above Benmore with a sound that could be no greater if the mountain shattered. Dark John ducked his head, with eyes for a second full of horror.

"By God!" said he, "did I not think it was the world's end, yon? and myself scarce ready. I wish I had not troubled you. Faith! there may be no more than words in Jib-boom's story, and no letters at all."

"What!" cried Anna with a sinking heart, but saw in a moment it was the coward spoke. "That settles it; if the sail was to Barra itself instead of out into the bay, I would not put it off another minute. Come down and launch the *Ron* with me, and I will go myself if you do not care to come."

She would listen to no protest; she went out in the darkness with no ears for him and all eyes for the light of the sloop, that to-night was more sweet for her than any star as it shone through the blurring rain. The thunder rolled more distant to the north over Eaval Mount; in a flash of lightning the chapel jumped to the eye, miraculous, steadfast, unafraid of the furies that terrorise mankind; it would have given Anna courage if she had it not by nature and the eagerness of her object. Very warm and thick the rain fell from the warring heavens like gouts of blood; the isle was full of scents, most marvellous fresh, most clear, scents of myrtle and heather-tip and flowers that in the common day have perfume only for the bee.

Anna went quickly through the darkness, the old man at her heels.

The sloop, when they reached her, was sound asleep, the gluck of the tide at her counter. A sea-bird rose with a cry from a spar, but no one hailed. Dark John climbed on board and crept to a companion aft. He stamped lightly on the deck-light, chewed dulse, and set a bleared, abstracted eye on the lamp that swung above the chains. Now, the thunder was remote and muttering, the rain completely gone, and in the cordage a cool breeze hummed. No one answered; he tried again, and some one moved below. There was a snap of steel, the deck-light glowed, and by-and-by the companion opened.

"It is I that am in it," said Dark John in a whisper. "She's with me, yon one."

"Oh, now the devil!" said Jib-boom, standing in the doorway in his breeches, shivering. "And I so snug! What put it in your head to choose a night like this? I made sure you would not trouble us till to-morrow or later maybe, and I hear of a notable merriment in Kintra for Wednesday. By the Book! what thundering was yonder!"

"It had to be to-night, or maybe not at all," said the old man. "Her brother went to Kilbride in the morning. On with your boots briskly, brave man!"

Jib-boom drew sea boots on, still grumbling, and at the business heard the voice of Anna. She called from the *Ron* she sat in, "You have some message for me, John tells me."

"Bad death on me if I care for the business!" muttered Jib-boom, stepping to the bulwark. "You're there," said he; "give me your hand," and helped her to the deck.

"I'm sorry to disturb you," said she.

"It's of no account," he assured her; "I meant to call at the white-house in the morning, but seeing you're here, I'll ask you to step into my cabin." She hung back a little dubious. "The men are forward," he explained, "and I'm here myself, in state, like MacNeil of Barra; at least we'll need a light to see what we are doing."

She stepped under the low companion and descended, the skipper close behind her. Dark John stayed on deck. The painter of the *Ron* was fastened to the rail; he loosened and threw it off. The boat drifted slowly from the side of the sloop; he could hear it, though he could not see it.

"O king!" said he; "will there not be searching of the sea to-morrow?"

CHAPTER XXVI

A Night's Voyage

THE sloop was like the grave, her only voice the ripple at her bows as she swung to her chain; the isle of Uist was asleep, with the thunder an echo far off, somewhere to the north-east, waking the glens in Skye. Dark John stood on the deck, fidgeting, all ears for a sound from below, when the skipper burst from the companion, ran past him in the dark, and bawled in the forepart of the ship upon his hands. They came up half-clad; he set them to the halyards, crying out his orders like a man demented with some sudden fear, and himself pulling at ropes as if his vessel was on a lee shore and her helm gone

"Skipper! skipper!" said one of the Macleods, spitting on his hands, "have you heard by any chance of a dancing anywhere that there should be such a devil's hurry, and us in the middle of our sleep?" But Jib-boom was not for argument or explanation, and aimed a blow at him that threw him up against the windlass. "When you're there anyway," said he, "just up with her anchor, and then you'll maybe waken." The smugglers, used to sudden alarms, wrought fast and hard; a south-west wind blowing briskly into the bay made their quittance easy; Dark John was still without a word of explanation when the *Happy Return* was sailing, froth at her bows and her sticks all creaking, along the island's edge, making for Benbecula. He was the only one on the ship beyond her skipper who knew they carried an unwilling passenger.

"Faith! you have not lost much time about it, whatever," said he at the first chance he got of a word.

Jib-boom was in a sweat. He stood under the lantern, mopping his face and glowering at the deck, like a man in some confusion of mind, though the navigation of his ship might have been expected more properly to engage him.

"This is the bonny business!" said he. "I took in hand with the pock-marked fellow up yonder in Creggans to carry your passenger, but little was it in my mind that this would be the sort of person I have here."

"Well, she came quiet enough with me, I'll warrant you," said John; "and so far as I could hear, she did not make much objection with yourself."

"And that's the cursed thing!" cried the skipper; "if she had made an uproar I could have managed to get up a spirit in myself; but there she's bolted in my cabin, the better of me with her eye and with her answer, and no more in fear of me than I'm in fear of yourself, John Dark. 'Haste ye with my letters, good man!' said she when she got down and saw me standing, something like an idiot I can tell you, for the sight of her there gave me the first true notion of what a business I had taken in hand with. – 'Haste ye with the letters, good man!' said she, I'm thinking just a bit dubious for the first time herself. 'They're not exactly what you would call here,' said I to her, and little in the humour, I assure you. 'Then,' said she, making to leave, 'I'm made a fool of; I might have known better than to put my trust in the words of an old rascal.'"

"Och! now the creature!" said Dark John, and felt for the solace of his pocket.

"'They're not here the letters,' said I; 'but I'm told they're yonder in Benbecula, and my orders were to bring you there and get them.' 'Whose orders?' said she, like the shutting of a knife. 'Just so!' I thought at that; 'get you on your high horse, mistress, and I'll be in better key to follow you.' 'The Sergeant's orders,' said I. 'It's his great desire to have a word with you up yonder in a place they call the Creggans.' 'I know it very well,' said she; 'the place and the man I have no desire myself to see, and I demand that I'm set ashore this instant.' I'll never deny that at that I swithered, for she was so cool. But she did a thing that made me keep my promise to the Sergeant; she looked about and saw a knife that was on a shelf, and thinking I did not see her, whips it under her plaid, with her face getting red. Thinks I, 'My lady, you are able to look after yourself!' and with that I steps back and locks the door on her. It's the first time ever there was a key turned in my command, and I'll warrant it's the last. She never gave a cry, and I'm not in the humour at all, at all!"

He turned round at a sound of flapping canvas, and damned his men for slack cloth.

"There's a gale behind us there," said he to the old man; "but I'll take the whole of it in my sails if I was blown over Benmore, for I'm anxious to get quit of my share of this affair that never came an honest smuggler's way before. Give me the Barra stuff, if it was gulping in the scuppers and all the country chasing me. I could make something of it; but here was I in my dreams so easy on's, and you drag me from my blanket to deal with a woman."

"They're the devil's own, I'll not deny it, little hero," said Dark John. "It's myself am as keen to be out of it as you. And we have had but the start of it. O king! amn't I glad I'm not the Sergeant, that has got to come round her with the coaxing?"

"Coaxing may come round her; but her like was never come round by anything like command," said Jib-boom, and went to the companion and bent his head to listen. There was never a sound from below. "She beats me clean!" said he. "If it wasn't for yon knife in the nook of her plaid, I would see you to the Worst Place before I would draw a bolt on her. I'm not the least bit in the key for such kidnapping, and what in the world's the meaning of it?"

Dark John took a chew of dulse. "There, good man!" said he, "you beat me, but I'm thinking it's all in the way of Corodale's courting."

"Oh, courting!" said Jib-boom. "Oh, now, if it was but the courting, it's a ploy that takes my fancy, and faith! when I think on it, there's no wonder Herself is so cool about it. But I wish you had made it up between you all to do the thing in better weather."

The sloop went through the dark like a drunk man stumbling; waves came over her bows and splashed in the seamen's faces, and wore like burns along the deck, for Jib-boom was taking out of her all the north he could. Rain began, and heavily, though it would be hard to guess what was rain and what the spray. The ship was full of noises, as if she was tormented. In every spar she strained; the shrouds were humming, points tap-tap-tapped on the canvas, and the clews tugged for freedom till the sheets were creaking. In her hold, in her cabin, strange hammerings; about her the hissing wash of the sea, and it on fire. Dark John's terror of the deep made him sick; he hung on a cleat with both hands, that never let go, except in a pause of the vessel's staggering, to make the sign of the Cross. The work of the ship went on about him, bustling – the cries at shifting of the tacks, the scamper of the men, barefooted; he was dead to all, and only conscious of the unstable, awful plank that heaved below him. Some of the men came up in a while and saw his horror in the light of the lantern, his face like skim-milk cheese, and his eyes bulging, even his seaweed forgotten, with its magic power gone. At first they were in the vein to mock him, but he was beyond a sense of it, and gibbered his Gaelic prayers – not the prayers of Stella Maris that come to Christians in their tribulation, but ancient heathen supplications long forgot in Uist, cried in the dark and in the tempests by brutes before the light came.

"Mary keep us! listen to yon! It will sink the sloop on us!" cried Maclean, and in a righteous fury shook Dark John till he lost his hold on the cleat and slid shapeless to the deck in a sort of stupor, where they left him. He lay some hours moaning under a tarpaulin that Jib-boom threw over him. When the wind abated, and he ventured to look up, the beginning of the day was over Eaval Mount in the east, and the sloop was going close to the shore of Aird. He sat up and looked about him with fishy eyes. She was soaked with sea, and every stitch of her dripping, and still the rain, in a cold, foggy drizzle, made Isle Benbecula like a swamp, wherein cattle waded and the inn of Creggans seemed to stand like a foundered vessel, with the water washing at its windows.

They anchored near the shore; gladly the old man got on his feet and drank with a glutton's eyes the view of the waving grasses, the flat, dark, steadfast sands. "In the mortal world," said he, "I never set eyes on a nobler prospect. *Oh, righ!* what a night! what a night! the like I have not passed since I touched the hand of death himself on Michaelmas."

"No more than a puff, I assure you," said Jib-boom; "that's what the weakest of us would be calling it in Skye, where north-west gales are begotten; the worst of it's to come for me, with this one here to be dragged ashore. I would sooner land a cargo of the cordial under the nose of Geordie's gentlemen, and every man a cutlass."

He had a tarred and blistered and unwieldy boat on chocks; he ordered her out and went below, dragging Dark John with him for company, – "for I can stand their tongues," said he, "but I cannot stand their weeping."

He was far from understanding his unwilling passenger to think of her in tears. If Anna had them, they were not for him to see. She had sat through the night in the noisy inwards of the sloop, racking her brain for some purpose in the outrage. That she should have an enemy in all the Outer Isles – Father Ludovick's sister! She felt at times it must be a dream, and tried in vain to wake herself, it was the climax of her nightmare, when, with the cabin still in the light of the lamp that had been left with her she heard a dubious step on the companion and the door unlocked. Up she sprang with a gasp, and stood with her hand in the nook of her plaid where the knife was. Jib-boom saw the act and rued his office. "On the soul of me!" he thought, "I wish you were ugly." He took off his seaman's hat.

"Carrying stuff for jollity, and for the old, and for the cold's my trade, and I have the name of taking a dram upon occasion; but that's, I'll take my oath on steel, the worst of me."

"You shall suffer for this night's work," cried Anna in English, breaking in upon his speech. "I have no idea what your purpose is; but you shall certainly not escape unpunished."

He scratched his head and looked foolish, and, still with what he meant for deference, "I have not much of the *Beurla,*" said he, "and I'm sure you have the most beautiful Gaelic."

"And I keep it for my friends, and honest folk," she answered, still in English; "the other tongue is good enough for such a vile transaction as this you are engaged in."

"I would not say but what you are quite right," cried Jib-boom, quite hearty, and laughed at her readiness "There was never a lady on my boat before – my grief to say it! and I'll not be sure of the manners for the occasion; but if I could be offering a glass of Barra for morning before you go ashore –"

"Ashore!" said Anna, trying hard to compose herself.

"Benbecula!" said Jib-boom. "It was all my contract bargained for that I should bring you here, and here you are, and if you will go back, myself will take you and put you into Boisdale Bay by dinner-time, not a hair the worse for it."

She looked about the cabin where she had passed the night and shuddered. "Not for all the world," she said. "Give me the shore, there's not a creature on the Long Isle would lay a hand on me."

She pushed past him, seeing he was no longer her jailer, and gave a little startled cry, with her heart at her mouth, when she stumbled on a figure crouching on the companion. She looked down and saw Dark John like a toad, his eyes shut up to slits, his jaws industrious, gave him a look more of repugnance than of blame, and stood upon the deck. Benbecula sure enough! – inhospitable, foreign, bleak, no place for the fluttering dove storm-driven from its home. The men on deck were astounded at the visitation; it was the first knowledge they had of a woman on board.

"Is it Boisdale, then, or here?" the skipper asked her again before she went ashore. "Last night I was the skipper, with the Sergeant here my master; now I'm Dan MacNeil."

"Ashore," she answered quickly, never looking at him nor at the men that gathered round.

He handed her into the boat, and took the oars himself; Dark John made to follow, but was thrust back by an oar. "You stay where you are, good man!" the skipper told him; "it is better for your health than the fog on Creggans." The old man cried and pleaded – wept, indeed – upon the bulwark, for this was to spoil all his plans in the interests of Col; but Jib-boom never heeded, rowed ashore, and landed Anna in a creek some hundreds of yards from Creggans Inn. There was no word passed between them till she stood on the sand and hesitated what she was next to do.

"Tell me this," said he, "and tell me no more. Are you here with your will or not?"

He had his answer only in the look she gave him.

"Then if you'll not come back," said he, "for the love of God keep clear of the inn and strike across for Gramisdale.

She ran across the sand. He watched her for a little and then rowed quickly back to the sloop. Her sails were down; he ordered them aloft again. "I'm not in the key," said he, "for argument with yon fellow."

CHAPTER XXVII

A Prisoner

ANNA ran to where the sand met the tufts of short salt grass, her spirit broken, and her limbs trembling under her now that she was free. She was heedless at first where she went, so long as she put distance between her and that dreadful vessel; and the first thing that brought her to her senses and made her think she was not out of danger yet was the crowing of a cock in Creggans. She was so close to the place she could have hailed it. She had thought herself safe anywhere on land, but she had only to look at this place – forlorn, ugly, aloof from all the world and silted to the eyes with sand – to think it dangerous, even if she had not unpleasant recollections of it and the warning of Jib-boom. It seemed the venue for wicked deeds, banished by itself from every neighbour, glooming under rotten bracken eaves, with curlews piping over it. A mile beyond it she could see the open ford with not a single figure on it (for the hour was early still), and in Creagory of Uist the smoke of morning fires was rising through the rain.

The day was fully come, but not a clear white summer light, rather a wandered dusk, disconsolate and a cold air that chilled to the marrow. In such a mitigate light, and at such an early hour, she hoped she might steal past the inn without observation, and so escape the need for a circuit that would bring her in among the impassable lochs that lay in that case between her and Gramisdale. She crept with caution past the outhouses of the inn, saw with satisfaction that there was as yet no smoke from its chimneys, and ran on again on the sand of the road leading to it, without courage to look behind her at its door and windows. She felt she had not far to go for safety, when something wakened all her apprehension.

The sand was wet with rain – it might have been the shore she moved on, so soaked it was; and there, plainly running from her very feet, was the print of some one else's walking! A man had passed in the same direction as she now followed; it must have been but lately, for the hollows of his steps were dry. In Creggans Inn, then, some one was assuredly afoot, no matter how early was the hour.

Her eyes followed the track away ahead of her; there was a feeling in her mind that if by some magic she could see far enough, – and it need not be very far either, – there would be the landlord of that dreadful house at the end of the footprints and waiting for her, a notion that had hardly formed itself in her mind till with a stifled little cry she saw a figure dimly in the distance. It was too far off to be certain whether it was man or beast; but Anna, terrified to think her enemy was already on her, turned without a moment's hesitation and ran back, convinced at last that her surest safety lay among the men of the smuggler's sloop. As she saw the inn and its door and windows now, it showed no sign of life, but the door was standing open! She had a fear that her very breathing would betray her: the house in its silence seemed the abode of evil, of things inhuman; its windows looked at her, dark and peering and intent. She was relieved to get out of sight of them round the gable-end, but how deep was her dismay to discover that the sloop was gone!

It slanted a long way from the land, as if it hurriedly fled, itself, from an outrage, – too far away already to hope for any help from it.

For the first time since she had been deceived and put on board the vessel, Anna wept. The *Happy Return*, that had been hateful to her a quarter of an hour ago, was now become, in the memory of her skipper's words, her last friend departed, and she was left alone to dangers the nature of which she could not guess. Where to could she fly now, with the open sea, the long flat sands where concealment was impossible, before her, and behind, this sinister inn and the person who was coming along the road that was her only way to safety?

A touch on her shoulder almost made her faint, she turned to see the Sergeant's wife.

"Oh, daughter!" cried the woman, in a trepidation that was plain in every feature, "what are you doing here? You could not be in a worse part of Isle Benbecula. Come back! come back! come back!" She caught Anna by the arm and drew her to the door of the outhouse, so much anxiety in her manner that Anna could not have a doubt her intention was a kind one.

"For Mary's love! my dear, you must hide yourself this moment: my man is coming on the road there, and once he sets an eye on you, I tell you that you're lost." She had the morning untidiness of the slattern born, her hair in wisps about her haffits, her buttons out of their places, and her feet unshod. Anna, looking at her, some-way lost her fear, and put up her hand to draw the woman's clothes together at the neck, as if it was a child. The Sergeant's wife dashed down the hand impatient, and panted new alarms, even weeping in the stress of her agitation.

"What does he want with me, your man?" asked Anna still with a feeling that wherever there was another woman and she the innkeeper's wife, there could be no great danger.

"Whatever he wants he'll get it, if it was your very life. Come in, come in, and I will hide you."

"In the house?" asked Anna, dubious, for now they were almost through the byre, and the woman led her to a door that gave entrance to the back of the house itself.

"It must be that or nothing. Look at the sand." She pointed through the byre-door behind them to the flat grey plain, that a glance could show every object on for miles. "And look at this." She showed the byre had no place that could hide so little as a bird, for half the roof was off it, and the morning light was in every cranny. "He has been, my man, for grass; the byre is the first place he will come to with it, and I must hide you up the stair. O God of Grace! I hear him coming!"

They dashed into the house and up the stair. "If he makes for the byre first, you will hear him, and I will cough, that you may come down the stair and out at the front and on your way." She had but time to say this before she drew the door softly after her and went down the stair.

Anna was left alone. She had a heart thundering as she sank in a chair and looked about her at the chamber where she had spent such hours of misery and of wakefulness on the night before her uncle's burial. Had it been some deep presentiment that had seized her then, that this was yet to be the place of danger for her? Sometimes she thought that this was still a part of the first experience there, and that all the months that lay between were only a dream. There from the window, soiled more foul than ever by the sea-birds, was the same long ford, her place of terror and romance, but vacant in the drizzling rain; the sand, the sand everywhere else around her, and far away in another clime, North Uist, a dirty dun in the sallow morning light, the mount of Eaval just a phantom in the mist. She pressed her hands on her heart to keep it still, and listened.

What hope she had of a flight from the front departed when she heard a footstep come in at the door.

The innkeeper threw his creel of grass on the kitchen floor and bawled on his wife for ale. She put it before him trembling, though she did her best to master it. He dragged the grass through the kitchen, threw it in the byre, and looked about him and over the empty sand and out to sea. The *Happy Return* was plain to view, yet he saw her with no surprise, but gave a muttered oath, and came hurriedly back to the kitchen. At a draught he emptied the can and ordered more, though plainly it was not the first he had had that morning. His wife, in tremors, gave him it; he stood with his back to the fire and his eye on the stair. Once or twice he chuckled, but a sullen look of drunken anger was his general aspect. The woman, nervous, thinking of her fugitive, went about her usual morning offices in a bustle, sweeping the sand from the hearthstone, stirring it into a cloud in the room by flicking a sloven's rag over stools and chairs.

"You're damned particular this morning," said he in English that she did not understand, though she surmised the meaning, and tried to make her industry no more zealous than on ordinary occasions. His words were plainly not meant for her only, and Anna up the stair could hear them. She felt that she was lost!

It was the cat and the mouse. "I wonder what I'll do next," he said, this time in the Gaelic.

"There's the cow to feed," his foolish woman ventured. Anna above could not but wonder at such simplicity, for the man's voice plainly made it clear that he suspected.

"Feed the cow!" he cried, and laughed most villainously. "A fine occupation for a gentleman that has sailed the oceans and has killed his men abroad like fish. You must think of something else, my love."

Even her poor intelligence told her now that there was something cunning in his manner. She answered him nothing, and he laughed at her again, a most ugly brute his face pitted as if some one in hobnails had trampled it. He turned from the scrutiny of her to glance at the stair; she was almost certain now that he knew; Anna had no doubt of it.

"I thought I saw some one yonder," said he at last.

"What!" said his wife, as grey in the face as a rag.

"What! what!" he mocked her. "I THOUGHT I SAW SOME ONE!" he roared in a fury at her evasion, and threw the empty vessel at her. She was used to that, and crouched in time to evade it, declaring that she had seen nobody.

"You saw nobody!" he cried, and caught at her by the arm. "Come here! come here!" He dragged her to the doors, both back and front, and pointed to the marks of Anna's footsteps on the sand. "You saw no one, daughter of the devil! for a cursed liar! Where's the girl?" His wife said nothing; Anna hurriedly looked at the window and tried it, to find its latticed space had never been built to open. The man's heavy step sounded on the stair. He came in with something bestial in his eye and mouth, the odour of the drunkard round him. His wife made an attempt to follow; when he turned to shut the door behind him, and saw her, he put his foot out and thrust her down the stair. She fell to the bottom with a cry of pain that he paid no heed to.

"Oh, you are a brute!" cried Anna, her fear lost in an indignation at the act.

"That's my way," said he, drunkenly laughing. "No argument, just the one heave and be done with it," and he threw himself in a chair with his back to the door. Anna kept on the other side of a table that filled the middle of the room. "Just the one heave," said he, with that satisfaction a man half-drunken has in a phrase that has come to him without consideration, as folk are said to find the happiest parts of poetry. "Just the heave!" he spoke in English, with an accent that was gathered from many breeds of them that speak English. He looked with a bullock's vacant eye, insane, at least with nothing human to be read in it, a wandering eye that settled on no one thing for a second. He made an effort, and seemed to catch the loose ends of his reason again, for in a bit his vision cleared and fixed itself on Anna's face.

"Just the one heave!" said he again, as if he had freshly discovered a pregnancy of meaning in it. "It's the only way with them. I would make her mind her own affairs if I had to break her back. Just the heave, like yon. Do you hear her whining?" He rose in a passion with oaths and his hand on the door, and then it seemed that his mind came back to Anna. He sat down again. The sobbing of the woman below filled the house.

"You cannot say I brought you here, anyway," he said pulling himself together again. "I'm out at my work and I come in, and here you are in my house and my wife hiding you. Now that you are here –"

"You know very well that I did not come here by my own will," interrupted Anna. "What is this about letters for me?"

He seemed to wonder for a moment, and then he laughed.

"Letters! From Corodale the stuck priest! It was not a bad plan, not a bad plan that, though it was not my own idea. You came here for letters; it's a pity you have made so long a journey for no end, because there's devil the letter I ken of, unless your own friend Col may have it."

"Very well," said Anna; "I must go; let me pass," and to try him, she took a step towards the door.

"Come, come!" said he, rising with a laugh, almost as if he were quite sobered at the idea of her escaping, and put out a hand to keep her back. "Sit down and talk. Now that you're here and there's something of a hurry, you know what I want."

"I have not the least idea," she replied.

"Oh, you can easily be guessing," said he with a leer; "it might be yourself, but it's not. Where's the money?"

"The money!" she repeated, sure that now he was mad indeed.

"The Loch Arkaig money, the *ulaidh*; you know very well what I'm meaning. Your uncle left it to you, your brother brags it'll never be handled, and I'm loth to let the mercies go to waste. If –"

"I know nothing about it," cried Anna, astounded that she should not sooner have divined the reason for this outrage on her liberty in a country where she had not a single enemy. "I know nothing about it."

"Not yet," said the Sergeant, "not yet perhaps, except the place where they hid it, and that's as much as I want to ken myself. The time is up at Michaelmas – twenty thousand sassenach! By God! to leave it so long was a madness. And his reverence says it's cursed, and you'll never touch it! Well, I'm not so dirty particular; I'll touch it. Come now! you will tell me where to look for it. You know."

"I can tell nothing," said Anna, and shut her lips in a way there was no mistaking.

"Let me get my hand on the stuff, and I'll put you back on the shore of Boisdale." His eye had grown quite clear and steady; he was almost sober with the thought that his purpose was about to be accomplished.

"I can tell nothing," Anna said again with firmness.

"But you know?" he cried, alarmed tremendously to think that after all perhaps she was as much in ignorance as himself of where the fifty-year fortune lay.

She did not answer for a little till she heard the sob of the woman down below. It might have frightened another, her it only angered. "I know; of course I know!" said she quickly, as if to punish him. "I'm the only one who does know, but I shall certainly never tell."

He laughed at that, relieved. "It's not the first time I had the secret under my roof," said he; "it went out the way it came in last time, but this time there'll be a difference. You'll never set foot across this door alive until you tell me."

"Then I'll go over it dead!" said Anna, without a moment's hesitation. "I would not tell if you tortured me."

He had drawn his chair up close to the table, on the other side of which she stood with her hand on it, looking down at him; he suddenly grasped her by the wrist. She struggled, but he freed her only far enough to get her fingers, and he crushed them till she nearly swooned with the pain, bending on her at the time a look that was half menace and half vanity of his own strength. She bit her under lip in agony, and the perspiration came upon her brow, but she did not utter word or cry.

"Tell me!" he said with an oath, and pressed harder. She gave a little catch at the throat, as if she tried to keep her tongue from being traitor. "No, no, no!" she cried, "not if you kill me!"

"We'll see about that," he said, releasing her. "Look at me; I have killed men."

Anna was comforted somewhat by the thought of the knife in the nook of her plaid.

"I have killed men. It has not troubled me more than if they had been rabbits."

CHAPTER XXVIII

The Price of Freedom

FOR a while he stared at her, to put her out of countenance or give her a frightened notion of his power. She met his glowering with a steadfast eye, convinced that, like every bully, he was one whose passions fed on other folk's fears. A fragile girl she looked in the morning light; but so trim in her garments, so dainty in the dressing of her hair, for all her night's adventures, that through his clouded senses and the vulgar greed that made him seek to terrify her, he felt at times the influence of a charm.

"There's one thing sure at any rate," said he to her, "you're uncommon dour for all that's of you. Well, so am I! and there's a pair of us. Ask the wife. It may be that you're thinking your friends will not be long of finding you in Creggans Inn: let me tell you that I laid my plans to send them looking for you in another place, and that's at the bottom of Boisdale Bay. They'll never dream of coming here for you. Or you may be thinking that I'll tire of keeping you a prisoner. Not a bit of me! so long as there's a handful of meal in the girnel; we have seldom company, and when it comes the way I'm loth to part with it I'm telling you, and there was never a fellow fonder of the ladies. In my time – in my time! Devil a foot on the sand there for weeks on end except Jib-boom's – a dog! I'll make him sweat for it, that did his best to let you slip from me in spite of what he promised."

She never answered. She looked at him either with a contempt that would have maddened him if he had any conceit of himself to understand it, or more often had her gaze on the cheerless prospect that was visible from the window – the rain streaming on the lattice lozens in blobs as if it had been oil, the desolate grey sand with birds, that were to be envied for their freedom, blown about upon it as they fed in a wind that swelled till it lashed the shore with breakers. A mist shut off the shore, the ford, the Isle of Uist, from her: if Creggans Inn was out of the world and forgotten at any time, 'twas now assuredly more than ever.

When she let her eyes stray to the window he thought he knew her thoughts, and that it was from that direction she hoped for her relief. "Take my word for it," he told her, "I have not seen a soul from that airt for a month. I could not get custom in this infernal place if I ran ale free from the spigot; I'm owing that to the priests that have given my inn a bad name, and your brother, by all accounts, as bad as anybody."

But it was not of her own distress she thought at all; it was on the vacant home in Boisdale, and her brother Ludovick distracted at her absence. She blamed herself most bitterly for coming away last night without leaving any hint behind of what had taken her. If it was true that something had been done to make them think that she was drowned, his condition at this moment would be terrible. At the very thought of it she felt like crying out her secret and securing her liberty, so that she might fly to him, but she was not yet subdued.

By-and-by she was left by her tormentor, who carefully locked the door and took the key with him. For more than an hour his voice came roaring up the stair in the foulest condemnation of his wife, whose fall, it seemed, had sorely bruised her. If Anna had the faintest hope of intercession from that quarter, she soon abandoned it; for it seemed indeed as if the wife had greater cause for terror than herself.

A dungeon could not well have been more cruel than this narrow, mildewed, dusty chamber under the bracken eaves; a dungeon could not have been more secure, of that she lost no time in making certain, and yet to make it all the safer her jailer never set a foot outside his kitchen-door. Once or twice his wife went out for peats or water, once in mournful cadence to cry upon her cow, that must have fed sparsely on that sandy plain. Anna wondered that there was never a glance up at the prison windows, until it struck her that the man could see his wife from the open kitchen-door, and that she dare not show her interest.

It seemed as if the place was in a perpetual dusk or dawn, so little did the passage of the day affect the light of it. No sun came through the mist, the rain was unceasing. Anna had no watch; she could not tell the hours. Her idleness was an agony to her; for very relief to her feelings she could have beat on the doors and cried aloud, but she knew that this would be useless, and the discovery of a half-knitted stocking with the wires in it provided a blessed relief, for it gave her an occupation. The sight of her thus engaged gave the man his first apprehension that, after all, perhaps she was not to be conquered. He had come up with food for her – at least he did not mean that she should perish of starvation.

Twice he returned, to find her spirit still unbroken. At the last, exasperated by indifference, he made to seize her; a cry broke from her, and she almost showed the knife, but his wife ran up the stair and drew on herself his anger. And so the day passed. The gloaming came, the room grew darker, night fell sudden and thick. Anna heard the woman rake the peats of the kitchen-fire and hum the smooring-hymn of the islands, that her man broke in upon with unbelieving blasphemy.

It was a night of storm. Gusts shook the inn, as if it would be levelled with the sand; in the cabin of the sloop itself she had not a greater feeling of insecurity. Over the island rang the shock of sea; the rain in spurts, as if it had been spindrift, thrashed upon the window. When sea-birds passed it was with mournful cries, as if they had been children pained; the odd humanity of their voices added to the girl's distress. She was to spend the night a prisoner, then, without the trivial solace even of a light, and she dreaded what might happen if she fell asleep. There was a great bedstead in the room; with a miracle of labour she dragged it across the door, and lay for long fighting against the drowsiness that was natural, seeing the previous night had brought no slumber, and at last she fell asleep.

A sound of breaking glass wakened her, and the dash of rain in her face. Through the broken window the wind drove in, possessing the chamber.

What had happened? Sitting on the bed, breathless, she listened; but only the fury of the storm was audible. All that was plain to her straining senses was that some one had thrown something at the window, and that it had fallen into the room. A sudden idea sent her quickly to her knees, and feeling about the floor till she came on a key. Manifestly the woman at last had come to her assistance. The key would not have been thrown in at the window unless there was a chance of her using it with a prospect of success, nor (she thought) could the woman have possessed herself of it if her husband were alert. And yet a long while Anna was irresolute, dreadful that it might, after all, be some device of the innkeeper. At last she gathered her courage and unlocked the door.

The storm drowned every sound except a stertorous breathing in the kitchen, where, to her dismay, was still a light. A score of strange surmises, fears, and plans alternative, held her for a while on the landing; but she reflected nothing was to lose by an endeavour at escape, and so she crept cautiously down the stair. At its foot, she knew, she must decide whether her safer way lay through the kitchen or the byre.

When she got to the foot she could see more than half the kitchen, and her eyes were held there, fascinated for a little at the sight of the Sergeant sitting by the fire on a chair, his feet on a stool and his face towards her. A crusie that hung on a joist lighted every way of escape for her; but the man was plainly asleep, his chin on his breast, his red hair with a bald patch conferring upon him an aspect curiously grotesque, an aspect elderly and innocent. Beyond him was a bed recessed in the wall, and his wife with a face of the greatest apprehension lay in it, signing to Anna that her flight must be by the byre-door.

The girl pushed open the door and drew it after her. She stood in the dark for a little, listening to the landlord's stertor; the byre was warm and odorous milkily; on the sheltered side of the house it had an air of peace and safety. She felt her way to the other door that lay between her and liberty; her hand was on the bar, when she stumbled against the foot of a ladder, that fell with a crash that shook her with terror. A wild fluttering of wings filled the byre, and the alarm of fowls that had been disturbed in their roosting. She plucked the door open and dashed into the night.

The innkeeper woke at the sound of his noisy poultry; divined the cause, and quickly made for the byre. The crusie light showed him the outer door was open: with an oath he ran back through the kitchen and out into the darkness before his house. He caught the fugitive as she came round the gable.

"A droll time to be leaving an inn!" said he, "but it's not the first time I've had a customer go in the dark and forget to pay the lawing." He drew her into the house, and seated her in the chair he had been sleeping in. "This is your work, is it?" he said to his wife, malignant. She shrank in her recess like an animal in its form, speechless and in terror of his anger, for still in Anna's hand was the key, for evidence of what the manner of her escape from her cell had been.

Luckily sleep had sobered him, and even put him in a humour to enjoy the chagrin of his prisoner's face and the mortal terror of his wife: he burst out laughing.

"Three o'clock in the morning," said he, in the tone of a genial friend; "it's the hour I was always at my best when a crack was going, and I'm not a bit vexed to have your company. I was gaming my head off here, and I suppose I fell asleep, and this one here in the bed that's whining took the chance. Just that! just that! that's a thing to deal with later. But tuts! to be flying like yon in a night like this! it was fair ridiculous!"

He drew himself a horn of ale, with something of a new assurance in his manner that Anna wondered at. He could not think her yielding, and yet in her heart she was, whenever she had thought of Ludovick's lamentation. That alone dauntoned her; otherwise, in the light, and with the presence of the woman, she was almost at her ease, assured that her jailer would not venture on desperate measures, and that sooner or later he must let her go.

The reason for his new complacency was soon apparent; in his sober mind had come an inspiration which would never have come to him tipsy, that he had all the time in his possession something to buy her secret with. Dark John had got her on board the smuggler with a tale of letters for her; the tale was not without some truth at its foundation, for letters for her there were, and one of them, filched by one thief from another, was at that moment in his pocket. He drew it suddenly out, without a word, and held it before her.

Freedom itself could not have given her a greater joy than she experienced at the sight of her own name in Duncan's handwriting: with a little cry she stretched to snatch her property.

"Oh no, stop a bit!" said the innkeeper. "You're thrawn, but I'm pretty thrawn myself too. There's plenty more letters where this one came from, and I could easily put you in the way of getting them – but on the one consideration."

Could she buy anything more precious with a single sentence – a sentence that left her none the poorer? The revelation hung on her lips, but it did not find expression.

"No," she told him firmly; "I cannot tell without the consent of my brother."

He laughed in her face. "A likely thing!" he cried. "And who's to go and ask him for it? I'll warrant it would be a ticklish errand. I wouldn't care to be the fellow myself would haggle with your brother for the twenty thousand pounds, and I have not seen the priest yet was such a fool as this you're thinking Father Ludovick, to let a fortune slip out of the family."

"My brother hates the very mention of it: I think he would believe he could not punish you worse than by putting you in the way of getting it."

"By the Lord! I wish he would try me," said the innkeeper, and then gave a startled cry. Anna jumped to her feet; outside somebody hailed the inn.

CHAPTER XXIX

The Surrender of the Secret

THAT a rap should come to Creggans in that hour of night, thundering its way through a house that seemed forgotten of the decent world, wholly given up to dark and secret passions, and to lonely desperate deeds, was more terrifying to the girl at first than all that had gone before. Only a moment she shrank, though, for a hope sprang quickly that for all its eerie solitude, and its sinister repute, the inn might now and then attract some honest traveller. The Sergeant glanced at her and saw she meant to cry. "Quiet, I'm telling you!" he hissed in her ear, and clapped a hand upon her mouth. She struggled, but he had sacked with ruffian corps in towns abroad; the warmth of her breath, the touch of her neck, stirred in him for a moment, even in his fear of the intrusion, old memories, foul appetites keener than the greed of wealth; the ancient elemental beast took in him command, and it was with an effort he restrained the instinct of his flesh to squeeze remorselessly and kill.

There was a confusion of muttering voices outside, and the shuffle of feet. Before the innkeeper could give words to an inquiry, Jib-boom, his skipper, cried for entrance in a voice that made it plain he was still his own master and in no mood for being kept long on the wrong side of any door he had a notion to make use of.

"I have my strength on me!" he bawled, beating with both of his open palms on the door till it dirled like a drum. "Are you hearing? I have my strength on me, and I'm angry, angry! Back with your bar, I'm telling you, this very instant, or Dan MacNeil will put his hands upon the lintel and the lum, and pull the house in pieces that would do for the ballast of a boat."

Anna's heart sank, she was still in the hands of the Philistines! The innkeeper let her go, and with an oath opened his door misgivingly. Jib-boom and the Macleods came into the light, glistening in oilskins, dripping with rain, irresistible to look on as if they had been cased in metal, surging upon the innkeeper impetuous like a tide as he stood before them on the middle of the floor, so that they did not at first see the woman shrinking behind.

"*Thrusdair!* Where's the girl?" cried the skipper, catching hold of the collar of the innkeeper's coat. "If she's a hair of her head the worse for you, I will take you out and give you death. Look at my face, – it's red. I could tear your heart out through your thrapple, and shred it on the yard to poison hens."

The innkeeper gave an ugly laugh, uncomfortable, his face ash-grey with anger, but knowing too well his skipper's strength and temper to make resistance.

"You have been at the Barra stuff again, Dan, I'm thinking," said he, drawing aside to show his wife and Anna in the dusk of the apartment.

"You're a liar there! I have not drunk to-day, I could not drink for thinking," cried the skipper; "it's just my natural strength in me," and stopped in a confusion at the sight of Anna standing gazing at him.

"God!" said he, "I'm fair affronted, lady! Did I not think – did I not think – what in the world was it I was thinking, lads?" He turned on his companions; the three stood dripping and glistening, their tarpaulin hats at once in their hands.

"Och! Put it in the English, skipper," said one of them; "in the Gaelic it was meaning that himself here was badly in need of killing, and yourself was the fellow, with a little help from Skye, could do it neat and cleanly." They shuffled their feet on the sandy floor awkwardly; the crimson paled on the face of Jib-boom; he was fast becoming the genial man who was daft about the dancing, and found his temper soft in the air of tavern rooms.

"Upon my word, a fine-like time of night to be disturbing us!" said the innkeeper, feeling himself master again, stretching out his arms, and trying to herd them out the way they had come in. Just another moment and they would have gone, for it looked indeed as if they were unwelcome intruders there to everybody; but the skipper saw something in Anna's face that stayed him.

"Och! to the mischief!" said he. "I wish I was out on the deep; all this carry-on is a confusion. Give me the deck and a rope's end, and no dubieties. I was in my red wrath with you since ever I let Herself ashore; did I not come here with gaiety to break every bone in your body?"

"And we were in the finest trim to give a hand at it, the two of us," said Calum. "It's a pity; it's a pity!"

"Let me get back to my boat out yonder, and I would give Dark John, if he was a generation younger, what he would not in a hurry be forgetting," the skipper went on, wondering at Anna's aspect. "I would never have been here but for his nonsense. First he said the lady was in Creggans with her own free will, and then he swore, when I would not let him follow her, the very life of her was in danger."

"In Creggans Inn!" cried the Sergeant. "Man! I have a wonder on me to hear you talking; the worst that could happen her here would be that she might choke with sand in the morning's milk, for my wife, this woman here, is too drowsy to be cleaning out her pails, and I have got shrimps before now in my porridge. Go back to your ship, good lads!" He tried again to push them out, as if they had been naughty children, and at that Anna caught the skipper's arm, with a cry to him not to leave her.

"Not a bit of me!" he promised heartily. "Was I not the fool to let you take your own way here yesterday morning? If it was not for that you might have been back long ago in Boisdale presbytery, and I would not be missing yon dancing in Kintra." He put her behind him, out of reach of the Sergeant, and faced that angry individual with something of the spirit he had brought to his entrance. "None of your dirty work for Dan MacNeil!" he told him. "I'm black ashamed that I had the share I had in this affair, and gave my word to take the lady here, not thinking it was much more than a ploy of Col Corodale's. Ships have I sailed for you, my speckled fellow, and run ankers of Barra for you, and missed many a noble entertainment at the dancing, and sang songs for you, but rot take me if I don't convoy Herself here back to where I took her from!"

The Sergeant shrugged his shoulders. "Faith, you're welcome!" said he. "The whole thing was no more than a prank of another man's, though I daresay I'll have to take the blame of it. It's lucky I'm not particular, and whatever way things turn out I need not care." He poured himself out a glass of spirits, gulped it at a breath, and scowled upon his wife, who all this time was either in a state of silent terror close upon a swoon, or whimpering stupidly, till Anna felt more pity for her than for herself. "There's a slut!" said her husband, and pointed a contemptuous finger at her. "One of the cursed gang of fools I have about me to do nothing else but bungle things and spoil me on every hand. Wasn't I the silly man?" He lifted his hand to her, carried away on his fury. Jib-boom gave a glad loud cry, and struck him with his fist upon the temple. He fell with a crash among the ashes of the hearth.

"There you are, master! Will you take another one?" cried the skipper. "This is better sport than any dancing: for seven years have I been craving the opportunity, and now I'm vexed I'm only in a half fury and dare not have a full indulgence. My God! I'm in my glory. Go back, boys, back to the boat, and take this lady with you: leave me here with Pock-marks, and you may take my very clothes. I'll never ask to leave so long as he can stand before me."

Anna tugged at his sleeve. "Oh come, come!" she pleaded. "You are but making matters worse for this poor woman. Let us go from this place." He was a child in her grasp; his eyes hungered for the innkeeper, who was getting to his feet, plainly in no fighting humour, but he moved at her pressure to the door.

To Anna's surprise the innkeeper began to don an oilskin coat. "If you're for starting now," said he to her, "then I'm going too; this thing demands an explanation."

"It's your own vessel; I can't hinder you," the skipper answered. "On my word it's only fair that you should come and take the blame for setting us to your dirty business."

They all went out of the inn except the wife. A faint bland breeze struck Anna's cheek and felt like the caress of liberty; she could have cried with joy, in spite of her rude companionship, to be free from the place of her fears and tortures, and yet her heart was heavy to think of the unhappy wretch, the wife for whom there never could be freedom nor caress. At the threshold she ran back impetuous, took the poor drab, that was her sister, in her arms and kissed her, then made for the shore with the sailors.

The sloop, that had hung all day irresolute off Aird, now lay at anchor in the creek; they went out to her in the small boat that had brought Anna to her prison, and weighed her anchor just about the hour of dawn. Anna thought, as she looked at the grey bars over flat Benbecula, that now they were leaving, that of late her ways had, at the intensest hours, been cast in chilly dawns, in the qualified melancholy half-lights when the meanings of nature are dim. A long time, with no bounds to it, seemed to have elapsed since she had been decoyed from home; how agonised a time it must have been for Ludovick ignorant of her fate! to herself it might have been months or even years, and it was with a shock she felt the reality that in truth it was but a matter of little more than a day when she saw, still chewing his dulse assiduous on the deck, Dark John, the wretch who had betrayed her. It was to him the innkeeper made his first advances whenever he got on board. They went muttering apart, putting their heads together. The skipper, looking to the handling of his vessel, and still defiant of his master, was annoyed at their communing, damned them heartily, and fell in conversation with the girl. She was glad of that comfort knowing him now really her friend, though he had played a part at first in her decoying. Sitting dead-weary on a water breaker, and he speaking to her now and then at every turn of what they call a smuggler's walk, it was vaguely she heard, and little she heeded what he said till he made some mention of the letters that had come for her. Till then he had been speaking with remorse of his own deceit; at the reference to the letters she was wide awake and eager in every nerve of her

"Yes, yes, the letters! how dared that man keep my letters?" she demanded, looking along the deck, where in the grey light the two conspirators sat on the fo'c'sle head.

"There you have me again!" said Jib-boom. "He got every one of them from myself. We were no sooner over the Minch than he was up the side and on the top of us demanding every scrap we carried; he made more ado about the letters sometimes than about the cargo. O king! what did I ken? I never had the schooling. At sailing the ships, at singing the songs, or at the dancing, there's very few my equal, but the scrape of a pen never yet but set me sweating. By the Book! if it was not my own singing of a song that cleared Corodale out of Uist."

"What!" cried Anna, wondering. "I do not understand."

"No more do I, but a woman in Dalvoolin, called Bell Vore, she told me that the song it was that did it, and it was the Sergeant's wife who told her. Have you not heard the 'Little Black Pot'?"

She shook her head.

He hummed the verse that Col had contrived –

> "Duncan, Duncan, what is your wishing?
> A crock of gold and an easy life."

"Stop! stop!" she cried in an anguish. "Do you tell me Mr Duncan heard that abominable thing?"

"He did, indeed, my shame to say it! I learned the words from the Sergeant here, and had a score or two of ready scholars of my own for it over in Boisdale Bay that night we burst the keg and had the fine carouse."

Through her mind the whole thing flashed; it was not ill for her to comprehend the story. She had heard the air herself that night, and Duncan when he left her must have heard the very words of this appalling ribaldry. It was clear to her now why he had gone away. The fiend who had devised the scheme could not have struck his blow with greater cunning if he had been in league with hell itself. How true had been her intuition that she had everything to fear from her lover's pride, if he had the slightest glimmer of light upon the scandalous things that Boisdale thought of him: his letter now was plain – he had gone from a delicacy that, though it had brought her pain, made him dearer to her than ever he was before.

"And have you any idea where the letters came from?" she asked, after thinking long.

"It's myself has not the smallest notion," said Jib-boom. "I did not even know they were from Mr Duncan till the Sergeant's woman blabbed her goodman's secret."

"Oh!" cried Anna, "I would give the world – I would give the world to know, and there's a rogue at the other end of this vessel could make me happy in a word!"

"And what in the universe is all his mischief for?" the skipper asked. "This roguery is not in the way of honest smuggling."

"He wants – he wants to get his hands on the Arkaig treasure."

Jib-boom was coiling a rope; at her words he let it fall at his feet.

"What is that you are saying?" he cried. "He is after the *ulaidh!*"

"He knows I could tell him where it is hidden," said Anna, "and all his plotting is to make me tell."

In the morning light she saw the skipper was amused at something in her answer, he shook with silent laughter till his earrings danced on his sunburnt neck. "*Mo chreach!*" said he, "the fifty-year fortune! Faith! I think myself you might do worse than tell him."

It was the very thought that was in her mind. The secret was her own; it had never brought her anything but misery, and the treasure seemed in some way more accursed in idleness than it could ever be if she renounced it altogether.

"You may not be believing me," said she impetuous "but as sure as I stand here I have it in the heart of me to do him an ill turn, and tell him of my own free will what he could never have got from me by force. Oh! it would be a just punishment for him, and it would be a relief to me; I do not think that even Ludovick would blame me."

"Indeed and I daresay not," Jib-boom agreed, so readily she had a little of her first distrust of him, and thought he shared his master's lust and counted on a portion of the plunder. With what a gang of rogues was she surrounded! how common and deep, she felt, was a vice she had never before met anywhere except in books!

Without another moment's hesitation, she left his side and went forward on the deck where the Sergeant and the other schemed.

The Sergeant was in a natural dread of the consequences of his plot, and Dark John shared his apprehension, for even in Uist girls were not to be trepanned with impunity. Father Ludovick's wrath, they felt, would follow them to the remotest of the Outer Isles.

"At any rate I'm done with Creggans," said the innkeeper; "that's the one thing certain: it'll have to be the mainland for me, and as fast as this black dog MacNeil can take us there after he has got rid of the woman. If there was not the need for that, I would knife him where he stood for daring to lift a hand to me. I –"

He started at a touch on his shoulder, and turned about to see Anna.

"Will you give me my letter?" she asked him, making a last trial at his better nature.

"Och! a bargain's a bargain!" he answered.

"I know," said she, "and I am quite agreeable.

"On my soul now, are you?" he cried; and drawing forth the letter, thrust it in her hand without a doubt of her meaning.

As her fingers closed on Duncan's letter she felt she was exchanging sorrow for her very heart's delight.

"You know Mingulay?" she said eagerly.

He wet a parched lip and nodded.

"It's in the Long Gallery in Mingulay, then, on the ledge below the blood of the Merry Dancers."

CHAPTER XXX

Anna's Return

KILBRIDE is over Cruachan and Hartabeck in the southeast corner of the island. Lost among heather, far from seas, though the ribbons of the sea come in among its pastures, and the scent of the tides is ever over it, and cattle wade in the heat of the day in wide inland waters, where silver-bellied trout and salmon play through the shoals of lythe and coaling, there is this township of St Bride, forgotten to the foolish world but darling to the Church. That Father Ludovick might bring the Host there to his people, where they worshipped in a hut, he had to travel once a fortnight. Welcome travelling it was to him, and the day when he went a true holiday, filling his soul with a gaiety deep and quiet. This small community, sharing none of the outer world's unrest loitering content and simple through heather and dream, ignorant of the great confusions elsewhere, was to him the jewel of his diocese. It was not only that he found there the lingering song of the women at the quern or waulking-wicker, the shearing ballad, the *ursguel* – the antic story of the folds, the old generous ways, and faith as passionate as his own; but that in Kilbride were still the ashes of revolt. The tale was done, the hope departed, but he loved to meet the men who had marched through English meadows fifty years ago, creatures kind of heart at home, shy as birds and always wondering; but to the Saxon towns they marched through with Prince Charlie creatures dim and terrible, alien as Mameluke or Arab, fancies of the pillow more than human folk, whereof the last had not been swallowed up in the mist whence they went out in a noble folly, whereto, when the sun fell on Drumossie Moor, they sorrowfully returned. Kilbride retained for him a ghost that mourned and could not be forgetting. He never left the place at evening to go home, his hat drawn down on his eyebrows, his plaid drawn high to his chin, but that he stood a moment on the verge of it, of the wilds and of the ancient days himself again, separate by some freak of the imagination from that new world of fretting influences that came with books and letters to the bay of Boisdale.

It was in Kilbride, the happy valley lacking distant prospects, where people were content and never had a doubt of God, that he was Lord of the Isles in a sense more deep than ever had been the old Macdonalds. He was the greatest man in the world for them – fond simpletons! – the knowledge of it made him glad and humble. That day of Anna's beguiling, a score at least of his people went part of the way with him when he left for home. He should have been happy, so cheerful the adieux – women frankly courting him, and men determinedly at their best with humour – but somehow the sense of a blow impending burdened him. Perhaps it was the portent of the sky, that ere he skirted Cruachan blackened suddenly, and the curious absence of the birds that ordinarily made the moorland busy and charmed his pilgrimages from Kilbride with chirp and song. A stagnant air was choking the islands; the pass was like a kiln for the heat; when he was over the slope of the hill and could see the ocean, it glinted to his vision like a metal tempering in fire, the horizon of a hue unusual.

He thought of thunder; he wished ardently for rain; soon the one was crashing on Benmore and the other pattered on him. Through the night he tramped with joy, possessed with that exultation that came to him always when tempest reigned, sometimes picturing to himself the hearth glowing and new-swept, the cheerful lamp, and Anna herself a benign domestic star. The hamlets round the rock of Stella Maris were dark and silent as he walked through them, more like memorial cairns than dwellings; far off he saw the light of the presbytery and hastened his pace.

It was almost with a lover's eagerness he opened the door. Anna was not downstairs. The lamp and fire were there, but lately tended; the table was set for his supper, their chairs drawn up to it, and the room was smelling of bog-myrtle she had plucked in rain, for still the drops were on it as it stood on the table with some wild roses.

"Anna!" he cried up the stair, even before he had his hat off: it was a common vanity of his to let her see him at his very wettest after such drenching pilgrimages. But he got no answer.

That night he searched in every house in Boisdale. He sought her in the chapel: he sought along the shore. At dawn, when she was far off in Benbecula, and shuddering at the sight of Creggans Inn, the quest was far and furious for signs of her. Like a madman he rode from township to township, from shearing to shearing, and late in the day he found himself at Corodale, knowing her heart was wont to be there.

Col took horse too, and together they went as far north as the ford. It was a day of rain and mist: like phantoms the two of them rode out of the fog and into hamlets, to amaze the children tending cattle; over moors, to meet women bearing peats on lonely tracks; along the shore, to startle men repairing the ravages of the dog-fish on their nets. No one had seen the girl on any path she might have taken to leave the presbytery's neighbourhood: it seemed – in one extravagant fancy of her brother's – as if, too soon angelic, she had taken wings. Her name was being cried on fields and mosses, resounding high on the moors, throughout the summer camps; the spinning stopped, the cattle were left untended, folk came hurriedly to the machar-land and joined the search.

Col found the company of the priest at last insufferable – the silent agony, the miraculous tirelessness, the foolish hopes that flared up on the flimsiest of suggestions, were an irritation to him; for judging the rest of the world was like himself, that envied her a knowledge so precious as the secret of the Arkaig treasure, he had, in a little while, in the bottom of his heart, a conviction that Anna's disappearance was in some way due to the very thing that had made her most attractive to himself. It was not grace and beauty and goodness that were lost to him it was a hidden store of lavish years he had been counting on; they were as assuredly stolen from him as if a robber had broken into the box upstairs in Corodale and taken the contents. The coarse chagrin of the expectant who is bitterly disappointed came out, someway, in his most trivial utterances; a shallowness in his spoken sentiments made the priest distrust him, and come at last to the sad conclusion that here was a vulgar mercenary, so they went their own ways searching.

Late in the afternoon, perhaps because he was the only one with wits untroubled by genuine distress, Col took a sudden thought and asked where the little boat the *Ron* was. It was customarily in the bay: he went with some others to look for it among the stranded skiffs and cobles; but the boat was gone, and at that discovery their searching was conducted in a different fashion and with new fears.

"I cannot understand it," cried Ludovick, distracted. "There was nothing in the world to send her out in a boat at any time, and more particularly on such a night as last night, and I am beat to think of any place she could have thought of going to by sea in any case. At any other time it might have been Dalvoolin round Kintra, on a sudden fancy; but she knew that all the folk are in Loch Eynort at the shearings."

"Let us go round the shore again, and take our boats this time," said some one, and for hours the island edge was searched, and every rock beyond it. Some fishermen, called by a smoke from Eriskay, cunningly rigged long lines with fishing hooks, and slyly grappled in the bay, but so as not to let her brother see them. Col cursed their folly, more certain than ever that he was right, and she was somewhere trapped for her secret, or fled of her own accord, – he had once the maddening notion that it might be to his brother Duncan, some of whose letters might have reached her, for all the care he and the Sergeant had taken to waylay them.

He rode hither and yond, as the saying goes, with every appearance of looking for the lady as ardently as the others did; but he was not like them, in that he never had a hope to find her in that neighbourhood. And yet it was his unexpecting eyes that first fell on the *Ron*. He came upon Anna's boat suddenly in a cleft of the rocks at Saltavik: it was with what was close upon a dread he left his horse and went down to look. There was little to see indeed, and no clue to its story as it lay there bright with paint, having something of a cheerful holiday aspect, the "hole-pins and oars in their places, to show that it had not gone adrift from the shore by accident.

Back he rode into Boisdale and told of his discovery. All the parish flocked to Saltavik and stood lamenting beside the little boat, the magic galley that had brought Anna to the fairy isle of Tir-nan-oig, the barge of her love and fancy. Father Ludovick looked at it, nodding carelessly on the edge of the sand, and turned on his people a stricken countenance. Over them swept a share of his apprehensions. A murmur rose among the fishermen, some foolish women in the background suddenly burst into the keening. The cadence of their wail had no sooner brought its meaning to his senses than he dashed among them, angrily commanding silence, and as they fell away abashed before him, he rode back to Stella Maris. The dusk was come; he went into the chapel; when, later, his people came they saw the wan glow of a single light, and did not venture to disturb him.

And so another night passed. A second dawn broke on his anguish. Haggard and grey he came out of the chapel when the first light rose in the east, and looked at the cold unpromising world.

It was the very hour when Anna gave up her secret. She saw the same dawn pale among the cordage of the vessel, spread quickly over Hecla and Benmore, flame at last fiery and golden through the Sound, the bars of the heavens crossed by myriad sea-fowl, the waves crashing milk-white on Orosay and the Barra Isles. She had gone aft when her secret was surrendered, the letter caught tightly in her hands.

"You have got it there?" said the skipper.

"Thank God!" she answered, and then had one short thought that sickened her, that after all she might again be cheated, the man had so readily seemed to trust her. The seal was broken, and she tore the paper open, to smile and sigh and murmur over its contents, though they were blaming her for her failure to acknowledge letters he had sent before. It was not the splendid day that gladdened her then, not the sunshine glorifying all the sea; it was the eager passionate words of remembrance, love, and hope in her lover's handwriting that made her brim with joy.

"Did you tell our speckled fellow yon?" asked Jib-boom, watching her countenance, and seemed greatly pleased with her answer.

"By the Book!" said he, "and you have made the finest bargain ever you made, then. In all my life I have not heard of a droller thing, and would sooner miss a hundred dances in Barra or the Isle of Skye than miss this that you're telling me."

The Sergeant, forward on the fo'c'slehead, looked aft at them, and had two thoughts in his head, – one that he had maybe parted with his letter for a fiction, and the other a conviction from Anna's solemn manner that he was truly at the door of fortune, but that he had not yet the key.

"What's this about the blood of the Merry Dancers?" said he, turning to the old man blinking beside him at the morning sun, cheerful at the thought of his feet again on the friendly land.

Dark John vowed he could not tell, that he did not know; aft to where Anna sat the Sergeant ventured then to ask an explanation, but there he found a check in the presence of Jib-boom. He waited for an opportunity, but he never had a chance to speak to her apart, so keen was her repugnance, and the shore slipped by: Orosay fell behind; here was Boisdale bay! Home seemed magically unchanged to Anna after her absence of tortured years. Greedily her eyes drank in the prospect, the familiar dwellings, the paths she knew with Duncan, oft frequented, the chapel on the rock. There was no one in the fields; but on the township tracks, so far as she could see, were people seemingly in some strange excitement, and at the curing-sheds were many men in groups, as if it had been Michaelmas and they balloted for the banks. She searched the whole visible isle for Ludovick, and saw him come at last to the chapel door. A fresh certainty of what he had endured in her absence gave her grief again, that drowned for a moment the sense of discovery and joy that she brought back with her.

The sloop swung round in the wind at the harbour mouth; Jib-boom prepared to set the girl ashore. "There you are," he told Dark John; "yourself, that took the lady from the shore, can take her back again: I'm not caring much to set a foot on Uist for a while to come until this thing blows over; I'm thinking to myself, O king! it would not be good for the health of Dan MacNeil." Helping Anna into the boat, he took the chance to whisper to her, "I have a bit of a surprise myself for this speckled fellow, more than any drubbing he would get from the Boisdale lads would be;" then gave a grimace of sly glee and pushed the boat from the sloop's side with a benediction.

Some of the men at the curing-sheds, seeing a woman's figure in the small boat from the smuggler, came quickly to the beach; a cry rose that Herself was safe and back again; the tidings went over the neighbourhood like a wave, and, like a wave returning, the folk poured on the shore at Anna's feet. Ludovick cleft the noisy band, that half-wept, half-laughed its welcome.

"I knew – I knew you were coming," said he. "Since the break of day I never had a doubt of it."

CHAPTER XXXI

Mingulay

COL had slept for the night in his friend the tacksman's at Dalvoolin He got up that morning with his mind resolved to relinquish this make-believe at searching and go home, where, his constant fears at any time of absence told him, things were certain to go contrary to his interests. For him, at all events, the new day came with no gladness; he was vexed with the conviction that everything went in opposition to his inclinations. The fortune his imagination had been feeding on for months further away than ever, his skipper and his sloop (or at least his share of these adventurers) vagrant without so much as "by your leave," and the priest manifestly dubious of him, – it was no wonder his patience was at an end. For decency's sake he would have to show face again at the presbytery and make an excuse for leaving, but that accomplished, he made up his mind he must be back in Corodale by noon.

Riding up the machar, busy with his thoughts, that were singularly heartless in the circumstances, he turned the point of the island just in time to see the sloop's arrival. "They will be on the hunt too, now," he thought, a grudging demon summing in a flash the cost of this new demand upon his property. He was too far off to see whom it was the vessel landed; but he could make plainly out that the shore was black with people in a manifest excitement, and the conviction came to him at once that Anna had returned.

Between him and the bay where the people were gathered was the figure of a man, half-walking half-running through the grass and sand. Col set his pony to a brisker progress; the closer he drew to the man approaching the more convinced he was that, in spite of an agility miraculous in one so old, it was no other than Dark John. A thought came to him then with a sense of revelation that this old wretch haunted him, a ghost in moments critical, led him first astray, and always spurred his interest in the fifty-years' fortune at any time the same might seem to flag.

"Corodale! Corodale!" Dark John cried, long before he neared him, waving his arms in a kind of frenzy. "Stop you there till I have my breath, for I have a story."

Col waited, wondering. The old man toiled through the bent grass, panting, the soil of two days' travelling in every furrow of his face. He caught Col's stirrup, and pointed back at the bay whence he had come so hurriedly; not at the folk cheering Anna as they accompanied her to the presbytery, but at the sloop, that was already putting about, as it seemed, to the open sea.

"A bad death on me, master," said he, "if yonder's not the last chance of the Arkaig *ulaidh*, and it at the turning of a tail on you!"

Col had a little saugh switch in his hand, cut from the tacksman's garden. In a sudden fury to have his unwelcomest thoughts brought back to him this way, he lashed the old man on the face with it and raised a weal.

"Master, master! Have I deserved it?" cried Dark John. "My God! here's pretty wages for all that I have done for you. Night and day have I been at the toiling for you, wanting meat and drink; listening, contriving, lying, taking the taunt for you, and you give me the willow withie! O king! have not I been the fool in my liking? For payment but the wand across the face! Black's the name of the willow that had no pity on the Son of God in His extremity, but, like the shivering-ash, held up its head, a braggart when the rest of the wood was trembling. No matter, master, no matter; yours is my hand, yours is my bosom, for I have said it: the cheek, O king! may go with it. See, I will give you the other side!"

He held up the other cheek for the lash, and Col rued his evil temper. "You come at the wrong hours always," he snarled. "But I am vexed I switched you. The life is worried out of me, these days, with many things. Has Herself come home yonder?"

"Faith! that has she," said Dark John, and caught again at the stirrup; "but not the way she went. Your friend, the speckled innkeeper in Benbecula, has got the best of her."

"What's that you're saying?" cried Col, jumping from his saddle. "Do you tell me she told him yon thing?"

"It cost him no more than a scrape of a pen from your brother Duncan. You might have kent the fellow; he kept a letter from the budget. Was ever a red-haired man, and he speckled, that swithered to give up a friend?"

"That red rogue turned traitor! May the brute die foreign and far from friends!" cried Col, all the new hopes built on the sight of Anna's home-coming toppling into the dust again. He looked blankly at the sloop, and his wits went wandering.

"In the Isles from here to Harris you have not a friend, O king! that is dependable, but myself. Am not I your man since yon night – Lord! – out there, and you so gallantly gripping me when the yellow of the end came in my eyes? They are saying that to drown is a pleasant dying, like the sweet half-dream of the morning, but they need not be telling that to me, for I have drowned and I know different: it is falling to a depth without a bottom, and the heart of you bursting, bursting!"

Col seemed as if he never heard him, glowering bewildered at the sloop. "Were you on the ship?" he asked, "and what were you doing there?"

"What but in your service? I would never have heard any more than yourself where the *ulaidh* was, if my wits did not keep me on the heels of the speckled fellow yonder."

"You know the place?" cried Col.

"No one better," he answered; "but the worst of it is the Sergeant knows nearly as well, and he's now on his way to the place in Mingulay."

He told the story hurriedly – of the shearing rumour that Duncan was returning, of the Sergeant's plan for squeezing the secret from Anna, of its failure at the first, and how at last the letter had compelled her, but never said a word about the share he had played, himself, in the decoying.

Col swore in English oaths, ever with an anxious eye on the sloop, that hung in the wind off Orosay, as if her mind was not made up on what her course should be. At last his brain came out of its fermentation. There was something to do, and the doing must be quickly settled on.

"Mingulay I know," said he, "and the arcades of it, and this dark quarter-mile they call the gallery I have been at the mouth of with my father once; but the Merry Dancers and their blood – it is beyond me! One might pick the saying up in a song of the country."

"There you are now! Did I not always say what a poor thing was this schooling, where a fellow blinds himself with books, and does not know the hemlock in his garden! Glad am I, *oh righ!* that I was not burdened with it, but was left with all my natural faculties. You do not know the *fuil nan Sluagh* – the blood of the Merry Dancers? Neither does the speckled fellow, and I would not tell him, but I could take you there to Mingulay and put your hand on it."

"At what price?" asked Col.

"For not a farthing! I would not take the Arkaig treasure if in depth it were to my knees and in width a pole, for a handful of dulse: a hundred times have I heard Master Ludovick call it cursed."

"But you do not care if the curse of it fall on me! That, by my faith, is droll friendship!"

Dark John held up an eager face to him. "Corodale," said he, "in the mornings, when I am newly wakened, and my innocence is still upon me, before the world takes hold, I will be thinking of that; thinking quick, and always certain that you were well to let it be. At night, too, when all the vigours are gone from my body, I have the same notion, that you would be the wiser not to set your mind on it, and I would be more your man to keep you from it. But when I am in my full possession, and with a taste – the littlest taste – of seaweed on my palate, I have another fellow in my skin, and if the stuff was at the other end of France I would carry you on my back to it. Yonder it goes!" He pointed to the sloop. "Oh love of men! have you not some notion of a way to get to Mingulay before him?"

"By the seven stars! and if I had a decent boat I would sail him for it," cried Col, plucking his Spanish beard, his eyes like lamps under shaggy eaves. His man stood helpless beside him, dog-tired, his eagerness slipping from him out of weariness. He had been sure that Col was capable even of miracles; here he was as useless as himself.

"A decent boat," said he, "and forty miles to Mingulay. Forty miles! and I am not liking the look of the weather at all, at all! There is a bit of a yawl of Baldy-Kate-Veg's in the creek down there at Dalvoolin –"

"The yawl!" cried Col. "I quite forgot her. With the yawl and this sou'-west wind as it is, I could easily make it – Mingulay before the nightfall; and Jib-boom, I'll warrant, could not make it any sooner. You will give me a hand, stout fellow?"

"Mingulay!" said John, and all his terror of the deep waters came over him.

Col waited no answer, but jumped into the saddle, and started for Dalvoolin, that he had so lately left. "Come along," he commanded, and the old man followed him.

Col turned his horse loose in the tacksman's field, and ran to the creek. Before the other joined him the sails were up, the yawl was ready for her voyage, and though the old man's fears cried out to him to remain on the steadfast land, he was, in his flesh, so much the agent of his master that he was at the jib-sheets without his will's consent, as it were, in a kind of trance.

The hour was seven. The sun was up in heaven, struck hot on the canvas, and brought the smell of bark and brine from it; the tar that coated the boat was blistering on the gunnel. Clear of the creek the sea beat on the island with a strength that marked its edge with white; high tide hid the lesser rocks that were scattered to the north of Eriskay, the green little isle tranquil within the beacons of Fearay.

On the wide sea or on the Sounds there was no other boat than this, and the sloop, that still hung dubious off Orosay.

"We have the start at any rate," said Col, looking back at her. "Now I'm wondering what is keeping them. Ah! yonder he goes! I thought he would not lose a minute longer if he saw us."

The sloop fell off; her sails, that had been idly flapping, filled in the brisk sou'-wester, and she made for the Sound of Barra leisuredly, as if treasure was a poor consideration to cause the tightening of a sheet.

"If that's the side of Barra that she's going to," said Col, astonished, "then Jib-boom is an odd man for a sailor. Are you sure, old man, it is Mingulay?"

"Am I sure, O king! my ears are on my head? I wish we were as certain to get there and back with the boat below us, for there's a gale at the brewing yonder." He pointed to the south, where black clouds with a yellow core lay thick between sea and sky.

"*Dhe!*" said Col, uneasy, "there's going to be a night of it, no doubt; it's plain Jib-boom is thinking the lee of Barra safest. Well, let him have it! it is longest too!"

He drew well out from Scurrival, and Grean Head, and Dorval, and still the weather favoured them. Barra swam at their counter, dazzling white with sands, all its bays murmuring; high over its mountains, birds; blue reek of shearing-fires on its upper levels, the townships on the plain forsaken. Col saw little of these things, that Dark John cherished and pined for with a landsman's eye. For Col the interest lay ahead of his ship; his heart was hammering at the doors of fortune in the long gallery of Mingulay, and when they rounded Doirlinn Head, and Mingulay was opened, he gave a gasp to think this was the reality, that somewhere in these rocks were stored the extravagant hours. If a wish could sink the *Happy Return* somewhere on the other side of the island, sailing too for treasure, she would lie with all her folk in the greenest depths of the Minch, rocking soft among the weeds and star-fish, that he might ride in the world above in wealth and splendour.

It was noon when they were come to Vatersay: the tide was on the turn; a calm that left the sails useless came suddenly, and for hours the two men laboured at the sweeps. There was no sight of the sloop; that was the one thought that made the travail at the oars to Col a mere diversion. His companion rowed in a kind of ecstasy, the sap of sea-weed sustaining him, though hours wanting food left him hungry. Col seemed to him gigantic, a marvel of endurance, so tireless that he might have rowed to the other side of the world, speechless – so full was he of thoughts. No sign of the sloop; and now a great space of empty sea behind them: the prize seemed in their grasp; if not, here came the wind again to help them.

It rose as sudden as it fell, gusty and fierce, catching the yawl at her bows, and throwing cold green seas to sluice along her ballast. Mingulay staggered a while beyond the spars, then leaped on them with the leaping wave, so large, so black, so terrible that the heart of the old man shrank to the size of a parched pea. "My end!" he cried; "we are gone, Corodale!" and caught the rigging. Col laughed. "No, nor gone," said he, "so long as I can hold a tiller." They passed in a second from the infuriate sea to a calm the ear could not believe in, but filled with a false commotion, the phantoms of all old sounds since the creation, the everlasting humming of the universe. The yawl was in a creek that lay like a broken cup in the thick of the cliffs of Carnan. Like oil the water lay around them; on every hand, except at the door they entered, the rock rose giddy over them, the seafowl white on its ledges.

CHAPTER XXXII

The Blood of the Merry Dancers

THE water was the water of a quarry-hole in this black creek of Mingulay, but with the scum of storms on it; no clean sea-foam, fresh spit of tempest, but a sickly yellow spume that saltly stank, streaking the surface on every side of the yawl, curdling like turned cream behind boulders, crusting with green decay the sides of the enormous rock in whose bowels it was prisoned. Dark John, at their entrance, lifted his face suddenly and sniffed. "My end, my hope, my loss, and my losing!" said he; "here is the sea-sap, the juice of the Long Isle ribs, and it at its simmering," – but then a loathing followed quick on his first gusto for seaweeds, and he grued. Enchantment held the place for him; it had an air familiar and alarming; he was come, he felt, on something he had known once long ago and quite forgotten. The stagnant air, the stillness, the drifting of the boat, the cliffs, stupendous over him and threatening, the smells of the rejected rags of tides, all stung him in the memory as acquaintances old and ominous. "O king! let us get out of it," he cried, and suddenly stood to his feet and pushed the oar down under water far above the loom, trying to check their entrance in a deep that had no bottom. Col took a foot-spar and rapped him on the knuckles. "Let her go!" he commanded, "or on my father's bones I'll throw you over." And John, grieving, strove again at the sweeps, but with abhorrence of the pool and of the walls confining it.

Of all the sea-birds gossiping on the high white ledges none seemed at any time to break the surface of that eerie water: it might be poisoned, by the way that they avoided it, and yet, rowing the boat to the inner end, Col and his companion could not but wonder at the life that tenanted the creek. Black-deep at the entrance, it shoaled sufficiently to make the bottom visible, though at no place could the oar fathom it, and looking over the side they could see the floor and its inhabitants – thickets of wrack, dark brown with waving leaves, and rank green undergrowth, and berried with fruit that must ripe and rot for God's purpose though beyond man's use or speculation, and glades of sand with crab and star-fish pondering in them, waiting for what to them was destiny. In the depths, too, they saw themselves, white-faced, across the gunnel; far below them, space, and the flying of cloud and sea-bird – another world as voiceless as the grave, but living in expectation.

Now that he was come to the place whose secret he had coveted so long, a melancholy fell on Col, made up of weariness and hunger, of apprehensions, too, that everything was but a dream, himself and his desires, and even this, the promise of fulfilment. Him, too, the creek of Carnan almost frightened, when he looked at the close arcades and caves recessed from either side of it. In them the water lapped like something living, something gluttonous; out of dark ravines that had the tide-mark green high up on them to where the dung of sea-fowl whitened on the rock, came the sob of the inner water.

The night was coming on, sooner here in the shades of the surrounding rock than elsewhere, a premature unnatural dusk, that stilled the birds of Carnan at an hour when in the outer sea they were still white-bellied in the sun, and joyous. There was a hum of wind above the hill, and evidence of a storm outside was in the rolling of the water, that never broke in waves, but swelled with a glassy surface as if it had been oil. A yellow dusk, in which the sea-fowl screamed, appeared to float like a vapour into the place, and Col came suddenly to himself, and bending to the oar, dragged madly for the long gallery. "Amn't I the fool to be lingering here, and maybe these fellows at our heels?" he said, remembering all at once that the secret of the *ulaidh's* hiding-place was not his alone.

If the creek was dark, darker was the gallery, the last ribbon of the sea recessed in Carnan Hill. It ran in a cleft that they pushed through with their oars against the rocks, which fell precipitous beside them, green with the slime of birds or with the weeds of the more adventurous tides. Col lifted his voice and cried into the way winding before them. Mactalla answered him – Mactalla, son of Earth, the old laugher, the old scorner, who was there the very first, and will be there the last, and remembers and understands. Col's challenge to the heart of the hill came back with a chuckling sound as of mockery. The tide was flowing, though in the gallery there was no apparent current. Bats flew in its crannies and the birds were far above; but otherwise life was gone, and the sky narrowed over them till they came at last to the end of the passage, where it broadened in a round inky pool that seemed the draining of the rock that rose dizzily on every hand. In the little bit of heaven they could see, a star for a moment burned, and then was hidden. All the rumour of the storm was somehow in this funnel of the hill; the wind sucked in it as it were in a gullet that swallowed every gale.

They stood in the boat and looked above them. "A kiln," said the old man; "just a kiln," and stretched his hand to pluck a shred of sea-weed growing with the barnacles on the rock. Col scanned the whole interior in one eager glance that covered everything to be seen in the dusk.

"Now we're here, old hero!" said he, "where's this blood of the Merry Dancers?"

Dark John searched the rock. "When the Merry Dancers light the north sky in winter-time," said he, "it is, as the old folk say, the strife of hosts who are there in a great enchantment. Their blood falls on the rock – that *is fuil nan sluagh*; that is the blood of the multitude. Look you, Corodale, for a red stain so long as daylight will let you. It must be – By the Book, Corodale, there it is!" He pointed to a red patch of mould or lichen, high on the rock before them, touched by the last wandering gleam of daylight, that but revealed it and went away. They could see that a ledge was below it. The situation was such an one as Col had sometimes seen in dreams.

"*Fuil nan sluagh*," he said, with his heart thundering. "Faith! now I mind of hearing the saying from my father when I was a boy. The very words were in his mouth when Father Ludovick was anointing him for the grave." He spoke in a whisper; his eyes pierced the dusk of the gallery, his head thrown back, calculating what height the ledge was from them and how it might be reached. At first it seemed a place that the goat or eagle only could mount to, so high it was and inaccessible. The rock might have been split with an axe, the riven sides of it appeared to fall so smooth and so precipitous to the very water; but that at some points soil had gathered on bosses and ledges, and was grown upon by rough herbage, ivy, and willow. But before the last of the light was gone and the chamber they floated in was wrapped in a more sombre dusk, he made out some terraces that, rising one above another on the right, wound round the funnel of the hill, until in every probability they reached the ledge below the lichen stain. It was thus, if anyway, the treasure must have been conveyed to its hiding-place.

He had such a gust of greed to see the gold come over him that he could not wait for daylight, though an ascent now was dangerous; in a fury he tore off his coat and waistcoat, pulled off his boots, and ordered his companion to keep the boat where she was till he had mounted. Dark John fastened the yawl with a pin in a cranny of the rock, crouched with his head in his hands, and began lamenting. He watched Col's preparations, and felt like one that was about to be deserted. Fear of the dark came over him, and of this crevice holding all the venom of the sea, his enemy; the tang of tide-waste rotting on the walls, the blackness of the depths, the hum of the wind in the funnel overhead, made all to him like an ocean cave where seamen's ghosts roved constantly.

"Corodale!" he cried hurriedly, "I have on me a penny; come, I am your fellow-man, I will toss you head or harp who bides in the boat and who goes climbing. On my word, if it was climbing for a week, I would sooner do it than remain with myself and my thinking here."

He got no answer, for Col, in a transport, already crept along the first of the terraces, the boat and his companion forgotten, but one thing singing in his veins. At first he found his climbing easy; but half-way to his goal the rock became more difficult, and was almost wholly dark, with a darkness that hid the boat below, and now it showed the sky above him only as a grey patch. With every foot of his progress his eagerness rose too; he felt that if the very mount had a soul that conspired against him he could master it. Startled in their sleep, birds rose from shelves beside him screaming, and some of them flapped across his face; he moved in an intuition more than by any judgment, crawling, clutching, slipping, rising from terrace to terrace, hanging sometimes by his hands above the abyss, in a passage that with a few hours' patience might have been made in ease and safety. But patience was gone from Col, in whose blood was boiling the fever of avarice. It was pitch-dark when he reached the ledge below the lichen stain. He knew he must be there, because it was the conclusion of the terracing.

A narrow ledge, by all appearance, from the water, it proved to be a broad platform when he reached it. The rock hung in a cornice over it, and on its breadth was a coarse grass and the litter of gulls. He climbed into it with hardly a breath left in his body, and lay for a little on his breast, panting with his labours.

From the depths he had left suddenly rose a cry – long, solemn, and craving – the expression of a grieving and abandoned soul, more searching than the boom of the wind, that up in this ledge of fortune was inconceivably loud, incredibly vociferous. He listened, startled when its echo died along the gallery and in the caves; the sea-birds silenced, the very wind that boomed above him lulled, or seemed to lull, a moment. Again it rose, that wailing cry, the cry of the soul of the sea imprisoned; a voice with no words, but infinitely sad, like women's voices crying cattle in on winter dusks on windy ebb-tide machars. Strange and yet familiar; he had heard something of the kind before, when Dark John plumbed the depths of Barra Sound and rose to the surface for the last time. Again he felt some fear of this old reprobate, who somehow had become so profound a part of his life. Well, this was the last of it, he thought; with the treasure secure, there was no longer need for intrigue with Dark John. Lying as he was, with his breast to the floor of the platform, he felt in the dark all over it. With his toes overhanging the edge he could reach its backmost wall. So far as he could discover this way, there was nothing on the ledge. He crawled on his knees, and blindly felt all round it.

Nothing!

The blood went to his head, its blows beat dull in his temples; the sweat soaked through his palms in a cold moisture.

Nothing! He must try again – this emptiness was a delusion: again his hands went over the floor and the wall behind it, finding only the soil, the crinkled lichen.

He had been deceived; there was no treasure here; an overmastering anger whelmed him. Climbing the face of the rock, his mind had been filled with the most glorious fancies. He had not felt fatigue; he had no more thought of danger than if he walked the flat sea-sand; wine could not have more exalted him, and this was what it came to!

He sat on the ledge, stunned at first, then in a tumult of fury at these untoward circumstances that were all bound up in some way with the old rogue wailing there below. No ease of mind had been for him since he dragged its prey from the sea, to be his spur to schemes that somehow seemed to end in foolishness and mockery. It was *trom-lighe* – it was Incubus he had lifted from the Barra Sound; there was something after all in the ancient proverb. The wail of his companion rose up again appealing; a horror of the creature for the moment drowned his vast chagrin at finding he was deceived and that there was no treasure.

The old man, left in the yawl below when Col ascended, sat listening for a while to the sound of his master climbing on the terraces. So long as he had that evidence of companionship he could master some of his fears; but in a little the man who climbed was high among the winds and out of hearing: the night, enormous and inimical, a tangible thing that clung, was round the yawl. He sat in the heart of tempest, in the core of the rock, where – as he fancied – winds were bred: though the yawl in her sheltered chasm had no movement, she was in the realm of night and storm and dream, unconscious of creation. For nearly a year, since he had tasted the bitterness of Barra Sound, he had felt himself the ocean's instrument, a slave of the sea he hated. To him it was not a lifeless element with wavering purposes, but a stupendous spirit moving abroad in a watery garment, scourging ships, striding the isles, hunting the souls of men, and here was he surely come into its cavern. The soul of the sea must be somewhere – in all the fearful coasts was anywhere more likely than in Mingulay and this black cleft in Carnan Hill? The dulse he plucked from the side of the rock had at last no savour for his palate; his taste was gone, but the other senses of him sharpened, so that in the blackness he could see the sky like smoke above him and hear the thrash of wings and smell the crawling depths. All trembling, he lifted up his voice and cried on Corodale. No human answer came to him, Col was in another world. Again and again he cried, his wail almost gave him comfort, but oh! the horror of its echo. He could stay where he was no longer, and leaving the boat, began to climb upon the terraces, crying as he went.

He came on the ledge when Col's chagrin was at its blackest, his cry rising close and suddenly and appalling under the eave of the rock. Col, lying on the ledge, heart-broken, heard his incubus, that comes in sleep and flies with the dawn on the window. 'Twas the man, he knew, and yet it was not; 'twas the ravished sea that cried in the old man's semblance, and he could not answer. Dark John, with his breast on the ledge, put out his hand and touched his master on the shoulder, felt along his neck, and drew his fingers lightly over his face. Col's flesh revolted at the touch, the odour and damp of the sea-cave were there. He started up, and with an oath thrust out his hand at his disturber. The consequence left him horror-stricken. For Dark John fell!

He fell with Corodale's name on his lips. He fell from terrace to terrace; he fell, as it seemed, eternally, for no sound came from below to tell of the end of his falling.

Col bent over the ledge and cried; no answer came to his question.

He cried again. Mactalla, the old scorner, chuckled in the rocks, the wind hummed overhead, the sea-birds clanged, but he got no answer. He dared not venture to descend in the darkness, for the hope that nerved his climbing was now gone. He cried again – coaxing, craving, threatening – and strained his ears for an answer. There came up, on a flaw of wind, a whiff of wrack, fresh bared by the turn of the tide in the gallery, and a wailing faint and distant immeasurably: that was all.

CHAPTER XXXIII

The Turn of the Tide

THE deed was so quickly done, and so simple was his share in it, that Col found it was not difficult to convince himself it was an accident. Murder was never in his thoughts, nor had he put himself in any way to that stress of mind or body that surely went to murder. It was dark; he had not dreamt the old man was so precarious upon the ledge; he had just pushed lightly with his hand, meaning to ward off his loathsome pawings, this lamentable catastrophe would never have happened to a man awake in mind and alert in body.

Then, again, – he contemplated, with his wits in more control, – doubtless the old fellow was no more than bruised, a broken rib at the worst, his falling checked in a measure by the terraces and the knobs of rock that bossed the cliff: with any luck at all he was lying halfway down as comfortably as Col himself lay. There came into his mind sometimes another picture – of his victim huddled as the last agony left him, swaying at the bottom of the pool among its weedy thickets, the star-fish and the crab indifferent to his presence; and that was a vision he thrust from him hastily each time that it took form. What thoughts he had had of fear and bitterness for Dark John were vanished miraculously; it gave him pleasure to think how carefully to-morrow he would take the old man home.

To-morrow! And home too! Home to Corodale, not a penny the better for this ridiculous adventure, and the knowledge that he had set out upon it common to all the Isles! The cursed thing was that he had shown his hand; it would be known that he had made this mad rush for Mingulay with the old man, in an enterprise whose shamefulness was obvious now to himself. It was that, at last, troubled him more than reflection on the old man, dead or injured.

Outside this funnel of Carnan Hill how the gale was blowing! Above him the wind was risen from its hum to a hooting, as if Pan played a giant pipe with Mingulay hollows for his instrument. Cold currents swept over the face of the rock; the tide, that had risen soundlessly, went back with chokings and retchings, sucked gluttonously by the sea. Then came rain – at first a drizzle, by-and-by in torrents, that soaked the litter of the ledge and drenched himself to the skin with icy water. It did him a service, too, for he was thirsty; his mouth as dry as a mill's hopper with the first fright of the accident. Greedily he scooped water, foul as it was, from the hollows of the ledge, and drank it from his palms. A great weariness burdened every part of him; the fancy seized him that it was the rock was living and that he himself was dead; the huge inscrutable night compressed him, and all his life came marshalling before him – its incidents, its ambitions, its failures – none of them due to his will or his devising. For a dozen years, since he came under the influence of the Sergeant's stories, and all his greeds uprose in him, he had worn the face of virtue and generosity, and all the time, below the shell of appearance, there was a man so different! If his father had not been a fool and had not spent in a fool's enterprises the fortune that had come to him, Col told himself he might have been a noble man. Heaven knew it was not for love of hypocrisy he was hypocrite, for any passion for wealth he was so parsimonious. Had luck been with him, and Dark John's story that the treasure was in Mingulay been true, he would, in a day, have sloughed the ancient sinner and come out clean and estimable.

But Dark John's information was wrong. No doubt he had himself been deceived, and the inn-keeper, with the true secret perhaps, was already in possession. Could it have been for any other reason the sloop had shown herself so indifferent to Mingulay, and sailed the other side of Barra? Eriskay – the Weaver's Stack – somewhere there was the fifty-year fortune.

With the storm possessing Carnan even to its hollows and its very roots, he lay the night long, waiting for the morning. In lulls of wind he sometimes tried the depths again for his own comfort, crying down the name of his companion, but always vainly. The night seemed the the last of nights, wherein sun and day are dreams only and never had reality. When at last a dun sky revealed itself over him, he was almost at the stage of an indifference. All will, all interest in things, were gone, washed out of him by the rain that poured the night long; and his hunger, one time frantic, was turned to pain, that almost revolted at the thought of eating again. Before the light was well in the funnel of the rock, and while there was still danger in descending, he prepared to leave, and it was then a thing happened that almost seemed the trick of a mischievous fate.

As he was going over the edge of the shelf that had so cruelly disappointed him, his hand on it for the last time, his fingers touched a coin. It lay among the litter of the gulls. His movements through the night had brought it to the surface, and when he rubbed it clean and found it a piece of French gold, a vexation swept through him that was more intense than any he had felt before, for there was the single evidence that after all Dark John was right, and this had been the hiding-place for the Arkaig *ulaidh*..

He stopped long enough to turn over every patch of grass and search every crack that was visible, and left only when it was plain that a bare floor and a bare back wall were before him. Then he quitted the ledge with reluctance, as if he thought he was the victim of enchantment, and that by-and-by, if he only waited, he would see the stuff that was now invisible. What a fool he had been to think old Dermosary or Father Ludovick would leave twenty thousand pounds tarnishing uselessly here for the sake of a sentiment!

So much did his vexation master him at this new discovery, that his anxiety about Dark John and the pangs of his hunger were forgotten for a while. The day was still but beginning, and the pool below invisible, till he came half-way down. What struck him oddly at first was that the old man was not to be seen: he had compelled his mind to think so much on him as waiting below, grumbling, that this was unbelievable. Clutching a willow-root, and bending over to look to the bottom of the cleft, he could scarcely convince himself that Dark John was not there. The thought that he was drowned after all filled Col again with horror; he had for some moments the agony of a second murder. He trembled in every limb; the willow-shrub he held shook in the cleft of rock it grew from, and losing his hold, he fell to the next terrace with a shock that sickened him.

When he sat up, new pains wrenched his body, and his right arm, he found, was useless. And yet he made a discovery then that gladdened him. It was that the yawl, as well as the old man, was missing. He had no thought of it till his eyes fell on the peg to which Dark John had fastened the boat, and when he saw it tethered nothing he gave a cry of astonishment. Across the pool, and deep into the gallery that led to it, he could see quite clearly; the water lay blackly in the wan dawn light, at ebb, with green slime showing on the walls for feet below high-water mark. Dark John was gone, and had taken the boat with him!

Col crept to the lowest terrace, racked in body, but for a while more eased in mind, for at least he was not guilty of manslaughter. Limpets scabbed the rock at the water edge; he loosened them with a knife, and gouged them out with his thumb, eating them without much relish, pondering the while what Dark John's object was and whether, if it was in a natural anger he went, he would have a speedy remorse and return. He counted much on the old man's fealty to him, so that for a little he was not greatly troubled by the thought of the difficulties of escape, though these were plainly manifest to him. There was but the one way out of the place for any living creature wanting wings – through the gallery and its quarter-mile of gloomy water of a depth unfathomed. It was some time before it came to him that, fine swimmer as he was this was not the swimming, even at his best, that he would willingly set out on, and with his injuries it was utterly beyond him.

For hours Col lay expectant, his eye on the mouth of the gallery, from which he could not let himself believe the yawl at any moment was not certain to return. Every circumstance sustained his hope: the terrors of the deep would not permit Dark John to venture alone on the open sea, that was still tempestuous, from the shelter of the creek, where he was trapped by his fears as surely as his master. And, besides, he dared not, even if he could make round for the habitable parts of Mingulay or the neighbour isles without Col, who had been seen to leave Dalvoolin with him.

These thoughts for hours were comforting, but nothing happened to confirm them. Once for a little, when the tide was at its first flowing, there was a sound in the gallery that filled Col with the jubilance of relief – the lap of water on clinker planks, the soft thud of timber, as if the yawl laboured to return in the narrow passage. He cried the name of his companion, but never got an answer and the hopeful rumour ceased, leaving a stillness more ominous than before.

The sun came out at midday. It glared from the eye of the hill on him – ardent, unnatural, small, and swift in passage. Not long it stayed, but stirred the thousand birds on the upper cliff into wild discordance, their multitude, their indifference to himself, amazing and disturbing Col. Their liberty to quit so easily the pit that prisoned himself spurred him even in his pains to try the upper ledges again, to seek if he had not overlooked some exit there. He crawled from terrace to terrace; but his broken body would not bear the exercise, and he was bound at last to return to the water-edge, and there thirst of the most anguishing kind assailed him, with no means of assuaging it; the brine of the shell-fish seemed to cake on his palate.

Night poured on Carnan and filled the cup of it with blackness. He slept till morning feverishly, hearing in nightmares Dark John's cries, far off and bitterly craving, now the accent of humanity, now the veritable voice of the sea; hearing, too, and that in moments half-awake, the lapping of the water on the boards of the yawl that had abandoned him. Hunger and thirst made the day that followed desperate. Black blanks came in among the hours of light; time was no more for him, nor hope, till one night there floated in on the high tide, among the scum of the stormy seas round Mingulay, the yawl herself, as black as death in the light of a moon that set the pool on fire. Her jib flapped as when he had left her to climb for fortune; the figure of Dark John sat propped against the mast.

Col raised himself on his arm and tried to cry, but his voice refused obedience. The boat floated in the middle of the pool without any help from wind or oar, the figure on her motionless. She was scarcely her own length from him, and swung her bow a moment, as if she meant to leave again and come no nearer. With one wild rallying of his senses he plunged into the water and swam for some tortured strokes till his hand was on her gunnel. There was a terror in the look of her, no innocent kindly boat was here, his agent of deliverance; it seemed some deadly craft of fever-wanderings, that sails unnatural seas.

And then the moon gave up her secret! For a second he saw Dark John's face turned round to look at him, the jaw fallen, the eyeballs withered, a body below it broken on the thwart where it had fallen from the cliff, the limbs spread out unnaturally. The boat, adrift from her tether had lingered in the gallery all these tides, and now – God over all! – 'twas Death come back for him!

The yawl heeled over with his weight; the body fell on his shoulders; the tide was sucking his feet, and he sank with his burden, with *trom-lighe* – incubus – spoil of the sea he had robbed at Michaelmas – to the dark, expectant, patient depths.

CHAPTER XXXIV

Conclusion

FOR days the islands lay in the very throat of storm, the Minch and Atlantic trying their best to break them, the Sounds continually white and furious or wrapped in fogs. Boats were lost on Barra Head; a ship from the sunny side of the world came in with all her folk on Eriskay, and they died on a Sunday on gaunt Rhu Breabadair, doubtless thinking of their orchards and their flowers. Boisdale presbytery sat in the shelter of Our Lady Star as snug as a nut in the noisy forest, full of happiness (except when thinking of the seaman on the tossing spar) and nothing knowing of the tragedies that lay beyond the channels.

When Anna was at her baking, Ludovick would come out to stand on the rock of Stella Maris and drink tempest, or tramp along the machar sand, surrendered in his mind to the ancient mother, and getting a gaiety of spirit so no other way available. Together they sat at night hearkening to the thousand ghosts of Ossian over Hecla and Benmore; his very sermons borrowed something from the season, and shook the chapel rafters. "Och! dear, now, isn't he fine, fine?" said the Boisdale people, and went home, themselves uplifted.

Came news from the other side of Uist that Col was unusually long from home; his horse was found in Dalvoolin, and some one had seen him set out on the yawl with Dark John, who was missing too, but this was not alarming: Col's business might have sent him into Barra or Benbecula, and the storm might readily have kept him there. To Ludovick sometimes came an apprehension that he was ashamed of, involving, as it did, a doubt of Col's last shred of honour: he never mentioned it to his sister, and yet it was on his tongue-tip often, when she was on the subject of her strange adventure at Creggans Inn. That he never blamed her for so easily relinquishing her secret did not much surprise her – that, indeed, was like him, – but she thought it curious that he never seemed to contemplate punishment for the wretches who had been responsible. He had had only a word – more sorrowful than angry – for Dark John when that old rogue came ashore from the sloop with her: for the innkeeper of Benbecula he had an odd pity that was half amusement.

"Let them go!" said he; "their punishment is in other hands," and hushed the islanders, who were furious for justice. It was a policy that pleased Anna, who was, herself, the very soul of forgiveness, perhaps because it was by her tribulations Duncan was to be restored. For he was coming back – she never let herself doubt it; coming back the more quickly when he should know how she had suffered, and was now the possessor of no unlucky fortune. When Ludovick was abroad, rain-battered shouting poetry on the sand, rejoicing in the tempest, she was praying for better weather as she bustled about her household offices, because these stormy seas cut Uist off entirely from the world where her hopes were, and her thoughts.

"Boreas," would she say to Ludovick, "have done, in pity, with thy gales!"

"What!" he would answer slyly, "for the sake of the drying of clothes?"

"Oh, I have other reasons, your reverence," she told him boldly; and he would smile, knowing them very well.

One night the storm blew as if its final breath was in it, and at daybreak it was the calm that wakened Anna, accustomed so long to sleep through the sounding of wind and sea. The Isles sparkled in sunshine, the sea laughed to its rim; in her bosom gushed a sense of wellbeing that presaged, as she felt, some speedy happiness.

It came, next day, with the sloop's return.

Not from the *Happy Return* had she looked for it – that vessel now ill-reputed more than ever; it amazed her indeed that it should so soon come back to a harbour where its influence had been so evil.

She and Ludovick stood at the porch and watched the sloop drop anchor. Her skipper came ashore alone, passed through the crowd of folk who jeered and threatened him, and boldly marched up to the presbytery.

"I'm here, Master Ludovick," said he, "and in all my life I have never run a better cargo."

"I hope it is one more willing than your last," said the priest.

"Willing enough, I'll assure you, and I'm here to make a bargain for it. I'm asking no more, Master Ludovick and Herself, than your forgiveness."

Ludovick put his hand on his shoulder. "Dan, Dan," said he, "you're a foolish fellow, the cat's-paw for a ruffian."

"By my faith! and I have got rid of him, then, and I'm in that droll state I cannot tell the name of my own ship's owner. But that is a small affair beside the other news that I have for you. Put your eye, Miss Anna, on the *Happy Return*, and tell me if you see a passenger."

Anna's heart leaped; his words could have but one meaning. "Not – not Mr Duncan?" she said, all red, and then quite pale for fear.

"Nobody else if Dan MacNeil has the use of his eyes and all his other faculties. Two or three splendid dances have I lost this week in Arisaig, that I might be the one to take him back. I'm not a bit complaining, though I'm the boy for the dancing; if it was twenty-and-three, and twenty to it, I would have come with yon fellow to Boisdale gaily. I made but the single pact with him – that he should let me have the chance to come the first ashore and tell you. It was the only way I thought I ever could make the face of me welcome again in Boisdale."

"Indeed," cried Anna, glad and trembling, "you are welcome," and took the skipper's hand.

Boisdale was merry that night: the piper fellow on Kinavreck played so lustily he almost burst the bag of his noble instrument, and there was dancing in the townships, such as Jib-boom delighted in – the dancing that may stop for supper but never for sleep.

"What do you say, my dear, to Tir-nan-oig?" asked Duncan. They fled from the sound of the revellers and together launched the *Ron*. She sat in his arm and heard his heart beat at her ear and felt his breath in her hair, and over him there came the birchen odour. A half-moon swung like a halbert-head among the stars; the Sound was filled with gold. Along the shores the little waves went lapping softly; burns tinkled down the sands. For long they sailed in silence, indulgent of their illusion that this indeed was Tir-nan-oig, where comes no grief nor ageing. They rounded Orosay, and heard the whooper swan in his sleep; the night was generous of its memories that came to them often again when they saw their children sail in the bay of Corodale.

"Oh!" she said at last, "how I wearied!"

"And I!" said Duncan. "The lad I tutored must have thought me crazy, walking my room till morning, thinking, thinking, and every separate thought a different grief. I had made up my mind that as you did not write to me you were determined to forget; and so I came to find out for myself."

"Oh!" she cried, and drew away from him; "was that your trust in me? I never doubted for a moment."

He drew her to his side again and looked into her eyes deep orbs that held the moon. "Not once?" he asked her softly.

"Only once, and briefly, when your brother came," she admitted. "Could you blame me?"

"I had in him, I'm sure, a firm defender," said Duncan.

"Indeed you had," she answered, remembering only all Col's crafty sentences, that seemed genuine to her innocence. "Poor Col! I fear I vexed him. I think he sometimes fancied, like yourself, that I was willing to forget."

"Forget! How lucky, maybe, was he then," said Duncan. "But you did not."

She nestled in his arms. "I did not, dear," said she. "Were we not together once in Tir-nan-oig? Who comes back from Tir-nan-oig?"

The *Ron* – oh happy galley! surely no other boat in all the world bore freight more precious than these two hearts – swam through the liquid gold; jewels from the deep came beaded on her sides, and broke profuse and glowing at her bow. Out to their doors came the elder folk of Boisdale, and looked on what had once been so familiar. "Herself is satisfied," said they, sharing her happiness. They heard her sing. Her voice came over the water from Orosay's lee, a sound enchanting – Bride's voice that hushes the children and wrings the hearts of men.

Father Ludovick left the revelry of his people and drew aside Jib-boom. "What have you done with your master?" he asked him.

"Master! I never had one; my name's MacNeil. But there was a fellow yonder sometimes paid me wages," said the skipper. "For him you may well be inquiring; he is gone for good, and a widow's at grass over yonder in Creggans."

"What! Not dead?" cried Ludovick.

"Not that I know of; but I'll swear there's a halter somewhere ready for him. I took him to the mainland, and there in a hurry he left me when he saw this gentleman of Corodale."

"What did you find in Mingulay?" asked the priest.

"We never went," said the skipper, "for I have been there before.

When Herself went ashore, 'Now let us slant for Mingulay,' says the Sergeant, 'for I have an object.' 'You need not trouble to go so far,' I told him. 'There has not been a coin of the Arkaig *ulaidh* on Mingulay for a dozen of years;' and I told him on my oath what there's not another in all the islands knows except myself – unless – unless – it might be Father Ludovick."

"I have known it," said the priest, "since old Corodale, who stole it, went to his death in an agony for the sin. And you are the other man who aided him? I always thought it might be you, but never asked."

"I was that same," confessed Jib-boom, "my shame to say it! And all I got, and all I asked for it, was the skippering of his sloop."

"In his crime, then, was but the one grace – that he never mentioned your name, but took the blame entirely on himself."

Behind them the sound of the pipes went blithely; out on the Sound the sails of the *Ron* were black against the gold of the moon. Ludovick saw the lovers, so happy because they did not know. Old Corodale – old rogue! – he had hoped to make amends for his sin by giving the Church a minister with the surplus of his thievings. The Church was saved that ill bequest; but what of Col's inheritance of the paternal avarice?

"I have a fear," said Ludovick to himself. "Father and son – father and son; both of them fools of the fifty-year fortune. To-morrow I'll go to Mingulay."

THE END